big NATE

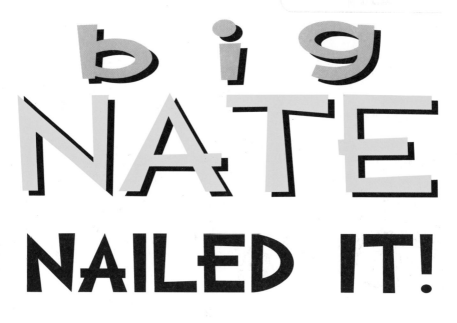

NAILED IT!

Complete Your *Big Nate* Collection

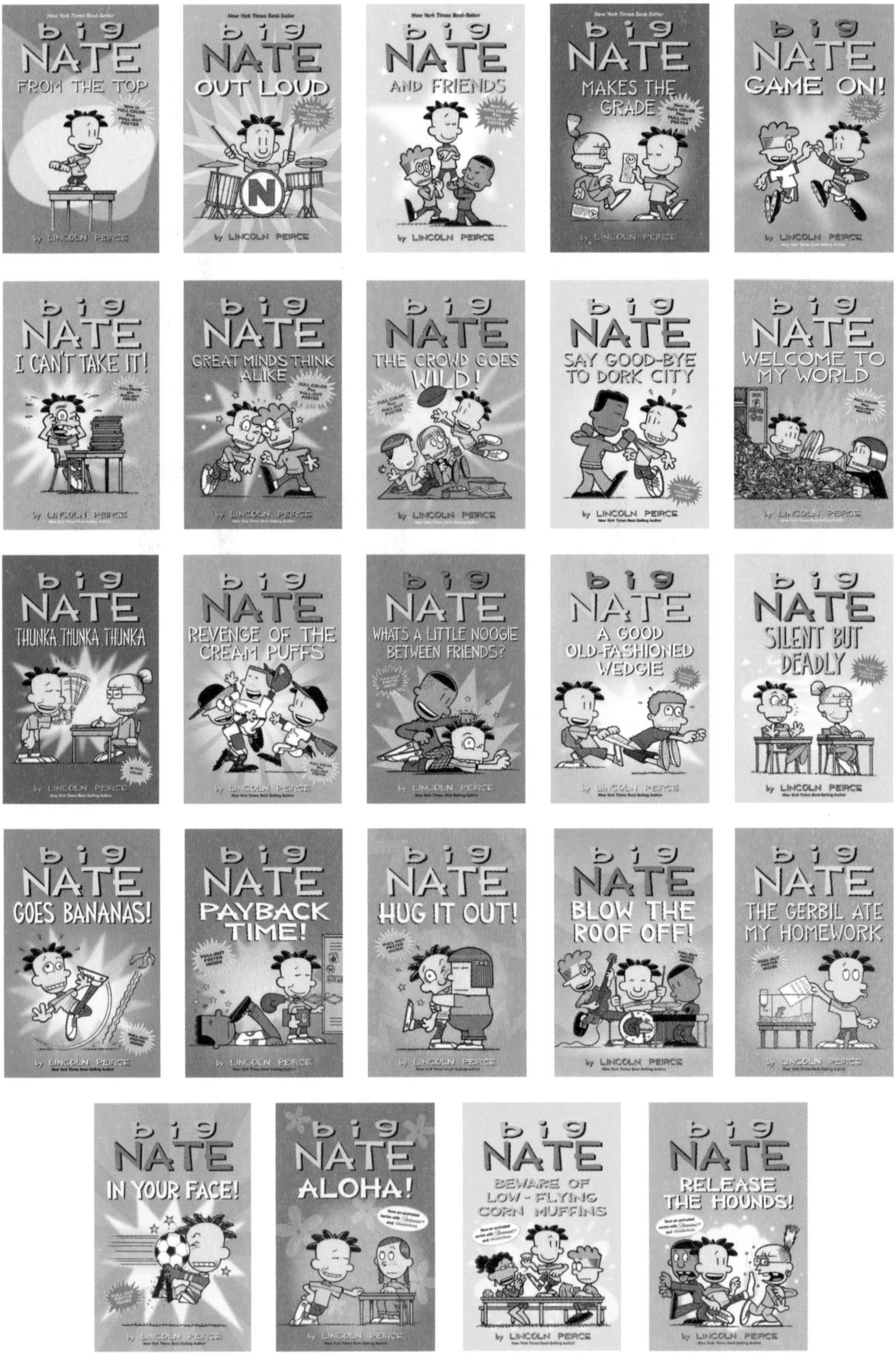
big NATE FROM THE TOP
by LINCOLN PEIRCE
big NATE OUT LOUD
by LINCOLN PEIRCE
big NATE AND FRIENDS
by LINCOLN PEIRCE
big NATE MAKES THE GRADE
by LINCOLN PEIRCE
big NATE GAME ON!
by LINCOLN PEIRCE
big NATE I CAN'T TAKE IT!
by LINCOLN PEIRCE
big NATE GREAT MINDS THINK ALIKE
by LINCOLN PEIRCE
big NATE THE CROWD GOES WILD!
by LINCOLN PEIRCE
big NATE SAY GOOD-BYE TO DORK CITY
by LINCOLN PEIRCE
big NATE WELCOME TO MY WORLD
by LINCOLN PEIRCE
big NATE THUNKA, THUNKA, THUNKA
by LINCOLN PEIRCE
big NATE REVENGE OF THE CREAM PUFFS
by LINCOLN PEIRCE
big NATE WHAT'S A LITTLE NOOGIE BETWEEN FRIENDS?
by LINCOLN PEIRCE
big NATE A GOOD OLD-FASHIONED WEDGIE
by LINCOLN PEIRCE
big NATE SILENT BUT DEADLY
by LINCOLN PEIRCE
big NATE GOES BANANAS!
by LINCOLN PEIRCE
big NATE PAYBACK TIME!
by LINCOLN PEIRCE
big NATE HUG IT OUT!
by LINCOLN PEIRCE
big NATE BLOW THE ROOF OFF!
by LINCOLN PEIRCE
big NATE THE GERBIL ATE MY HOMEWORK
by LINCOLN PEIRCE
big NATE IN YOUR FACE!
by LINCOLN PEIRCE
big NATE ALOHA!
by LINCOLN PEIRCE
big NATE BEWARE OF LOW-FLYING CORN MUFFINS
by LINCOLN PEIRCE
big NATE RELEASE THE HOUNDS!
by LINCOLN PEIRCE

big NATE
NAILED IT!

by LINCOLN PEIRCE

Andrews McMeel
PUBLISHING®

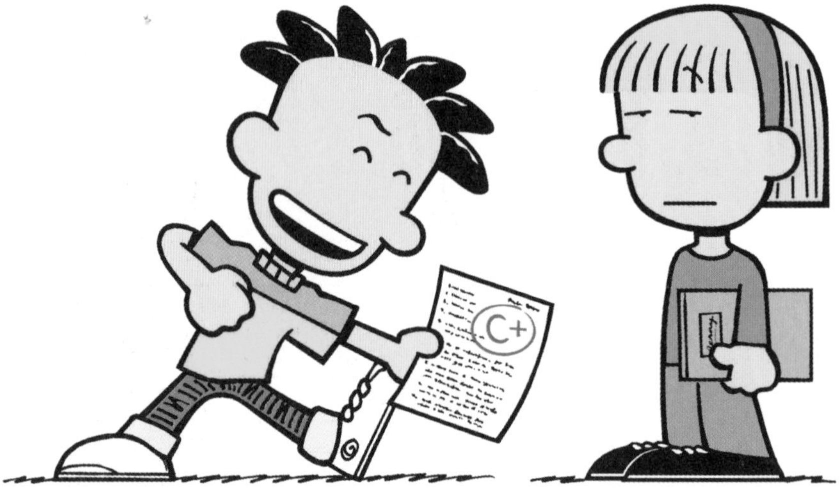
C+

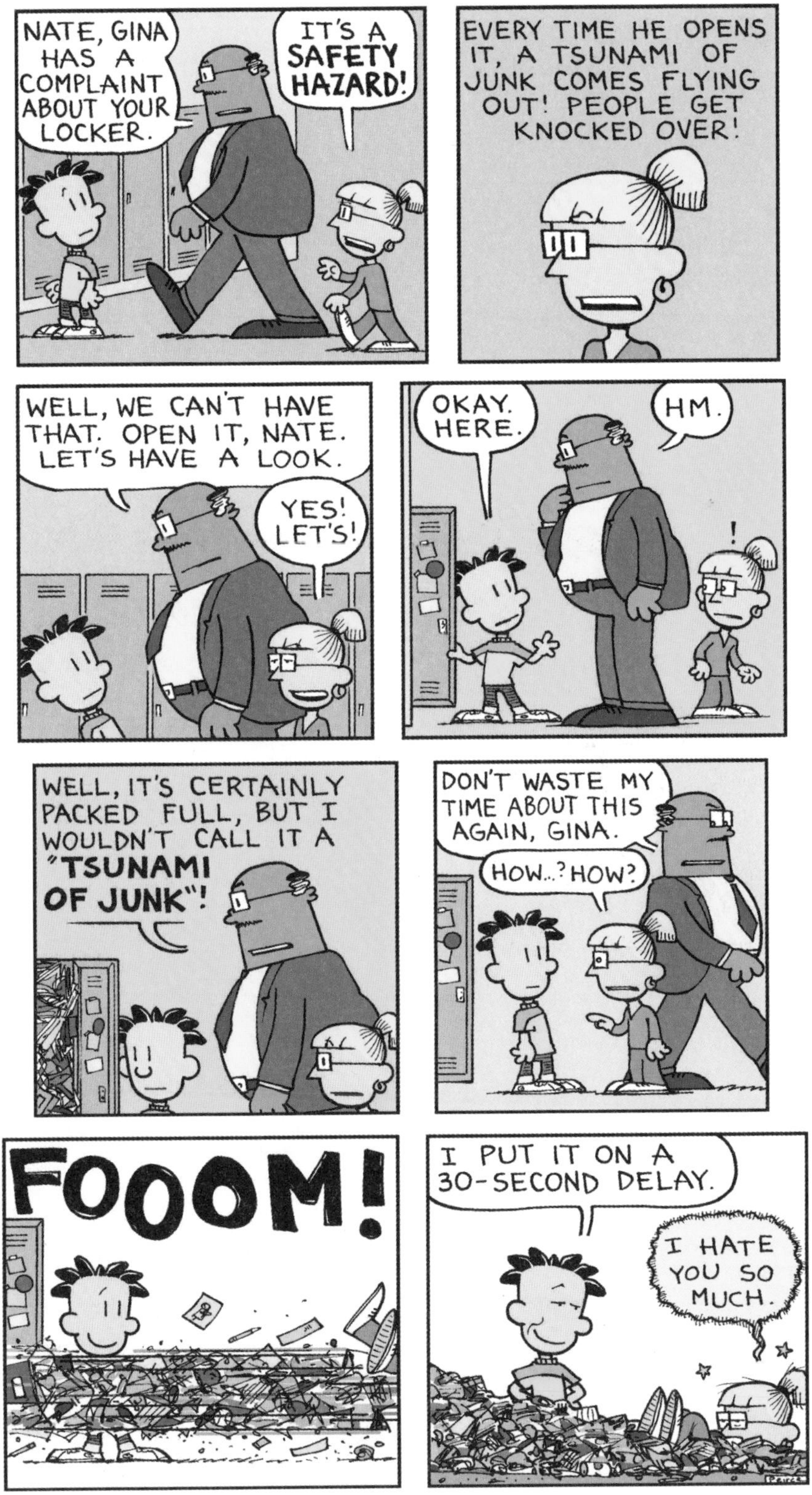
NATE, GINA HAS A COMPLAINT ABOUT YOUR LOCKER.
IT'S A **SAFETY HAZARD!**
EVERY TIME HE OPENS IT, A TSUNAMI OF JUNK COMES FLYING OUT! PEOPLE GET KNOCKED OVER!
WELL, WE CAN'T HAVE THAT. OPEN IT, NATE. LET'S HAVE A LOOK.
YES! LET'S!
OKAY. HERE.
HM.
!
WELL, IT'S CERTAINLY PACKED FULL, BUT I WOULDN'T CALL IT A "**TSUNAMI OF JUNK**"!
DON'T WASTE MY TIME ABOUT THIS AGAIN, GINA.
HOW...? HOW?
FOOOM!
I PUT IT ON A 30-SECOND DELAY.
I HATE YOU SO MUCH.

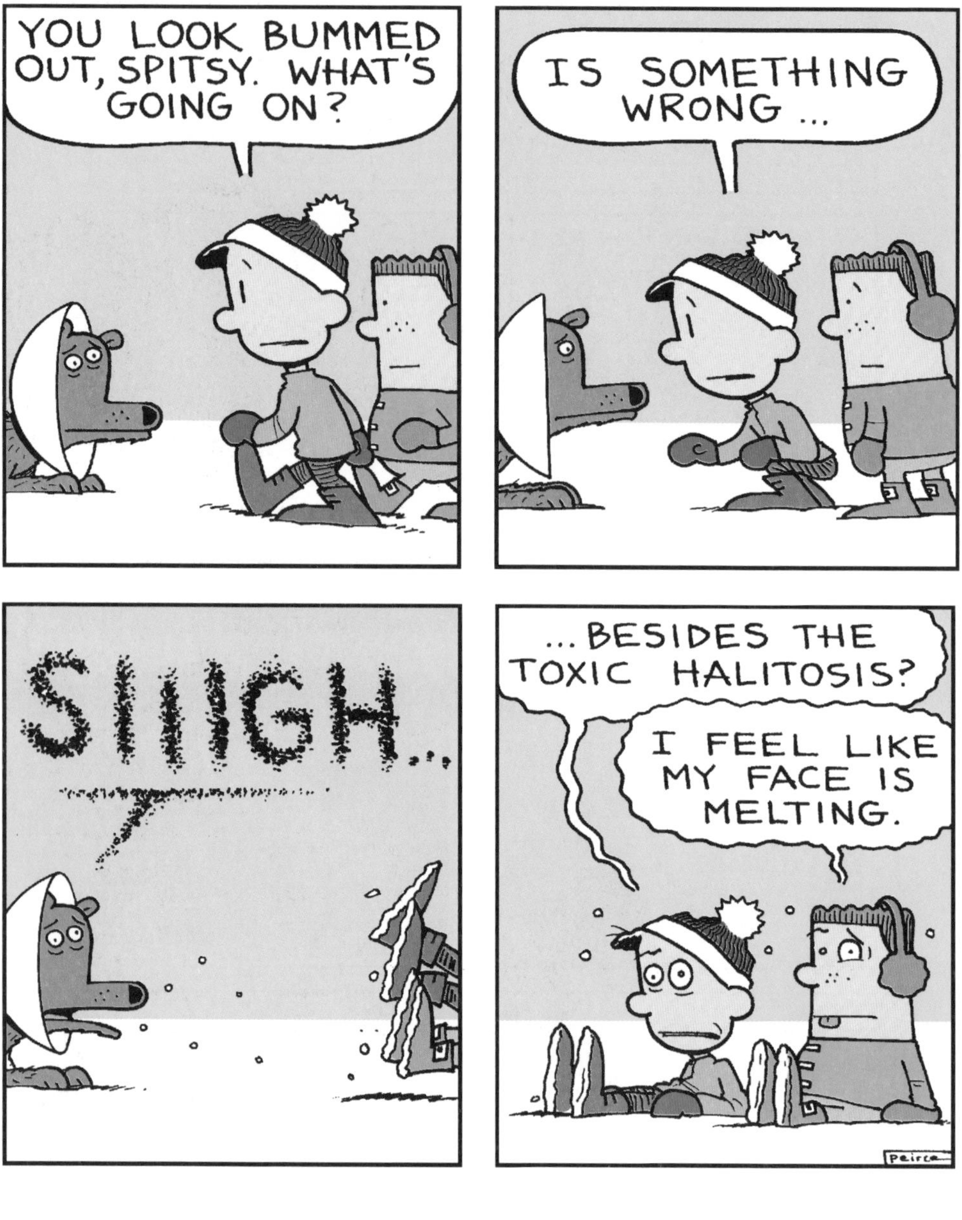
YOU LOOK BUMMED OUT, SPITSY. WHAT'S GOING ON?
IS SOMETHING WRONG ...
SIIIGH...
... BESIDES THE TOXIC HALITOSIS?
I FEEL LIKE MY FACE IS MELTING.
Peirce

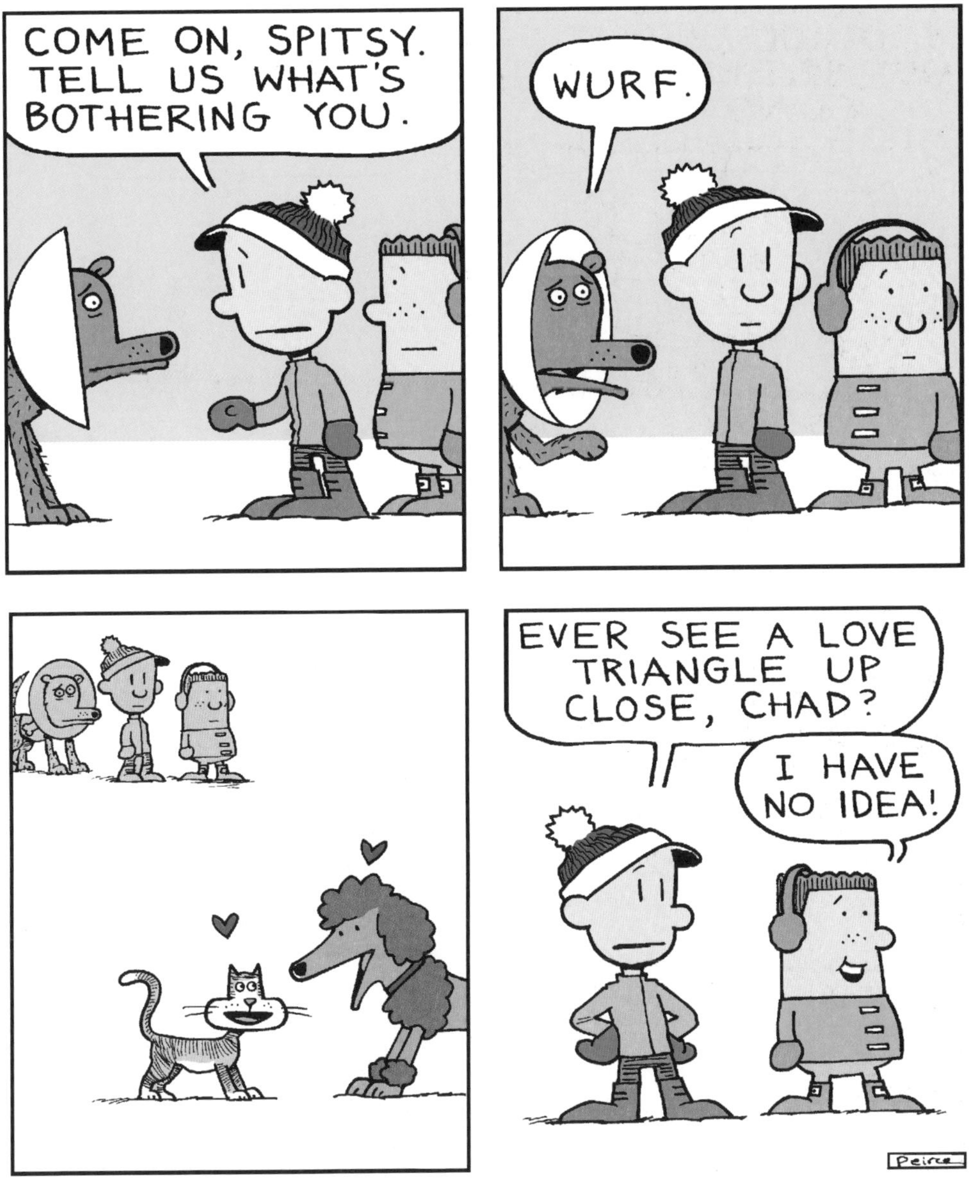
COME ON, SPITSY. TELL US WHAT'S BOTHERING YOU.
WURF.
EVER SEE A LOVE TRIANGLE UP CLOSE, CHAD?
I HAVE NO IDEA!
Peirce

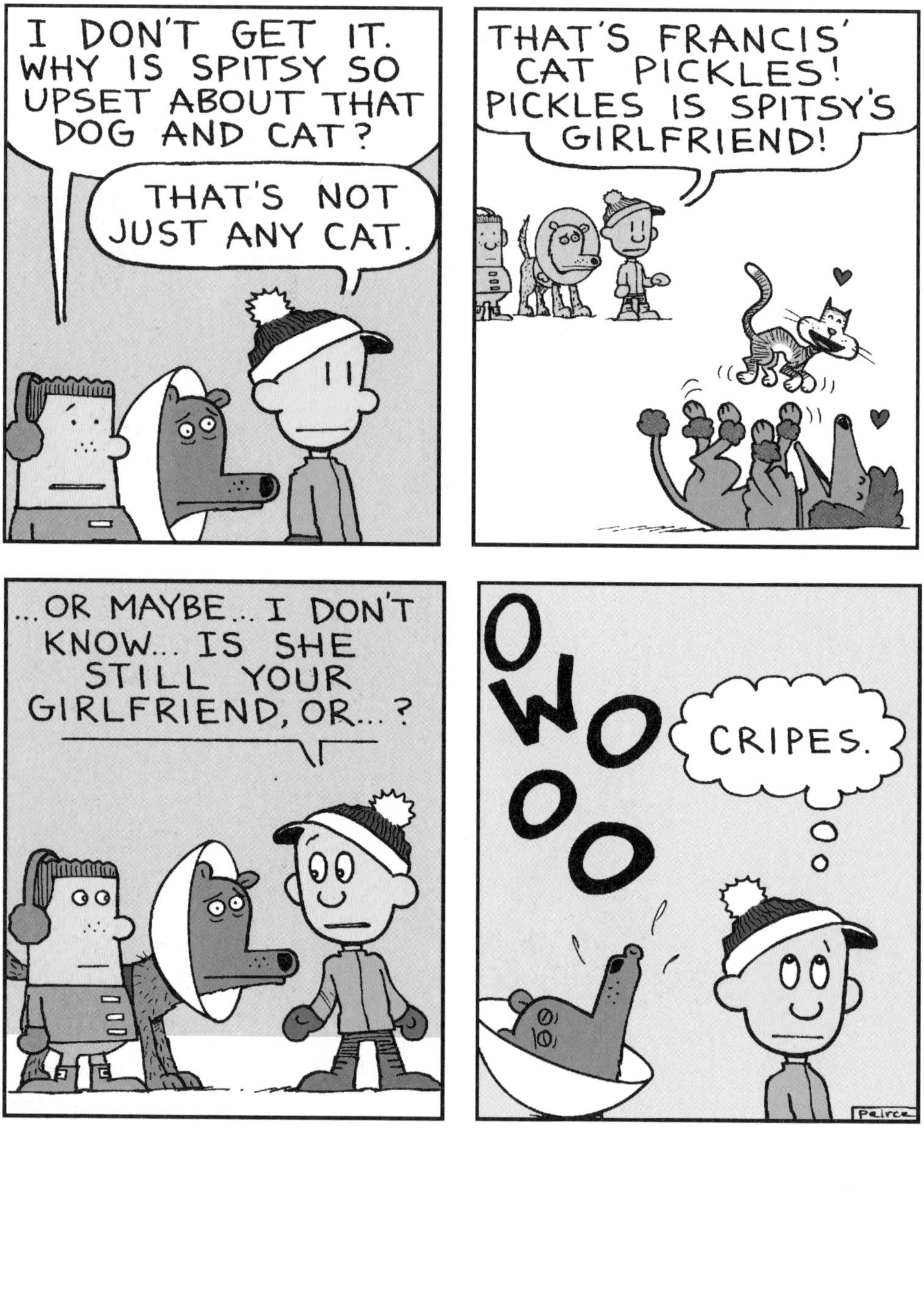
I DON'T GET IT. WHY IS SPITSY SO UPSET ABOUT THAT DOG AND CAT?
THAT'S NOT JUST ANY CAT.
THAT'S FRANCIS' CAT PICKLES! PICKLES IS SPITSY'S GIRLFRIEND!
...OR MAYBE... I DON'T KNOW... IS SHE STILL YOUR GIRLFRIEND, OR...?
OWOOO
CRIPES.
PEIRCE

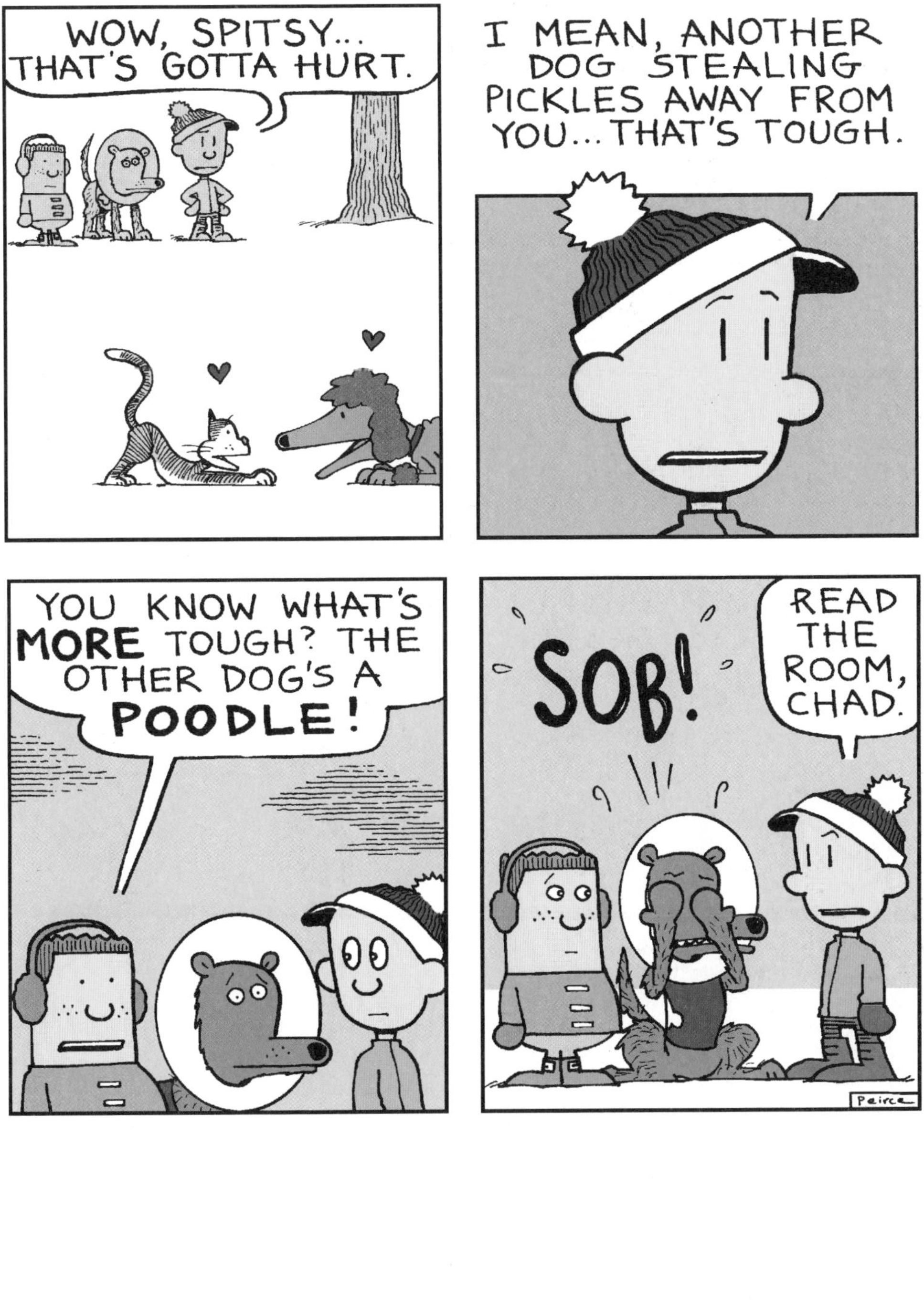
WOW, SPITSY... THAT'S GOTTA HURT.
I MEAN, ANOTHER DOG STEALING PICKLES AWAY FROM YOU... THAT'S TOUGH.
YOU KNOW WHAT'S **MORE** TOUGH? THE OTHER DOG'S A **POODLE**!
SOB!
READ THE ROOM, CHAD.
Peirce

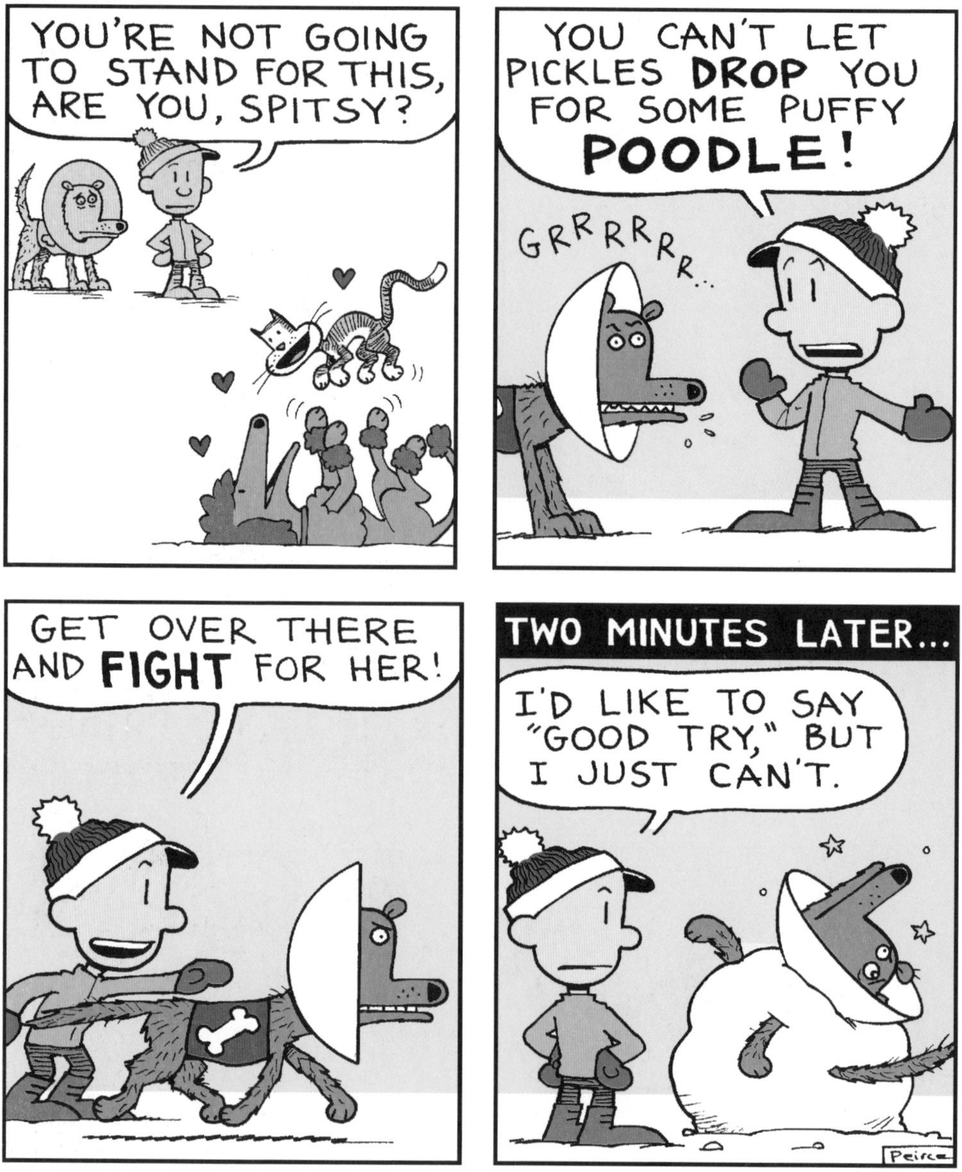
YOU'RE NOT GOING TO STAND FOR THIS, ARE YOU, SPITSY?
YOU CAN'T LET PICKLES **DROP** YOU FOR SOME PUFFY **POODLE!**
GRRRRRRR...
GET OVER THERE AND **FIGHT** FOR HER!
TWO MINUTES LATER...
I'D LIKE TO SAY "GOOD TRY," BUT I JUST CAN'T.
Peirce

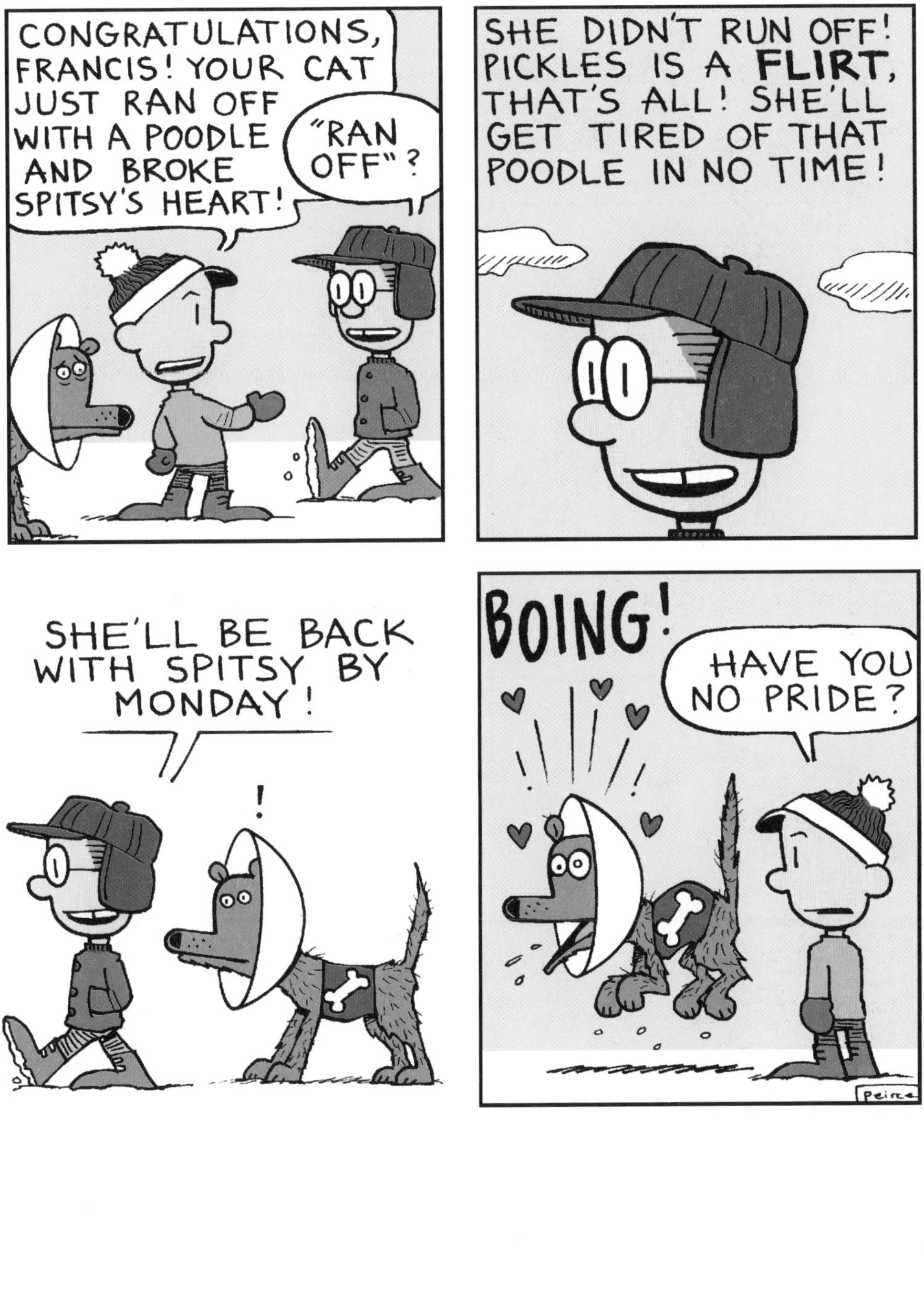
CONGRATULATIONS, FRANCIS! YOUR CAT JUST RAN OFF WITH A POODLE AND BROKE SPITSY'S HEART!
"RAN OFF"?
SHE DIDN'T RUN OFF! PICKLES IS A **FLIRT**, THAT'S ALL! SHE'LL GET TIRED OF THAT POODLE IN NO TIME!
SHE'LL BE BACK WITH SPITSY BY MONDAY!
!
BOING!
HAVE YOU NO PRIDE?
Peirce

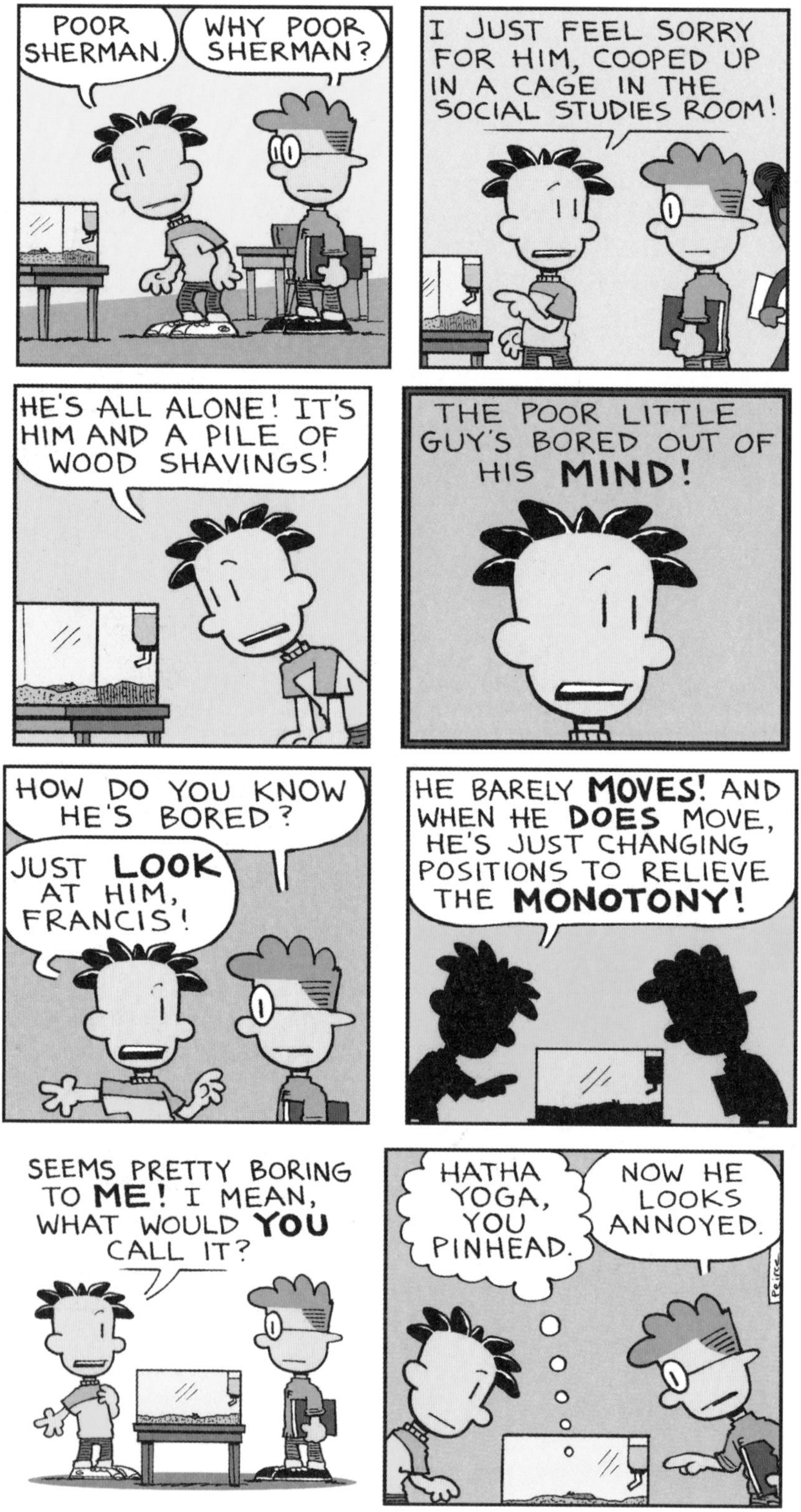
POOR SHERMAN.
WHY POOR SHERMAN?
I JUST FEEL SORRY FOR HIM, COOPED UP IN A CAGE IN THE SOCIAL STUDIES ROOM!
HE'S ALL ALONE! IT'S HIM AND A PILE OF WOOD SHAVINGS!
THE POOR LITTLE GUY'S BORED OUT OF HIS **MIND**!
HOW DO YOU KNOW HE'S BORED?
JUST **LOOK** AT HIM, FRANCIS!
HE BARELY **MOVES**! AND WHEN HE **DOES** MOVE, HE'S JUST CHANGING POSITIONS TO RELIEVE THE **MONOTONY**!
SEEMS PRETTY BORING TO **ME**! I MEAN, WHAT WOULD **YOU** CALL IT?
HATHA YOGA, YOU PINHEAD.
NOW HE LOOKS ANNOYED.

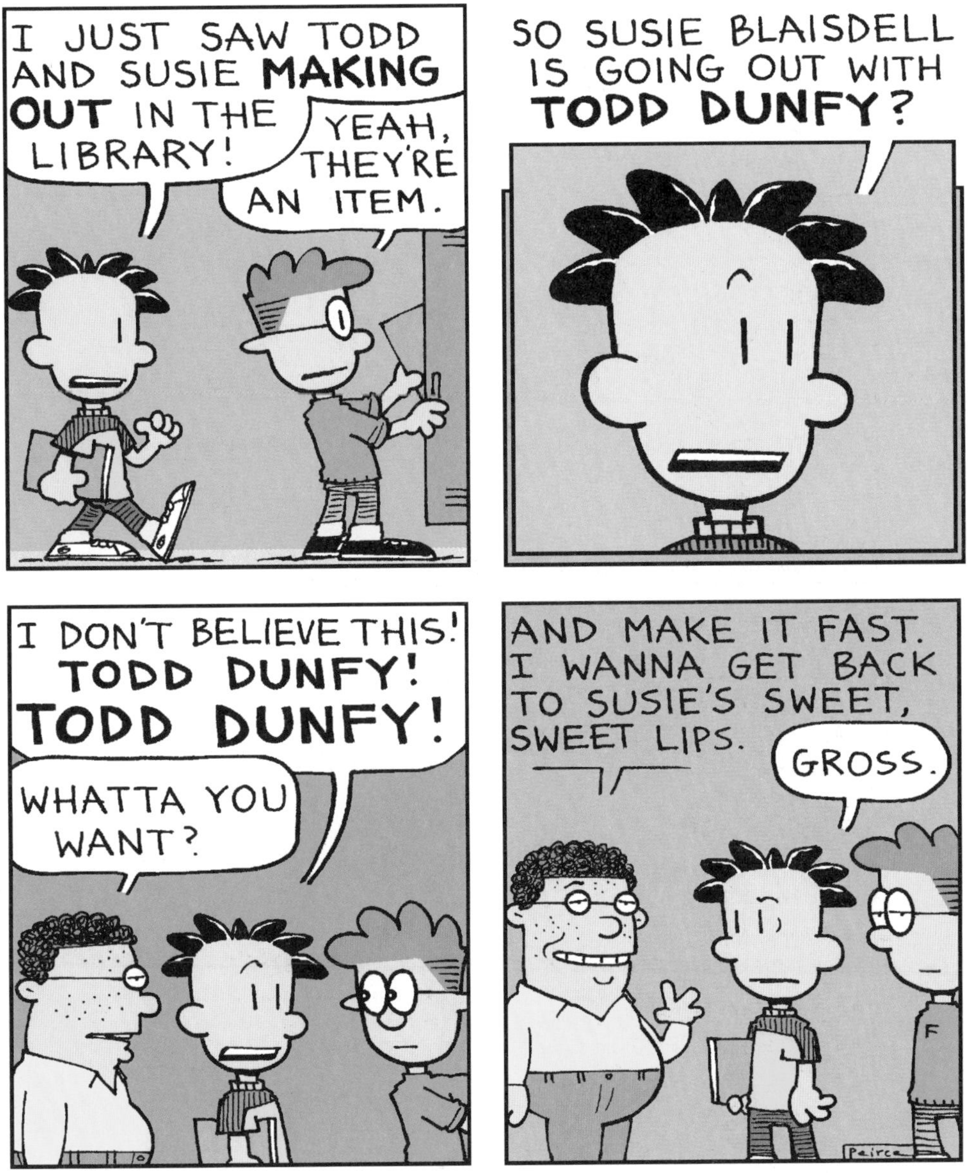
I JUST SAW TODD AND SUSIE MAKING OUT IN THE LIBRARY!
YEAH, THEY'RE AN ITEM.
SO SUSIE BLAISDELL IS GOING OUT WITH TODD DUNFY?
I DON'T BELIEVE THIS! TODD DUNFY! TODD DUNFY!
WHATTA YOU WANT?
AND MAKE IT FAST. I WANNA GET BACK TO SUSIE'S SWEET, SWEET LIPS.
GROSS.
Peirce

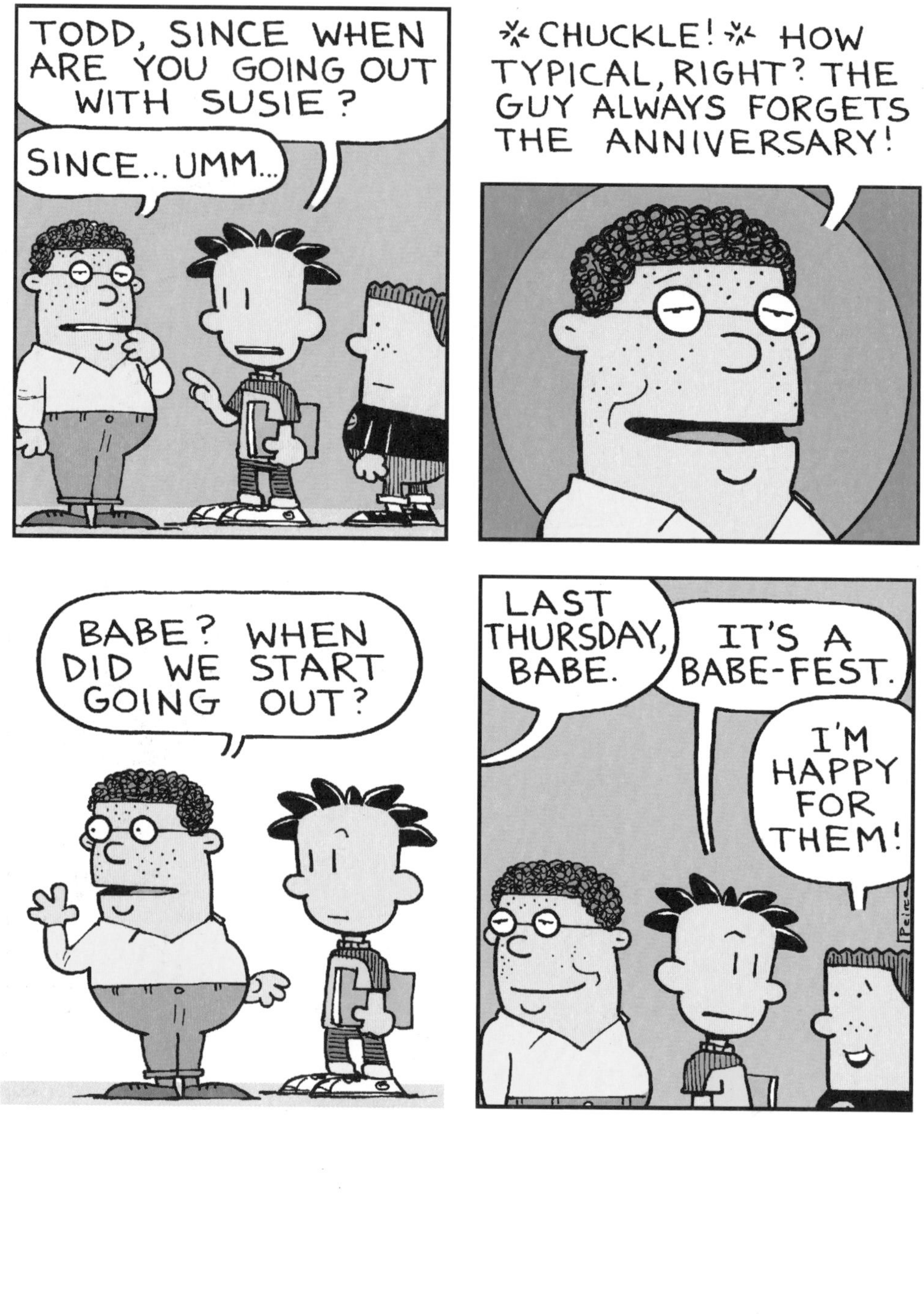
TODD, SINCE WHEN ARE YOU GOING OUT WITH SUSIE?
SINCE... UMM...
CHUCKLE! HOW TYPICAL, RIGHT? THE GUY ALWAYS FORGETS THE ANNIVERSARY!
BABE? WHEN DID WE START GOING OUT?
LAST THURSDAY, BABE.
IT'S A BABE-FEST.
I'M HAPPY FOR THEM!

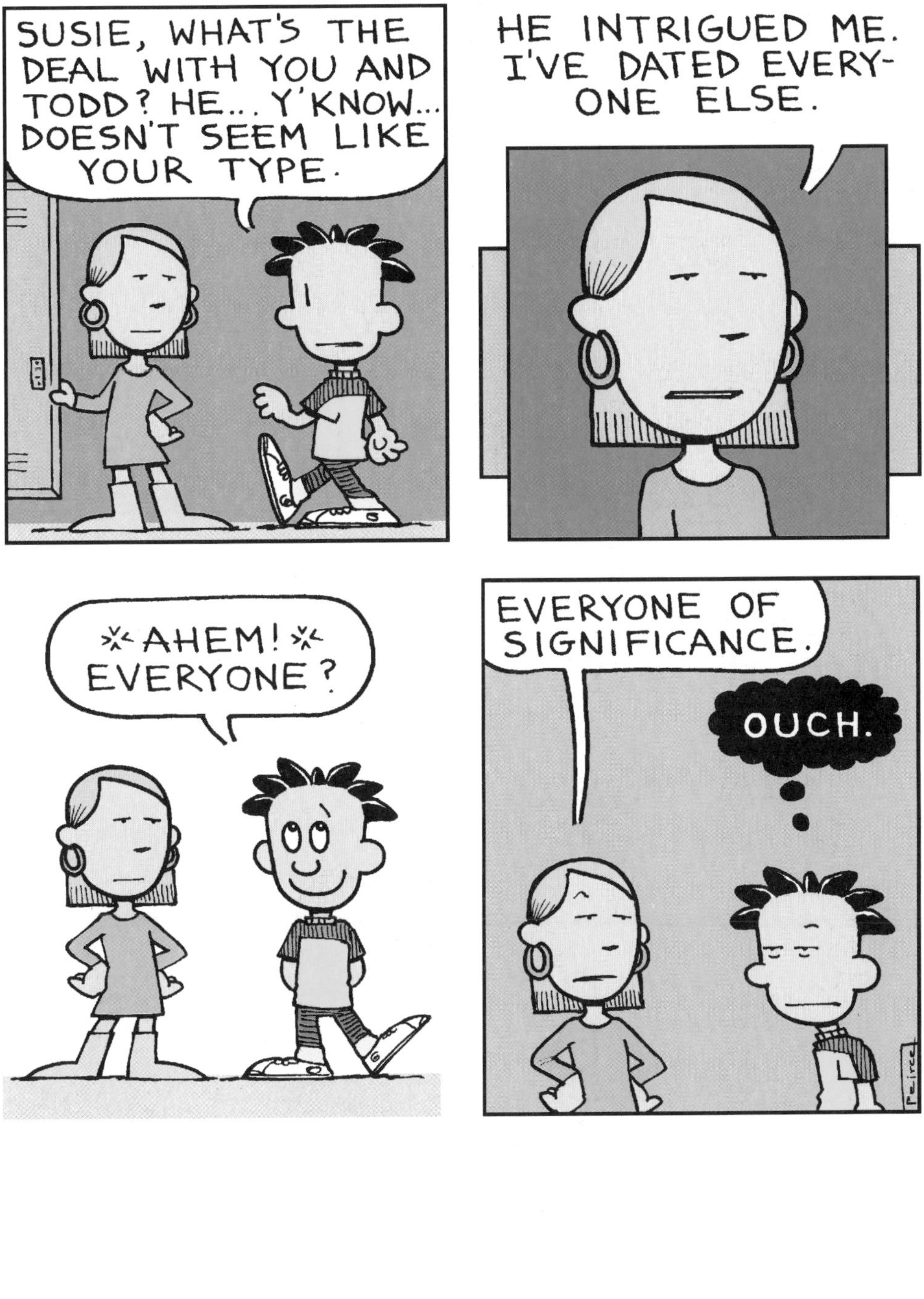
SUSIE, WHAT'S THE DEAL WITH YOU AND TODD? HE... Y'KNOW... DOESN'T SEEM LIKE YOUR TYPE.
HE INTRIGUED ME. I'VE DATED EVERY-ONE ELSE.
AHEM! EVERYONE?
EVERYONE OF SIGNIFICANCE.
OUCH.
Peirce

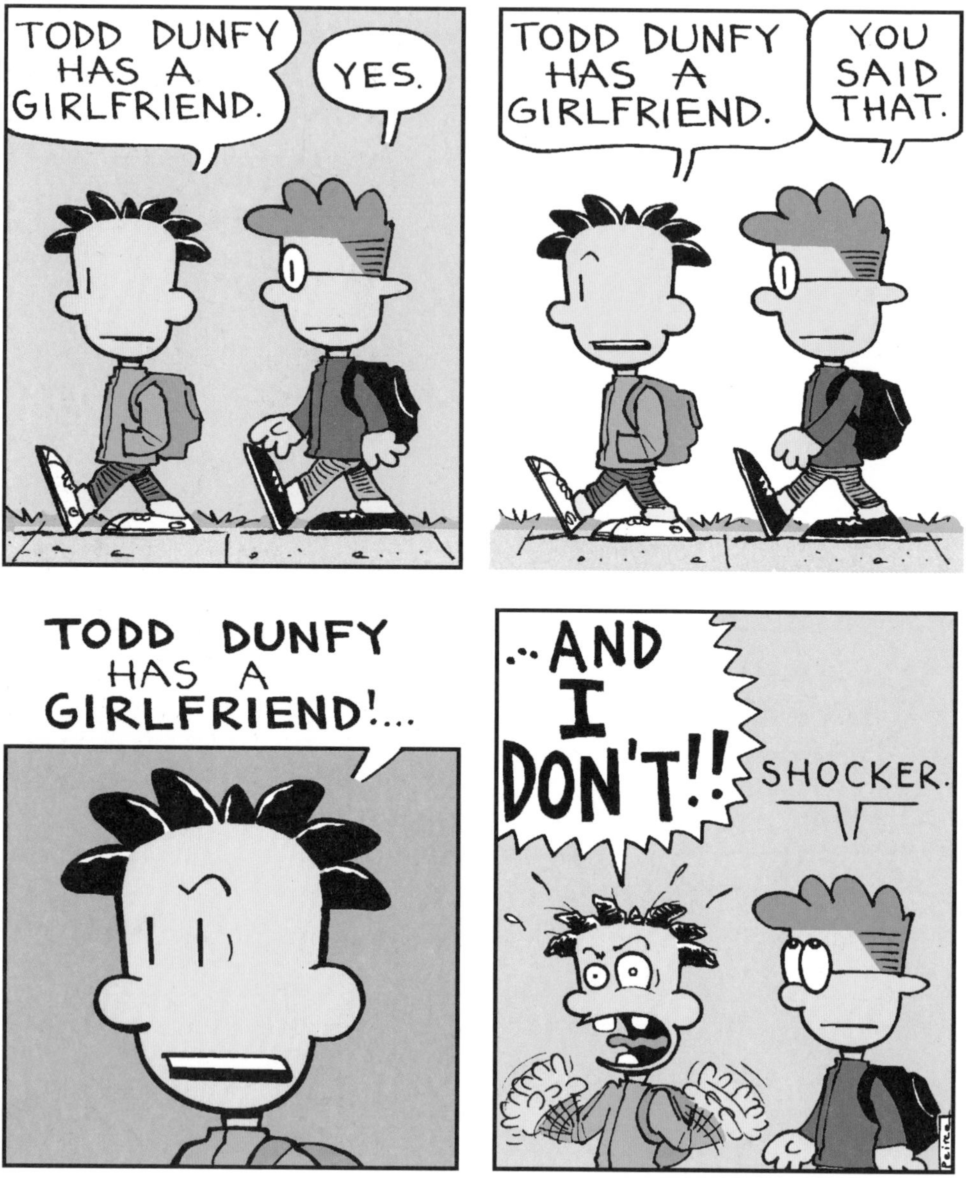
TODD DUNFY HAS A GIRLFRIEND.
YES.
TODD DUNFY HAS A GIRLFRIEND.
YOU SAID THAT.
TODD DUNFY HAS A GIRLFRIEND!...
...AND I DON'T!!
SHOCKER.

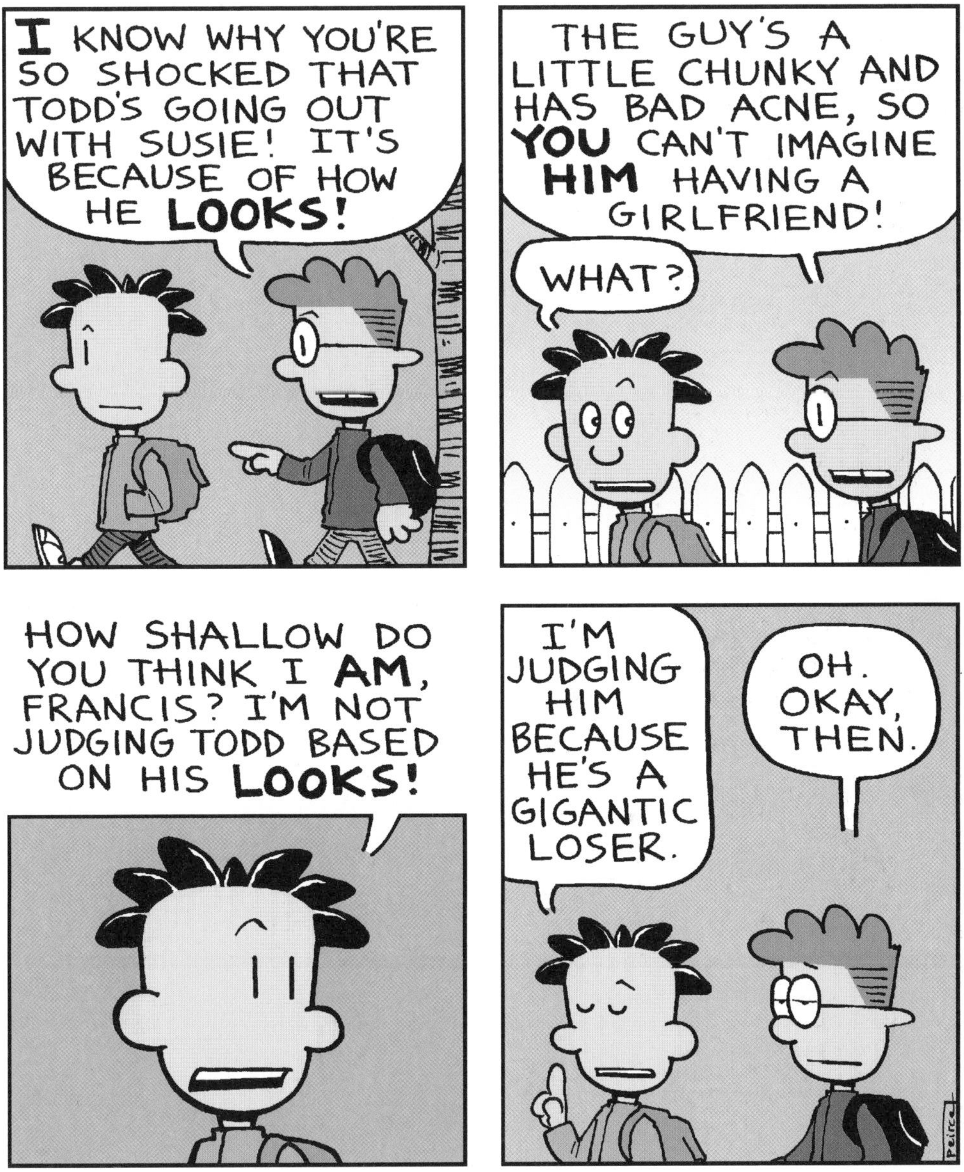
I KNOW WHY YOU'RE SO SHOCKED THAT TODD'S GOING OUT WITH SUSIE! IT'S BECAUSE OF HOW HE **LOOKS**!
THE GUY'S A LITTLE CHUNKY AND HAS BAD ACNE, SO **YOU** CAN'T IMAGINE **HIM** HAVING A GIRLFRIEND!
WHAT?
HOW SHALLOW DO YOU THINK I **AM**, FRANCIS? I'M NOT JUDGING TODD BASED ON HIS **LOOKS**!
I'M JUDGING HIM BECAUSE HE'S A GIGANTIC LOSER.
OH. OKAY, THEN.
PEIRCE

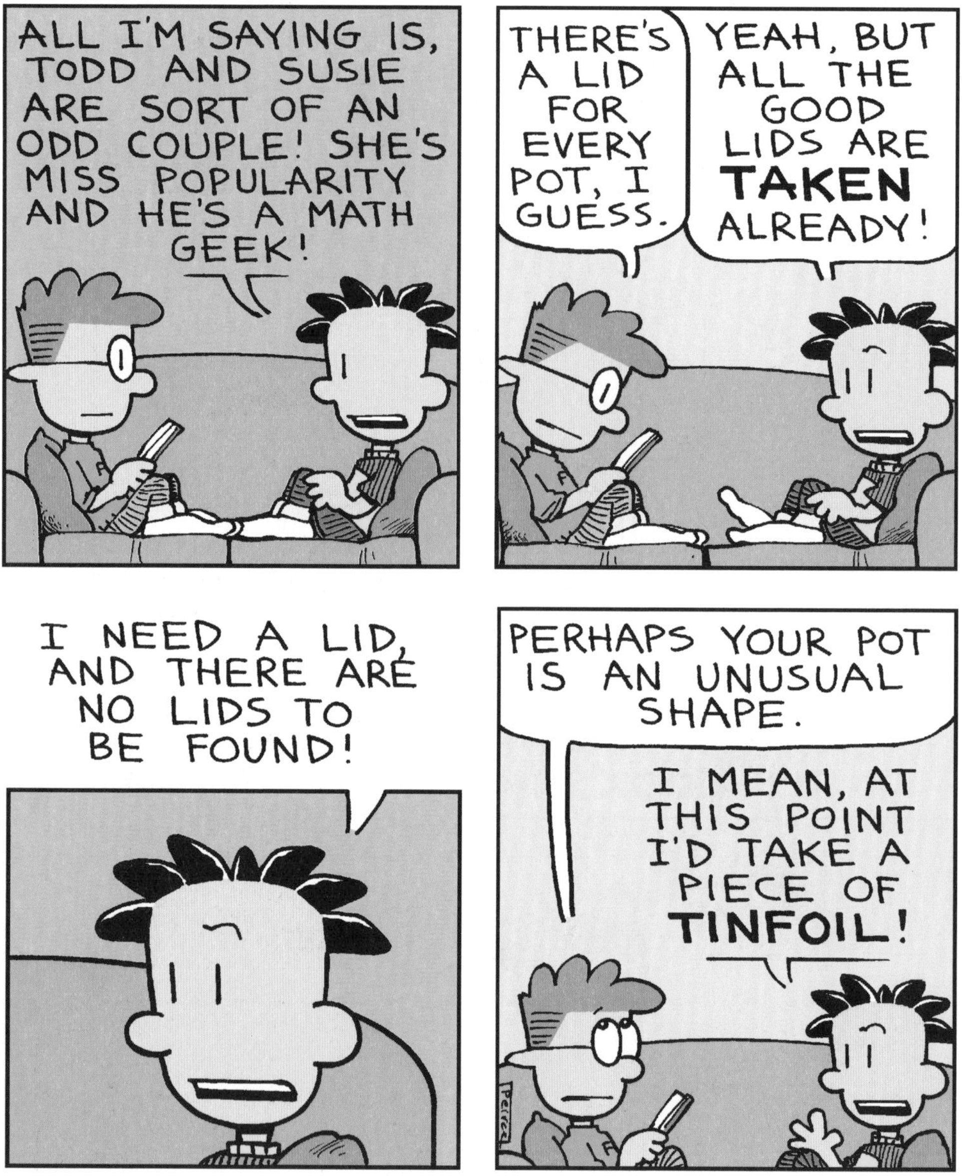
ALL I'M SAYING IS, TODD AND SUSIE ARE SORT OF AN ODD COUPLE! SHE'S MISS POPULARITY AND HE'S A MATH GEEK!
THERE'S A LID FOR EVERY POT, I GUESS.
YEAH, BUT ALL THE GOOD LIDS ARE **TAKEN** ALREADY!
I NEED A LID, AND THERE ARE NO LIDS TO BE FOUND!
PERHAPS YOUR POT IS AN UNUSUAL SHAPE.
I MEAN, AT THIS POINT I'D TAKE A PIECE OF **TINFOIL**!

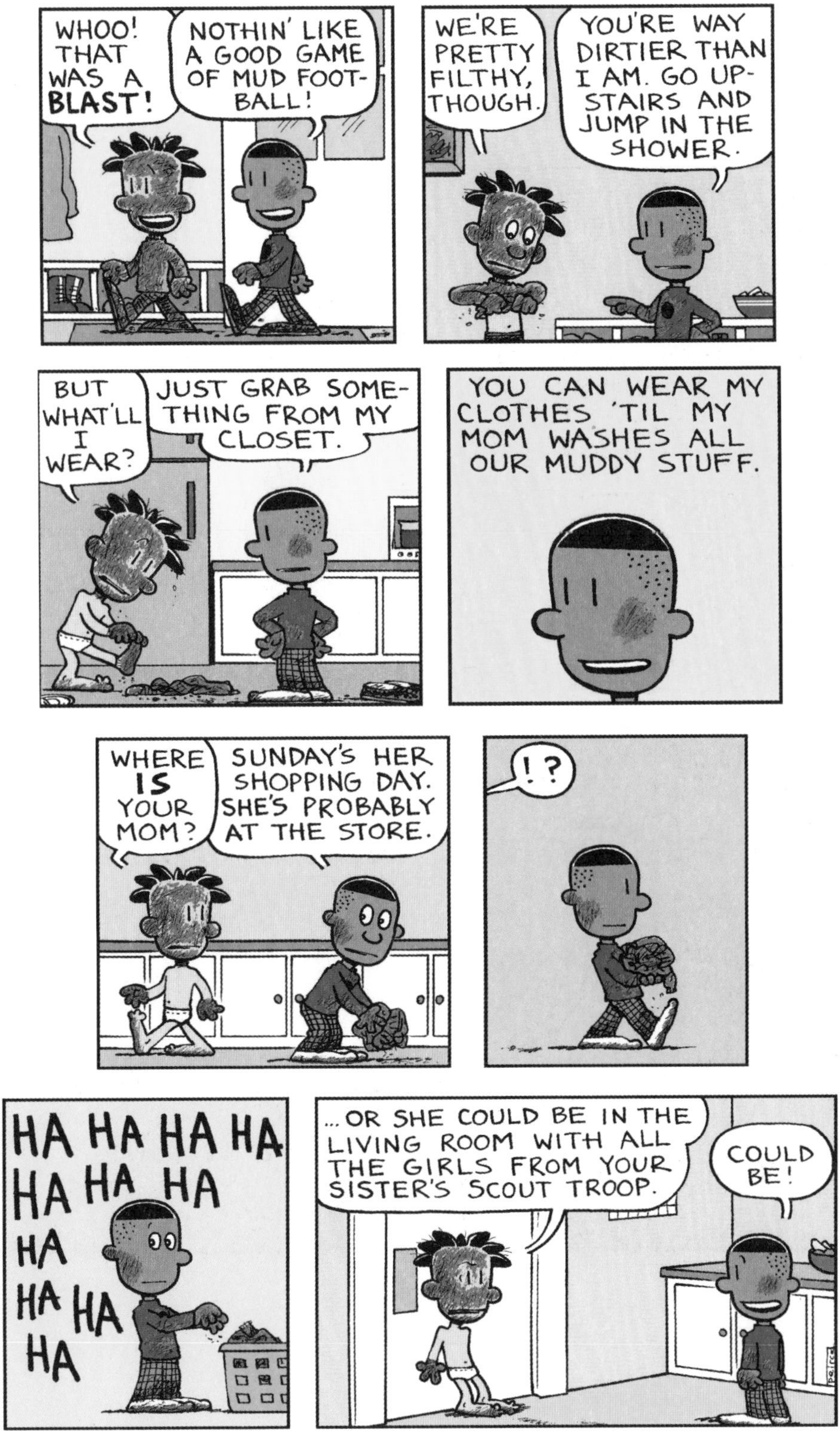
WHOO! THAT WAS A BLAST!
NOTHIN' LIKE A GOOD GAME OF MUD FOOT-BALL!
WE'RE PRETTY FILTHY, THOUGH.
YOU'RE WAY DIRTIER THAN I AM. GO UP-STAIRS AND JUMP IN THE SHOWER.
BUT WHAT'LL I WEAR?
JUST GRAB SOME-THING FROM MY CLOSET.
YOU CAN WEAR MY CLOTHES 'TIL MY MOM WASHES ALL OUR MUDDY STUFF.
WHERE IS YOUR MOM?
SUNDAY'S HER SHOPPING DAY. SHE'S PROBABLY AT THE STORE.
!?
HA HA HA HA HA HA HA HA HA HA HA
...OR SHE COULD BE IN THE LIVING ROOM WITH ALL THE GIRLS FROM YOUR SISTER'S SCOUT TROOP.
COULD BE!

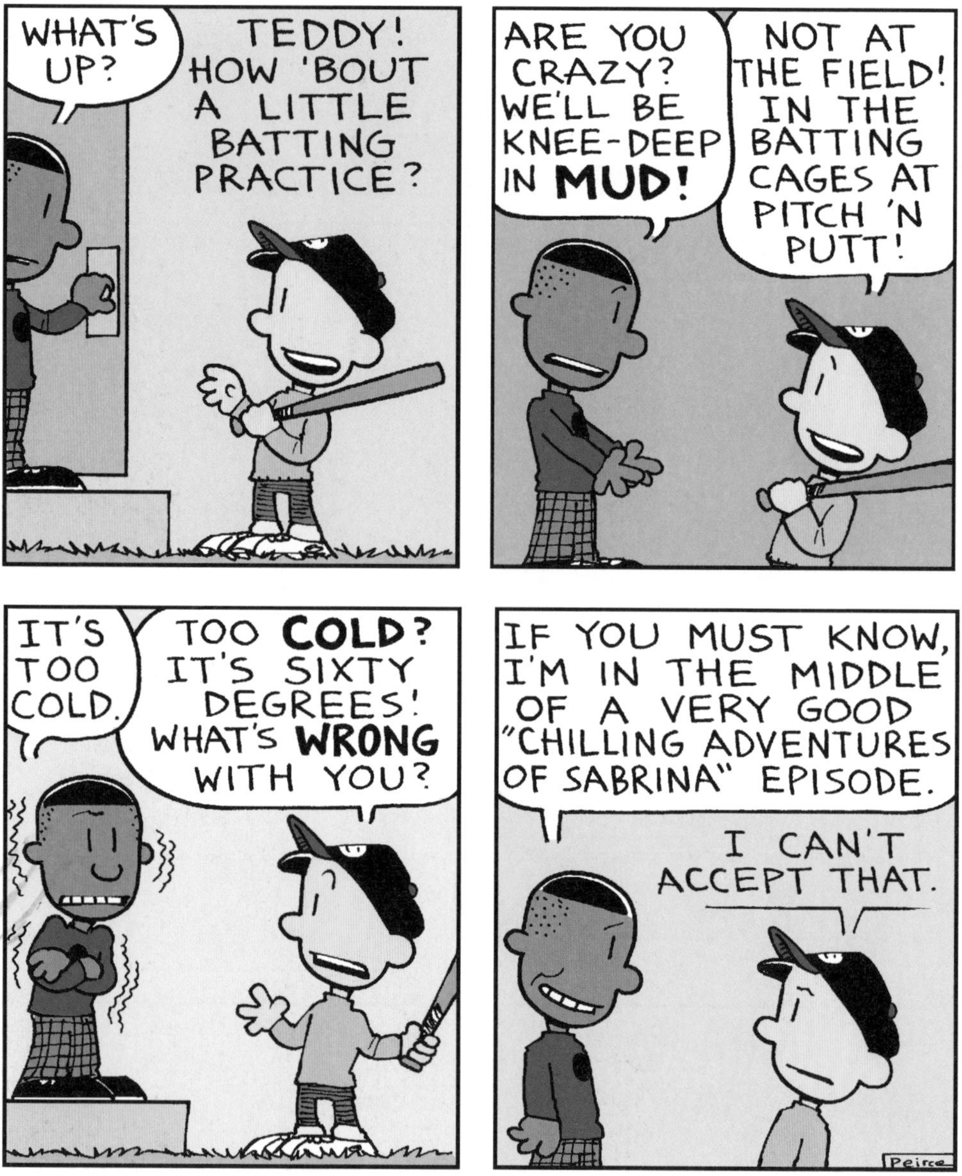
WHAT'S UP?
TEDDY! HOW 'BOUT A LITTLE BATTING PRACTICE?
ARE YOU CRAZY? WE'LL BE KNEE-DEEP IN **MUD!**
NOT AT THE FIELD! IN THE BATTING CAGES AT PITCH 'N PUTT!
IT'S TOO COLD.
TOO **COLD**? IT'S SIXTY DEGREES! WHAT'S **WRONG** WITH YOU?
IF YOU MUST KNOW, I'M IN THE MIDDLE OF A VERY GOOD "CHILLING ADVENTURES OF SABRINA" EPISODE.
I CAN'T ACCEPT THAT.
Peirce

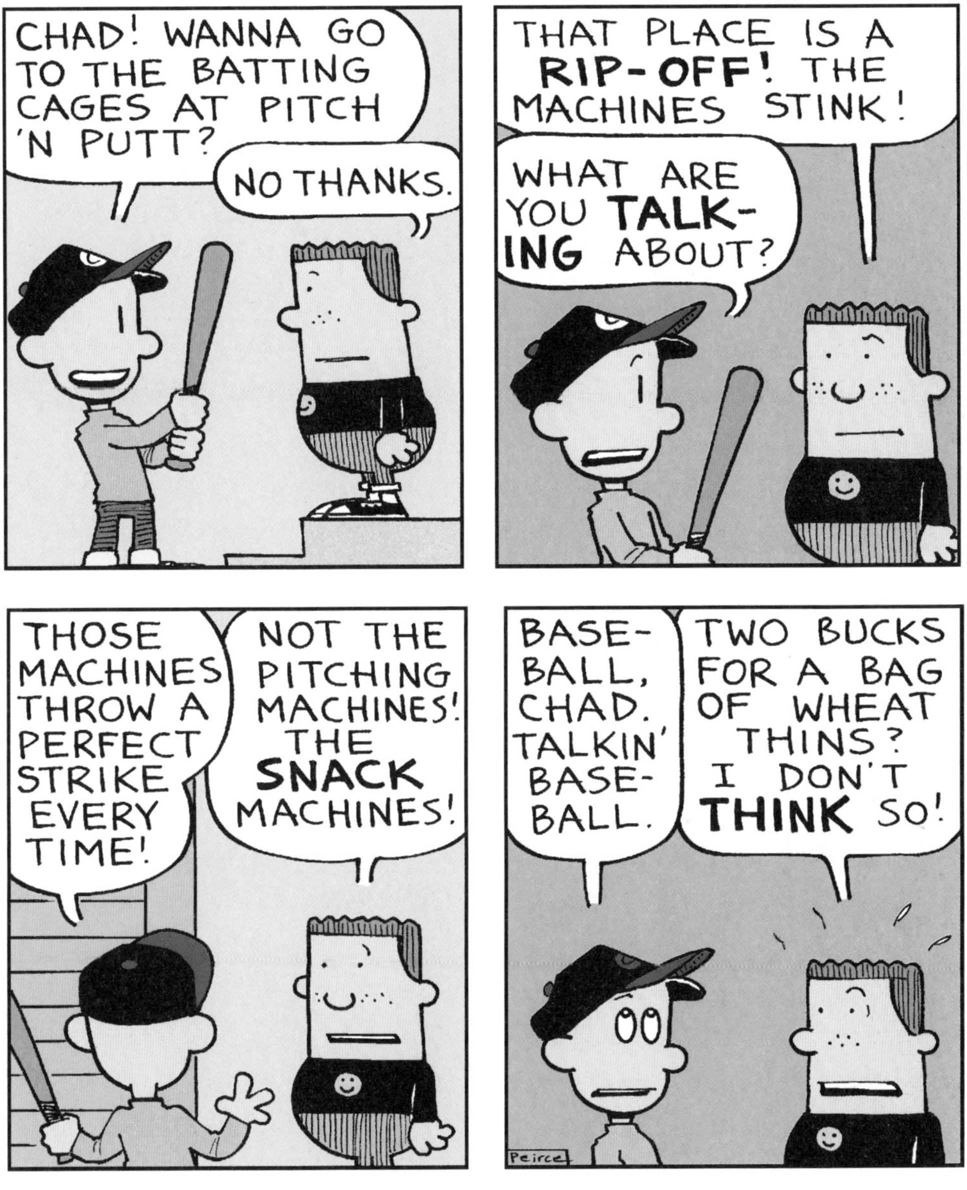
CHAD! WANNA GO TO THE BATTING CAGES AT PITCH 'N PUTT?
NO THANKS.
THAT PLACE IS A **RIP-OFF**! THE MACHINES STINK!
WHAT ARE YOU **TALKING** ABOUT?
THOSE MACHINES THROW A PERFECT STRIKE EVERY TIME!
NOT THE PITCHING MACHINES! THE **SNACK** MACHINES!
BASEBALL, CHAD. TALKIN' BASEBALL.
TWO BUCKS FOR A BAG OF WHEAT THINS? I DON'T **THINK** SO!
Peirce

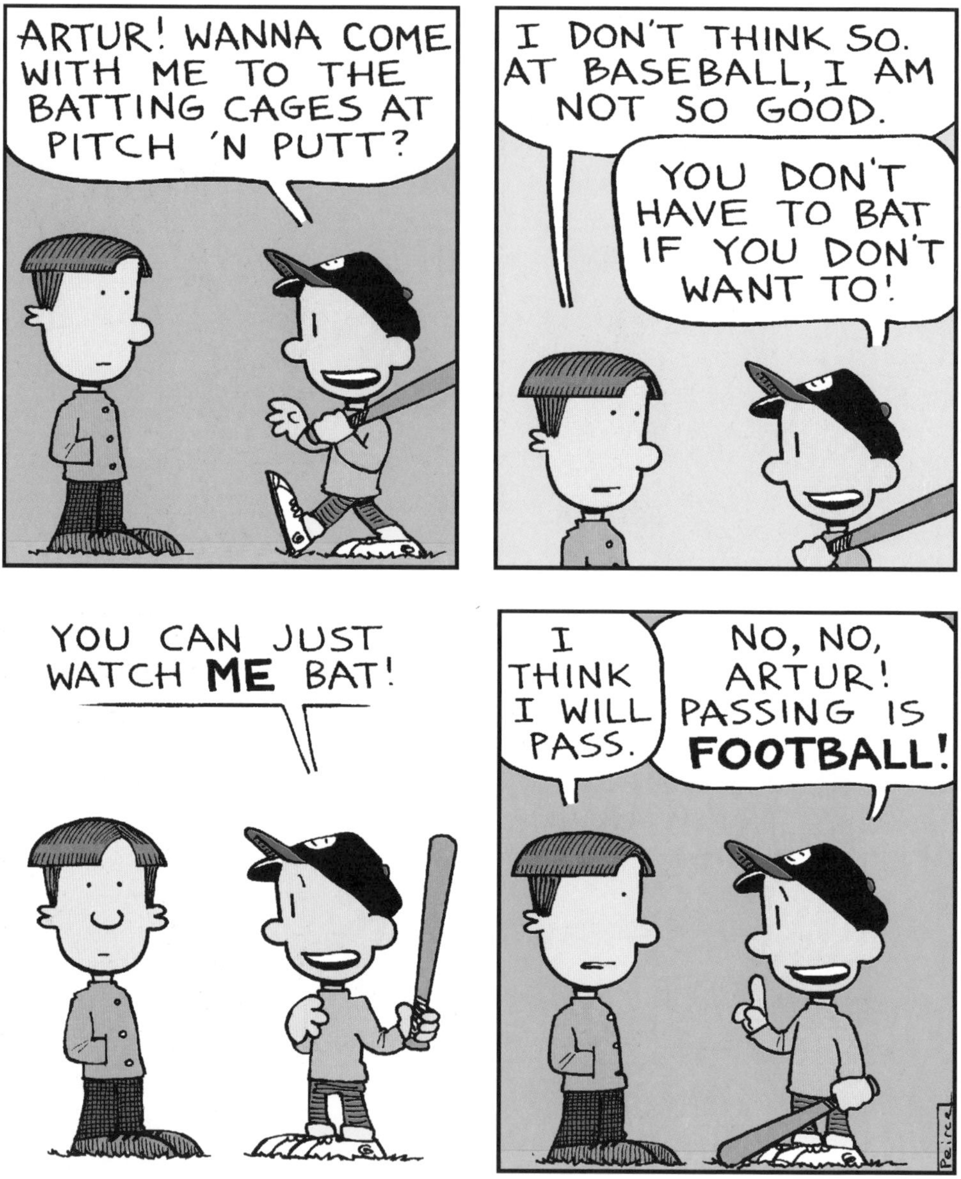
ARTUR! WANNA COME WITH ME TO THE BATTING CAGES AT PITCH 'N PUTT?
I DON'T THINK SO. AT BASEBALL, I AM NOT SO GOOD.
YOU DON'T HAVE TO BAT IF YOU DON'T WANT TO!
YOU CAN JUST WATCH **ME** BAT!
I THINK I WILL PASS.
NO, NO, ARTUR! PASSING IS **FOOTBALL**!
Peirce

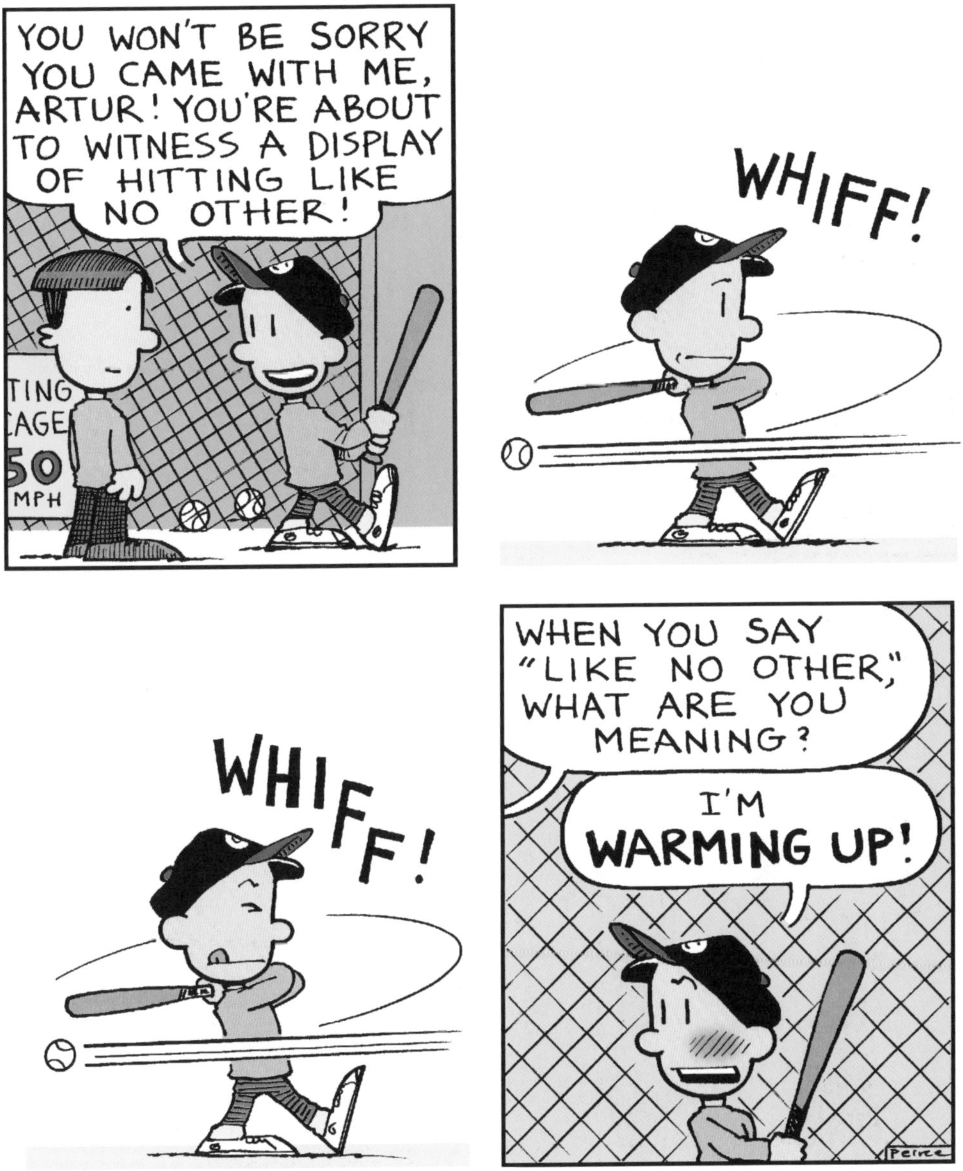
YOU WON'T BE SORRY YOU CAME WITH ME, ARTUR! YOU'RE ABOUT TO WITNESS A DISPLAY OF HITTING LIKE NO OTHER!
TING
AGE
50
MPH
WHIFF!
WHIFF!
WHEN YOU SAY "LIKE NO OTHER," WHAT ARE YOU MEANING?
I'M **WARMING UP!**
Peirce

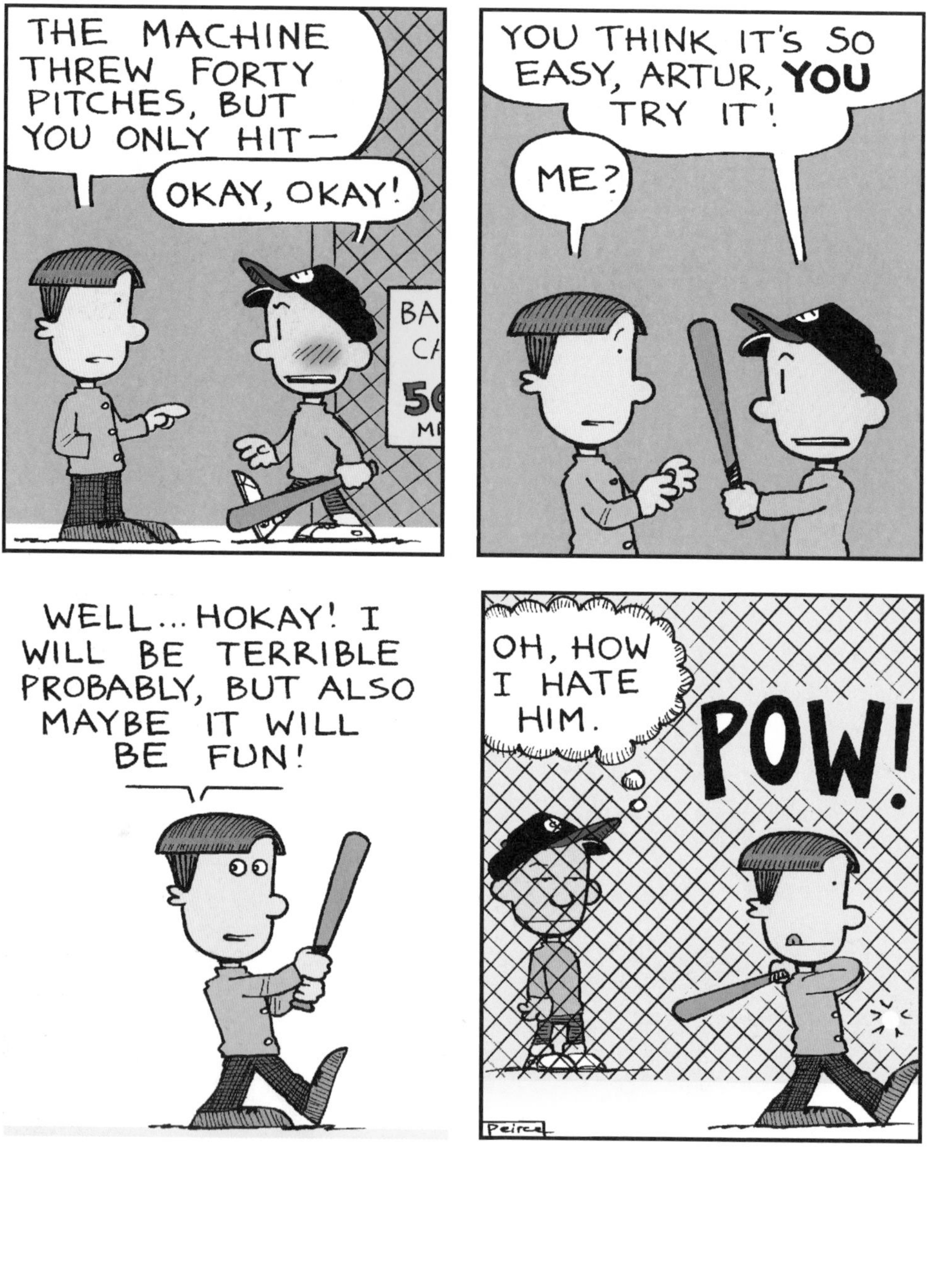
THE MACHINE THREW FORTY PITCHES, BUT YOU ONLY HIT—
OKAY, OKAY!
YOU THINK IT'S SO EASY, ARTUR, **YOU** TRY IT!
ME?
WELL... HOKAY! I WILL BE TERRIBLE PROBABLY, BUT ALSO MAYBE IT WILL BE FUN!
OH, HOW I HATE HIM.
POW!
Peirce

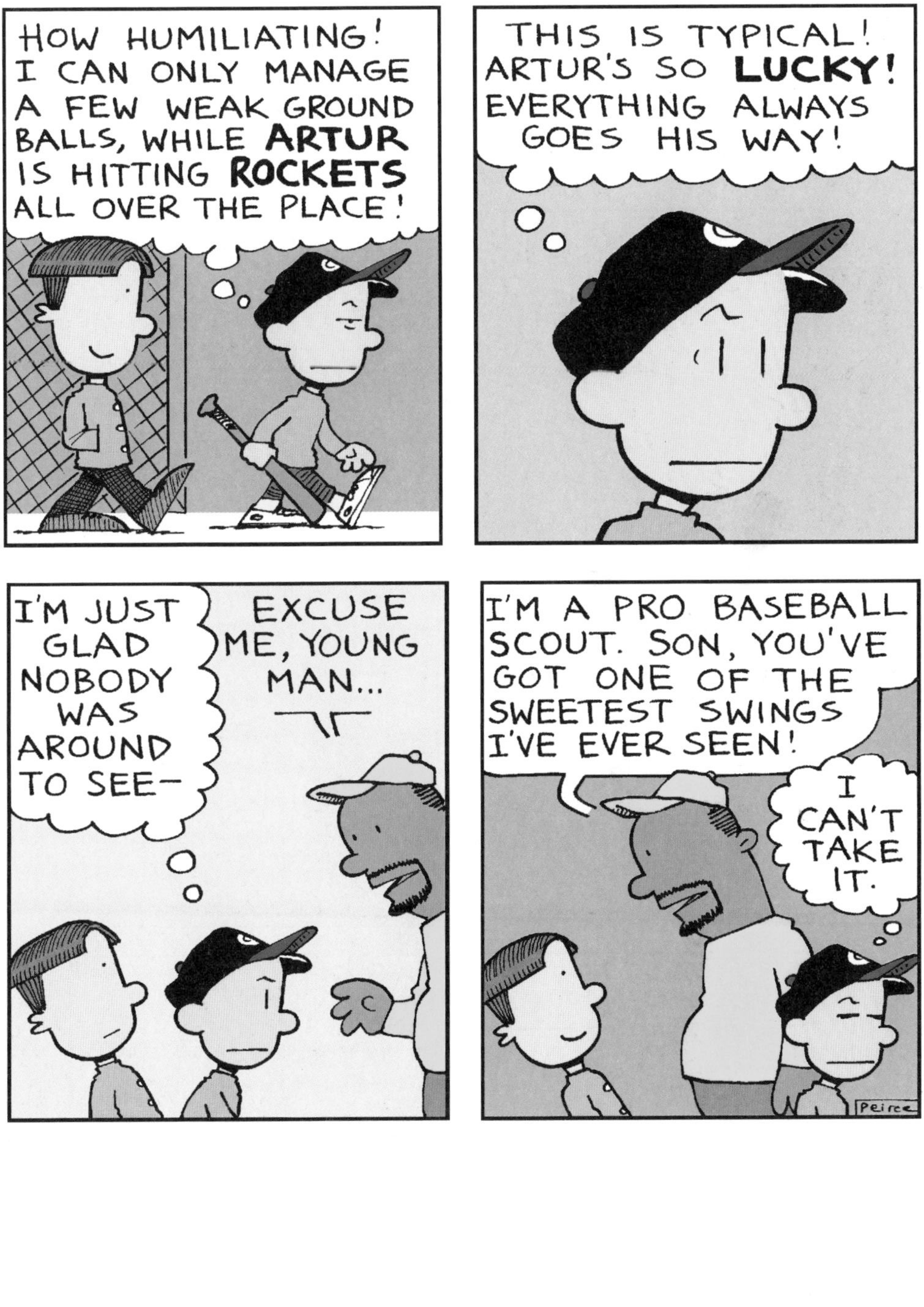
HOW HUMILIATING! I CAN ONLY MANAGE A FEW WEAK GROUND BALLS, WHILE ARTUR IS HITTING ROCKETS ALL OVER THE PLACE!
THIS IS TYPICAL! ARTUR'S SO LUCKY! EVERYTHING ALWAYS GOES HIS WAY!
I'M JUST GLAD NOBODY WAS AROUND TO SEE-
EXCUSE ME, YOUNG MAN...
I'M A PRO BASEBALL SCOUT. SON, YOU'VE GOT ONE OF THE SWEETEST SWINGS I'VE EVER SEEN!
I CAN'T TAKE IT.
Peirce

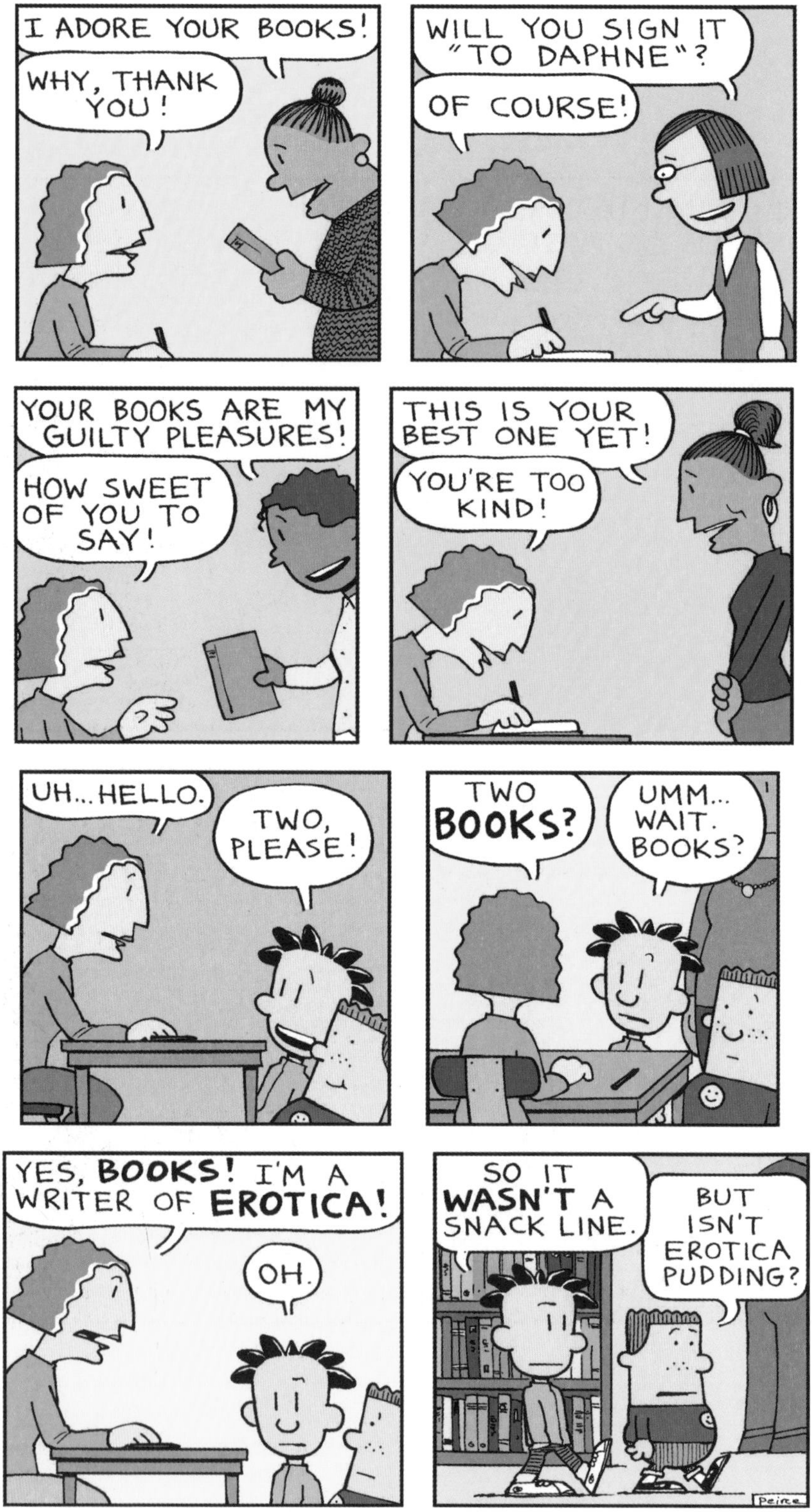
I ADORE YOUR BOOKS!
WHY, THANK YOU!
WILL YOU SIGN IT "TO DAPHNE"?
OF COURSE!
YOUR BOOKS ARE MY GUILTY PLEASURES!
HOW SWEET OF YOU TO SAY!
THIS IS YOUR BEST ONE YET!
YOU'RE TOO KIND!
UH... HELLO.
TWO, PLEASE!
TWO **BOOKS?**
UMM... WAIT. BOOKS?
YES, **BOOKS!** I'M A WRITER OF **EROTICA!**
OH.
SO IT **WASN'T** A SNACK LINE.
BUT ISN'T EROTICA PUDDING?
Peirce

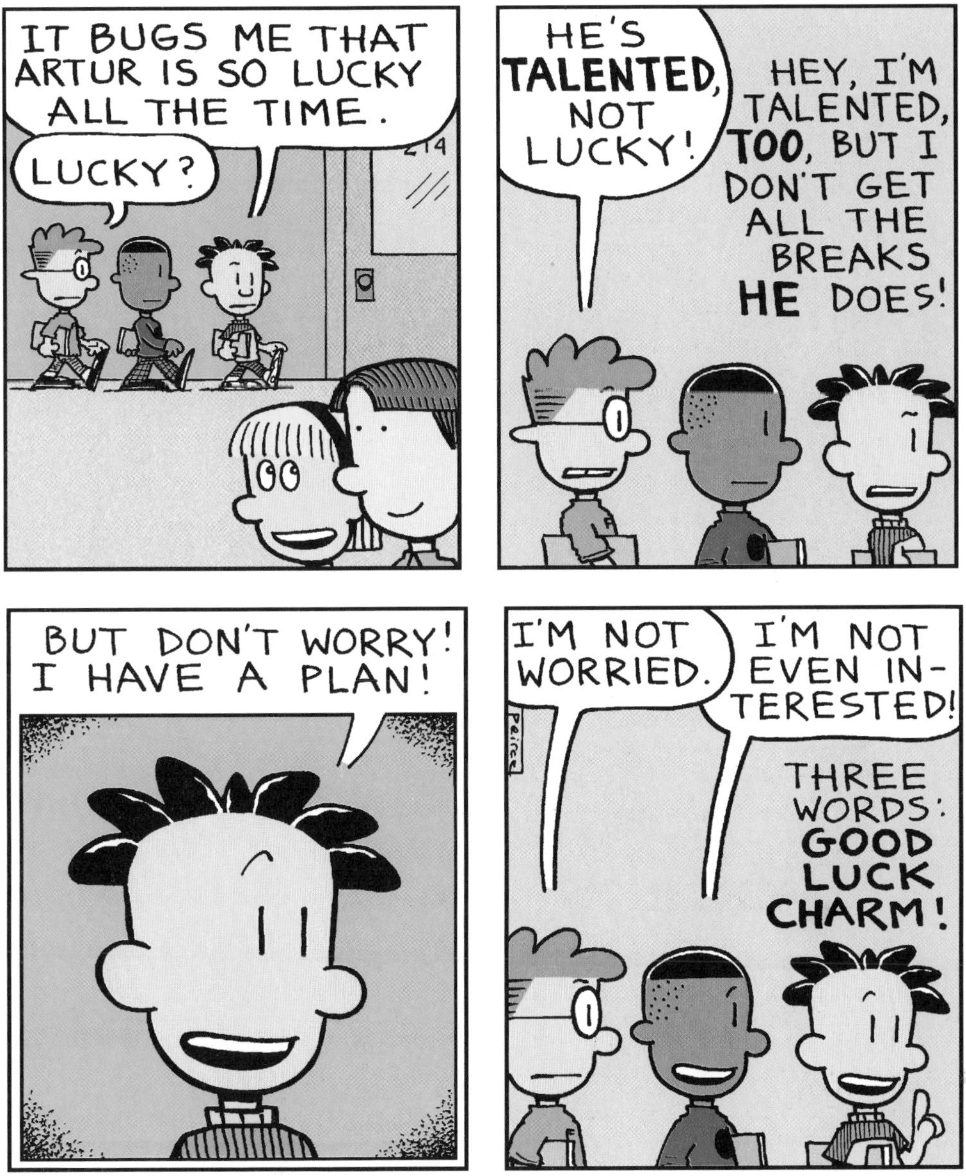

IT BUGS ME THAT ARTUR IS SO LUCKY ALL THE TIME.
LUCKY?
HE'S **TALENTED**, NOT LUCKY!
HEY, I'M TALENTED, **TOO**, BUT I DON'T GET ALL THE BREAKS **HE** DOES!
BUT DON'T WORRY! I HAVE A PLAN!
I'M NOT WORRIED.
I'M NOT EVEN INTERESTED!
THREE WORDS: **GOOD LUCK CHARM!**
Peirce

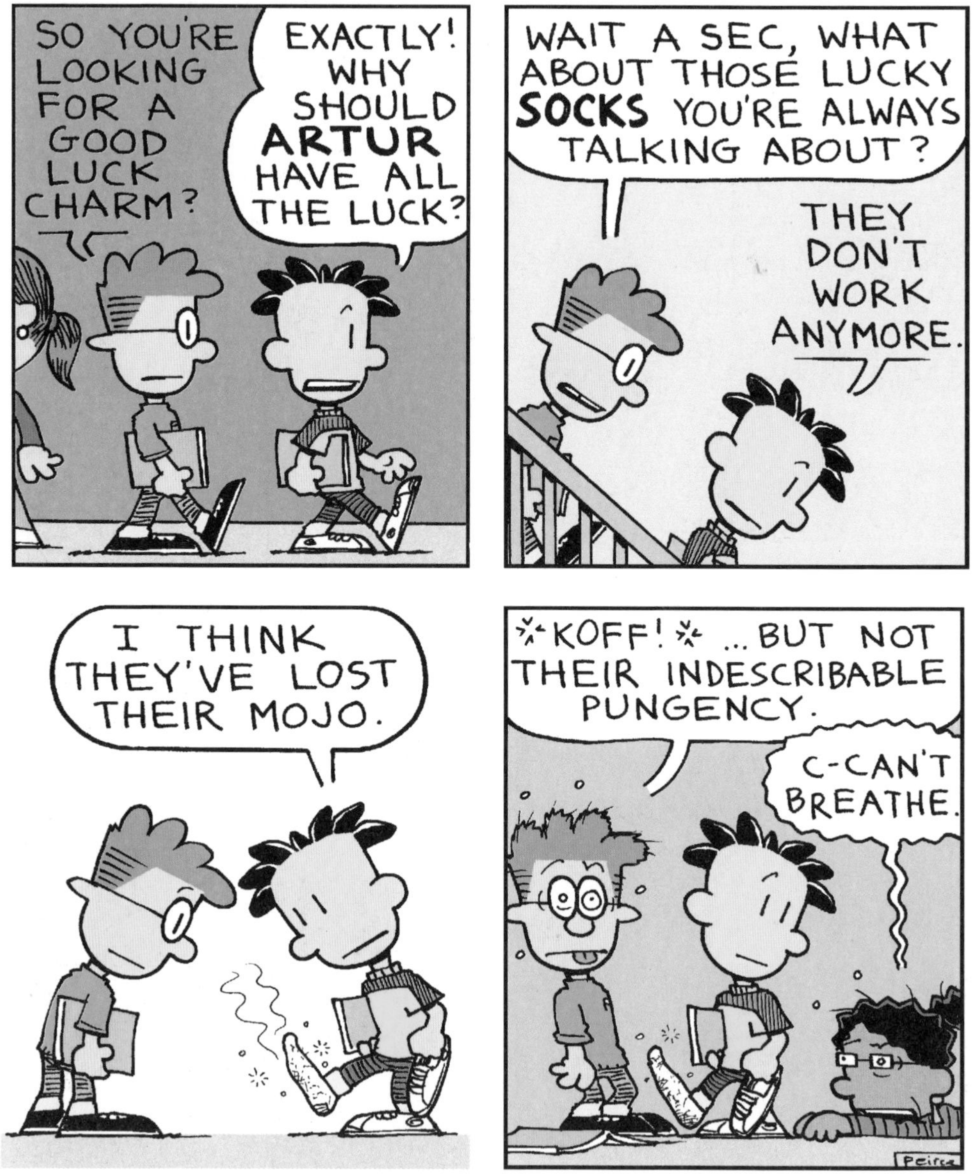
SO YOU'RE LOOKING FOR A GOOD LUCK CHARM?
EXACTLY! WHY SHOULD ARTUR HAVE ALL THE LUCK?
WAIT A SEC, WHAT ABOUT THOSE LUCKY SOCKS YOU'RE ALWAYS TALKING ABOUT?
THEY DON'T WORK ANYMORE.
I THINK THEY'VE LOST THEIR MOJO.
KOFF! ... BUT NOT THEIR INDESCRIBABLE PUNGENCY.
C-CAN'T BREATHE.
PEIRCE

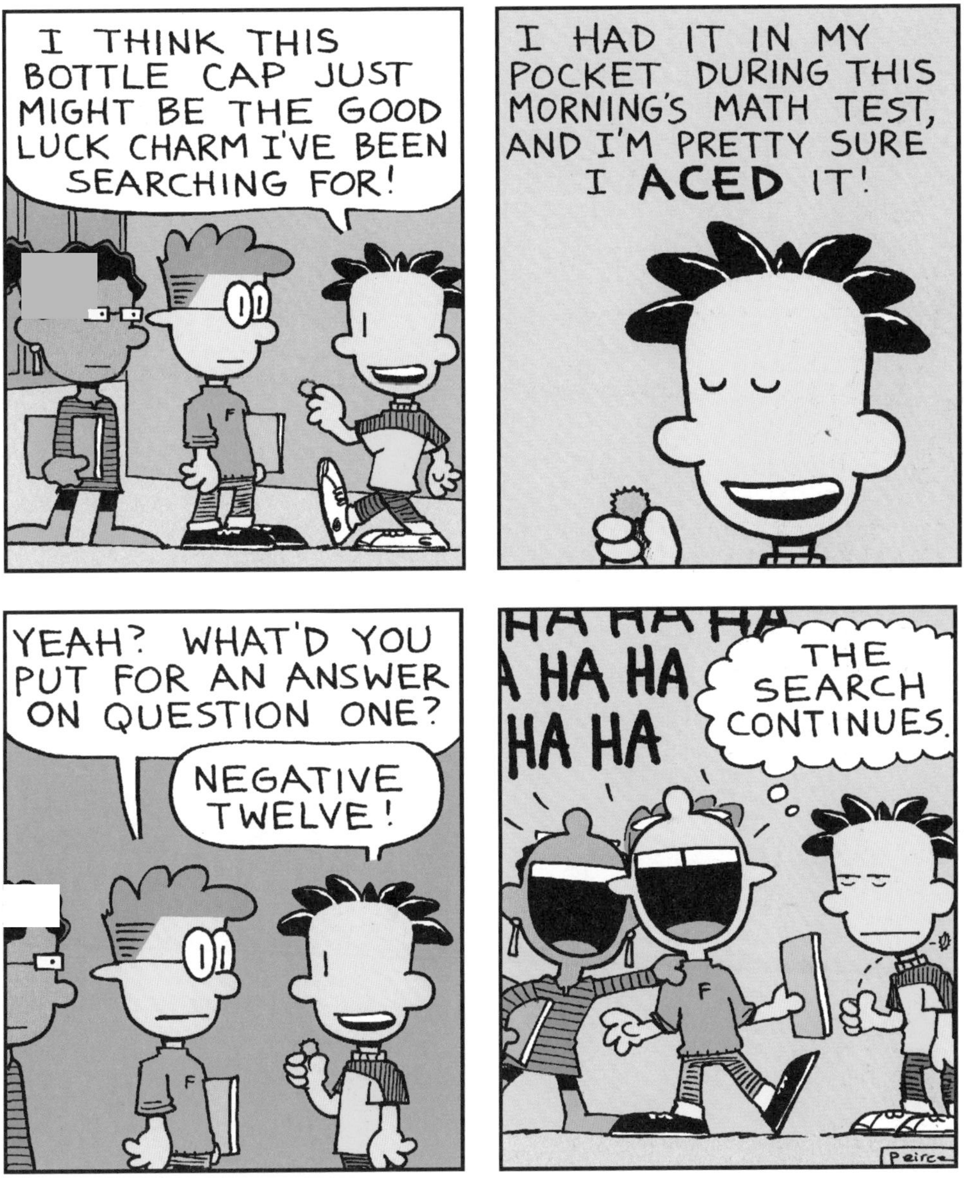
I THINK THIS BOTTLE CAP JUST MIGHT BE THE GOOD LUCK CHARM I'VE BEEN SEARCHING FOR!
I HAD IT IN MY POCKET DURING THIS MORNING'S MATH TEST, AND I'M PRETTY SURE I **ACED** IT!
YEAH? WHAT'D YOU PUT FOR AN ANSWER ON QUESTION ONE?
NEGATIVE TWELVE!
HA HA
HA HA
THE SEARCH CONTINUES.
Peirce

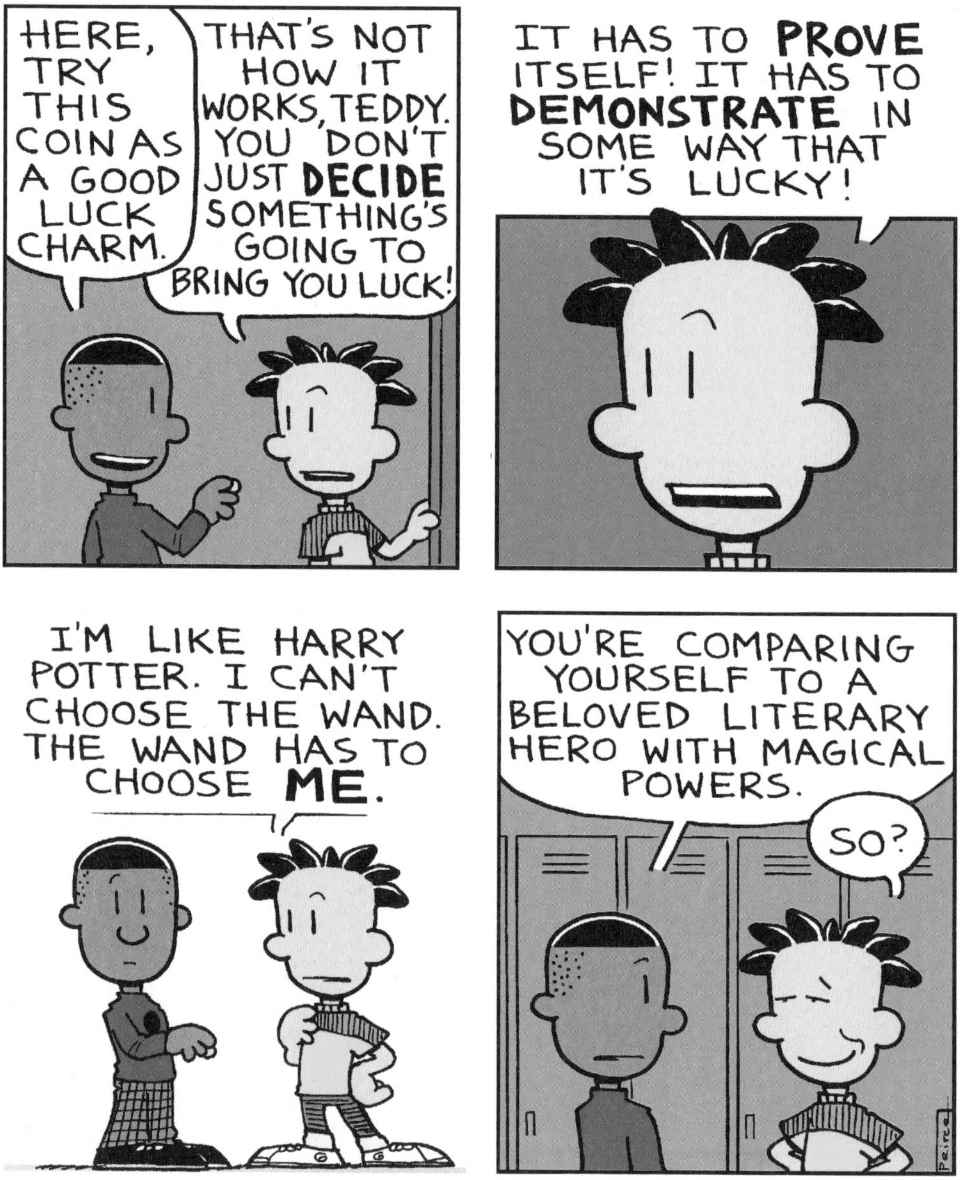
HERE, TRY THIS COIN AS A GOOD LUCK CHARM.
THAT'S NOT HOW IT WORKS, TEDDY. YOU DON'T JUST **DECIDE** SOMETHING'S GOING TO BRING YOU LUCK!
IT HAS TO **PROVE** ITSELF! IT HAS TO **DEMONSTRATE** IN SOME WAY THAT IT'S LUCKY!
I'M LIKE HARRY POTTER. I CAN'T CHOOSE THE WAND. THE WAND HAS TO CHOOSE **ME**.
YOU'RE COMPARING YOURSELF TO A BELOVED LITERARY HERO WITH MAGICAL POWERS.
SO?
Peirce

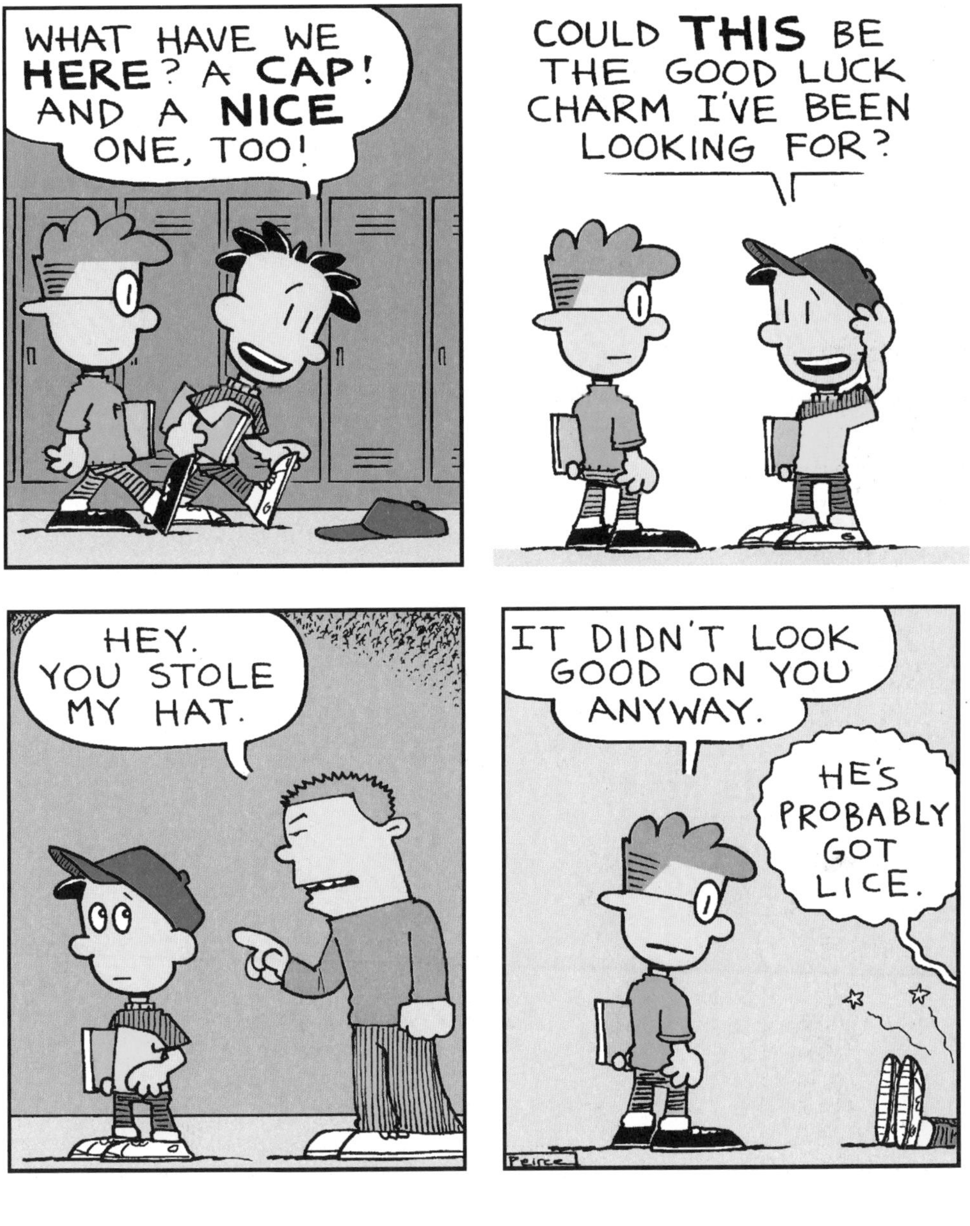
WHAT HAVE WE HERE? A CAP! AND A NICE ONE, TOO!
COULD THIS BE THE GOOD LUCK CHARM I'VE BEEN LOOKING FOR?
HEY. YOU STOLE MY HAT.
IT DIDN'T LOOK GOOD ON YOU ANYWAY.
HE'S PROBABLY GOT LICE.
Peirce

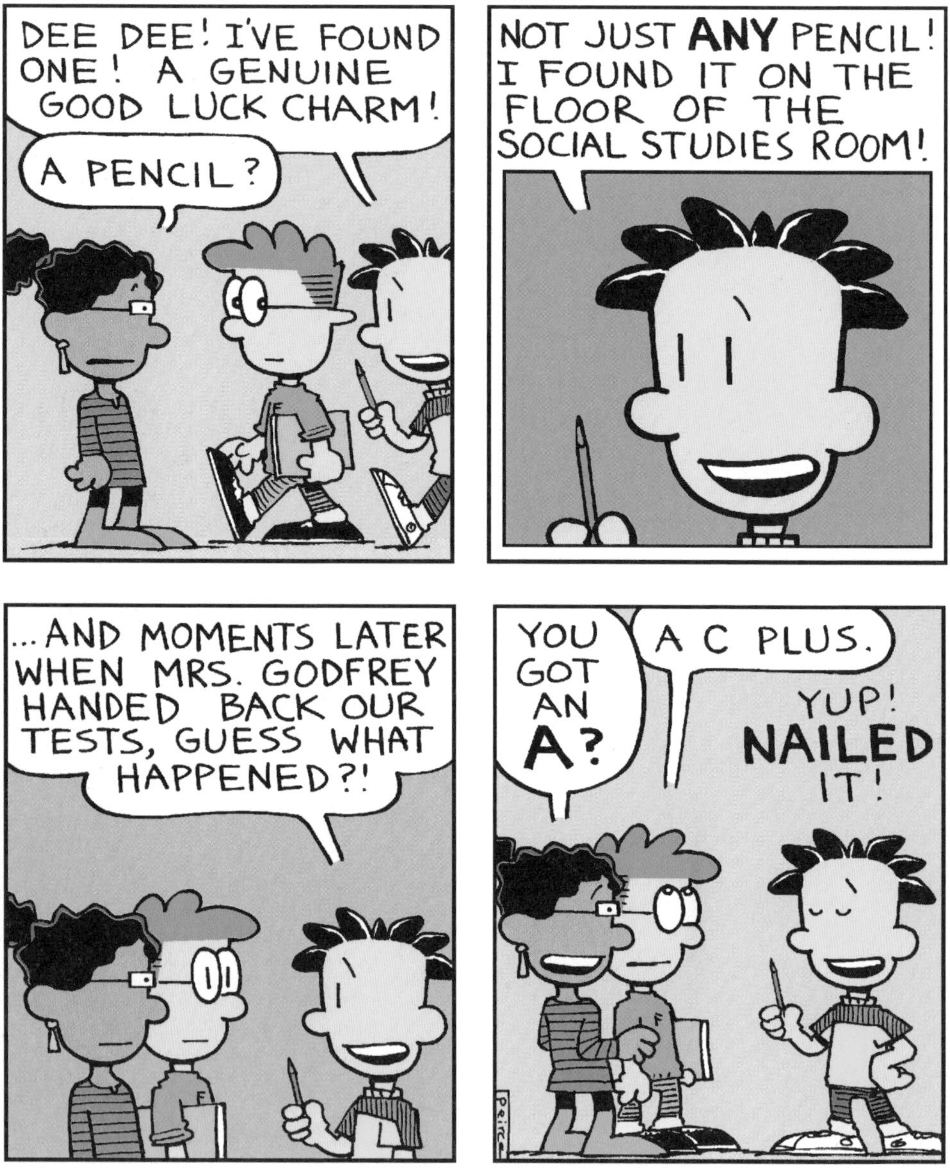
DEE DEE! I'VE FOUND ONE! A GENUINE GOOD LUCK CHARM!
A PENCIL?
NOT JUST **ANY** PENCIL! I FOUND IT ON THE FLOOR OF THE SOCIAL STUDIES ROOM!
...AND MOMENTS LATER WHEN MRS. GODFREY HANDED BACK OUR TESTS, GUESS WHAT HAPPENED?!
YOU GOT AN **A?**
A C PLUS.
YUP! **NAILED** IT!
Peirce

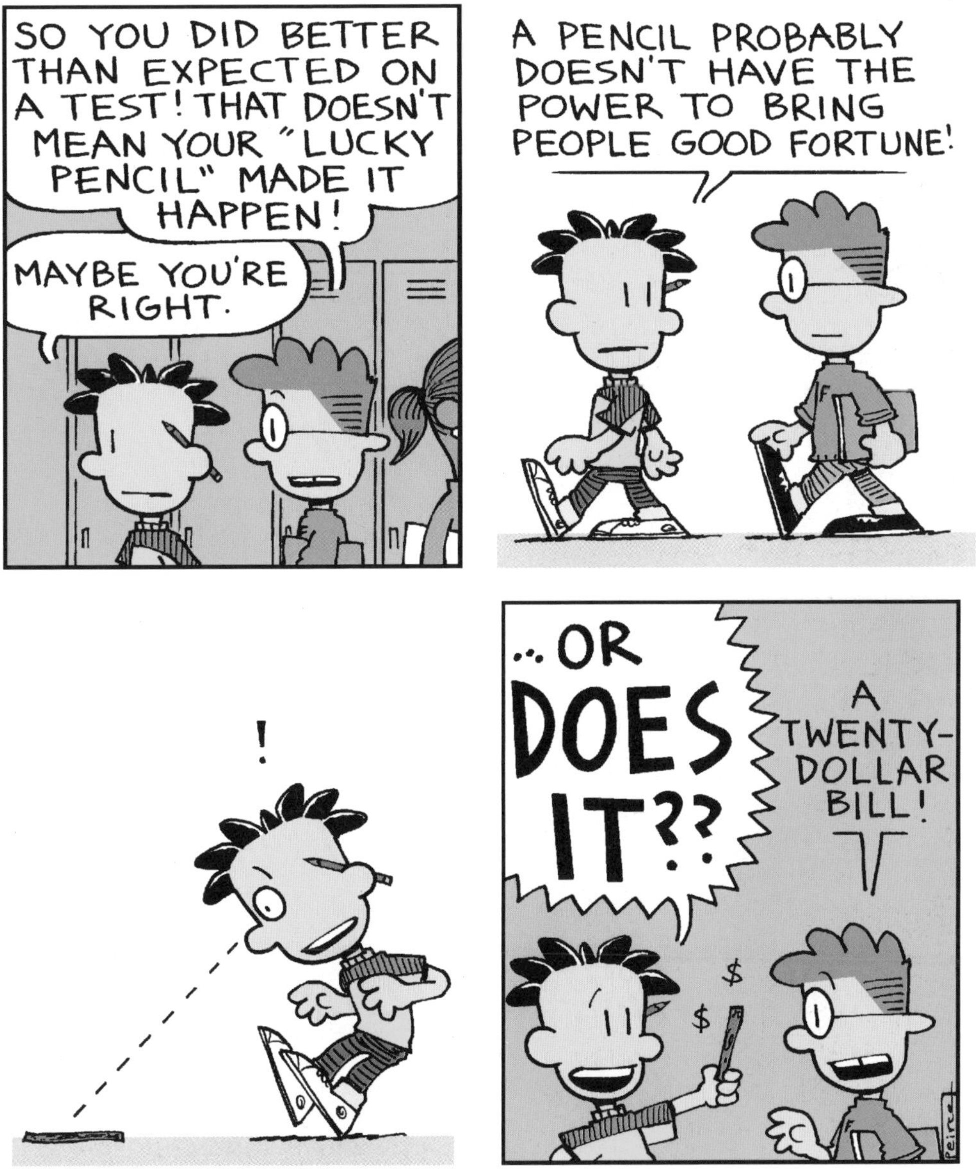
SO YOU DID BETTER THAN EXPECTED ON A TEST! THAT DOESN'T MEAN YOUR "LUCKY PENCIL" MADE IT HAPPEN!
MAYBE YOU'RE RIGHT.
A PENCIL PROBABLY DOESN'T HAVE THE POWER TO BRING PEOPLE GOOD FORTUNE!
!
...OR DOES IT??
A TWENTY-DOLLAR BILL!
$
$
PEIRCE

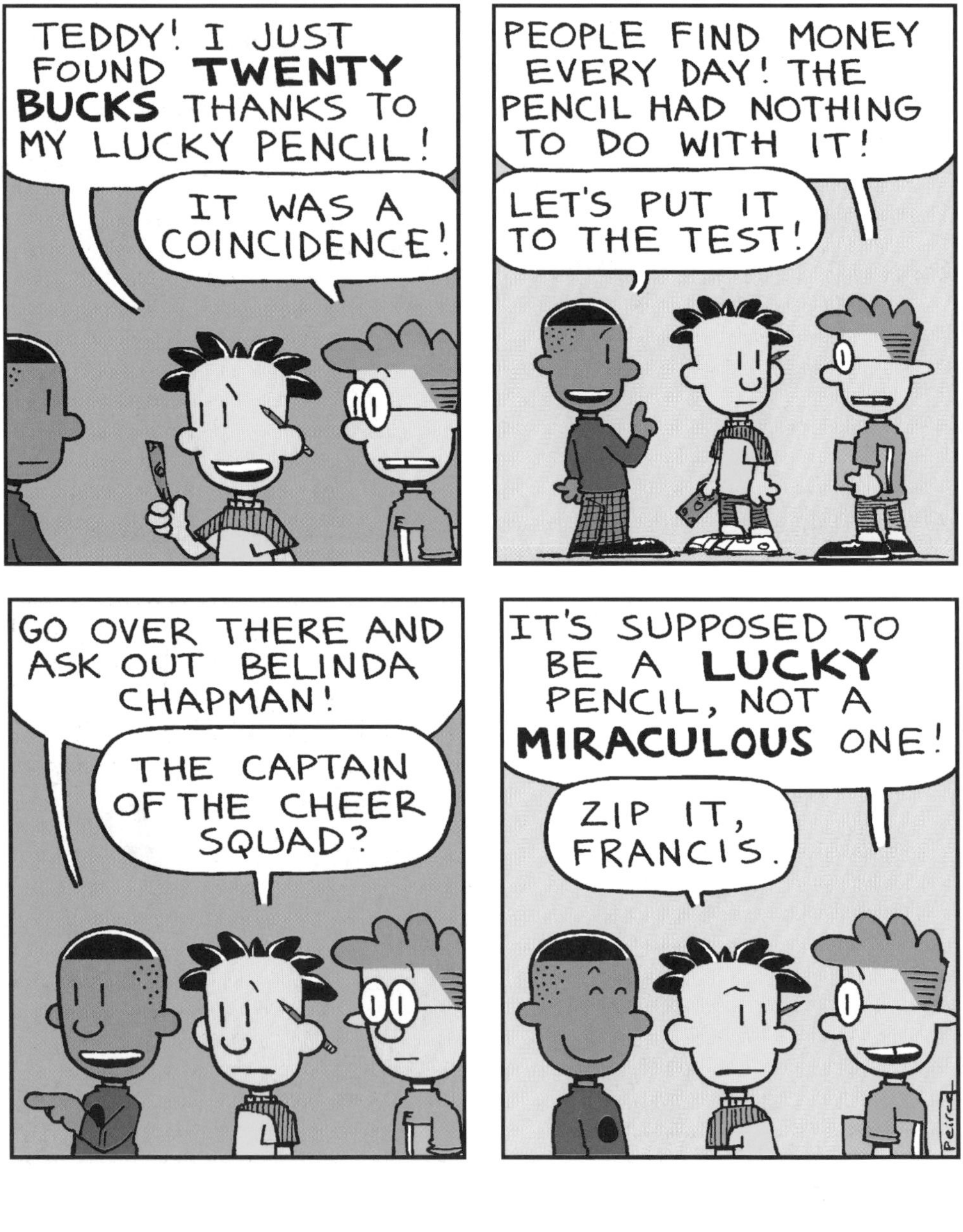

TEDDY! I JUST FOUND **TWENTY BUCKS** THANKS TO MY LUCKY PENCIL!
IT WAS A COINCIDENCE!
PEOPLE FIND MONEY EVERY DAY! THE PENCIL HAD NOTHING TO DO WITH IT!
LET'S PUT IT TO THE TEST!
GO OVER THERE AND ASK OUT BELINDA CHAPMAN!
THE CAPTAIN OF THE CHEER SQUAD?
IT'S SUPPOSED TO BE A **LUCKY** PENCIL, NOT A **MIRACULOUS** ONE!
ZIP IT, FRANCIS.
Peirce

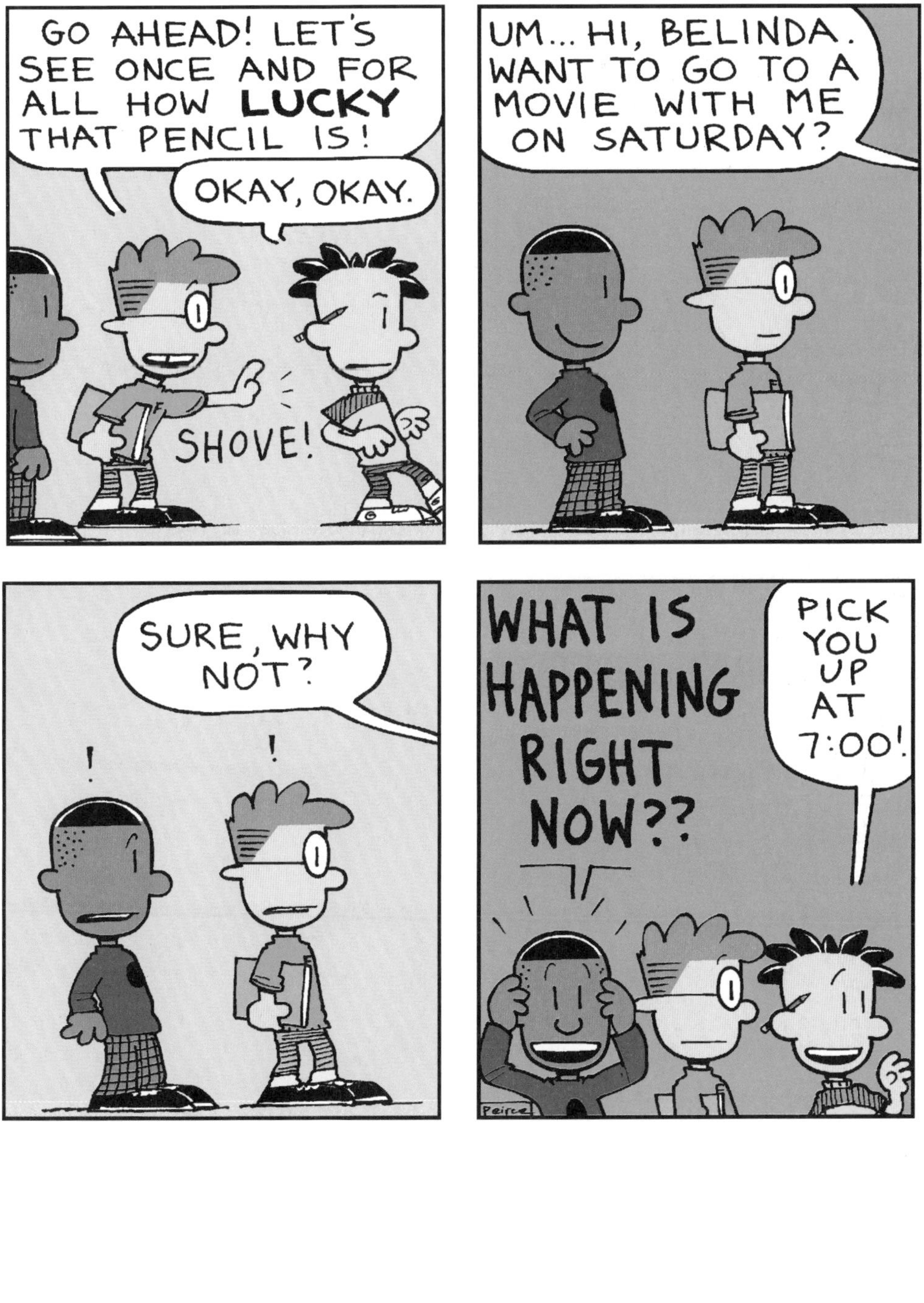
GO AHEAD! LET'S SEE ONCE AND FOR ALL HOW **LUCKY** THAT PENCIL IS!
OKAY, OKAY.
SHOVE!
UM... HI, BELINDA. WANT TO GO TO A MOVIE WITH ME ON SATURDAY?
SURE, WHY NOT?
!
!
WHAT IS HAPPENING RIGHT NOW??
PICK YOU UP AT 7:00!
Peirce

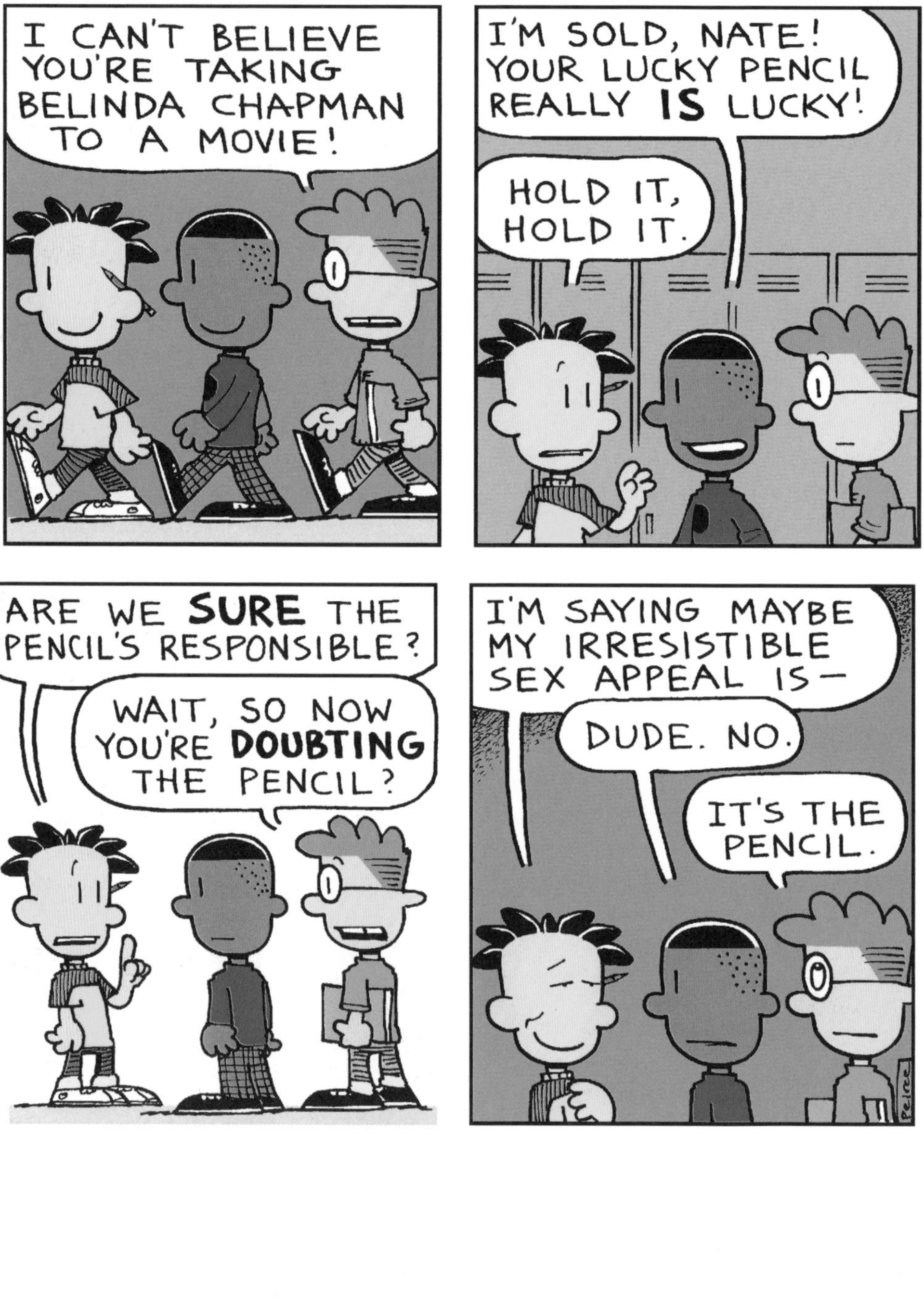
I CAN'T BELIEVE YOU'RE TAKING BELINDA CHAPMAN TO A MOVIE!
I'M SOLD, NATE! YOUR LUCKY PENCIL REALLY **IS** LUCKY!
HOLD IT, HOLD IT.
ARE WE **SURE** THE PENCIL'S RESPONSIBLE?
WAIT, SO NOW YOU'RE **DOUBTING** THE PENCIL?
I'M SAYING MAYBE MY IRRESISTIBLE SEX APPEAL IS—
DUDE. NO.
IT'S THE PENCIL.
Peirce

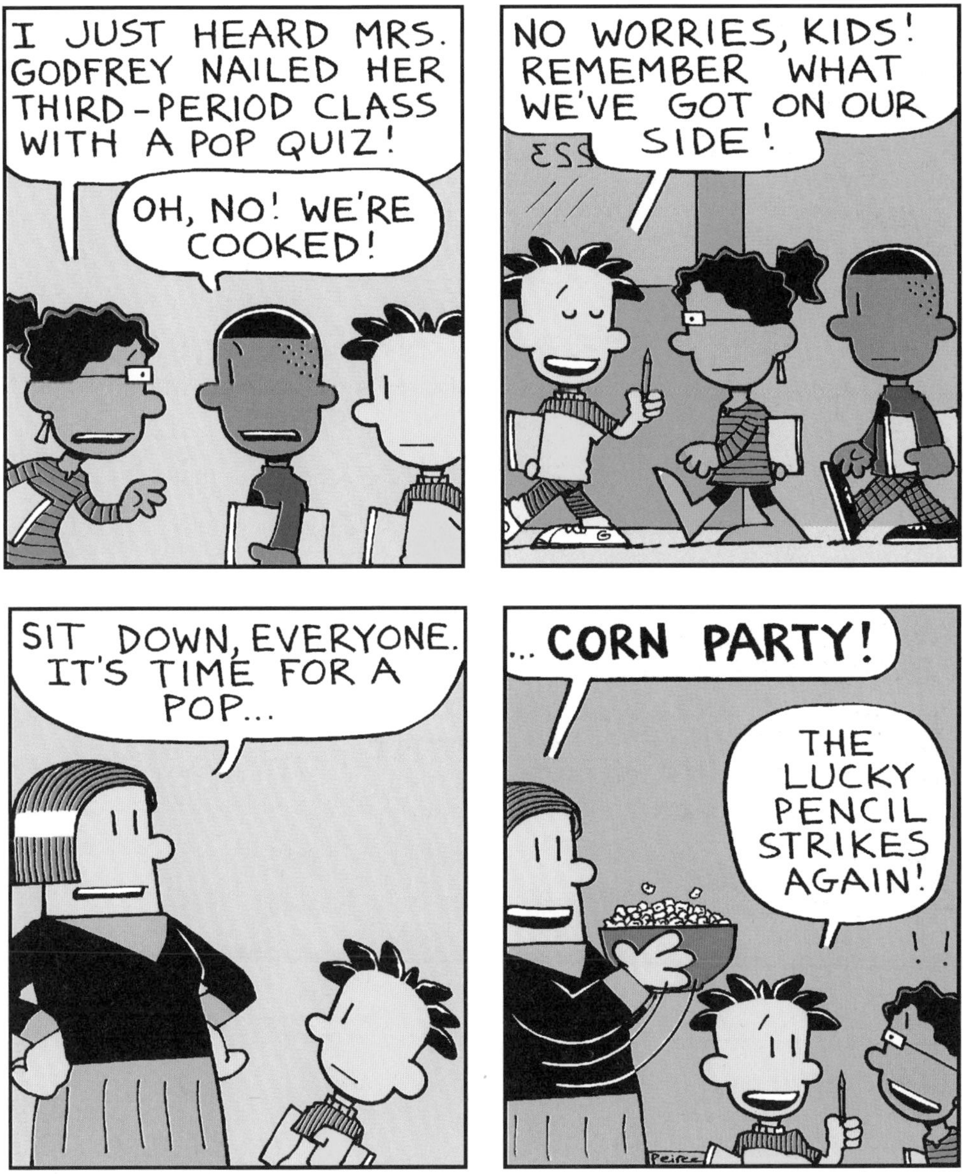
I JUST HEARD MRS. GODFREY NAILED HER THIRD-PERIOD CLASS WITH A POP QUIZ!
OH, NO! WE'RE COOKED!
NO WORRIES, KIDS! REMEMBER WHAT WE'VE GOT ON OUR SIDE!
SIT DOWN, EVERYONE. IT'S TIME FOR A POP...
...CORN PARTY!
THE LUCKY PENCIL STRIKES AGAIN!
! !

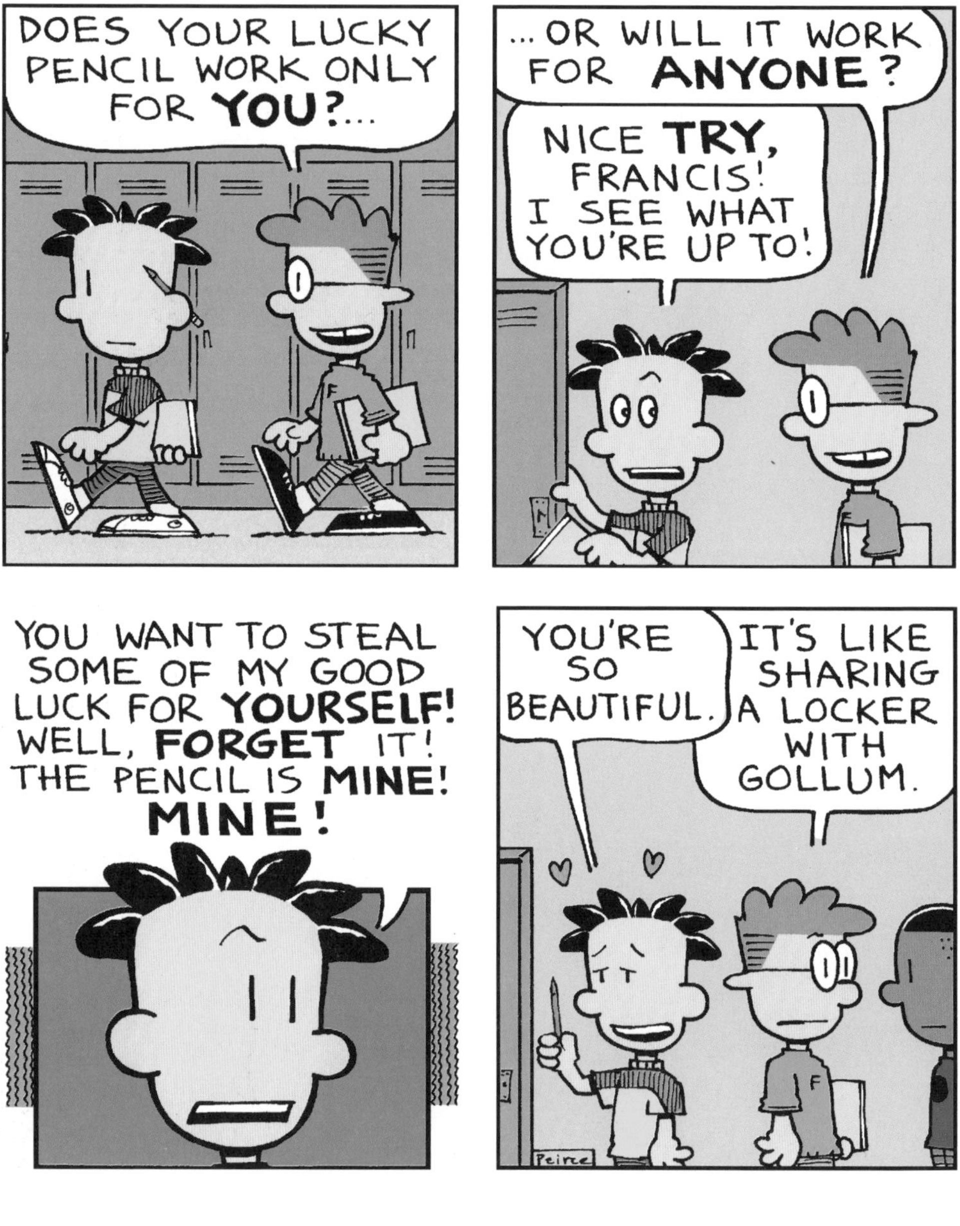
DOES YOUR LUCKY PENCIL WORK ONLY FOR **YOU?**...
...OR WILL IT WORK FOR **ANYONE**?
NICE **TRY**, FRANCIS! I SEE WHAT YOU'RE UP TO!
YOU WANT TO STEAL SOME OF MY GOOD LUCK FOR **YOURSELF!** WELL, **FORGET** IT! THE PENCIL IS **MINE! MINE!**
YOU'RE SO BEAUTIFUL.
IT'S LIKE SHARING A LOCKER WITH GOLLUM.
Peirce

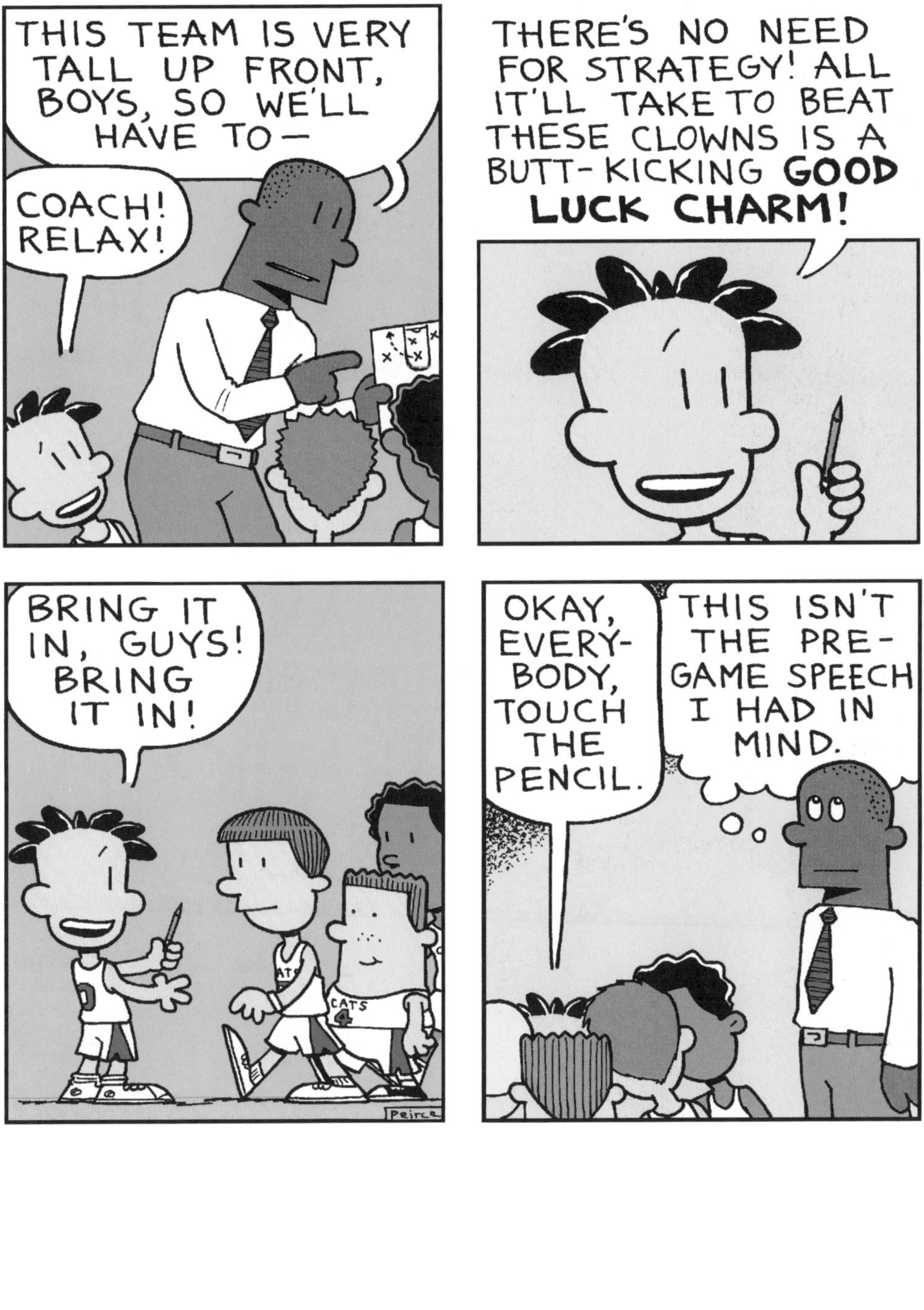
THIS TEAM IS VERY TALL UP FRONT, BOYS, SO WE'LL HAVE TO—
COACH! RELAX!
THERE'S NO NEED FOR STRATEGY! ALL IT'LL TAKE TO BEAT THESE CLOWNS IS A BUTT-KICKING GOOD LUCK CHARM!
BRING IT IN, GUYS! BRING IT IN!
CATS
4
Peirce
OKAY, EVERY-BODY, TOUCH THE PENCIL.
THIS ISN'T THE PRE-GAME SPEECH I HAD IN MIND.

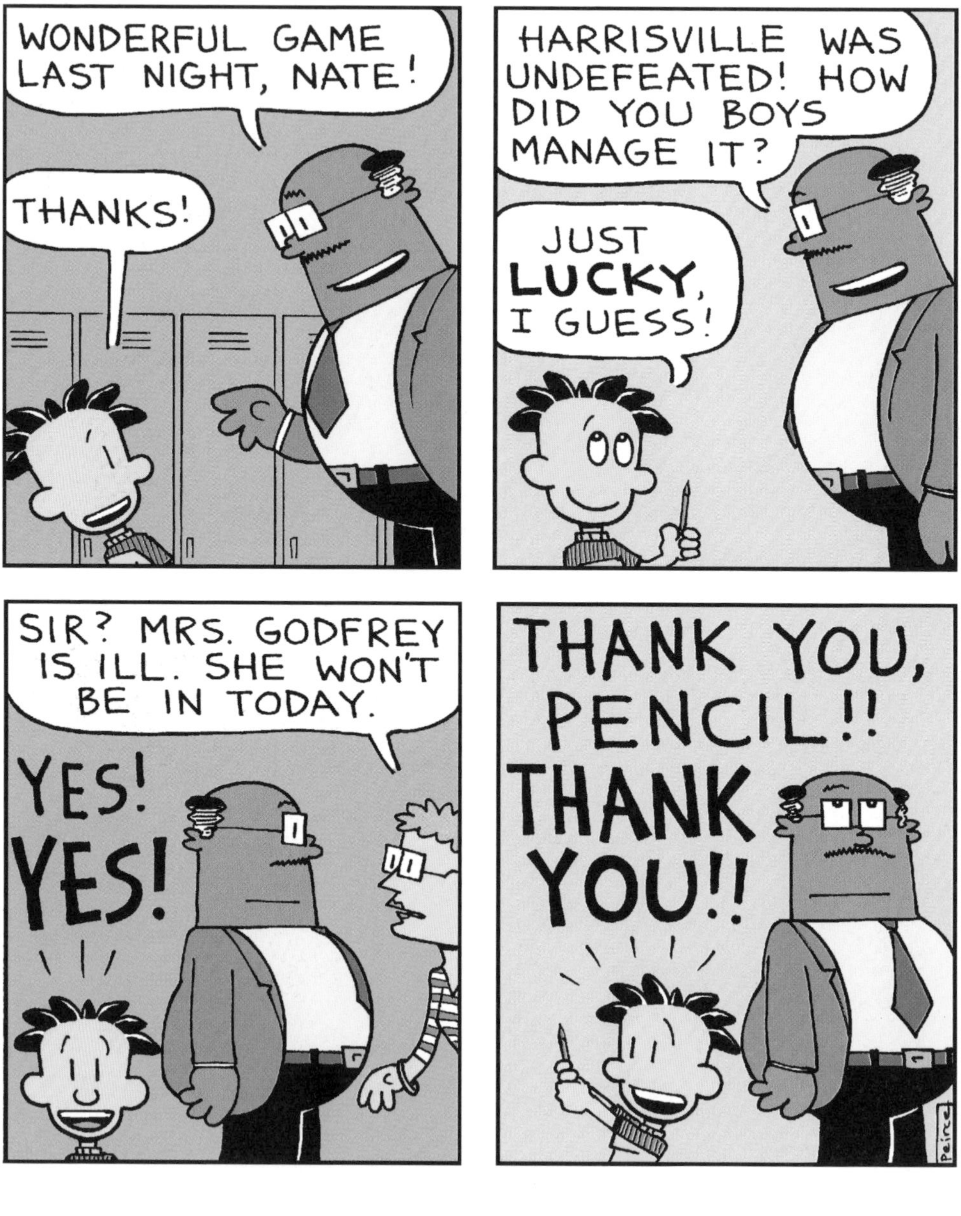
WONDERFUL GAME LAST NIGHT, NATE!
THANKS!
HARRISVILLE WAS UNDEFEATED! HOW DID YOU BOYS MANAGE IT?
JUST **LUCKY**, I GUESS!
SIR? MRS. GODFREY IS ILL. SHE WON'T BE IN TODAY.
YES! YES!
THANK YOU, PENCIL!!
THANK YOU!!
Peirce

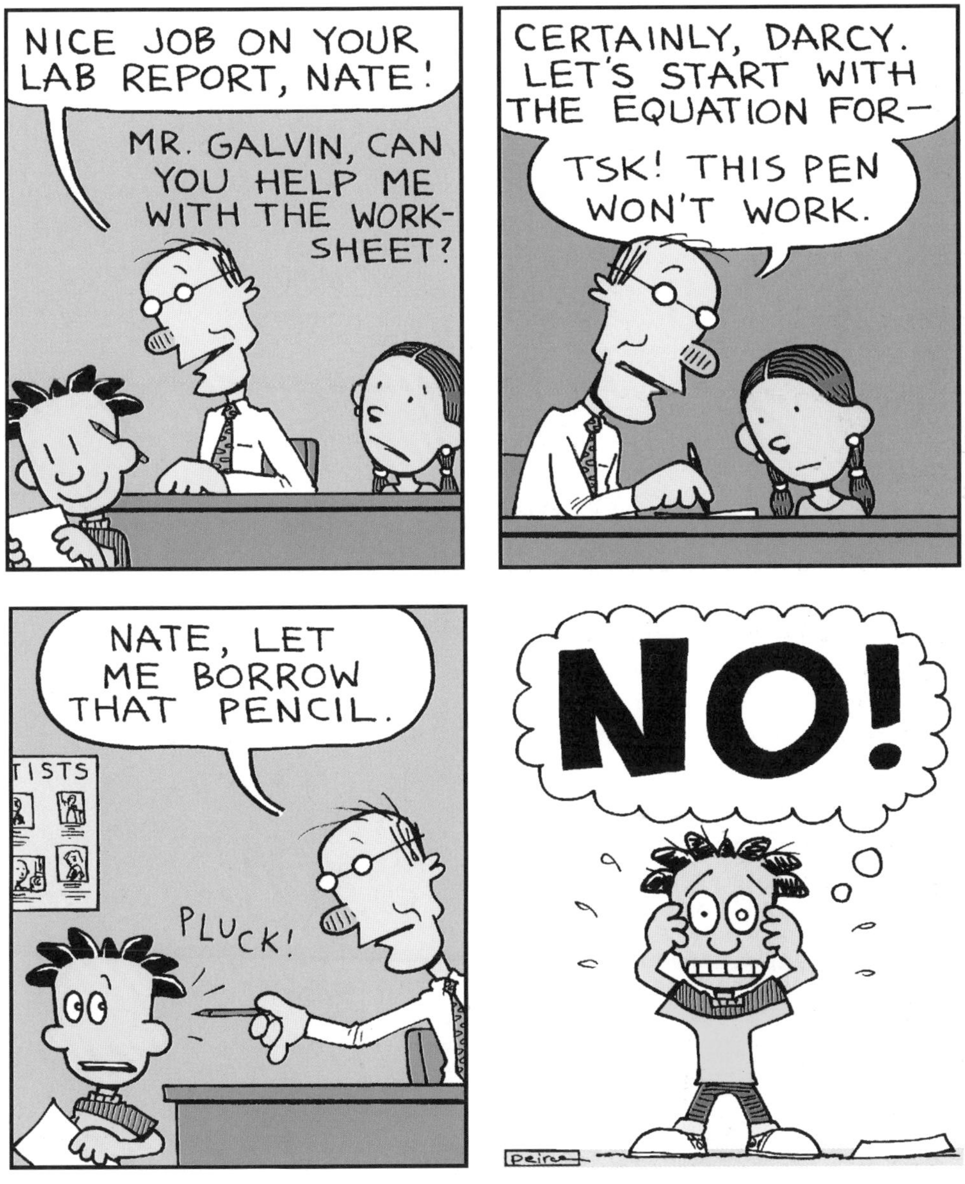
NICE JOB ON YOUR LAB REPORT, NATE!
MR. GALVIN, CAN YOU HELP ME WITH THE WORK-SHEET?
CERTAINLY, DARCY. LET'S START WITH THE EQUATION FOR—
TSK! THIS PEN WON'T WORK.
NATE, LET ME BORROW THAT PENCIL.
TISTS
PLUCK!
NO!
peirce

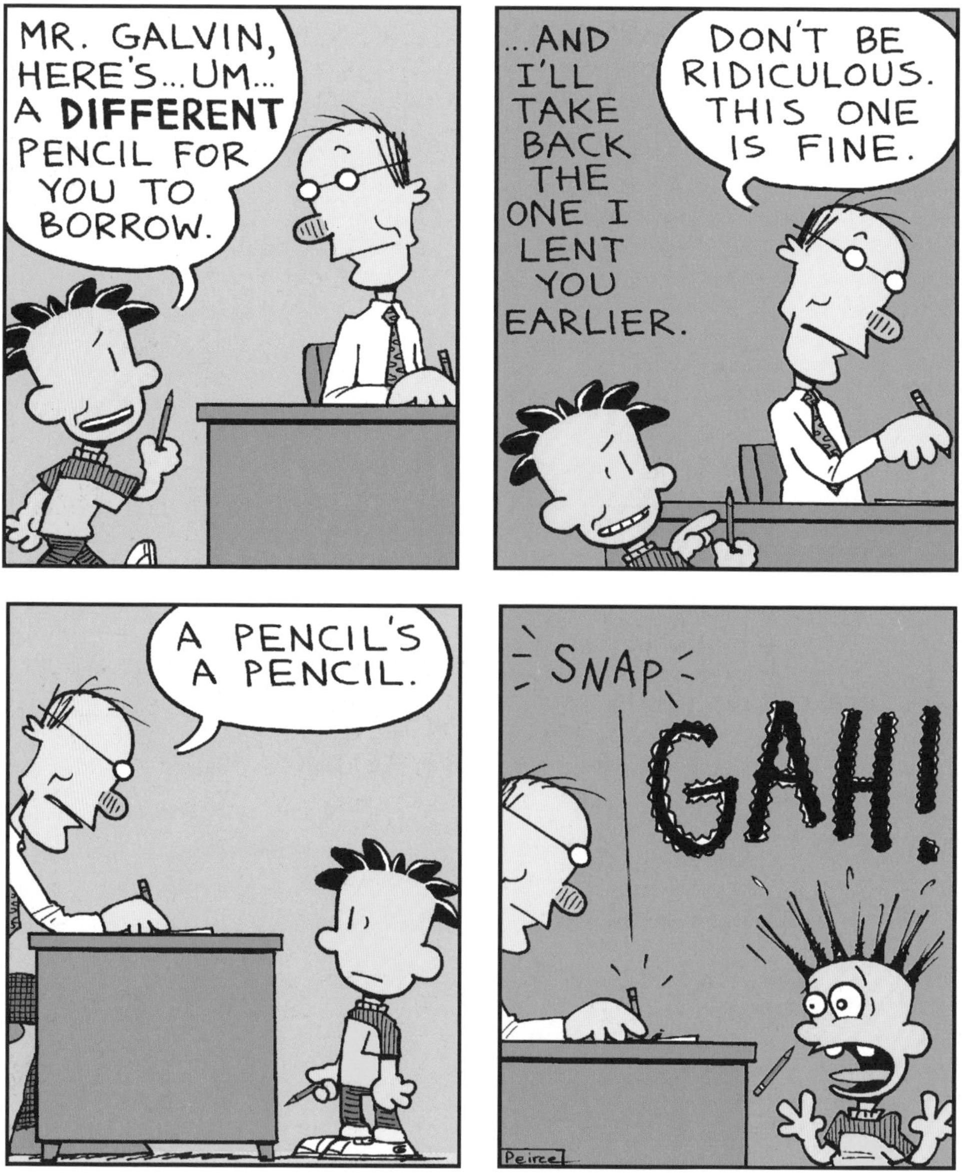
MR. GALVIN, HERE'S...UM... A **DIFFERENT** PENCIL FOR YOU TO BORROW.
...AND I'LL TAKE BACK THE ONE I LENT YOU EARLIER.
DON'T BE RIDICULOUS. THIS ONE IS FINE.
A PENCIL'S A PENCIL.
SNAP
GAH!
Peirce

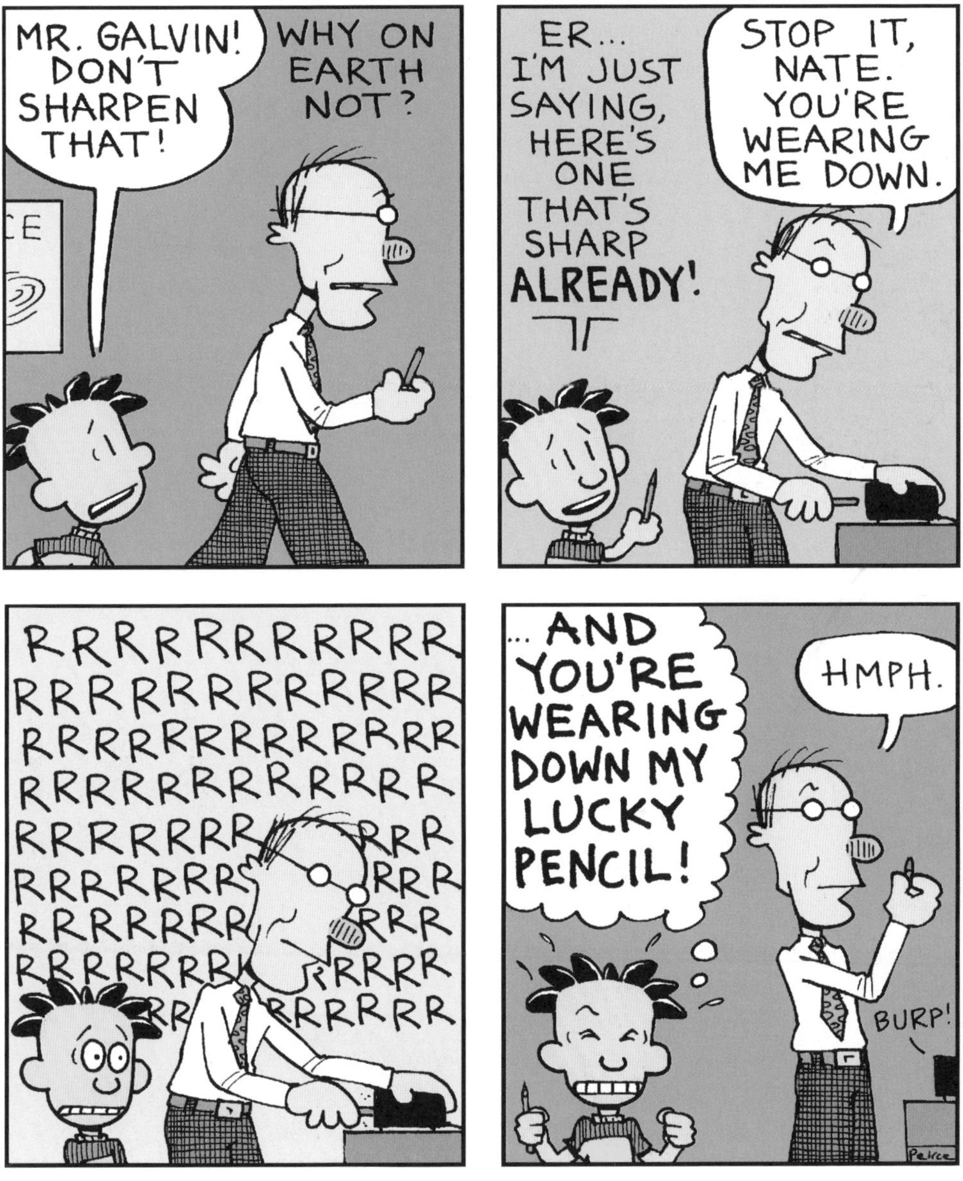

MR. GALVIN! DON'T SHARPEN THAT!
WHY ON EARTH NOT?
ER... I'M JUST SAYING, HERE'S ONE THAT'S SHARP **ALREADY**!
STOP IT, NATE. YOU'RE WEARING ME DOWN.
RRRRRRRRRRR
RRRRRRRRRRRR
RRRRRRRRRRRR
RRRRRRRRRRR
RRRRRRR RRR
RRRRRRR RRR
RRRRRRR RRR
RRRRRRR RRRR
RR RRRRRR
... AND YOU'RE WEARING DOWN MY LUCKY PENCIL!
HMPH.
BURP!
Peirce

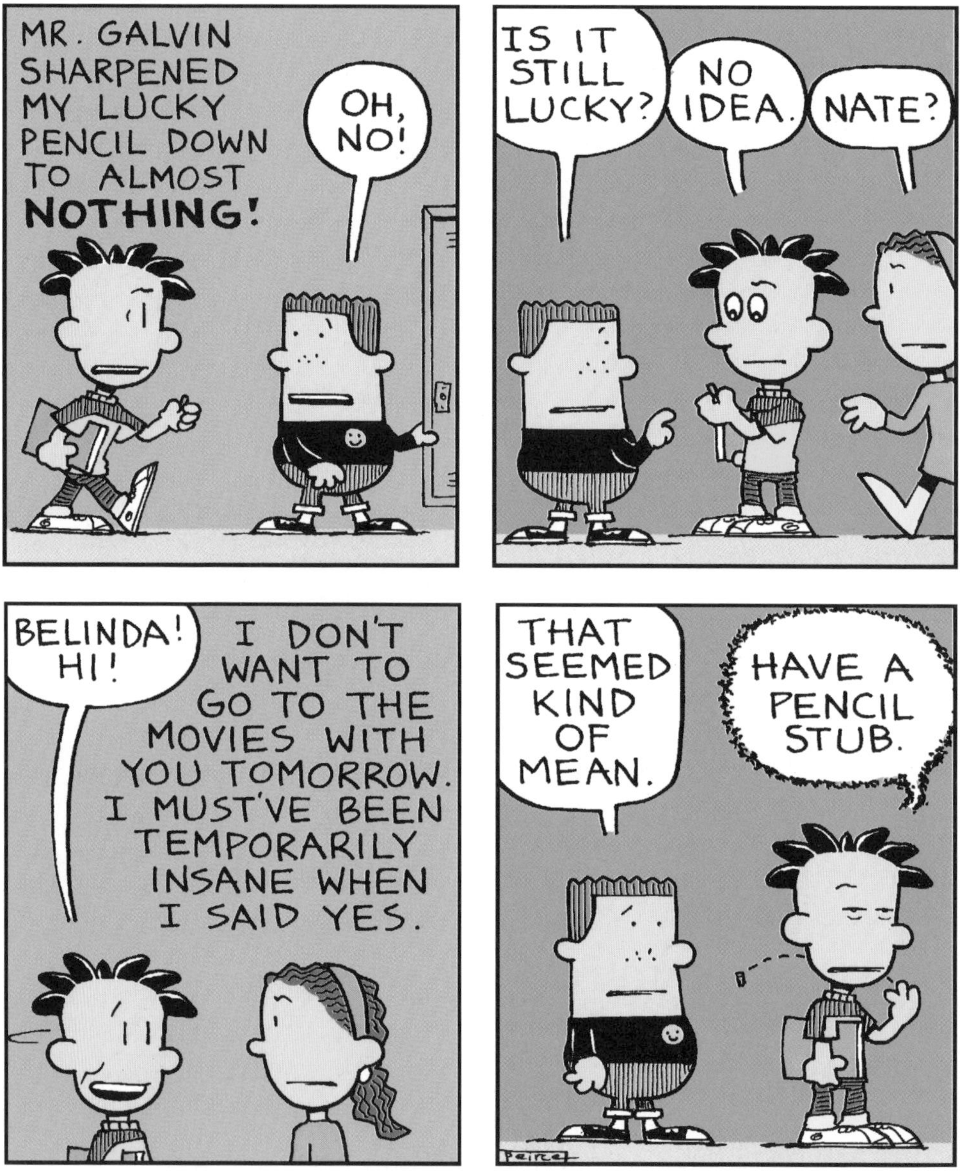
MR. GALVIN SHARPENED MY LUCKY PENCIL DOWN TO ALMOST **NOTHING!**
OH, NO!
IS IT STILL LUCKY?
NO IDEA.
NATE?
BELINDA! HI!
I DON'T WANT TO GO TO THE MOVIES WITH YOU TOMORROW. I MUST'VE BEEN TEMPORARILY INSANE WHEN I SAID YES.
THAT SEEMED KIND OF MEAN.
HAVE A PENCIL STUB.

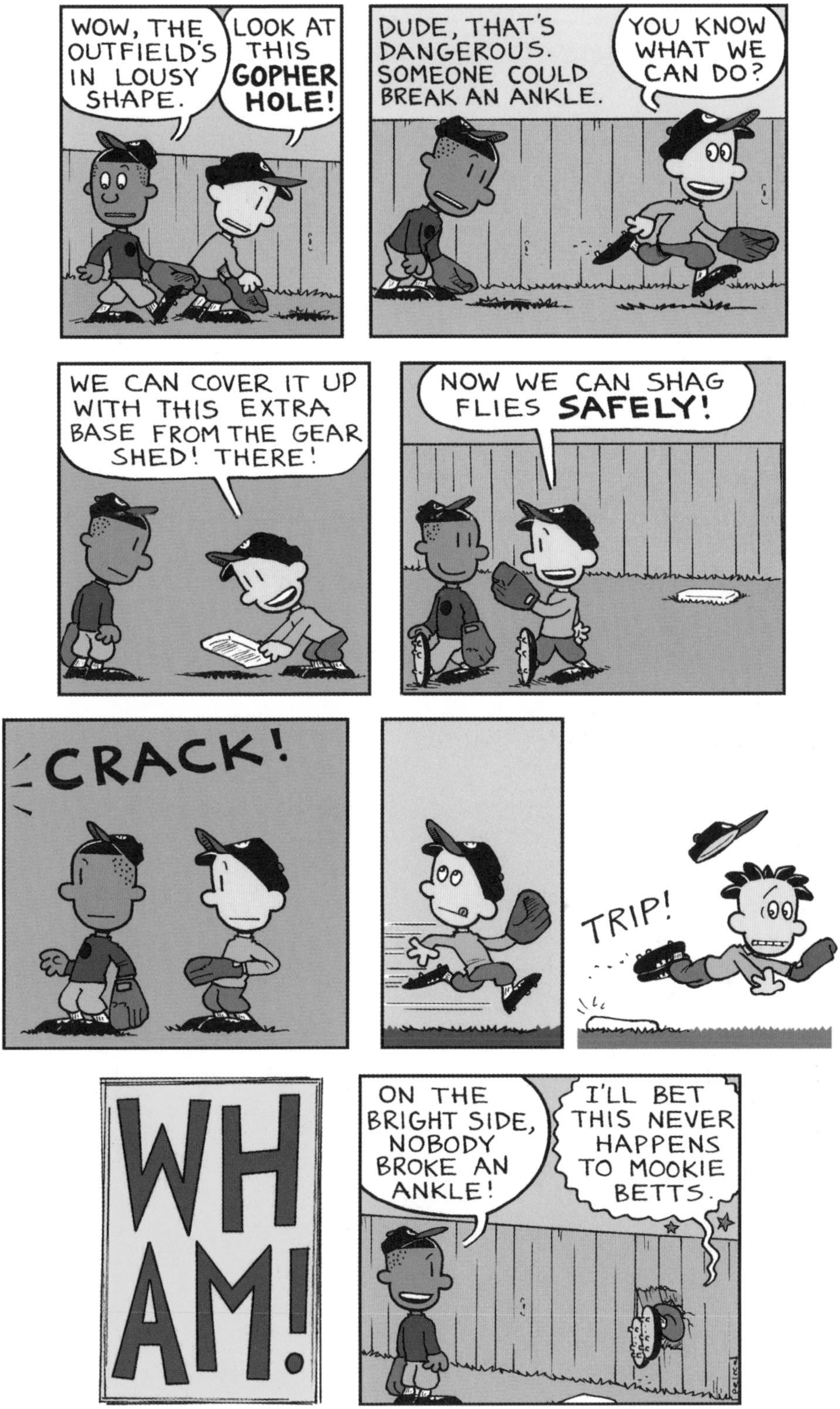
WOW, THE OUTFIELD'S IN LOUSY SHAPE.
LOOK AT THIS **GOPHER HOLE!**
DUDE, THAT'S DANGEROUS. SOMEONE COULD BREAK AN ANKLE.
YOU KNOW WHAT WE CAN DO?
WE CAN COVER IT UP WITH THIS EXTRA BASE FROM THE GEAR SHED! THERE!
NOW WE CAN SHAG FLIES **SAFELY!**
CRACK!
TRIP!
WHAM!
ON THE BRIGHT SIDE, NOBODY BROKE AN ANKLE!
I'LL BET THIS NEVER HAPPENS TO MOOKIE BETTS.

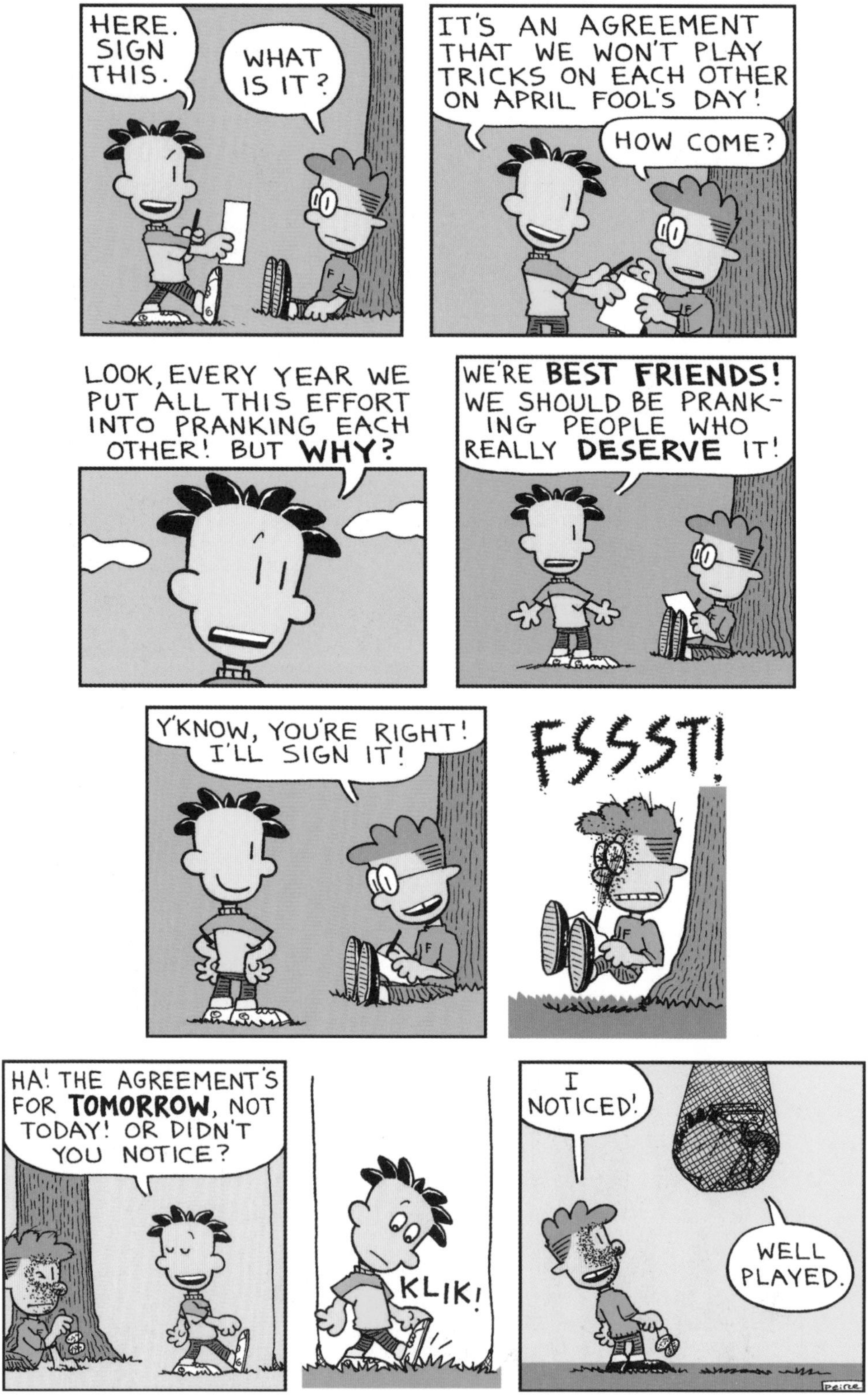
HERE. SIGN THIS.
WHAT IS IT?
IT'S AN AGREEMENT THAT WE WON'T PLAY TRICKS ON EACH OTHER ON APRIL FOOL'S DAY!
HOW COME?
LOOK, EVERY YEAR WE PUT ALL THIS EFFORT INTO PRANKING EACH OTHER! BUT WHY?
WE'RE BEST FRIENDS! WE SHOULD BE PRANKING PEOPLE WHO REALLY DESERVE IT!
Y'KNOW, YOU'RE RIGHT! I'LL SIGN IT!
FSSST!
HA! THE AGREEMENT'S FOR TOMORROW, NOT TODAY! OR DIDN'T YOU NOTICE?
KLIK!
I NOTICED!
WELL PLAYED.
PEIRCE

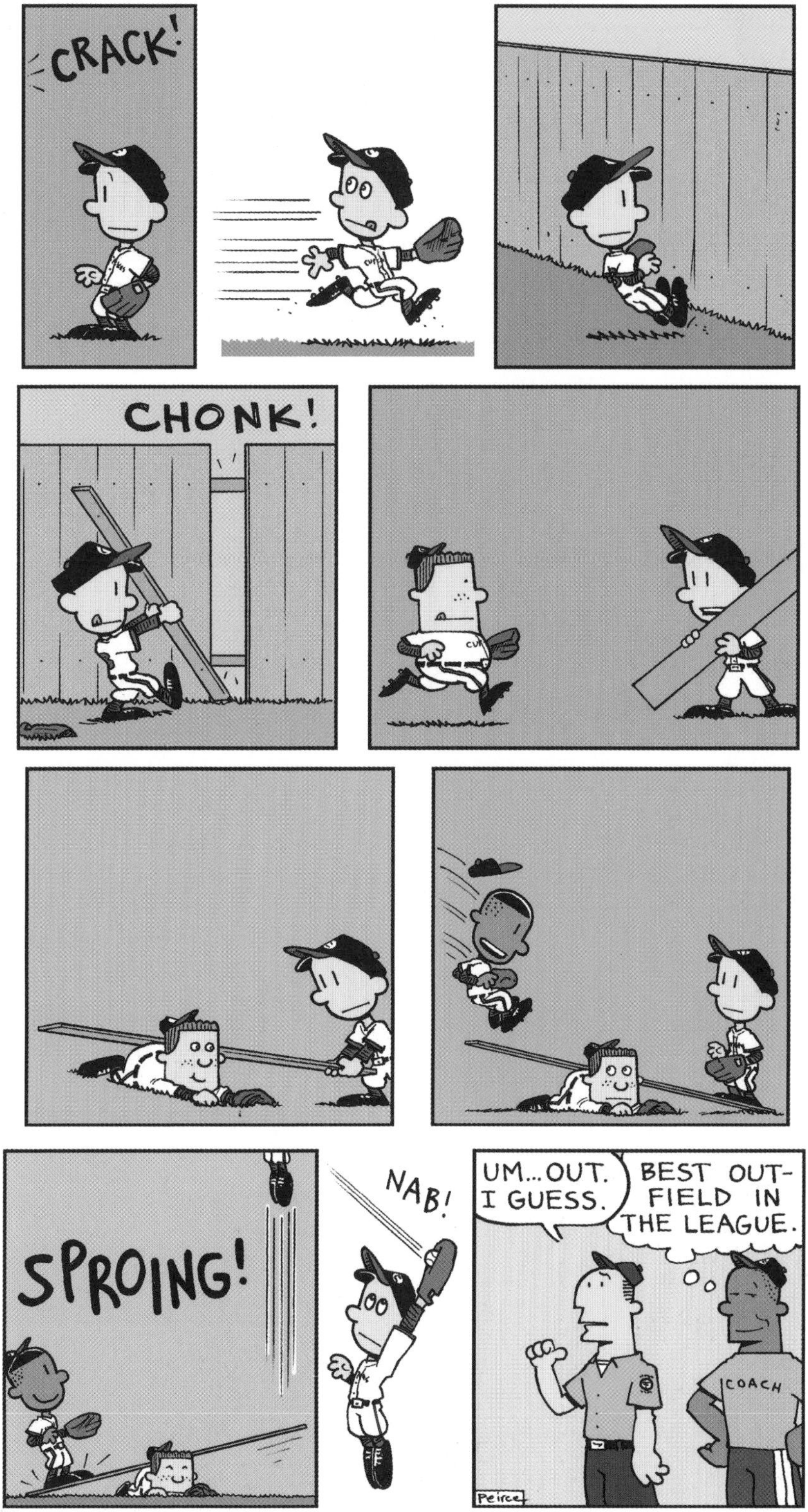
CRACK!
CHONK!
SPROING!
NAB!
UM...OUT. I GUESS.
BEST OUT-FIELD IN THE LEAGUE.
COACH
Peirce

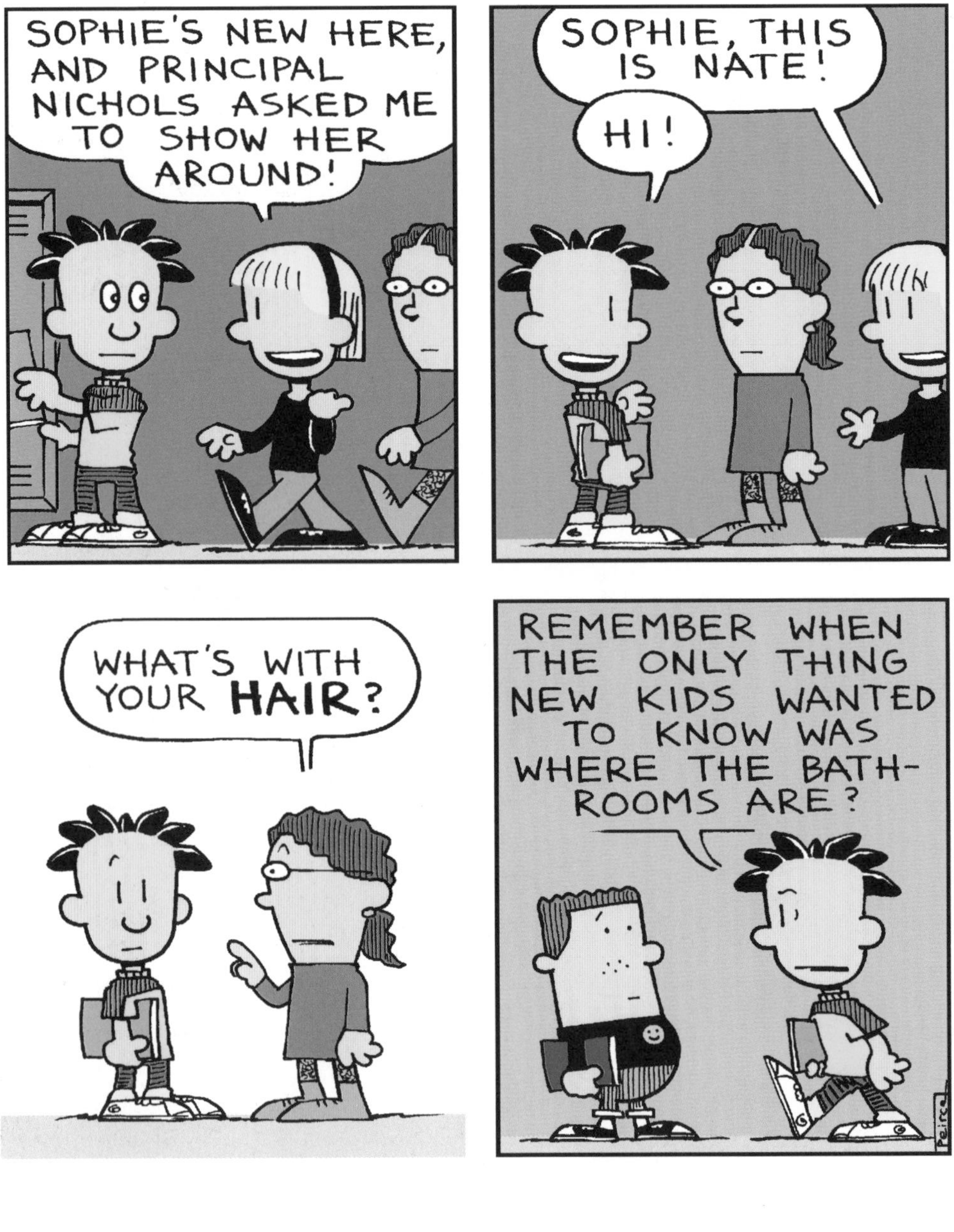
SOPHIE'S NEW HERE, AND PRINCIPAL NICHOLS ASKED ME TO SHOW HER AROUND!
SOPHIE, THIS IS NATE!
HI!
WHAT'S WITH YOUR **HAIR**?
REMEMBER WHEN THE ONLY THING NEW KIDS WANTED TO KNOW WAS WHERE THE BATH-ROOMS ARE?
Peirce

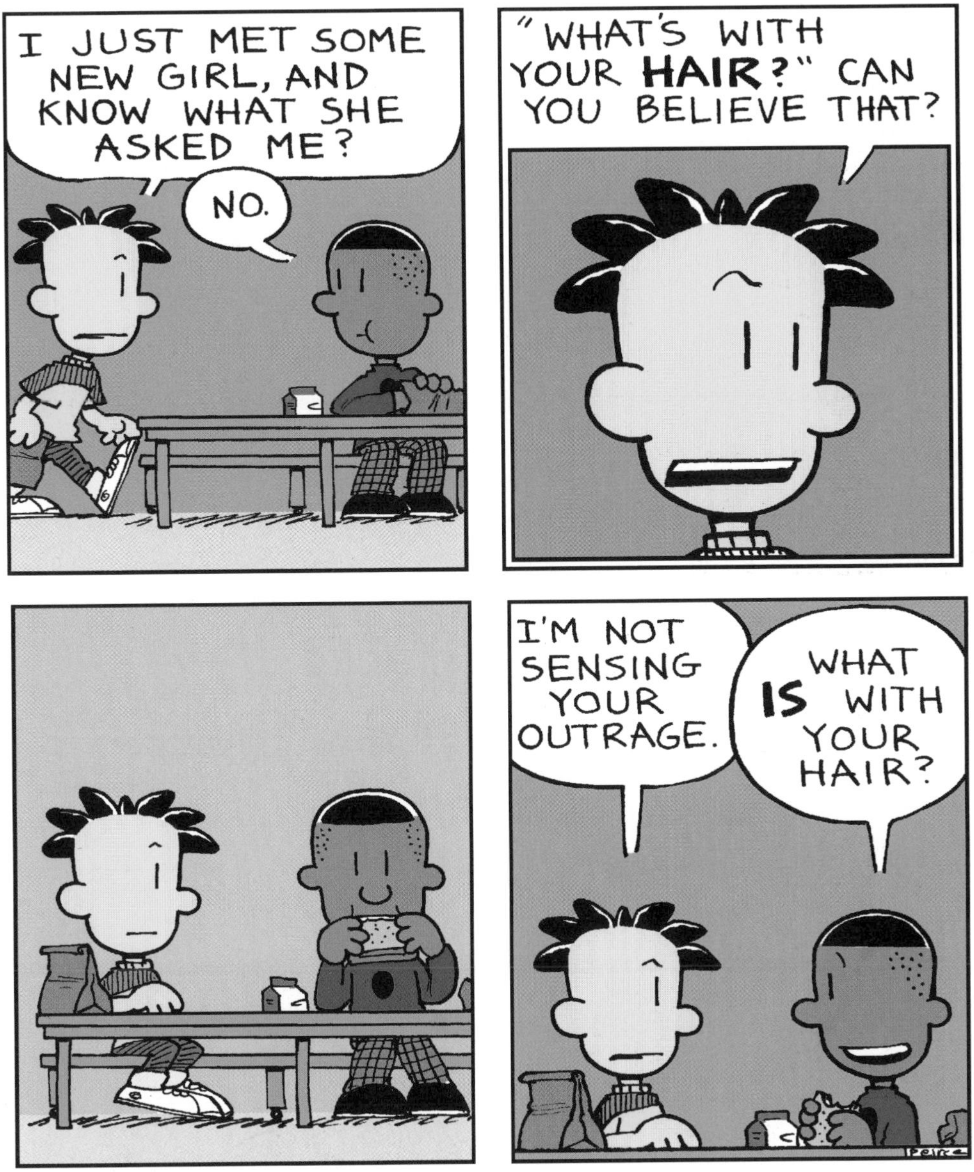
I JUST MET SOME NEW GIRL, AND KNOW WHAT SHE ASKED ME?
NO.
"WHAT'S WITH YOUR **HAIR?**" CAN YOU BELIEVE THAT?
I'M NOT SENSING YOUR OUTRAGE.
WHAT **IS** WITH YOUR HAIR?

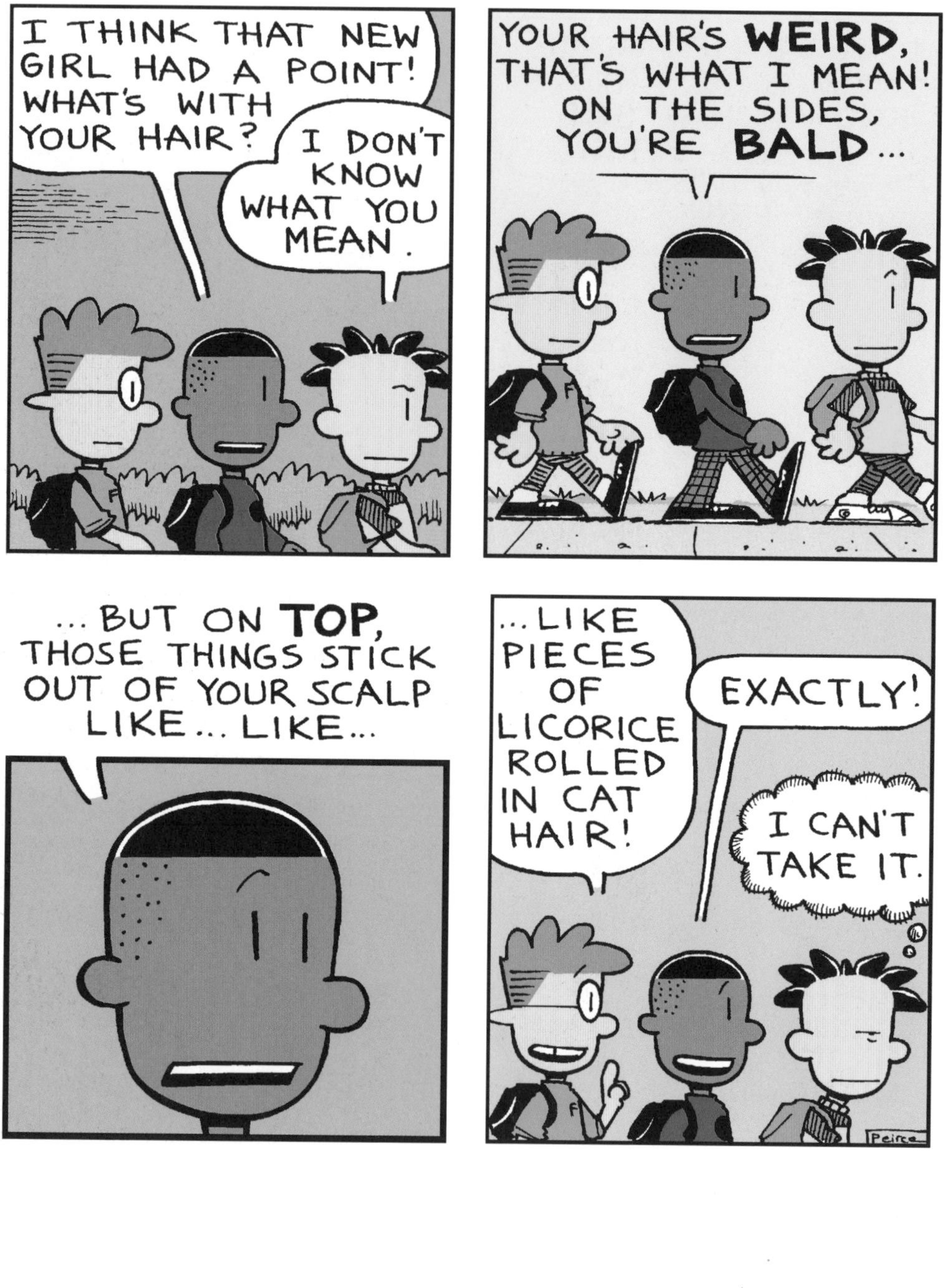
I THINK THAT NEW GIRL HAD A POINT! WHAT'S WITH YOUR HAIR?
I DON'T KNOW WHAT YOU MEAN.
YOUR HAIR'S **WEIRD**, THAT'S WHAT I MEAN! ON THE SIDES, YOU'RE **BALD**...
... BUT ON **TOP**, THOSE THINGS STICK OUT OF YOUR SCALP LIKE... LIKE...
... LIKE PIECES OF LICORICE ROLLED IN CAT HAIR!
EXACTLY!
I CAN'T TAKE IT.
Peirce

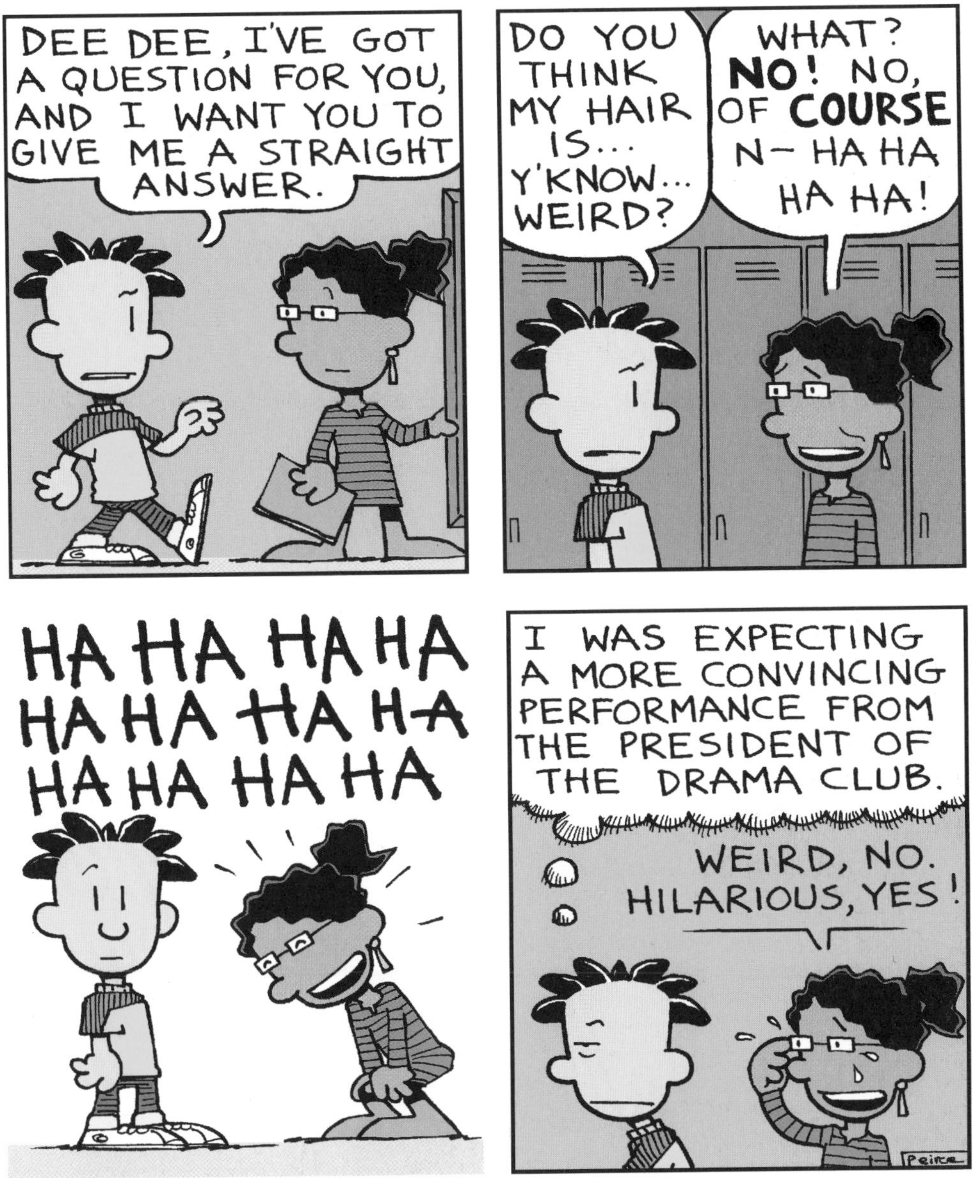
DEE DEE, I'VE GOT A QUESTION FOR YOU, AND I WANT YOU TO GIVE ME A STRAIGHT ANSWER.
DO YOU THINK MY HAIR IS... Y'KNOW... WEIRD?
WHAT? **NO!** NO, OF **COURSE** N- HA HA HA HA!
HA HA HA HA HA HA HA HA HA HA HA HA
I WAS EXPECTING A MORE CONVINCING PERFORMANCE FROM THE PRESIDENT OF THE DRAMA CLUB.
WEIRD, NO. HILARIOUS, YES!
Peirce

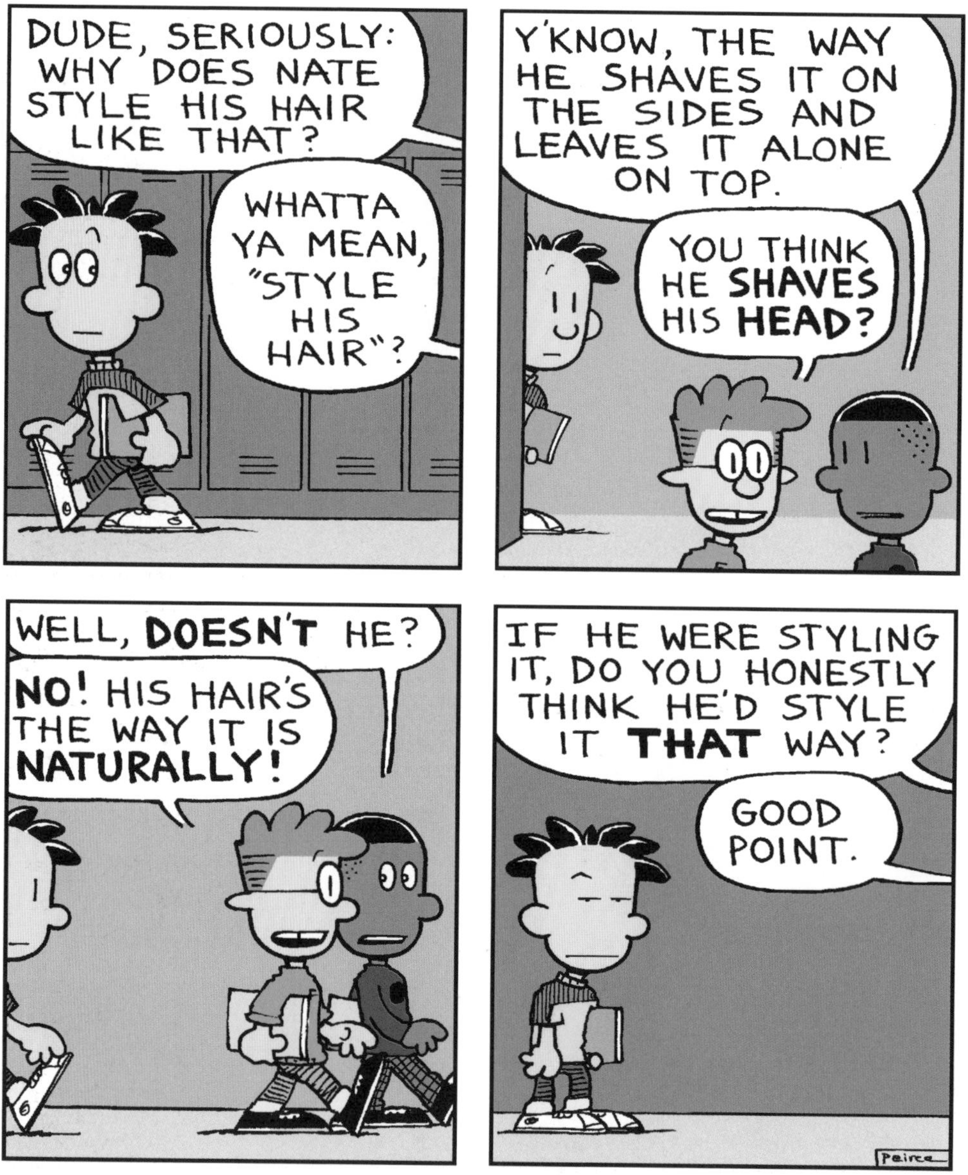
DUDE, SERIOUSLY: WHY DOES NATE STYLE HIS HAIR LIKE THAT?
WHATTA YA MEAN, "STYLE HIS HAIR"?
Y'KNOW, THE WAY HE SHAVES IT ON THE SIDES AND LEAVES IT ALONE ON TOP.
YOU THINK HE SHAVES HIS HEAD?
WELL, DOESN'T HE?
NO! HIS HAIR'S THE WAY IT IS NATURALLY!
IF HE WERE STYLING IT, DO YOU HONESTLY THINK HE'D STYLE IT THAT WAY?
GOOD POINT.
Peirce

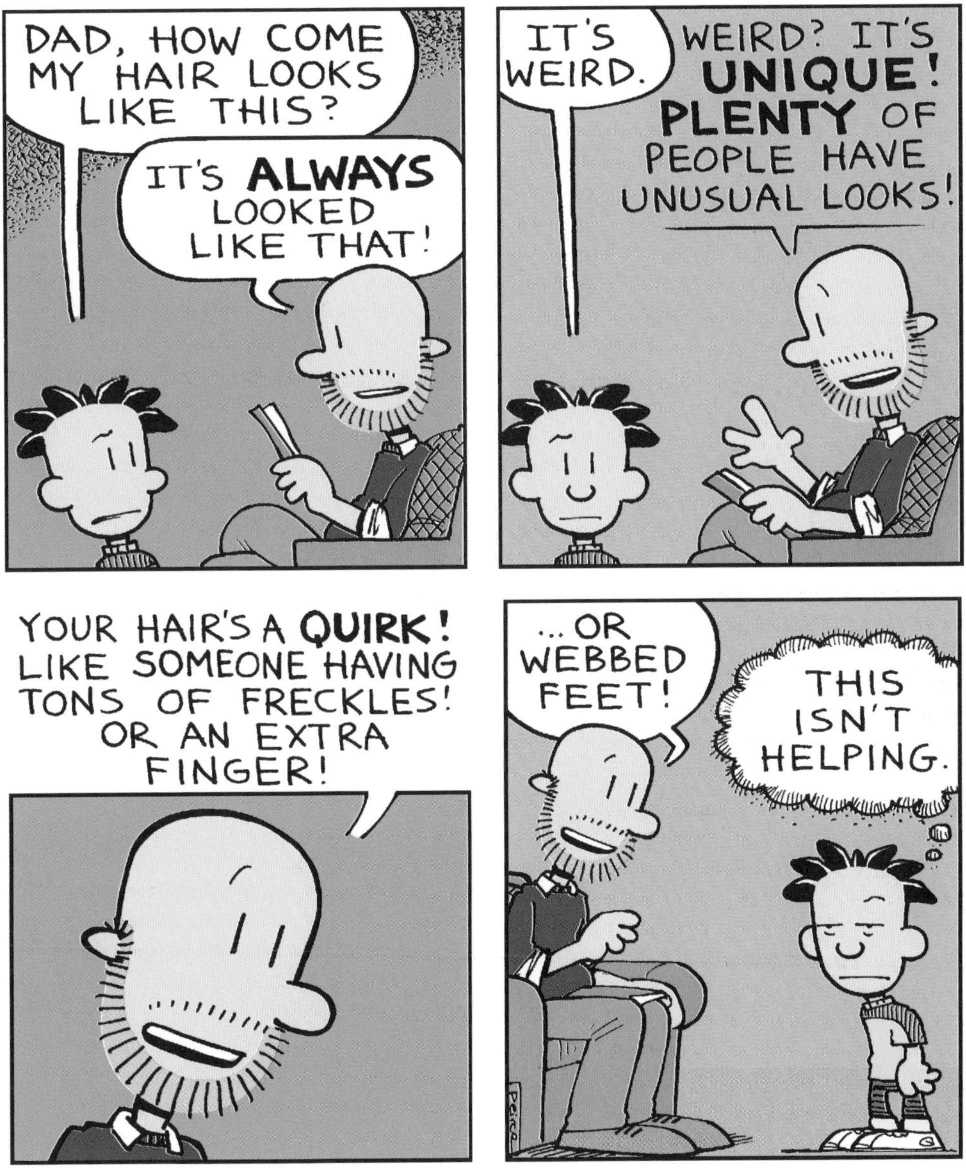
DAD, HOW COME MY HAIR LOOKS LIKE THIS?
IT'S ALWAYS LOOKED LIKE THAT!
IT'S WEIRD.
WEIRD? IT'S UNIQUE! PLENTY OF PEOPLE HAVE UNUSUAL LOOKS!
YOUR HAIR'S A QUIRK! LIKE SOMEONE HAVING TONS OF FRECKLES! OR AN EXTRA FINGER!
...OR WEBBED FEET!
THIS ISN'T HELPING.
Peirce

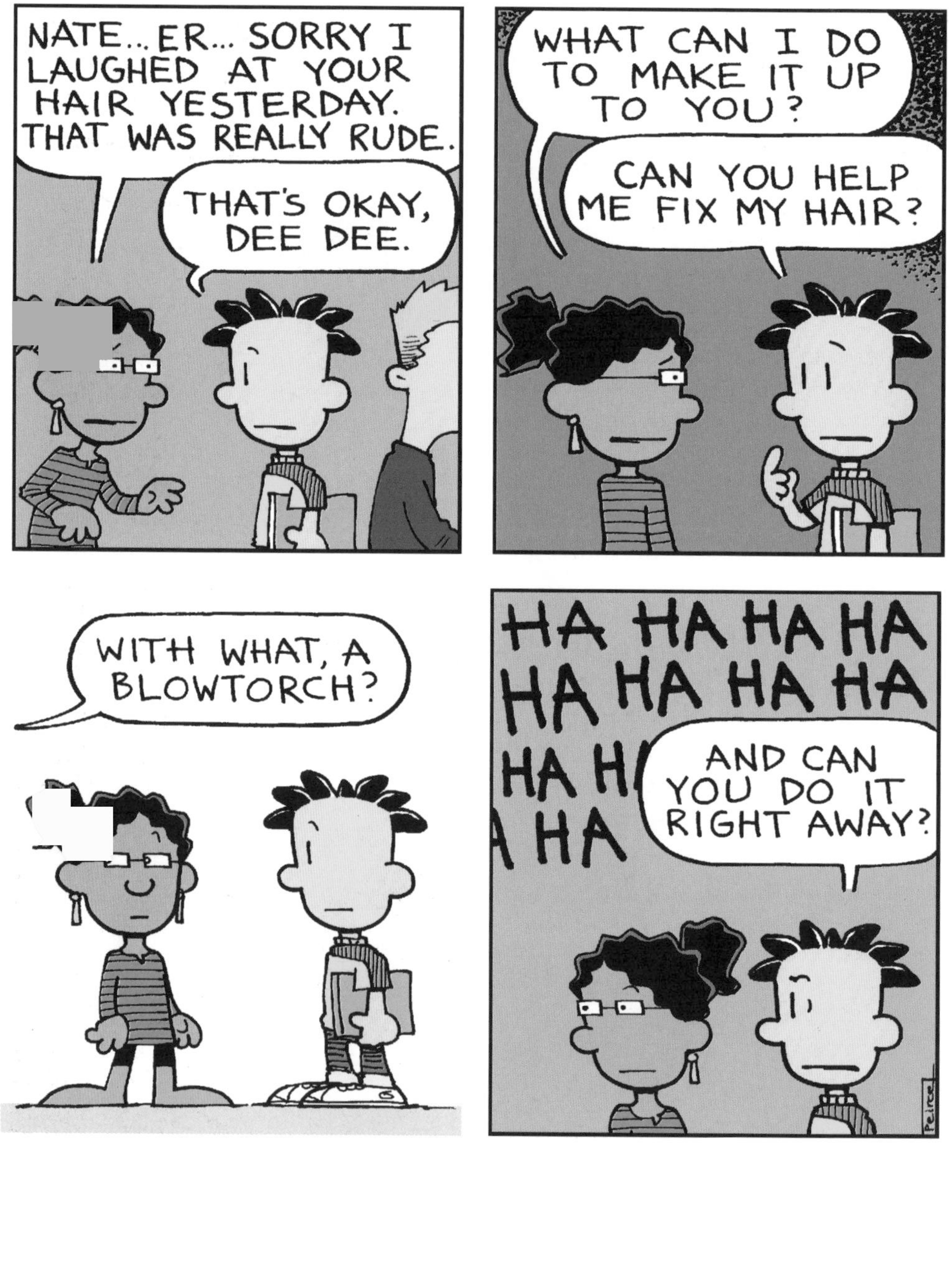
NATE... ER... SORRY I LAUGHED AT YOUR HAIR YESTERDAY. THAT WAS REALLY RUDE.
THAT'S OKAY, DEE DEE.
WHAT CAN I DO TO MAKE IT UP TO YOU?
CAN YOU HELP ME FIX MY HAIR?
WITH WHAT, A BLOWTORCH?
HA HA HA HA HA HA HA HA HA HA HA HA HA HA
AND CAN YOU DO IT RIGHT AWAY?
Peirce

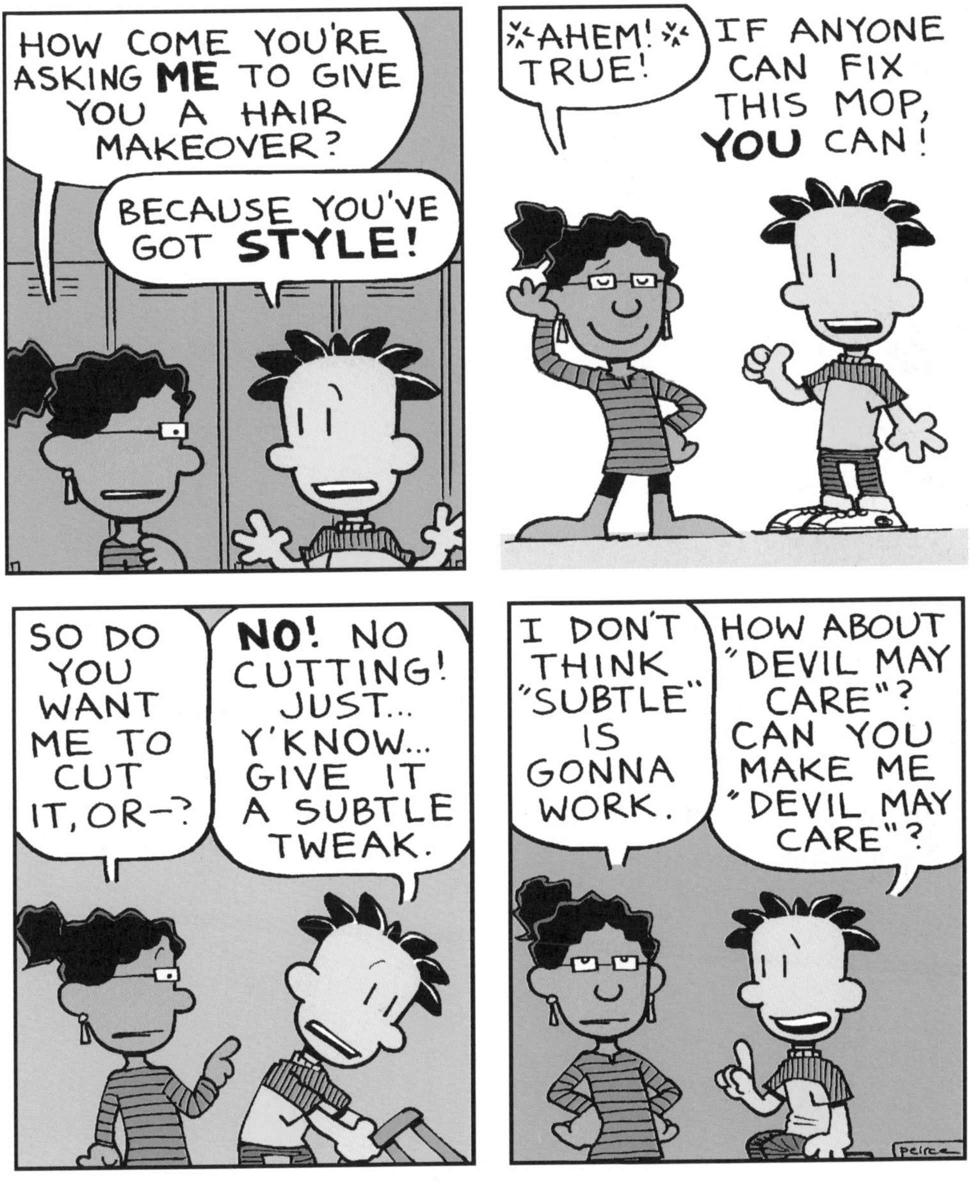
HOW COME YOU'RE ASKING **ME** TO GIVE YOU A HAIR MAKEOVER?
BECAUSE YOU'VE GOT **STYLE!**
AHEM! TRUE!
IF ANYONE CAN FIX THIS MOP, **YOU** CAN!
SO DO YOU WANT ME TO CUT IT, OR-?
NO! NO CUTTING! JUST... Y'KNOW... GIVE IT A SUBTLE TWEAK.
I DON'T THINK "SUBTLE" IS GONNA WORK.
HOW ABOUT "DEVIL MAY CARE"? CAN YOU MAKE ME "DEVIL MAY CARE"?
peirce

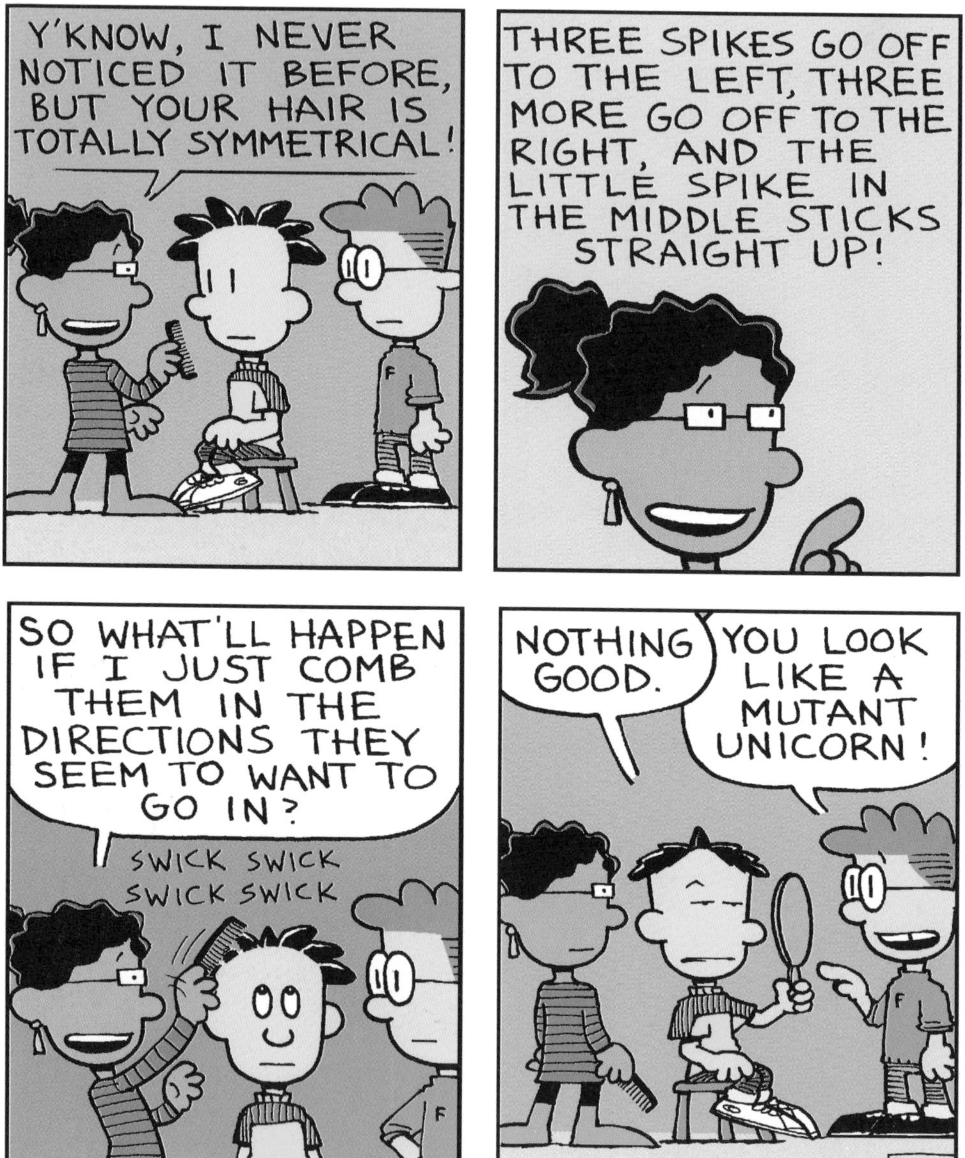
Y'KNOW, I NEVER NOTICED IT BEFORE, BUT YOUR HAIR IS TOTALLY SYMMETRICAL!
THREE SPIKES GO OFF TO THE LEFT, THREE MORE GO OFF TO THE RIGHT, AND THE LITTLE SPIKE IN THE MIDDLE STICKS STRAIGHT UP!
SO WHAT'LL HAPPEN IF I JUST COMB THEM IN THE DIRECTIONS THEY SEEM TO WANT TO GO IN?
SWICK SWICK SWICK SWICK
NOTHING GOOD.
YOU LOOK LIKE A MUTANT UNICORN!
Peirce

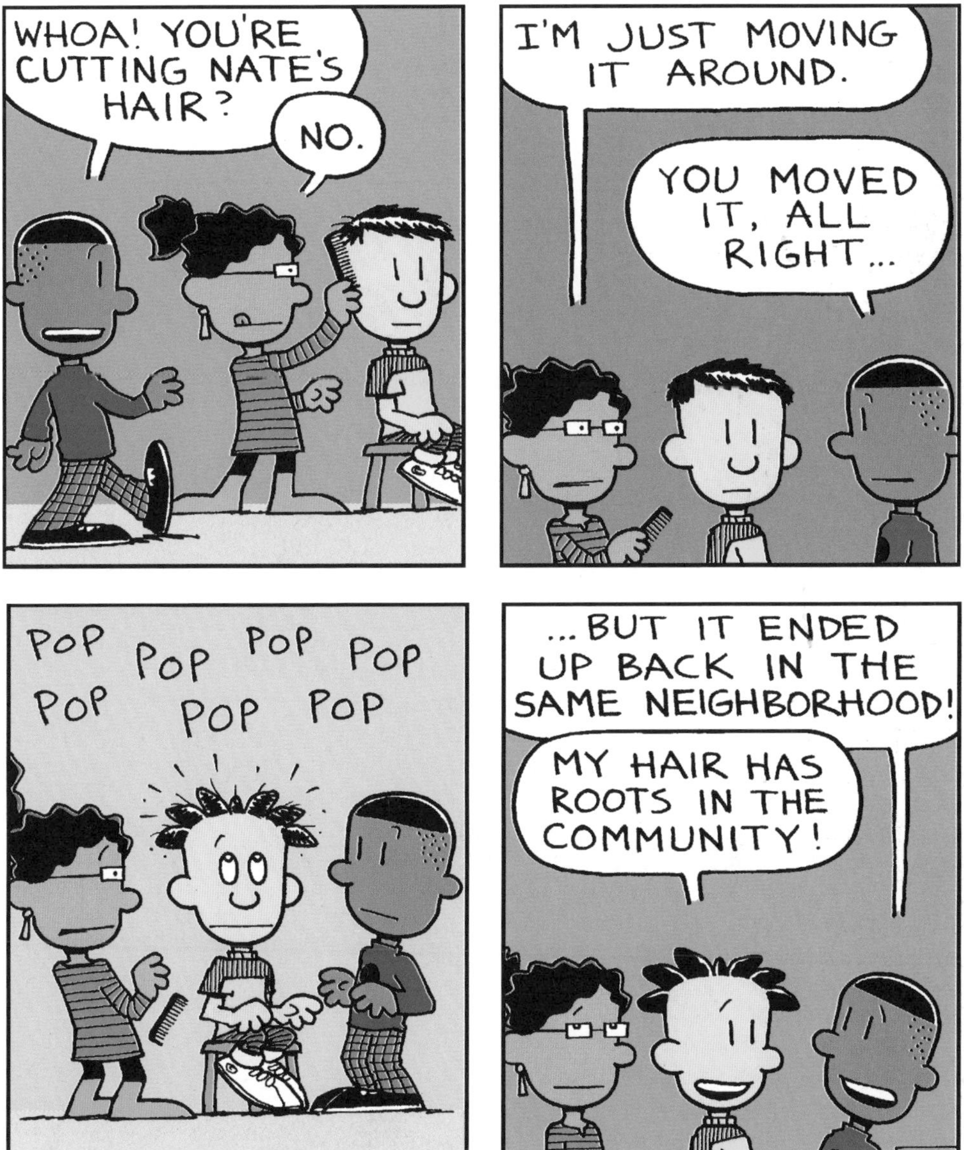
WHOA! YOU'RE CUTTING NATE'S HAIR?
NO.
I'M JUST MOVING IT AROUND.
YOU MOVED IT, ALL RIGHT...
POP POP POP POP POP POP POP
...BUT IT ENDED UP BACK IN THE SAME NEIGHBORHOOD!
MY HAIR HAS ROOTS IN THE COMMUNITY!
Peirce

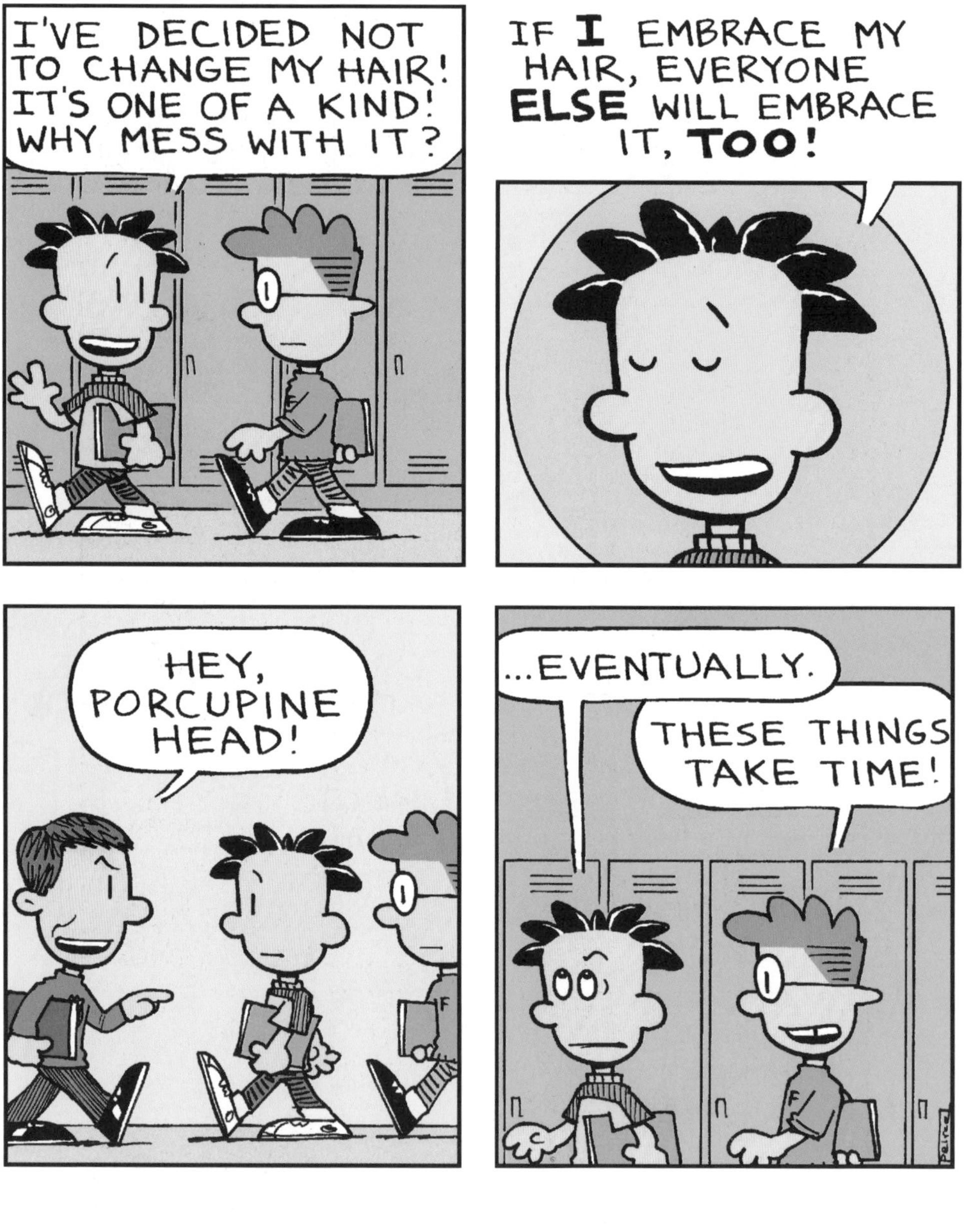
I'VE DECIDED NOT TO CHANGE MY HAIR! IT'S ONE OF A KIND! WHY MESS WITH IT?
IF I EMBRACE MY HAIR, EVERYONE ELSE WILL EMBRACE IT, TOO!
HEY, PORCUPINE HEAD!
...EVENTUALLY.
THESE THINGS TAKE TIME!
PEIRCE

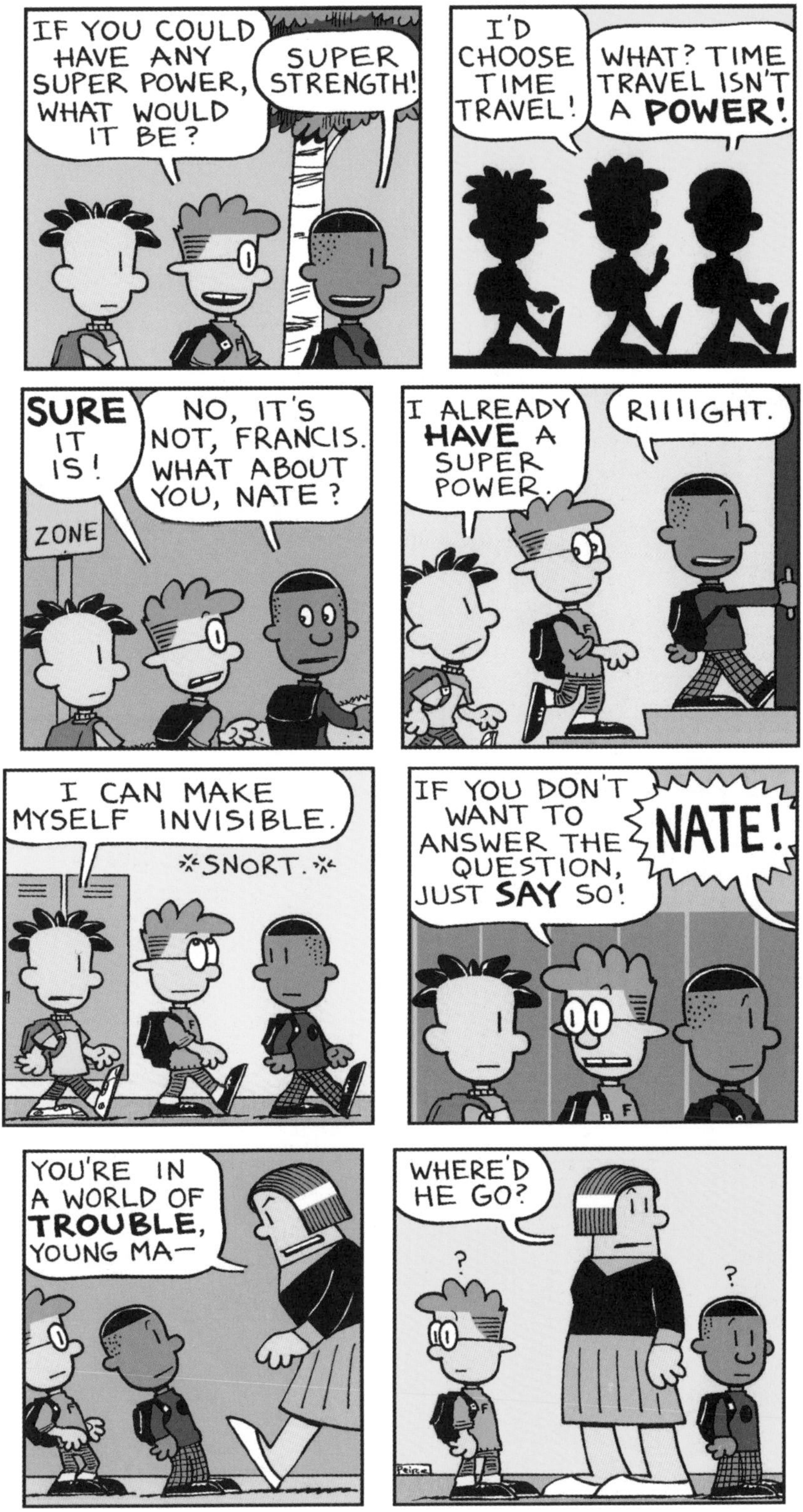
IF YOU COULD HAVE ANY SUPER POWER, WHAT WOULD IT BE?
SUPER STRENGTH!
I'D CHOOSE TIME TRAVEL!
WHAT? TIME TRAVEL ISN'T A **POWER**!
SURE IT IS!
NO, IT'S NOT, FRANCIS. WHAT ABOUT YOU, NATE?
ZONE
I ALREADY **HAVE** A SUPER POWER.
RIIIIGHT.
I CAN MAKE MYSELF INVISIBLE.
SNORT.
IF YOU DON'T WANT TO ANSWER THE QUESTION, JUST **SAY** SO!
NATE!
YOU'RE IN A WORLD OF **TROUBLE**, YOUNG MA—
WHERE'D HE GO?
?
?

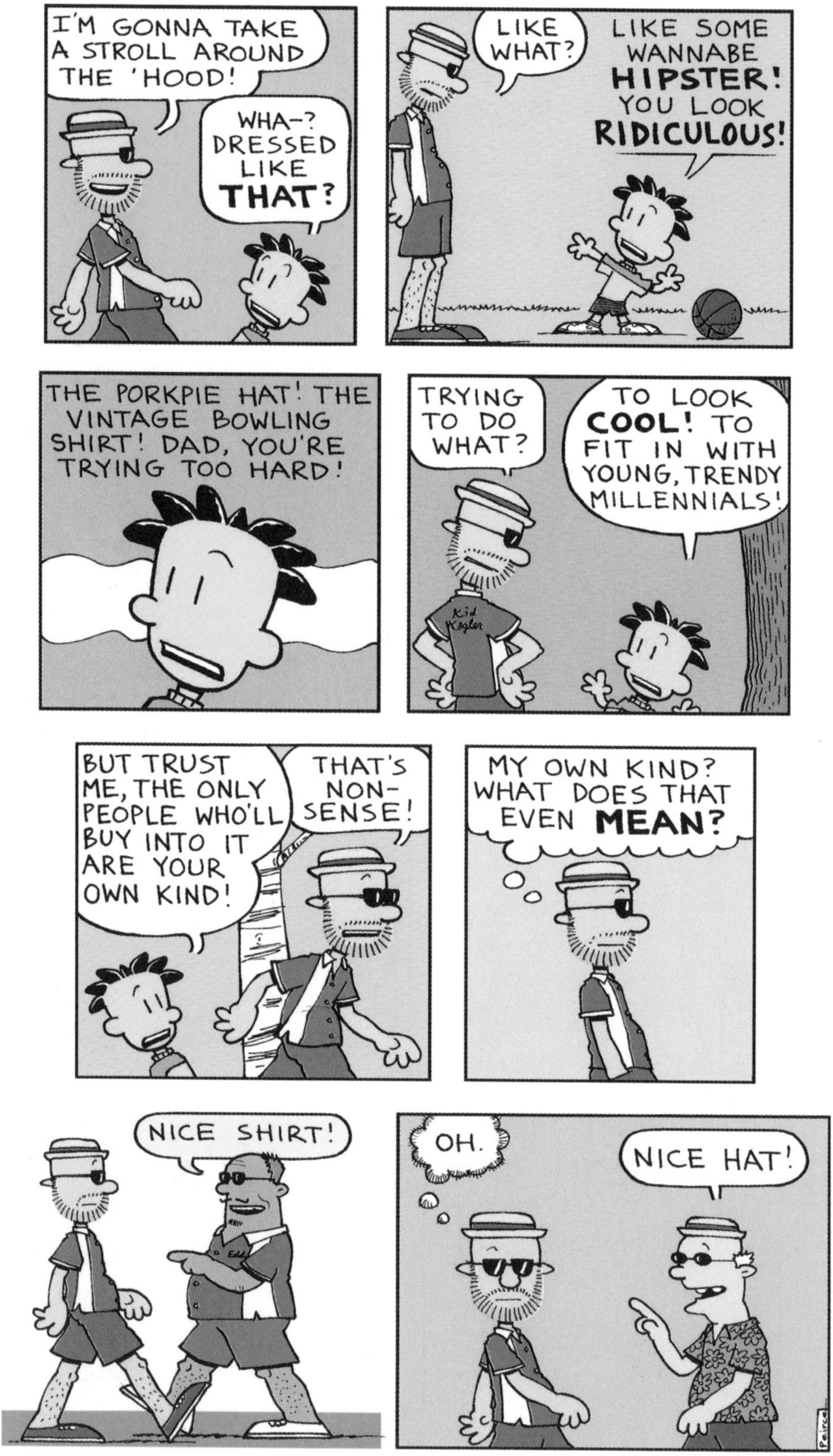
I'M GONNA TAKE A STROLL AROUND THE 'HOOD!
WHA-? DRESSED LIKE **THAT**?
LIKE WHAT?
LIKE SOME WANNABE **HIPSTER**! YOU LOOK **RIDICULOUS**!
THE PORKPIE HAT! THE VINTAGE BOWLING SHIRT! DAD, YOU'RE TRYING TOO HARD!
TRYING TO DO WHAT?
TO LOOK **COOL**! TO FIT IN WITH YOUNG, TRENDY MILLENNIALS!
Kid Kegler
THAT'S NONSENSE!
BUT TRUST ME, THE ONLY PEOPLE WHO'LL BUY INTO IT ARE YOUR OWN KIND!
MY OWN KIND? WHAT DOES THAT EVEN **MEAN**?
NICE SHIRT!
OH.
NICE HAT!
Peirce

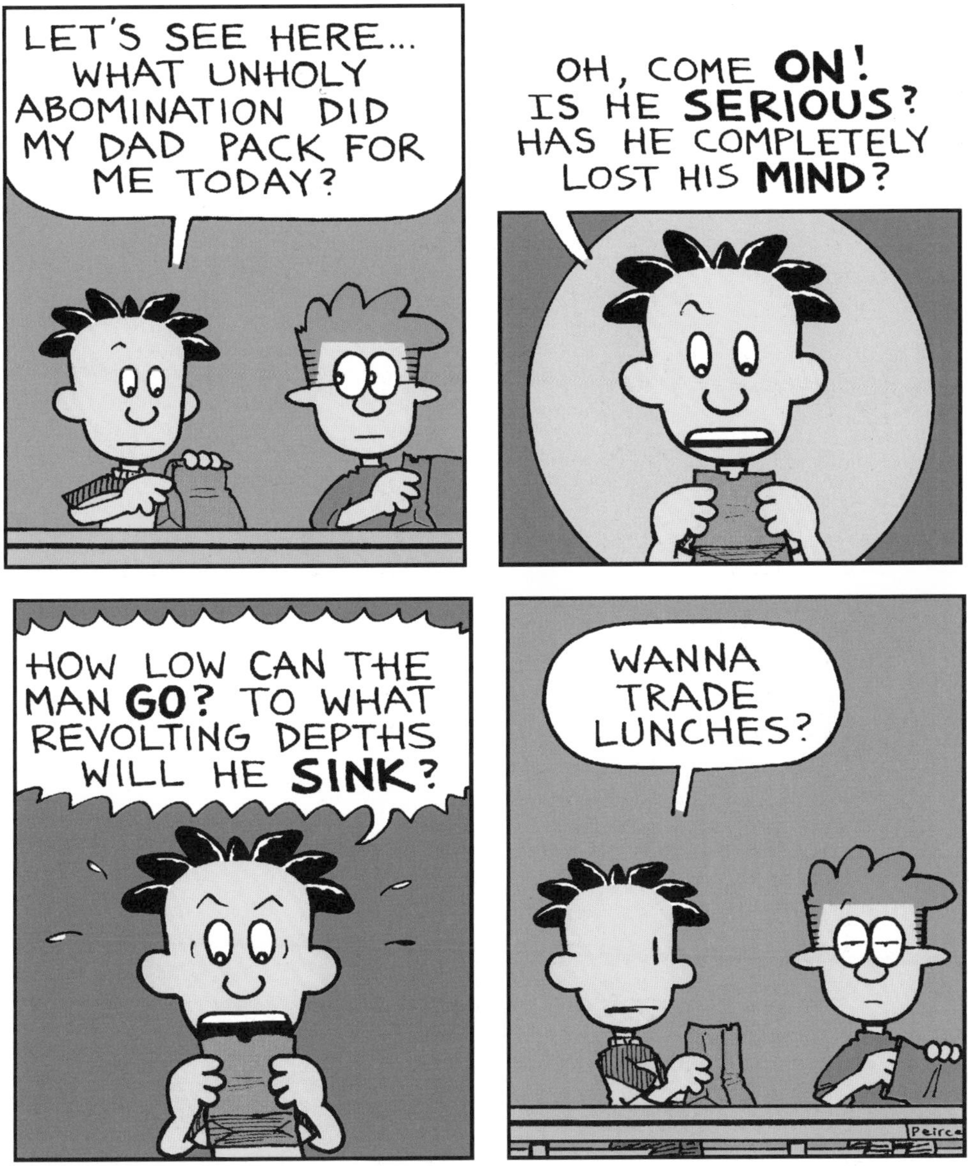
LET'S SEE HERE... WHAT UNHOLY ABOMINATION DID MY DAD PACK FOR ME TODAY?
OH, COME ON! IS HE SERIOUS? HAS HE COMPLETELY LOST HIS MIND?
HOW LOW CAN THE MAN GO? TO WHAT REVOLTING DEPTHS WILL HE SINK?
WANNA TRADE LUNCHES?
Peirce

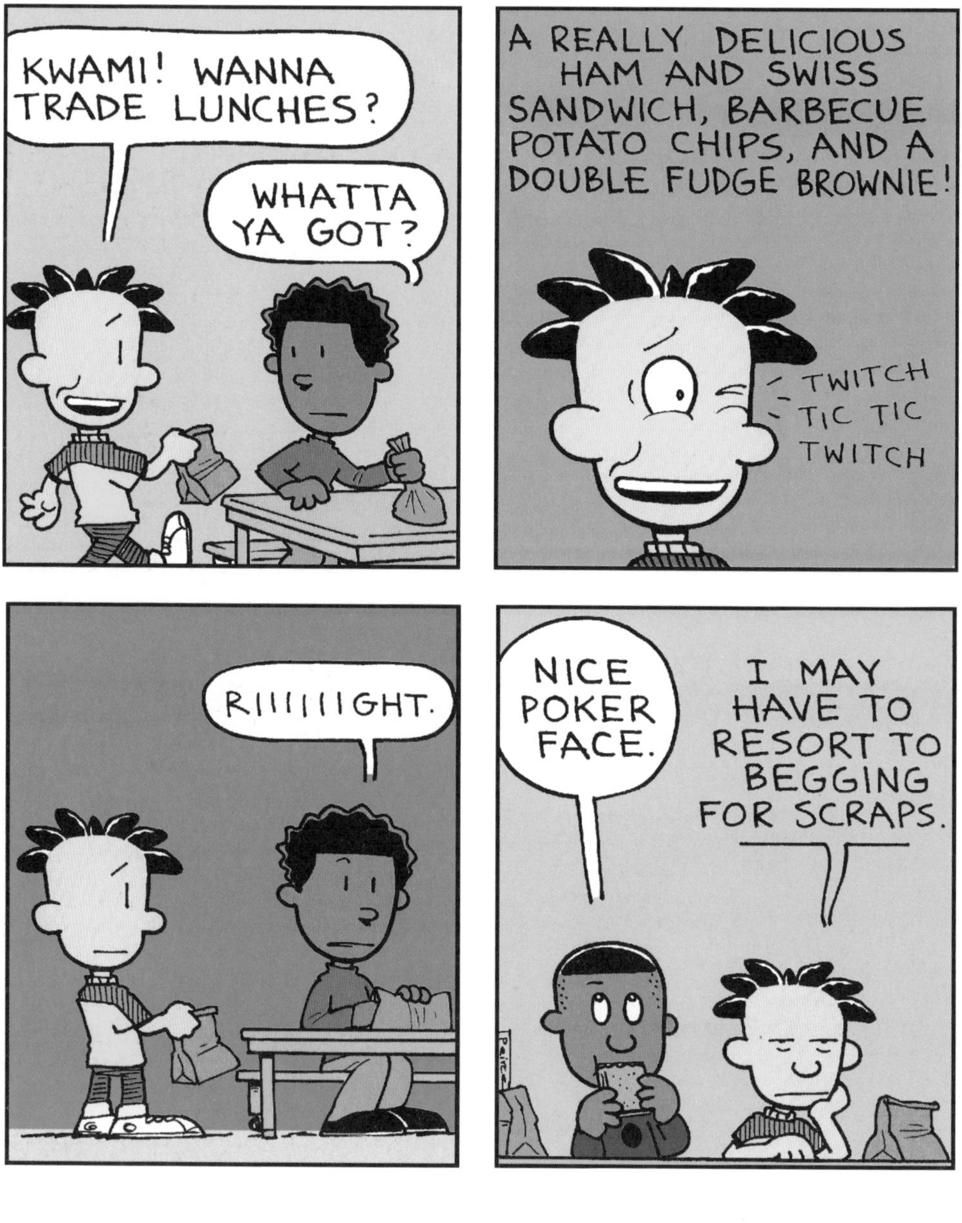
KWAMI! WANNA TRADE LUNCHES?
WHATTA YA GOT?
A REALLY DELICIOUS HAM AND SWISS SANDWICH, BARBECUE POTATO CHIPS, AND A DOUBLE FUDGE BROWNIE!
TWITCH TIC TIC TWITCH
RIIIIIIGHT.
NICE POKER FACE.
I MAY HAVE TO RESORT TO BEGGING FOR SCRAPS.

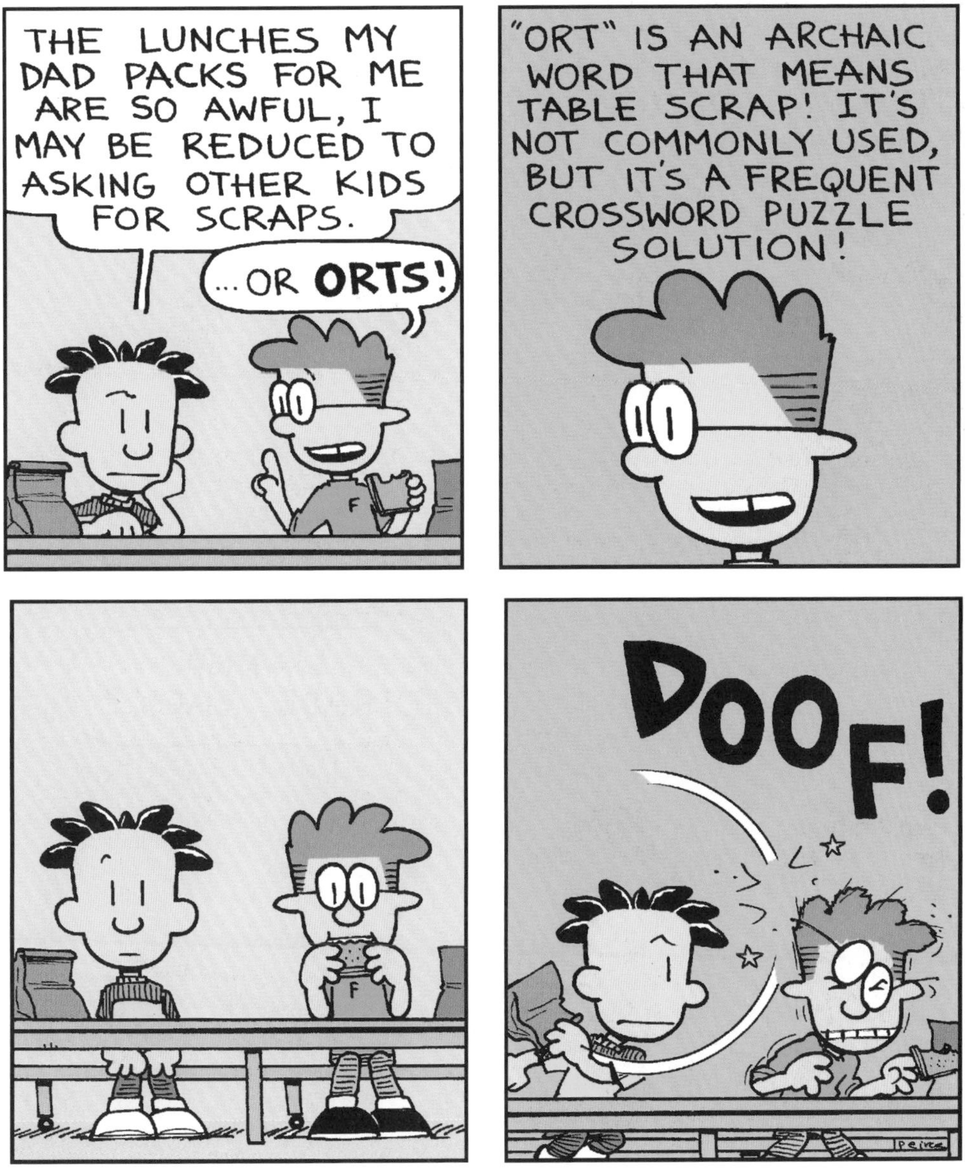
THE LUNCHES MY DAD PACKS FOR ME ARE SO AWFUL, I MAY BE REDUCED TO ASKING OTHER KIDS FOR SCRAPS.
...OR ORTS!
"ORT" IS AN ARCHAIC WORD THAT MEANS TABLE SCRAP! IT'S NOT COMMONLY USED, BUT IT'S A FREQUENT CROSSWORD PUZZLE SOLUTION!
DOOF!
Peirce

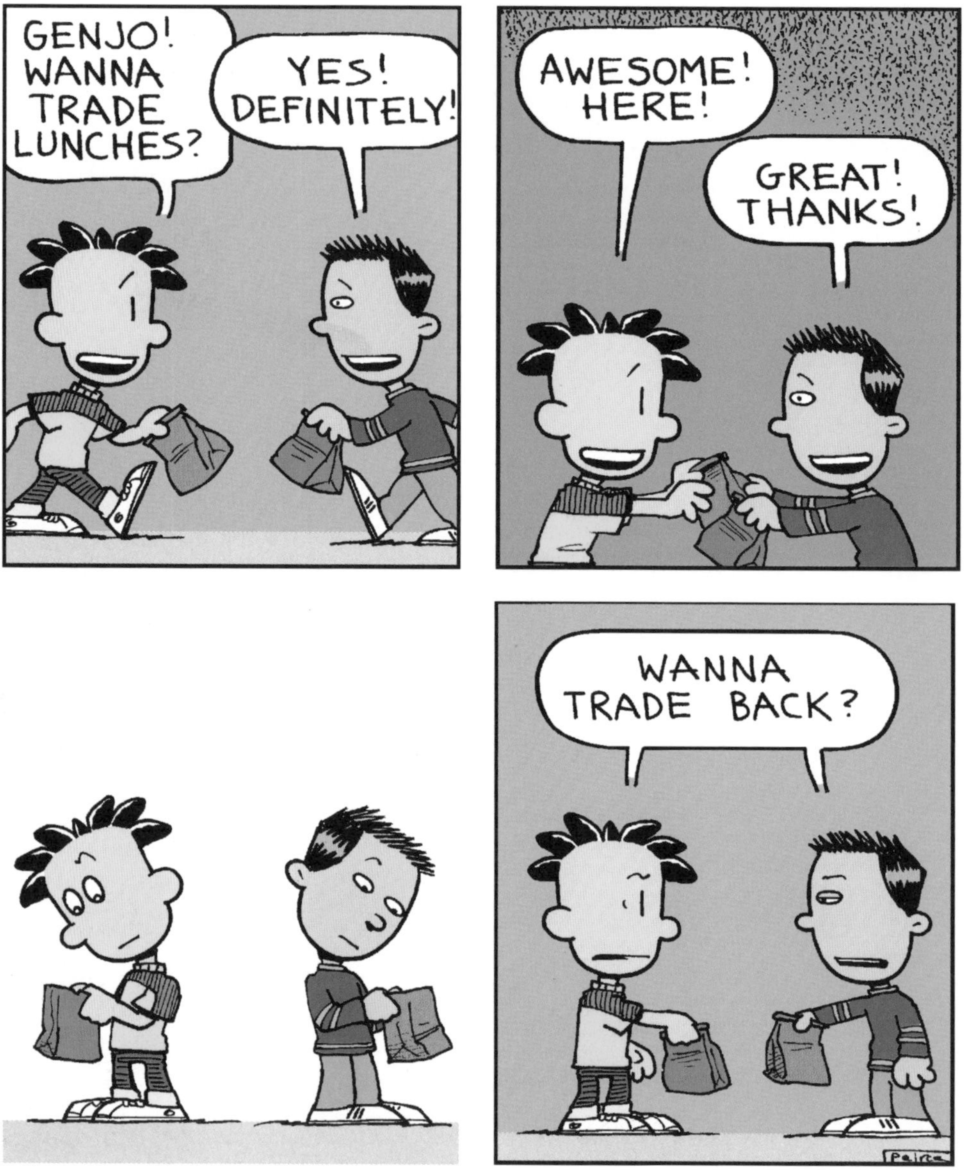
GENJO! WANNA TRADE LUNCHES?
YES! DEFINITELY!
AWESOME! HERE!
GREAT! THANKS!
WANNA TRADE BACK?
Peirce

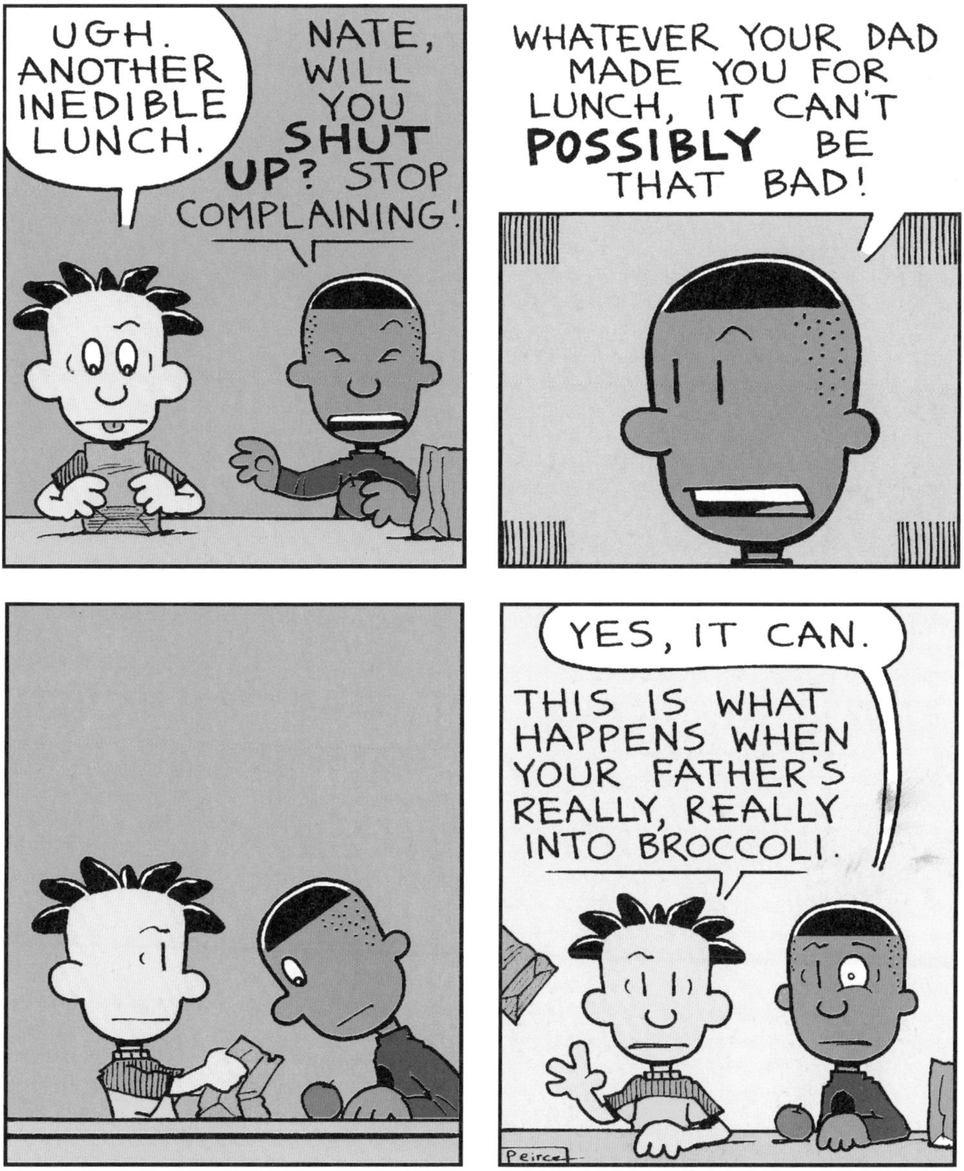
UGH. ANOTHER INEDIBLE LUNCH.
NATE, WILL YOU SHUT UP? STOP COMPLAINING!
WHATEVER YOUR DAD MADE YOU FOR LUNCH, IT CAN'T POSSIBLY BE THAT BAD!
YES, IT CAN.
THIS IS WHAT HAPPENS WHEN YOUR FATHER'S REALLY, REALLY INTO BROCCOLI.
Peirce

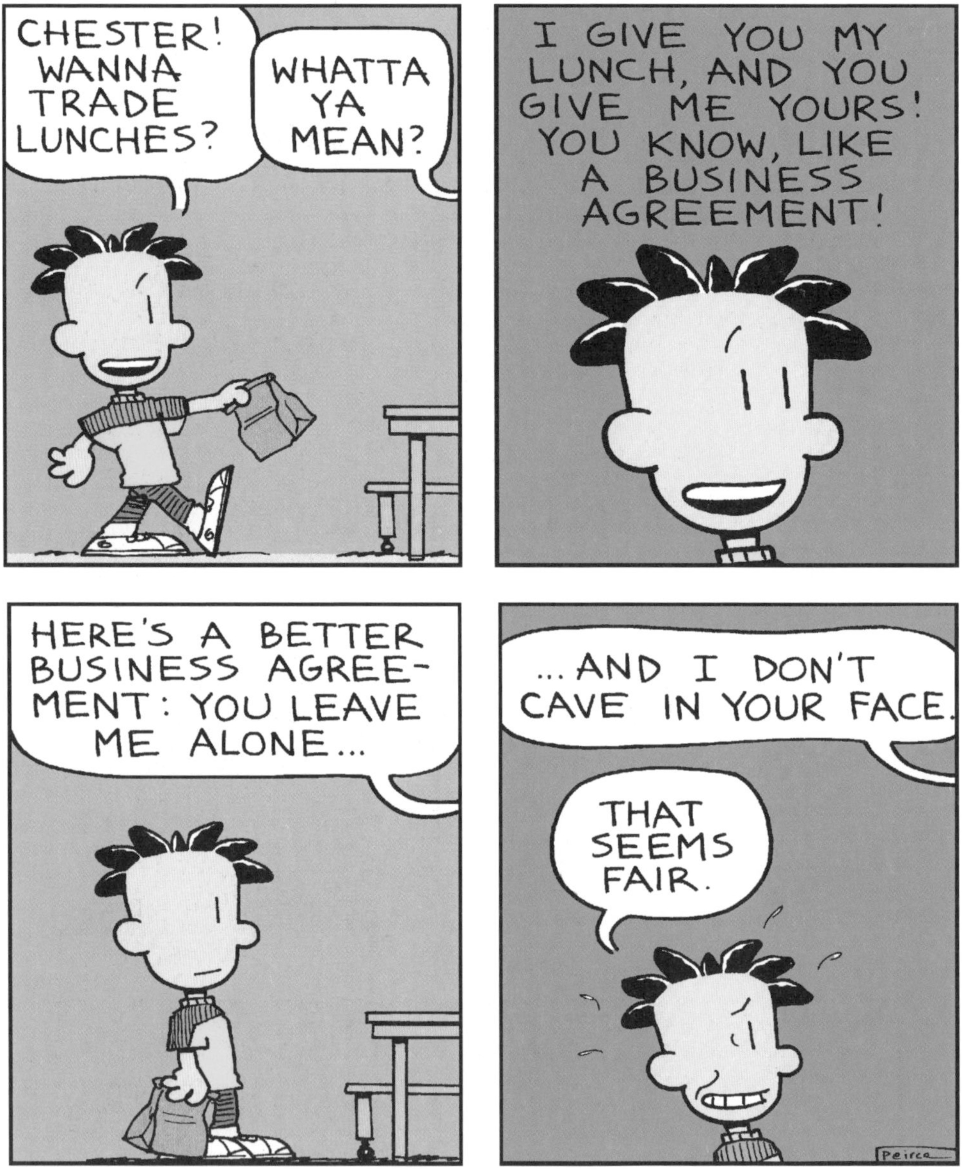
CHESTER! WANNA TRADE LUNCHES?
WHATTA YA MEAN?
I GIVE YOU MY LUNCH, AND YOU GIVE ME YOURS! YOU KNOW, LIKE A BUSINESS AGREEMENT!
HERE'S A BETTER BUSINESS AGREE-MENT: YOU LEAVE ME ALONE...
...AND I DON'T CAVE IN YOUR FACE.
THAT SEEMS FAIR.
Peirce

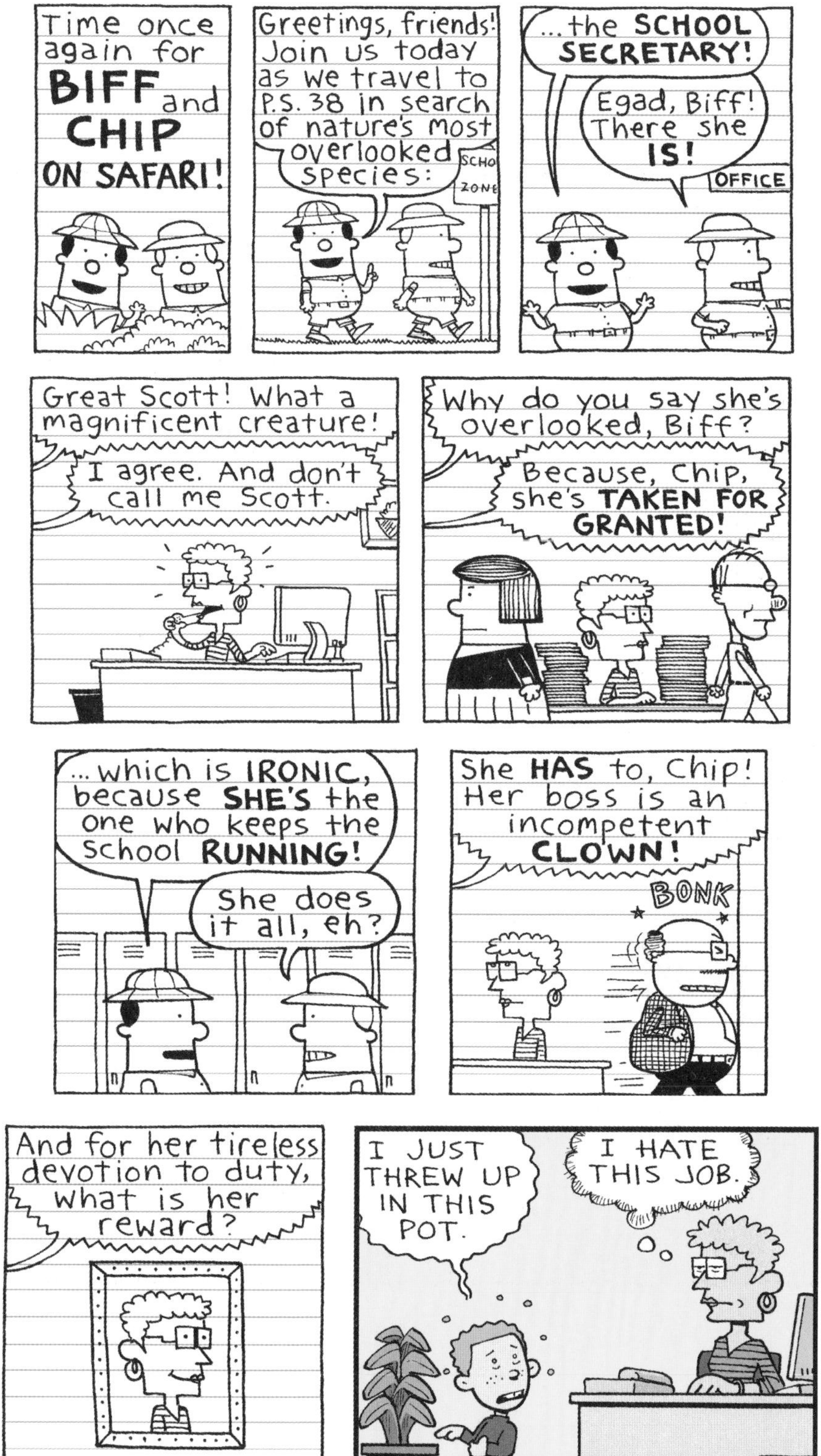
Time once again for BIFF and CHIP ON SAFARI!
Greetings, friends! Join us today as we travel to P.S. 38 in search of nature's most overlooked species:
SCHO ZONE
...the SCHOOL SECRETARY!
Egad, Biff! There she IS!
OFFICE
Great Scott! What a magnificent creature!
I agree. And don't call me Scott.
Why do you say she's overlooked, Biff?
Because, Chip, she's TAKEN FOR GRANTED!
...which is IRONIC, because SHE'S the one who keeps the school RUNNING!
She does it all, eh?
She HAS to, Chip! Her boss is an incompetent CLOWN!
BONK
And for her tireless devotion to duty, what is her reward?
I JUST THREW UP IN THIS POT.
I HATE THIS JOB.
Peirce

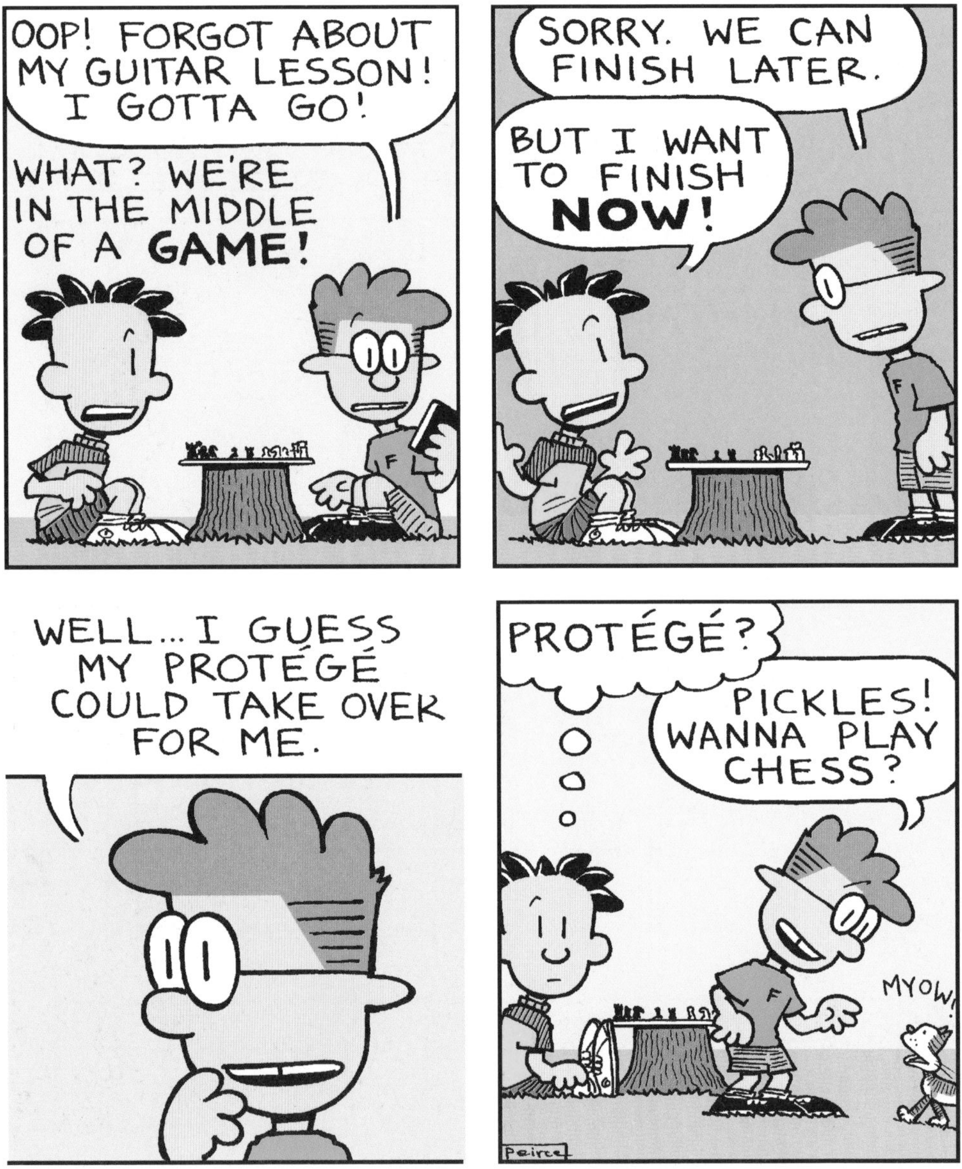
OOP! FORGOT ABOUT MY GUITAR LESSON! I GOTTA GO!
WHAT? WE'RE IN THE MIDDLE OF A **GAME**!
SORRY. WE CAN FINISH LATER.
BUT I WANT TO FINISH **NOW**!
WELL... I GUESS MY PROTÉGÉ COULD TAKE OVER FOR ME.
PROTÉGÉ?
PICKLES! WANNA PLAY CHESS?
MYOW!
Peirce

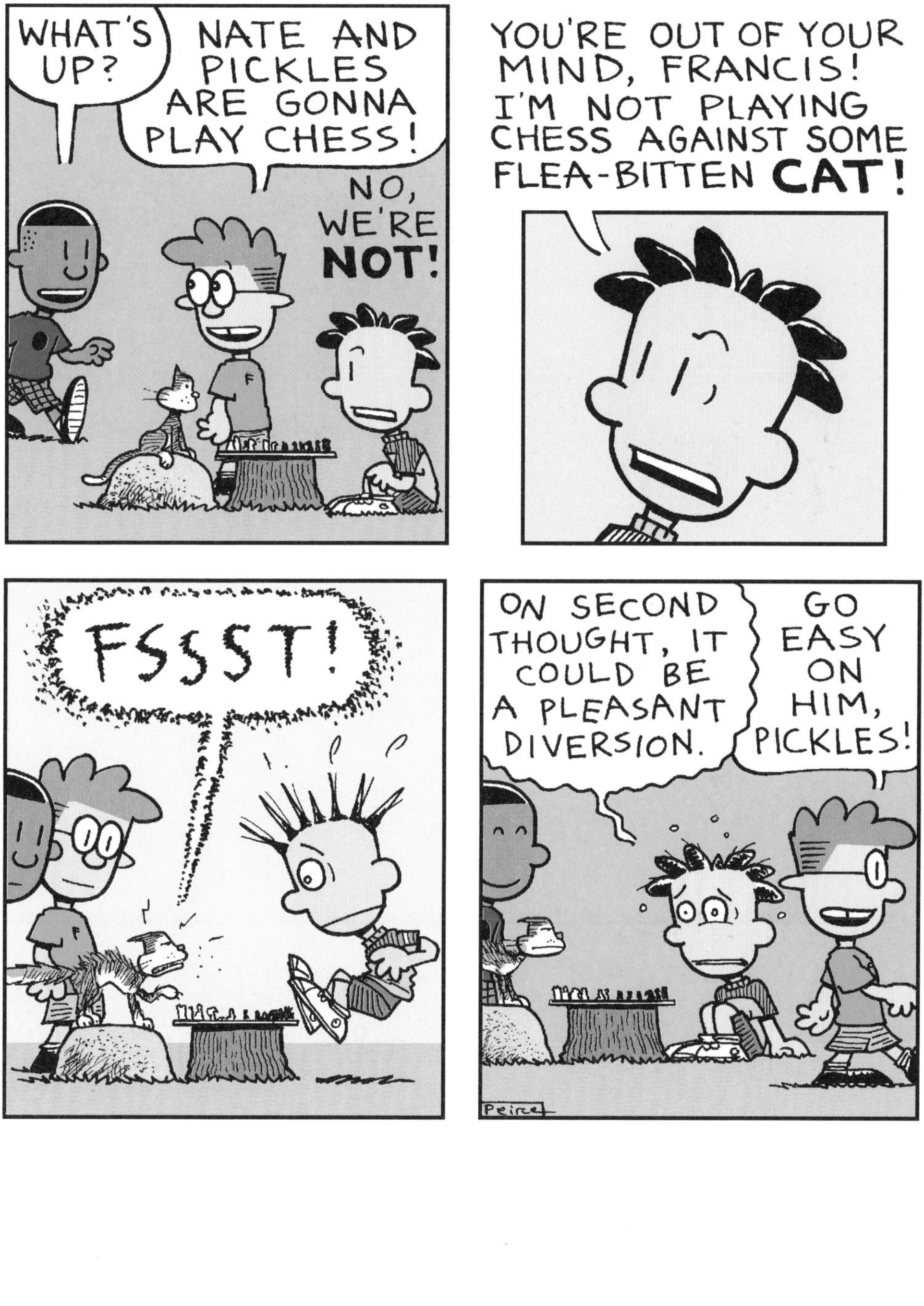
WHAT'S UP?
NATE AND PICKLES ARE GONNA PLAY CHESS!
NO, WE'RE **NOT!**
YOU'RE OUT OF YOUR MIND, FRANCIS! I'M NOT PLAYING CHESS AGAINST SOME FLEA-BITTEN **CAT!**
FSSST!
ON SECOND THOUGHT, IT COULD BE A PLEASANT DIVERSION.
GO EASY ON HIM, PICKLES!
Peirce

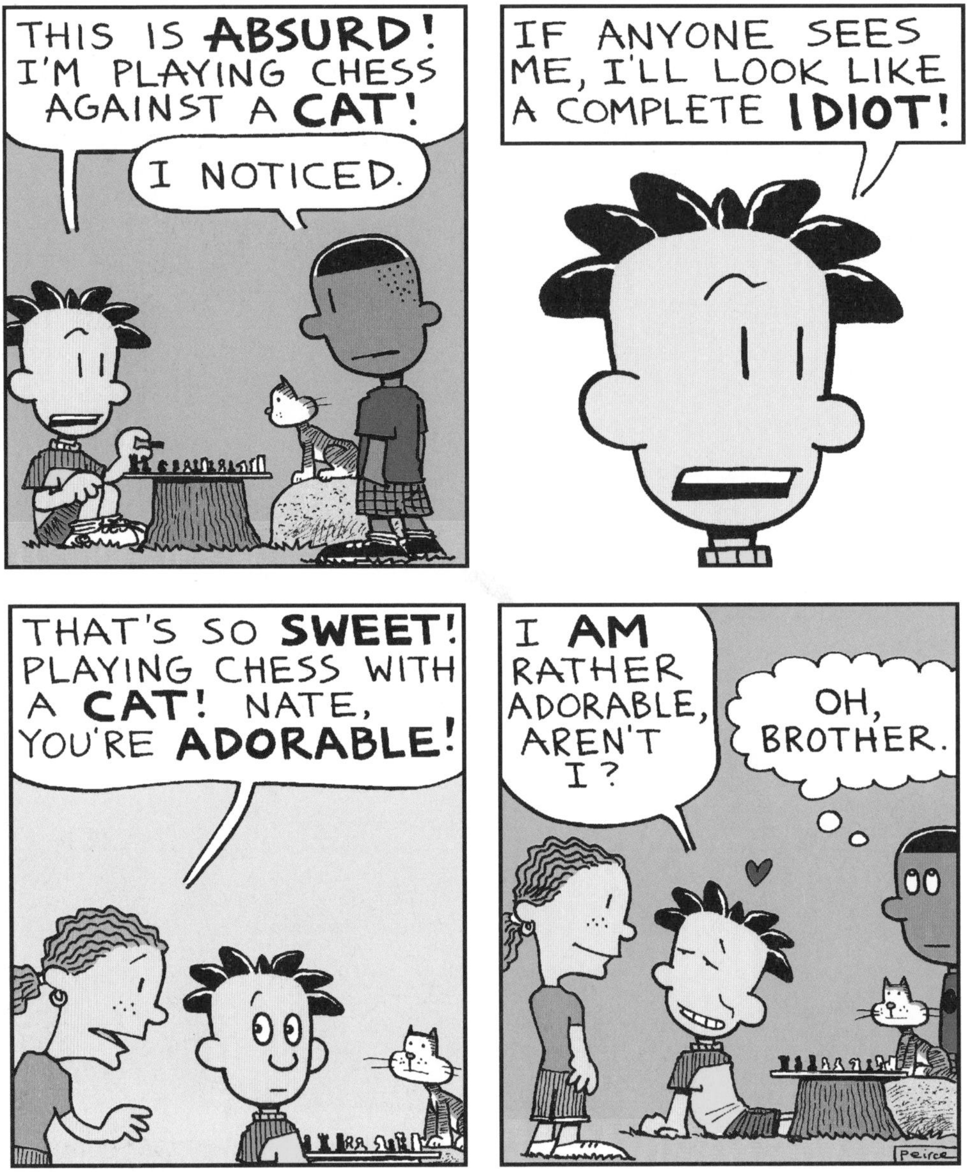
THIS IS ABSURD! I'M PLAYING CHESS AGAINST A CAT!
I NOTICED.
IF ANYONE SEES ME, I'LL LOOK LIKE A COMPLETE IDIOT!
THAT'S SO SWEET! PLAYING CHESS WITH A CAT! NATE, YOU'RE ADORABLE!
I AM RATHER ADORABLE, AREN'T I?
OH, BROTHER.
Peirce

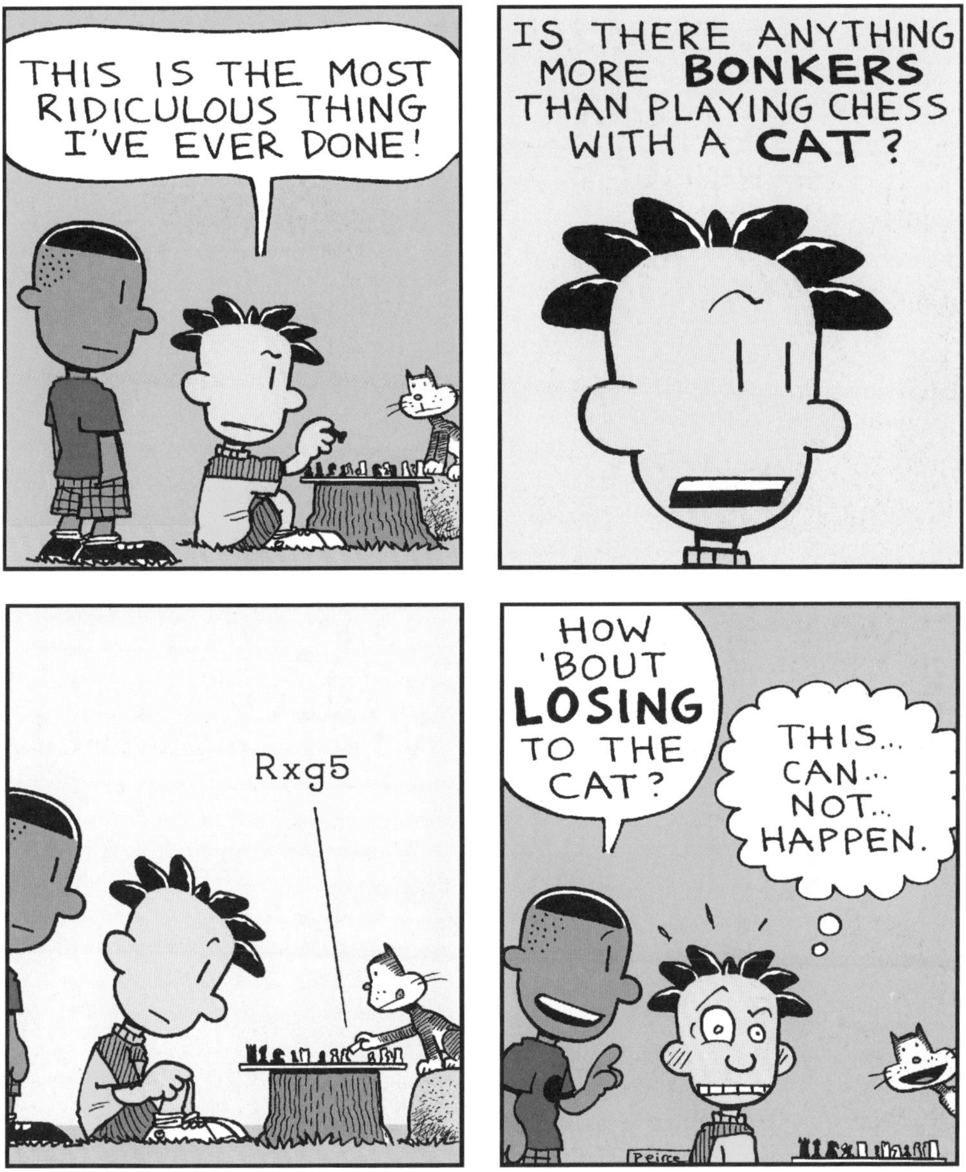
THIS IS THE MOST RIDICULOUS THING I'VE EVER DONE!
IS THERE ANYTHING MORE **BONKERS** THAN PLAYING CHESS WITH A **CAT**?
Rxg5
HOW 'BOUT **LOSING** TO THE CAT?
THIS... CAN... NOT... HAPPEN.
Peirce

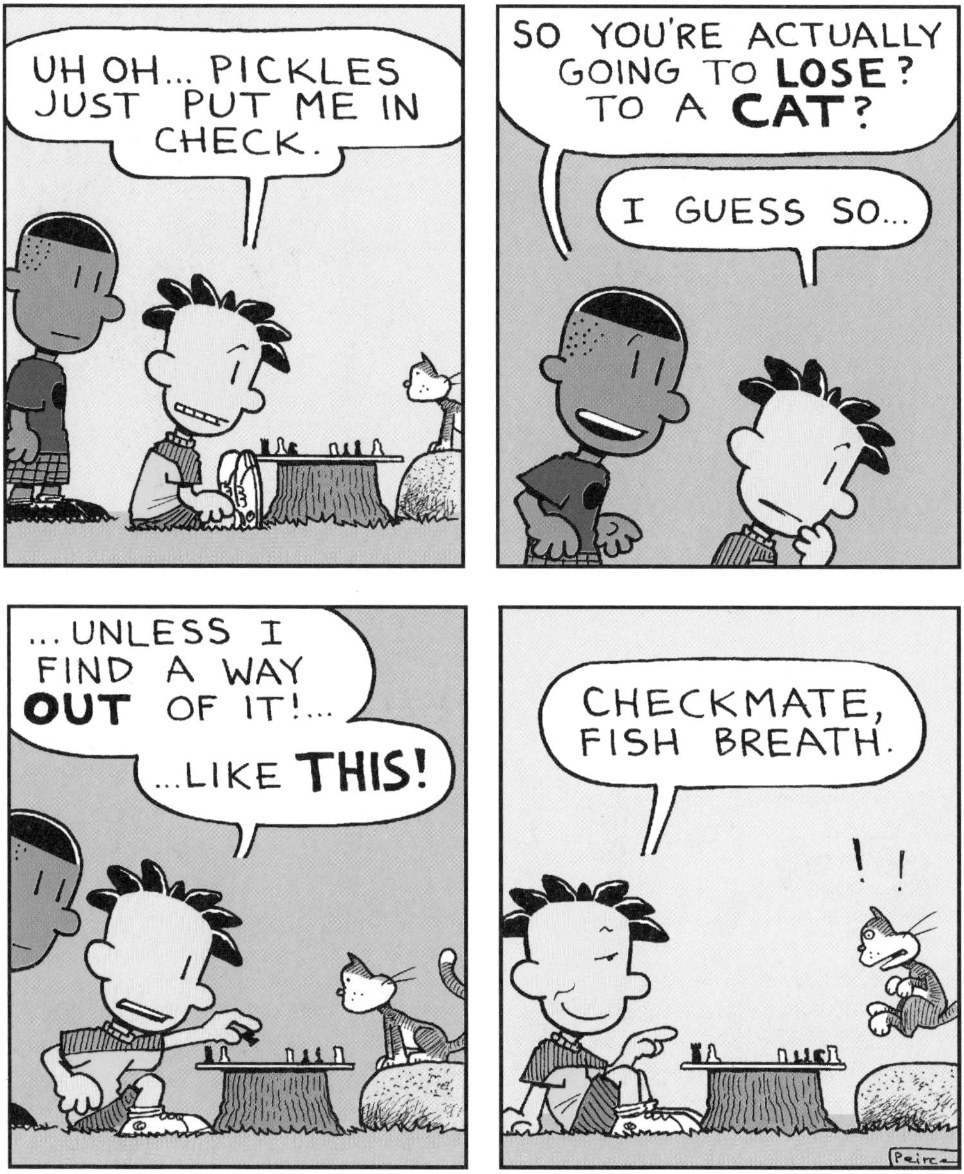
UH OH... PICKLES JUST PUT ME IN CHECK.
SO YOU'RE ACTUALLY GOING TO **LOSE**? TO A **CAT**?
I GUESS SO...
...UNLESS I FIND A WAY **OUT** OF IT!...
...LIKE **THIS!**
CHECKMATE, FISH BREATH.
! !
Peirce

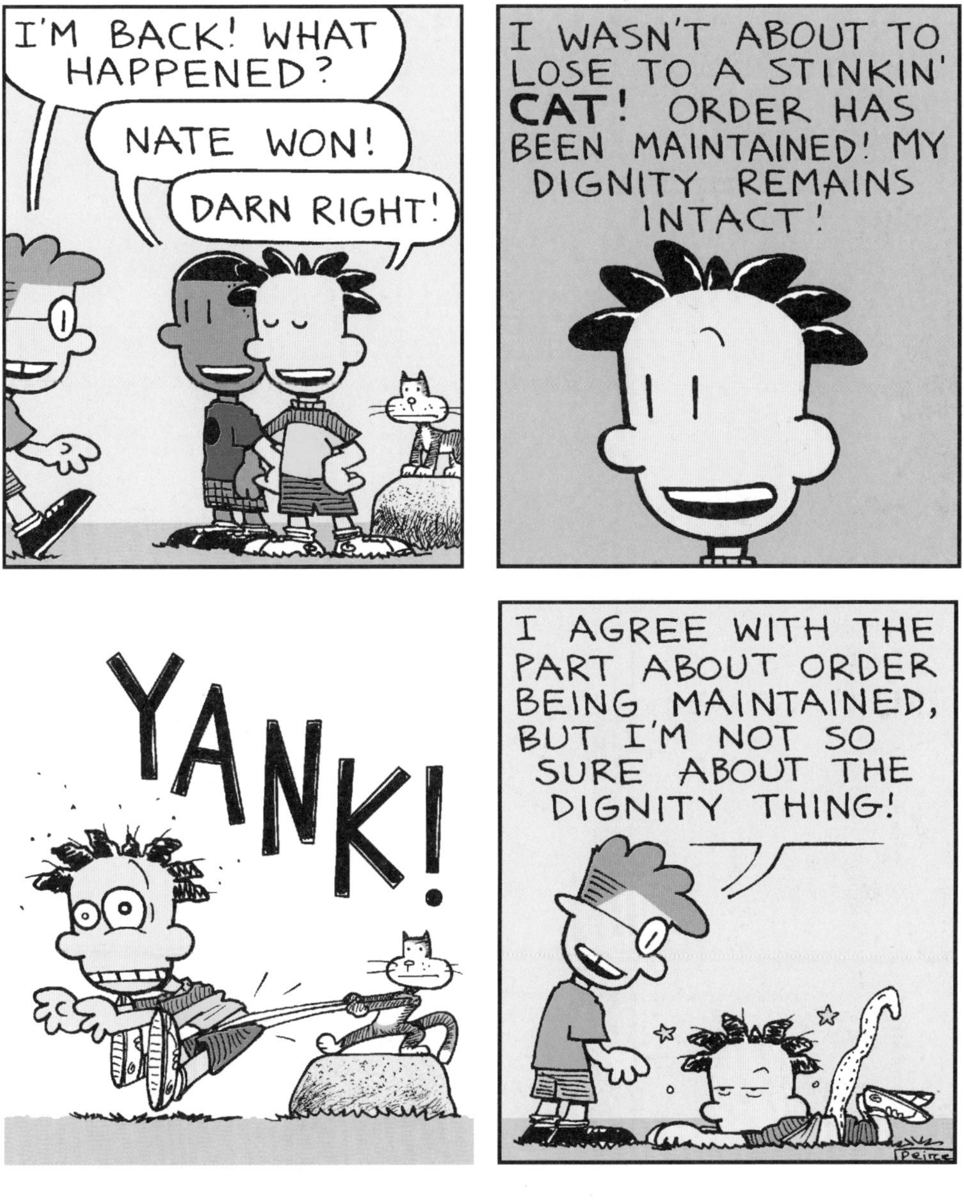
I'M BACK! WHAT HAPPENED?
NATE WON!
DARN RIGHT!
I WASN'T ABOUT TO LOSE TO A STINKIN' **CAT**! ORDER HAS BEEN MAINTAINED! MY DIGNITY REMAINS INTACT!
YANK!
I AGREE WITH THE PART ABOUT ORDER BEING MAINTAINED, BUT I'M NOT SO SURE ABOUT THE DIGNITY THING!
Peirce

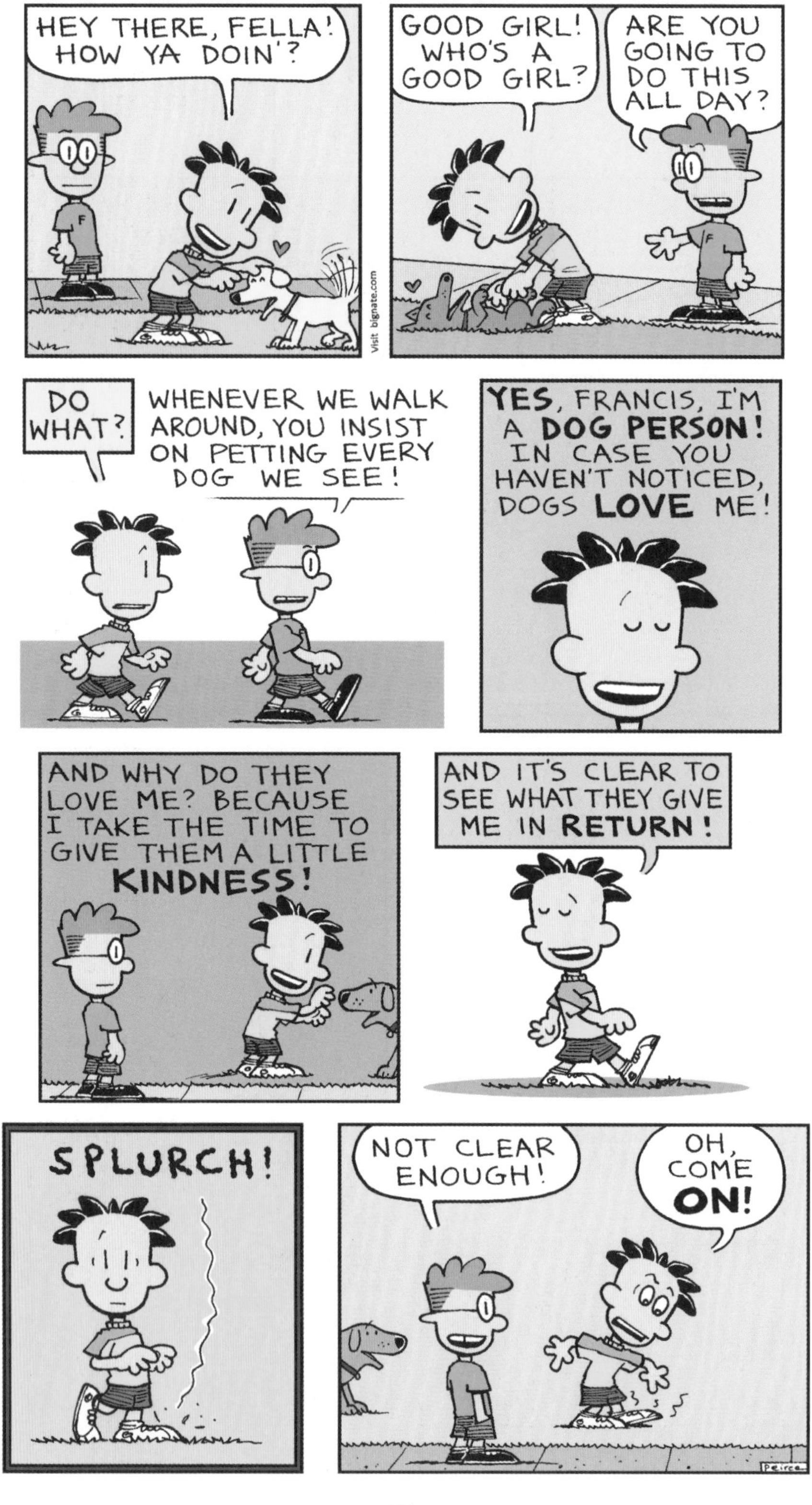
HEY THERE, FELLA! HOW YA DOIN'?
Visit bignate.com
GOOD GIRL! WHO'S A GOOD GIRL?
ARE YOU GOING TO DO THIS ALL DAY?
DO WHAT?
WHENEVER WE WALK AROUND, YOU INSIST ON PETTING EVERY DOG WE SEE!
YES, FRANCIS, I'M A DOG PERSON! IN CASE YOU HAVEN'T NOTICED, DOGS LOVE ME!
AND WHY DO THEY LOVE ME? BECAUSE I TAKE THE TIME TO GIVE THEM A LITTLE KINDNESS!
AND IT'S CLEAR TO SEE WHAT THEY GIVE ME IN RETURN!
SPLURCH!
NOT CLEAR ENOUGH!
OH, COME ON!
Peirce

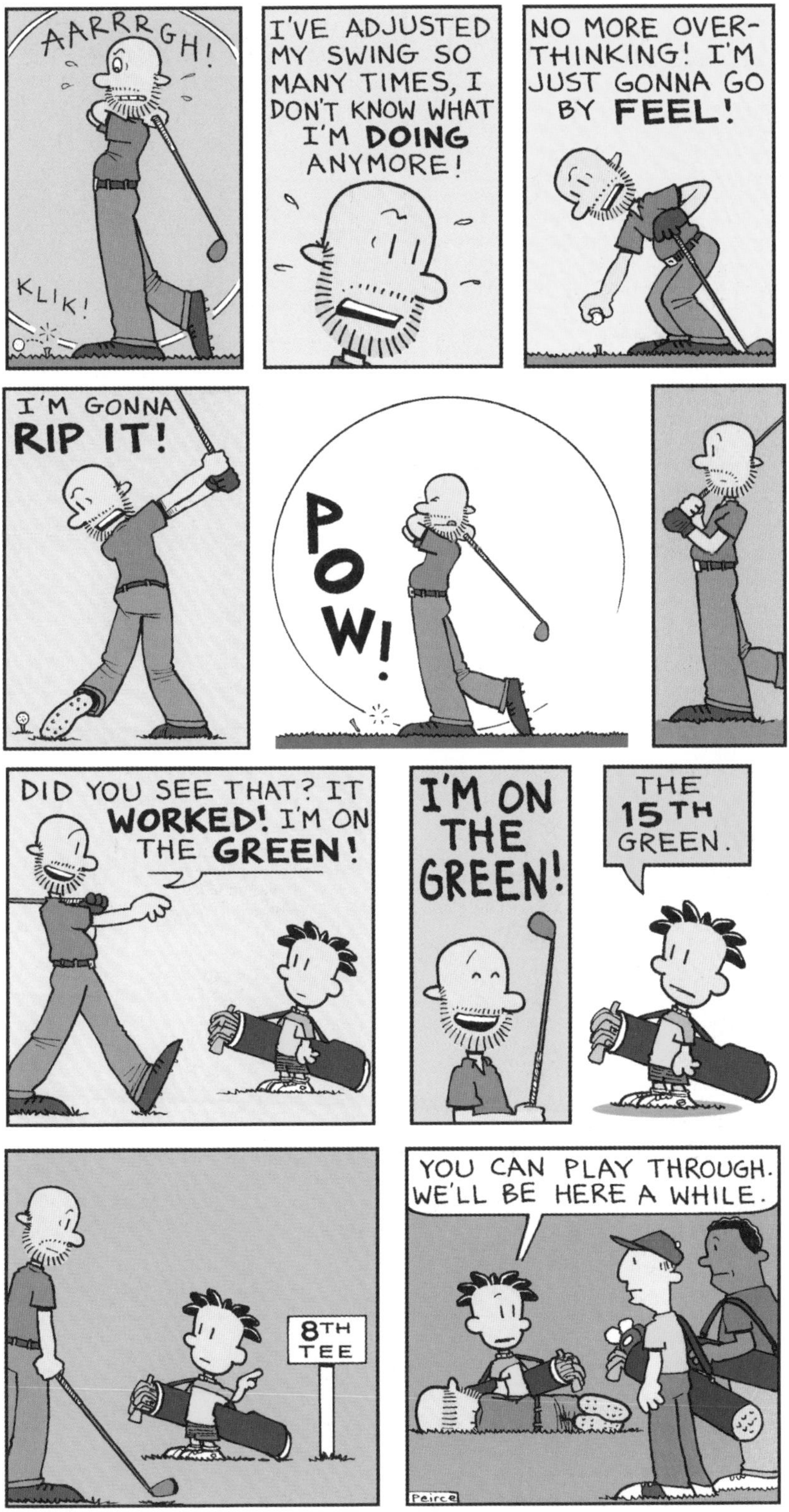
AARRRGH!
KLIK!
I'VE ADJUSTED MY SWING SO MANY TIMES, I DON'T KNOW WHAT I'M **DOING** ANYMORE!
NO MORE OVER-THINKING! I'M JUST GONNA GO BY **FEEL**!
I'M GONNA **RIP IT!**
POW!
DID YOU SEE THAT? IT **WORKED!** I'M ON THE **GREEN**!
I'M ON THE GREEN!
THE 15TH GREEN.
8TH TEE
YOU CAN PLAY THROUGH. WE'LL BE HERE A WHILE.
Peirce

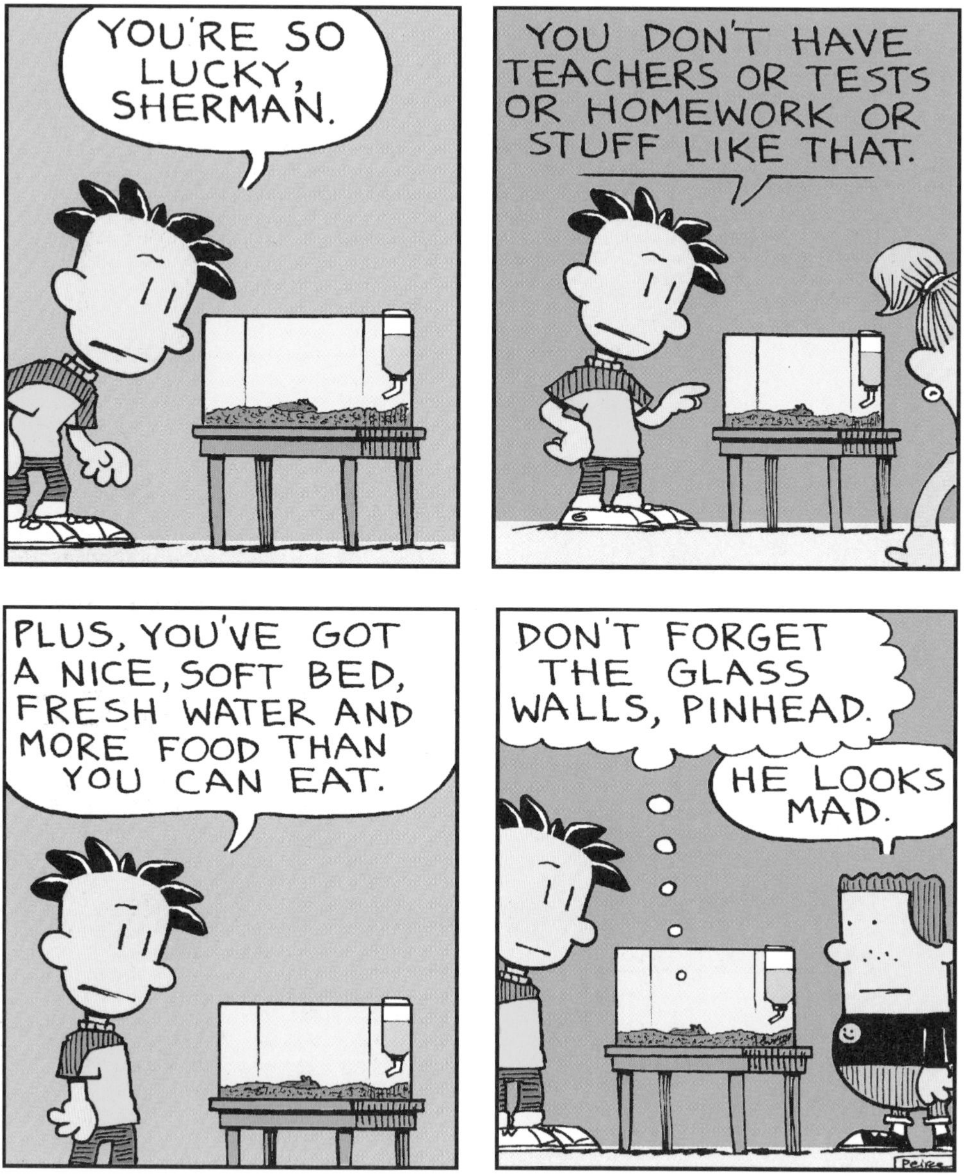
YOU'RE SO LUCKY, SHERMAN.
YOU DON'T HAVE TEACHERS OR TESTS OR HOMEWORK OR STUFF LIKE THAT.
PLUS, YOU'VE GOT A NICE, SOFT BED, FRESH WATER AND MORE FOOD THAN YOU CAN EAT.
DON'T FORGET THE GLASS WALLS, PINHEAD.
HE LOOKS MAD.
Peirce

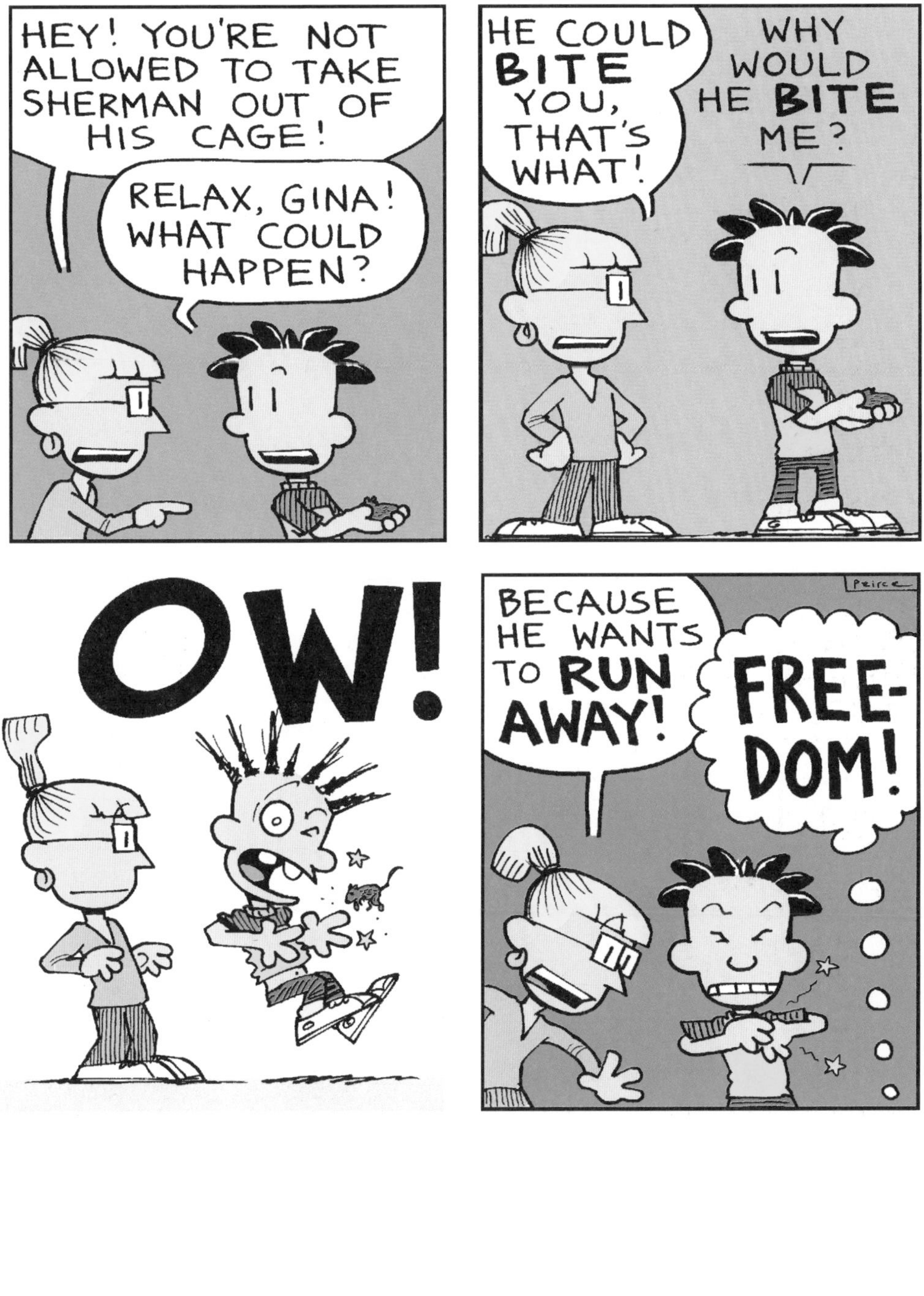
HEY! YOU'RE NOT ALLOWED TO TAKE SHERMAN OUT OF HIS CAGE!
RELAX, GINA! WHAT COULD HAPPEN?
HE COULD BITE YOU, THAT'S WHAT!
WHY WOULD HE BITE ME?
OW!
Peirce
BECAUSE HE WANTS TO RUN AWAY!
FREE-DOM!

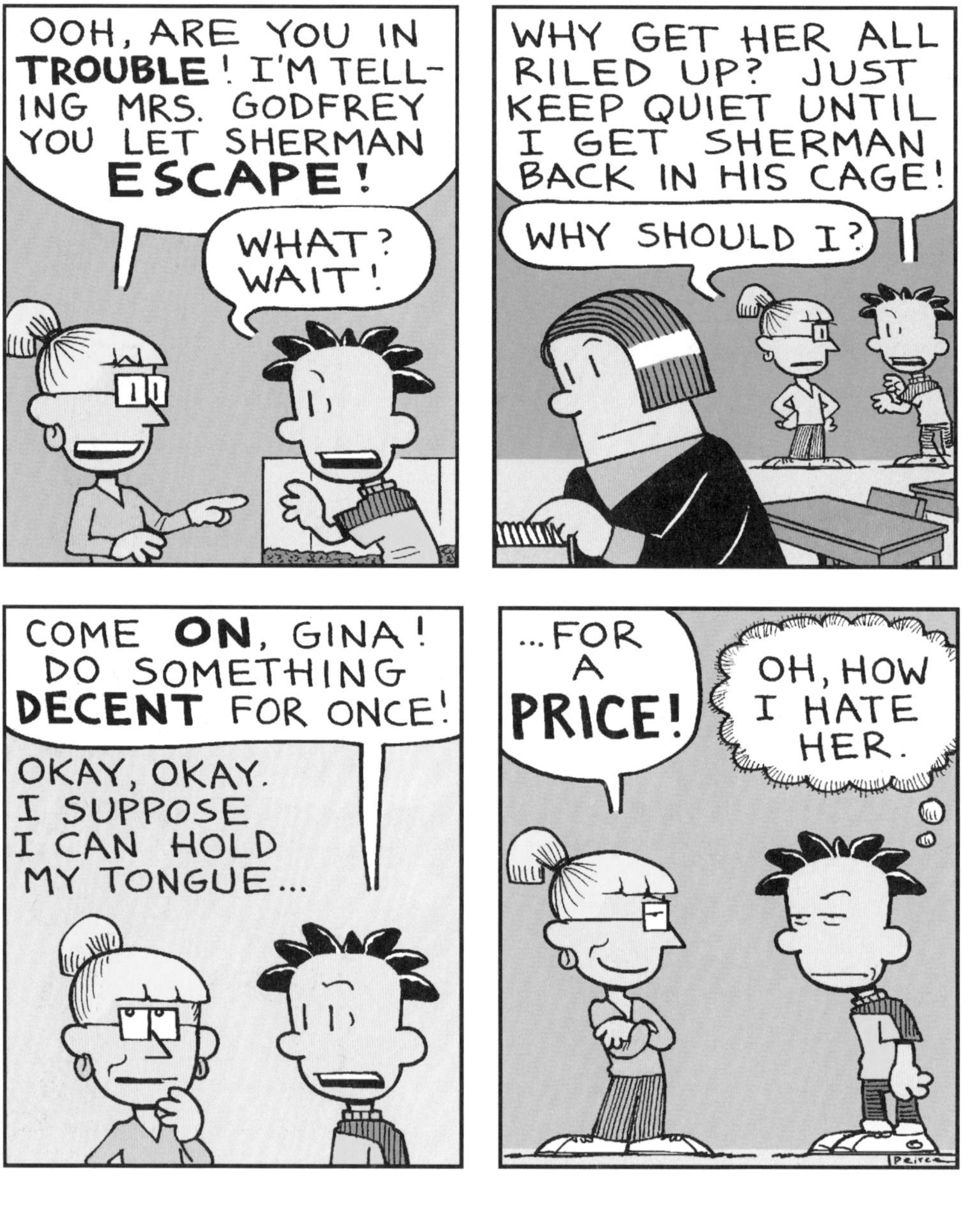
OOH, ARE YOU IN TROUBLE! I'M TELLING MRS. GODFREY YOU LET SHERMAN ESCAPE!
WHAT? WAIT!
WHY GET HER ALL RILED UP? JUST KEEP QUIET UNTIL I GET SHERMAN BACK IN HIS CAGE!
WHY SHOULD I?
COME ON, GINA! DO SOMETHING DECENT FOR ONCE!
OKAY, OKAY. I SUPPOSE I CAN HOLD MY TONGUE...
...FOR A PRICE!
OH, HOW I HATE HER.
PEIRCE

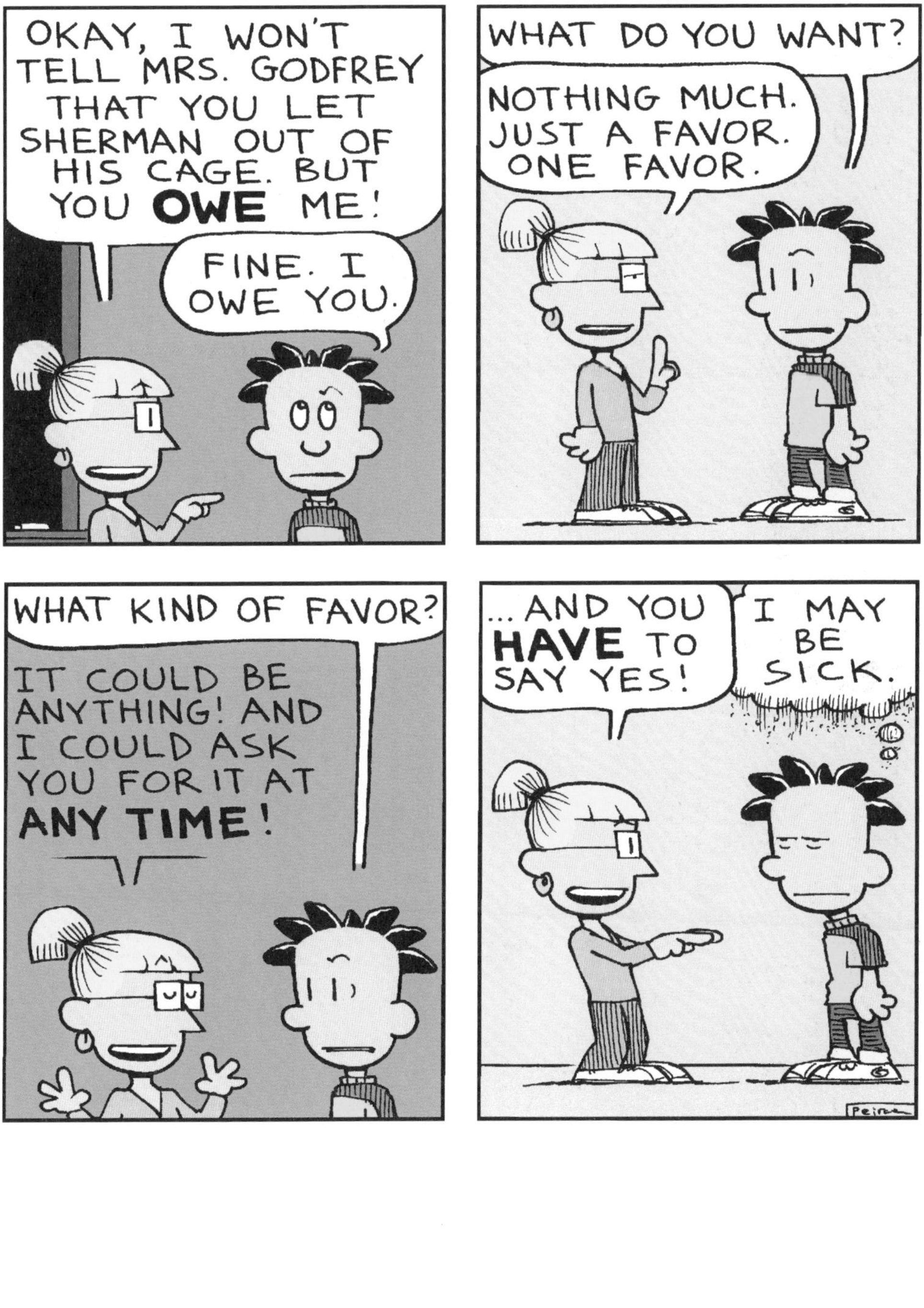
OKAY, I WON'T TELL MRS. GODFREY THAT YOU LET SHERMAN OUT OF HIS CAGE. BUT YOU **OWE** ME!
FINE. I OWE YOU.
WHAT DO YOU WANT?
NOTHING MUCH. JUST A FAVOR. ONE FAVOR.
WHAT KIND OF FAVOR?
IT COULD BE ANYTHING! AND I COULD ASK YOU FOR IT AT **ANY TIME**!
...AND YOU **HAVE** TO SAY YES!
I MAY BE SICK.

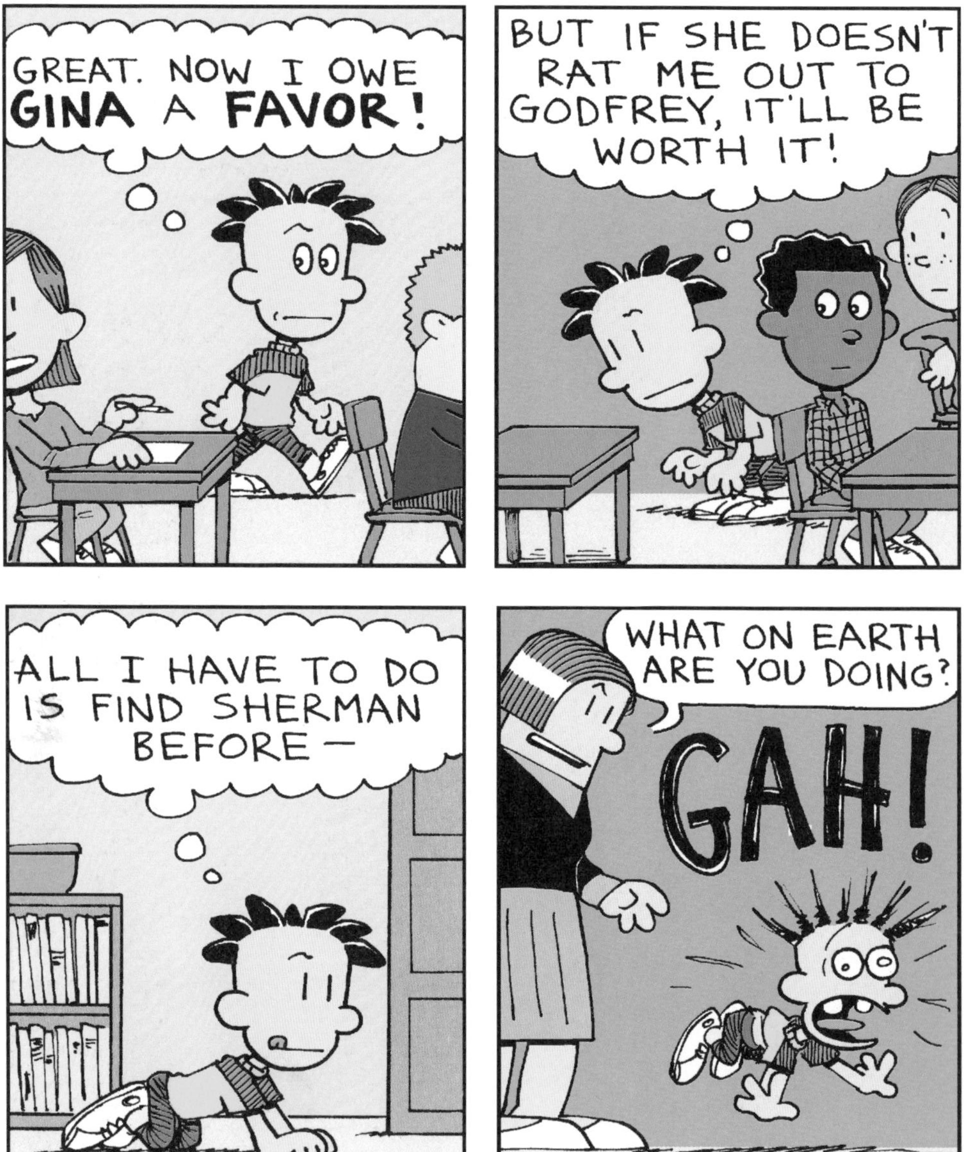
GREAT. NOW I OWE GINA A FAVOR!
BUT IF SHE DOESN'T RAT ME OUT TO GODFREY, IT'LL BE WORTH IT!
ALL I HAVE TO DO IS FIND SHERMAN BEFORE—
WHAT ON EARTH ARE YOU DOING?
GAH!
Peirce

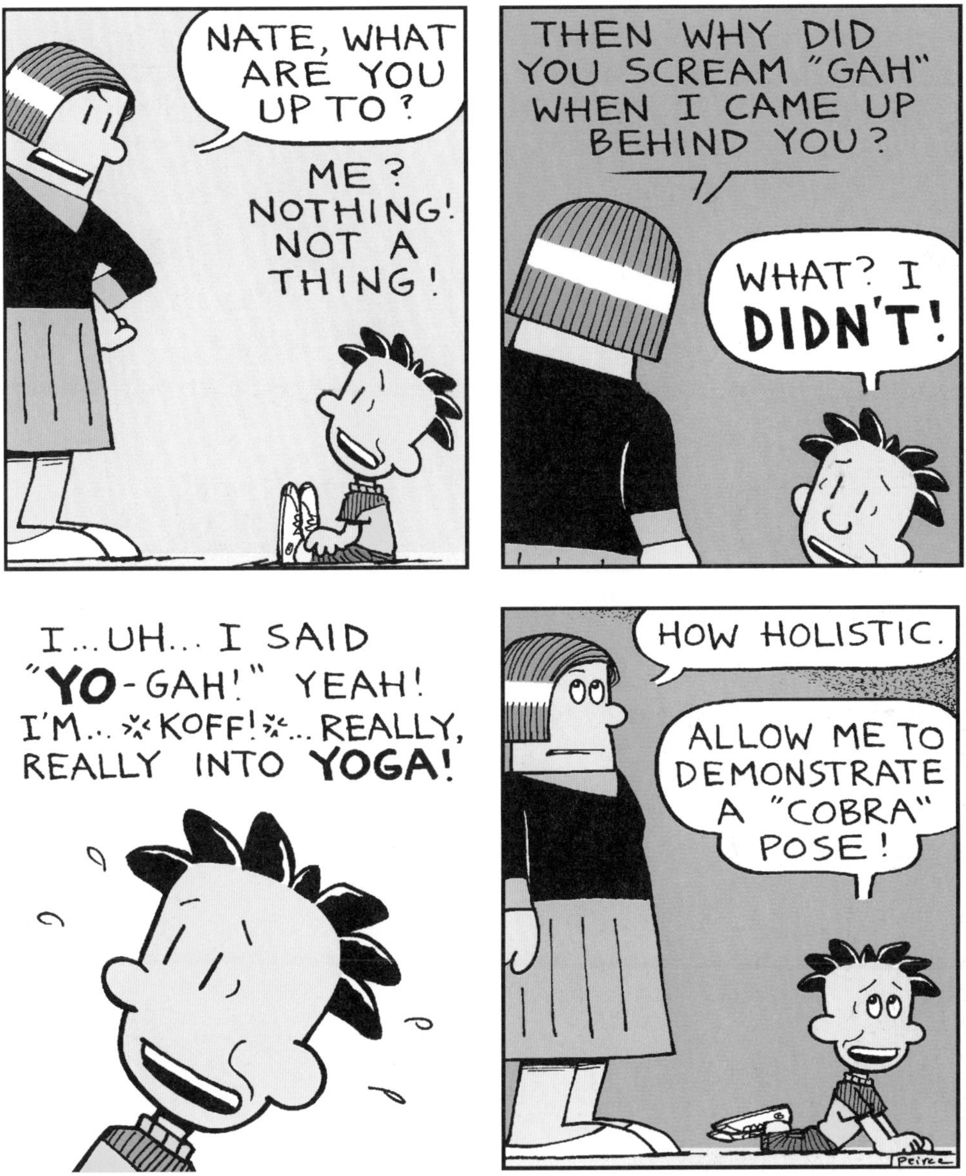
NATE, WHAT ARE YOU UP TO?
ME? NOTHING! NOT A THING!
THEN WHY DID YOU SCREAM "GAH" WHEN I CAME UP BEHIND YOU?
WHAT? I **DIDN'T!**
I... UH... I SAID "**YO**-GAH!" YEAH! I'M... *KOFF!*... REALLY, REALLY INTO **YOGA**!
HOW HOLISTIC.
ALLOW ME TO DEMONSTRATE A "COBRA" POSE!
Peirce

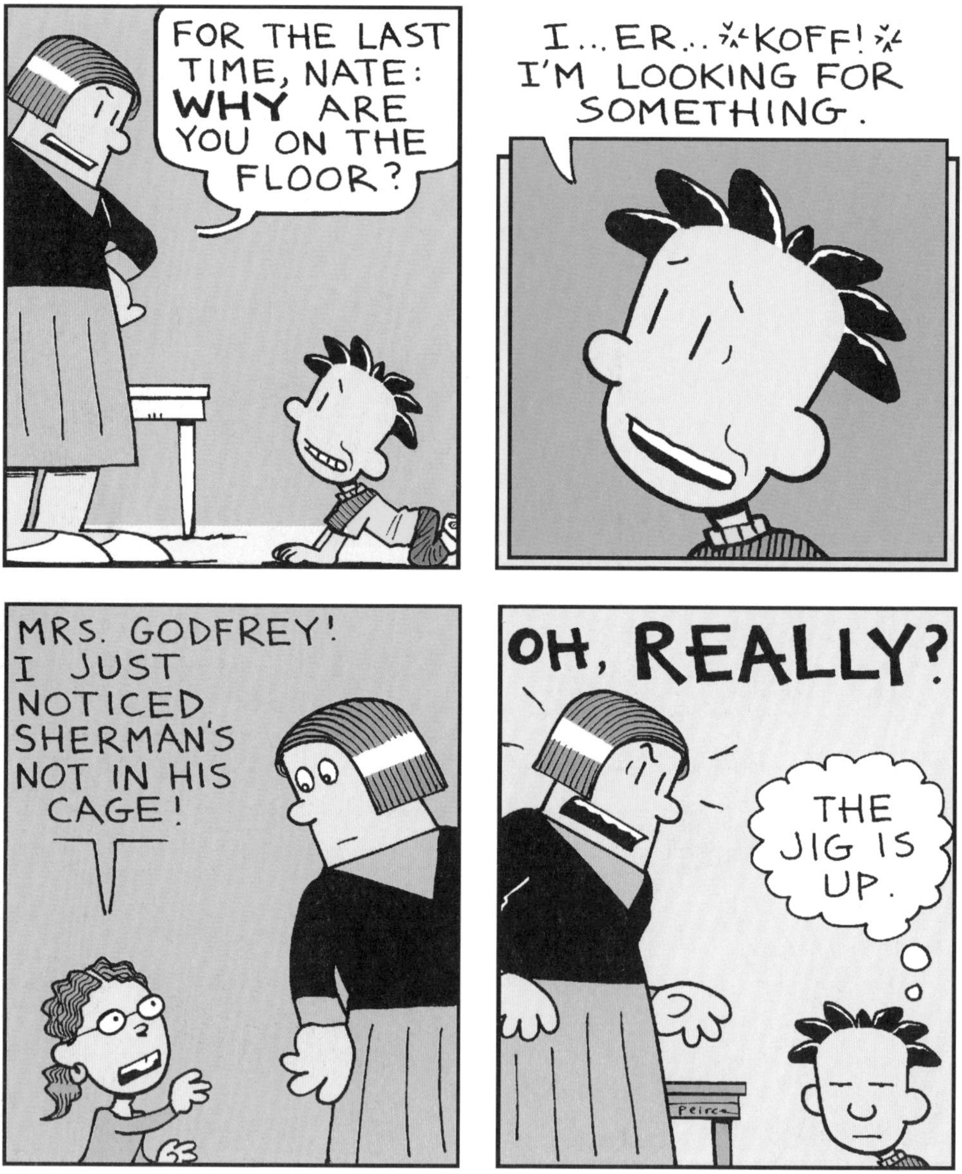
FOR THE LAST TIME, NATE: WHY ARE YOU ON THE FLOOR?
I... ER... *KOFF!* I'M LOOKING FOR SOMETHING.
MRS. GODFREY! I JUST NOTICED SHERMAN'S NOT IN HIS CAGE!
OH, REALLY?
THE JIG IS UP.
Peirce

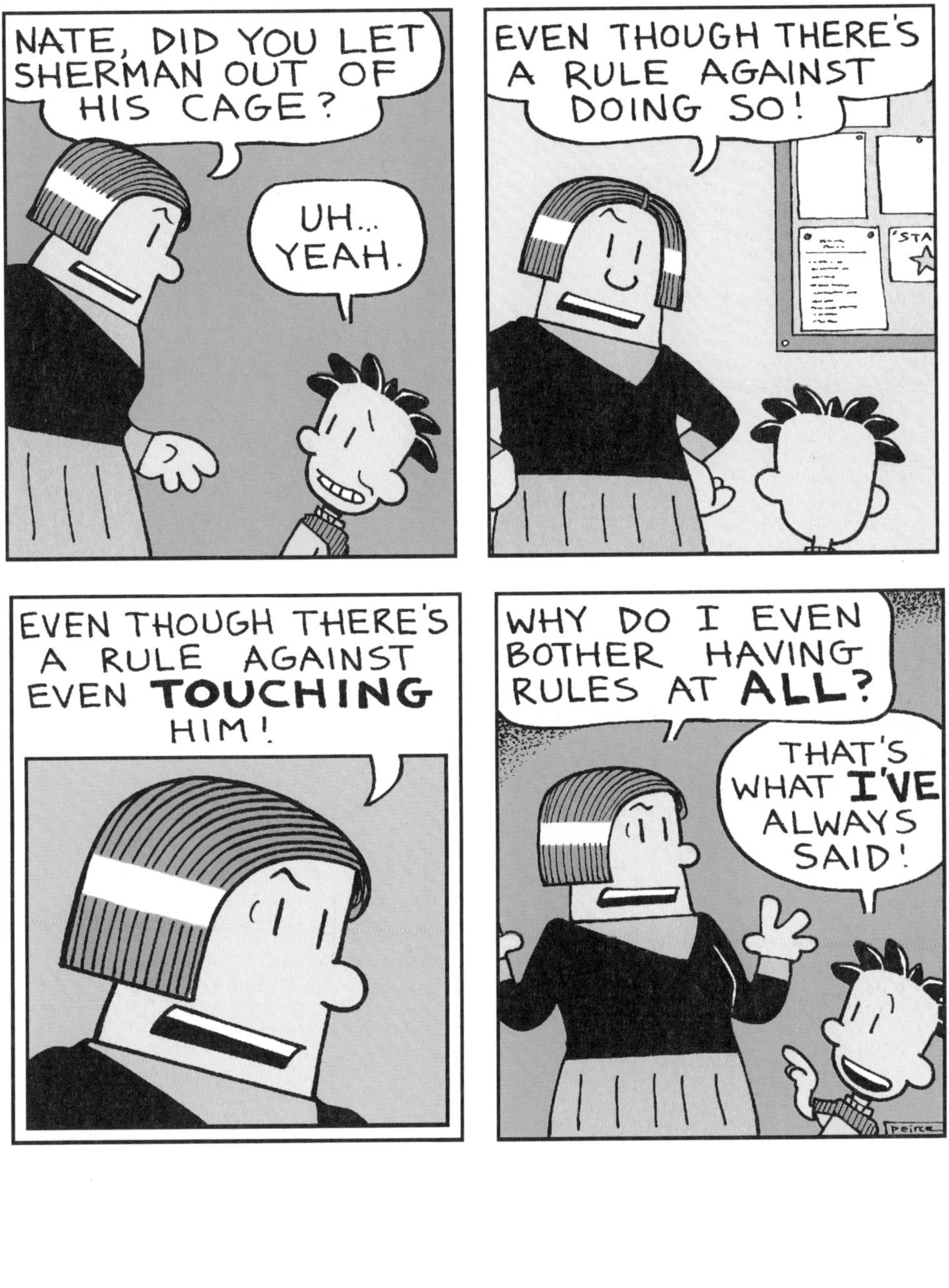
NATE, DID YOU LET SHERMAN OUT OF HIS CAGE?
UH... YEAH.
EVEN THOUGH THERE'S A RULE AGAINST DOING SO!
EVEN THOUGH THERE'S A RULE AGAINST EVEN **TOUCHING** HIM!
WHY DO I EVEN BOTHER HAVING RULES AT **ALL?**
THAT'S WHAT **I'VE** ALWAYS SAID!
peirce

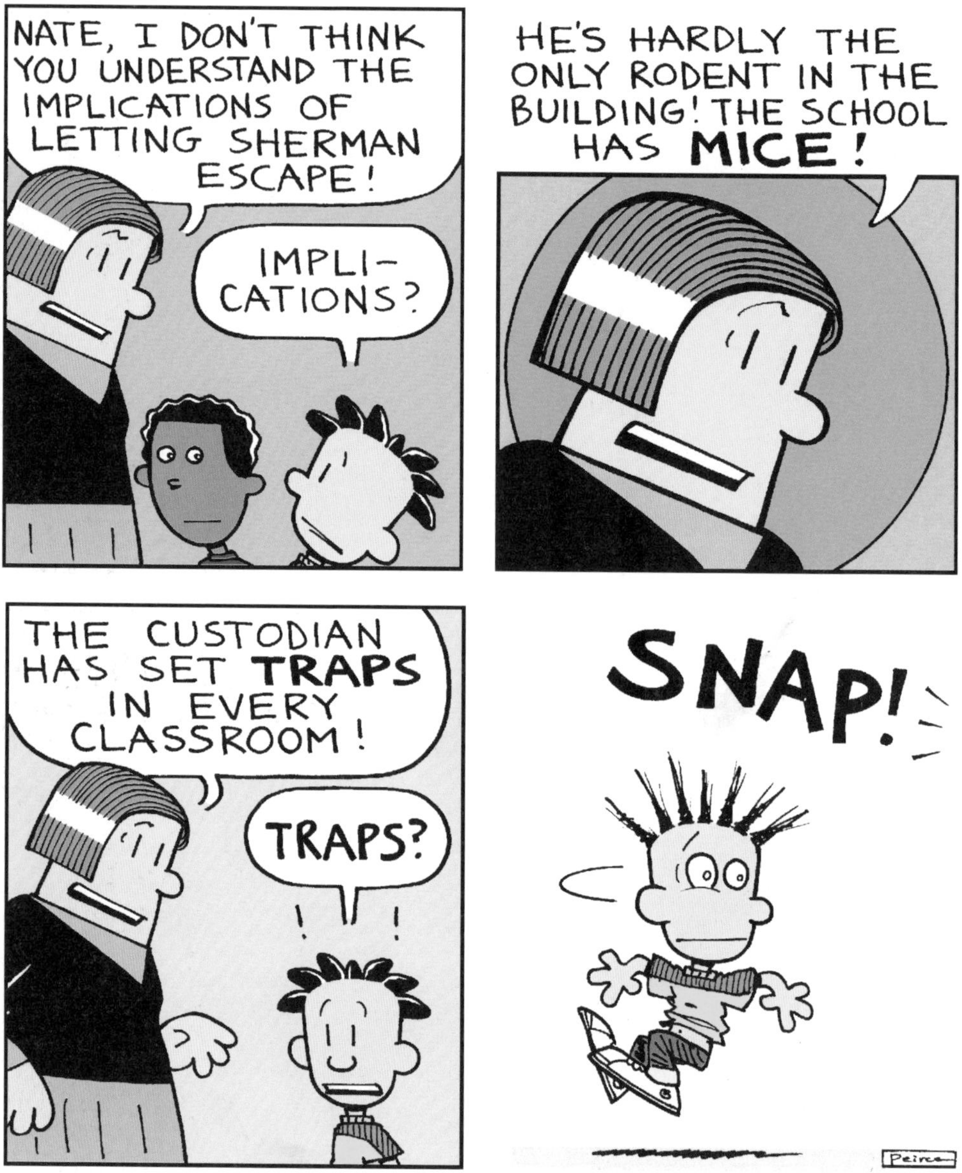
NATE, I DON'T THINK YOU UNDERSTAND THE IMPLICATIONS OF LETTING SHERMAN ESCAPE!
IMPLI-CATIONS?
HE'S HARDLY THE ONLY RODENT IN THE BUILDING! THE SCHOOL HAS **MICE**!
THE CUSTODIAN HAS SET **TRAPS** IN EVERY CLASSROOM!
TRAPS?
! !
SNAP!
Peirce

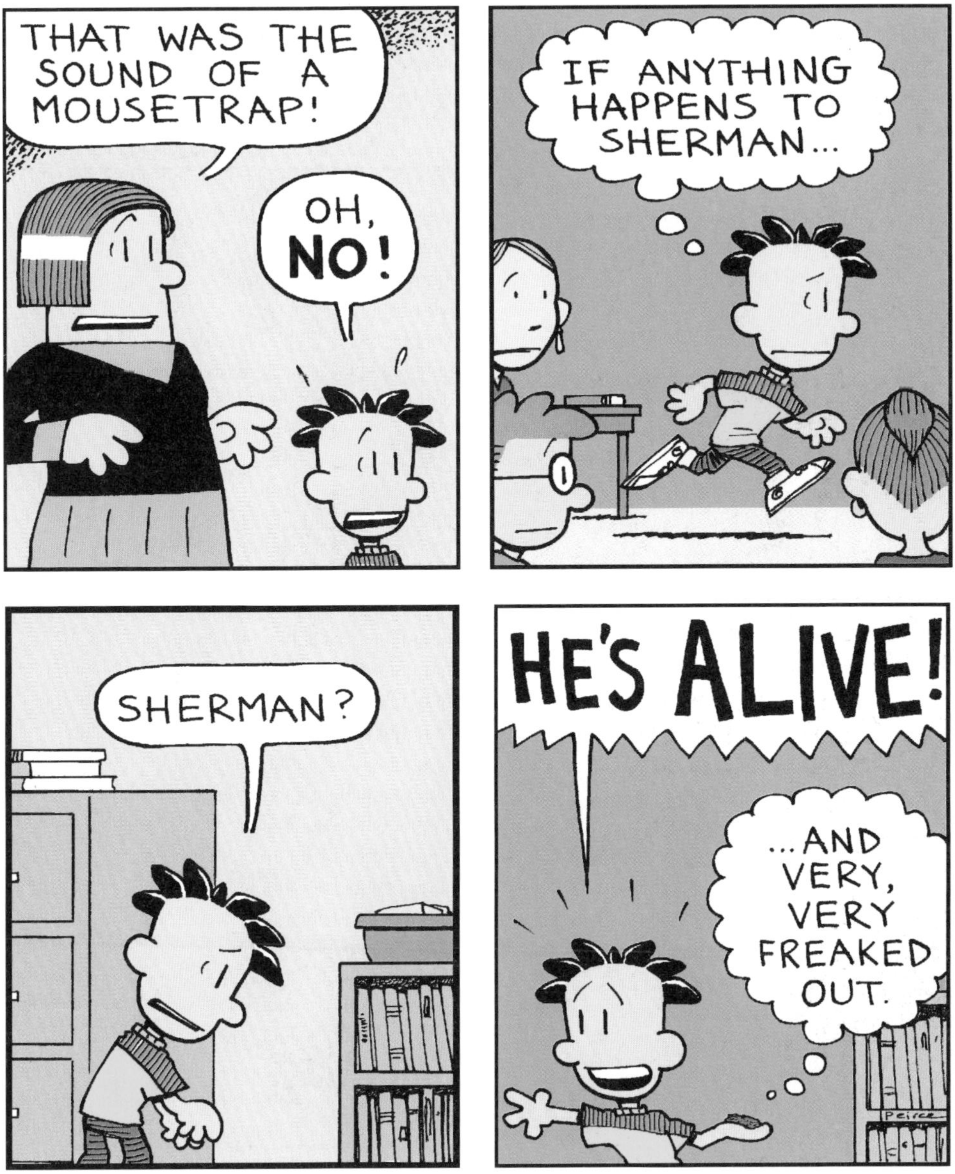
THAT WAS THE SOUND OF A MOUSETRAP!
OH, NO!
IF ANYTHING HAPPENS TO SHERMAN...
SHERMAN?
HE'S ALIVE!
...AND VERY, VERY FREAKED OUT.
Peirce

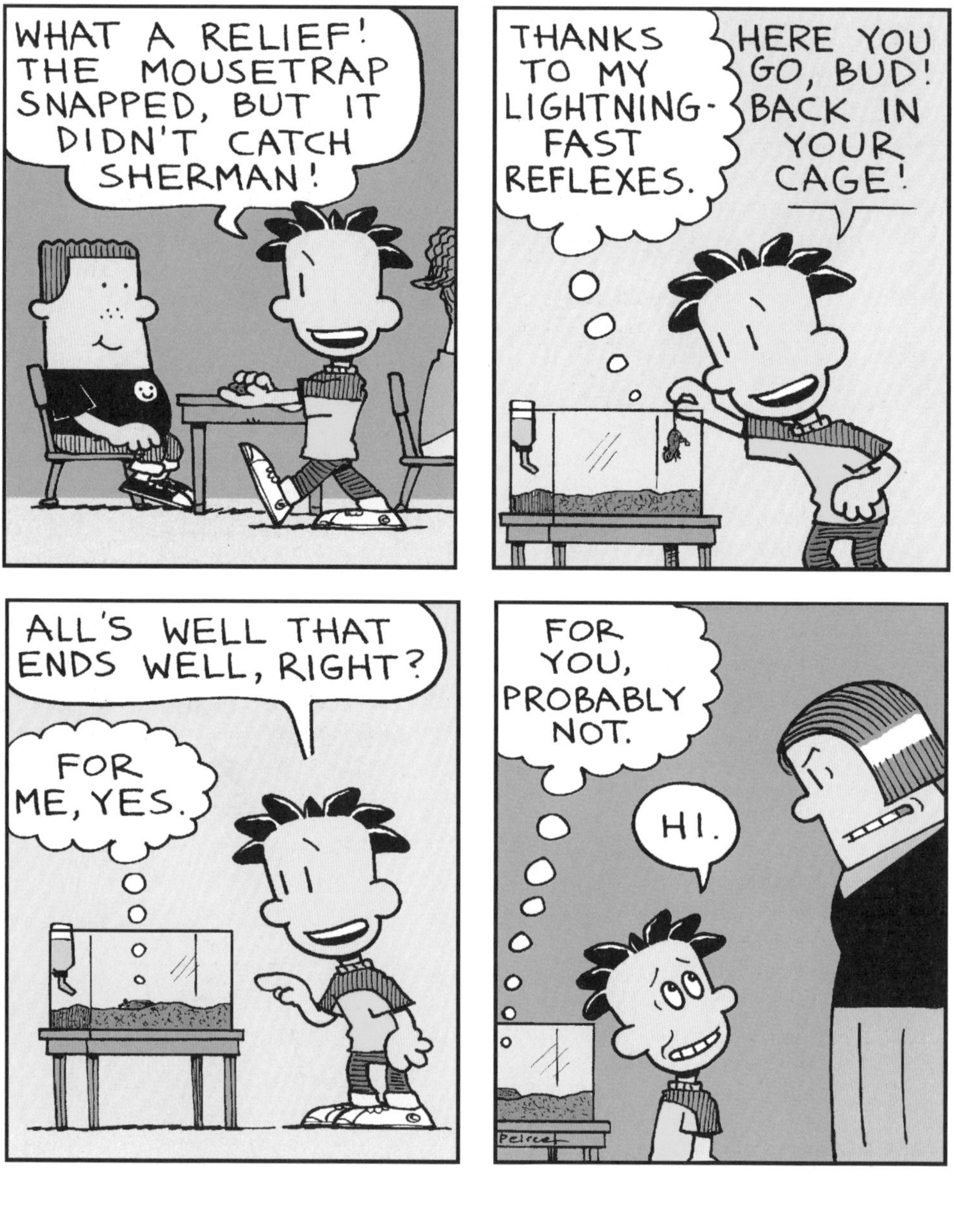
WHAT A RELIEF! THE MOUSETRAP SNAPPED, BUT IT DIDN'T CATCH SHERMAN!
THANKS TO MY LIGHTNING-FAST REFLEXES.
HERE YOU GO, BUD! BACK IN YOUR CAGE!
ALL'S WELL THAT ENDS WELL, RIGHT?
FOR ME, YES.
FOR YOU, PROBABLY NOT.
HI.
Peirce

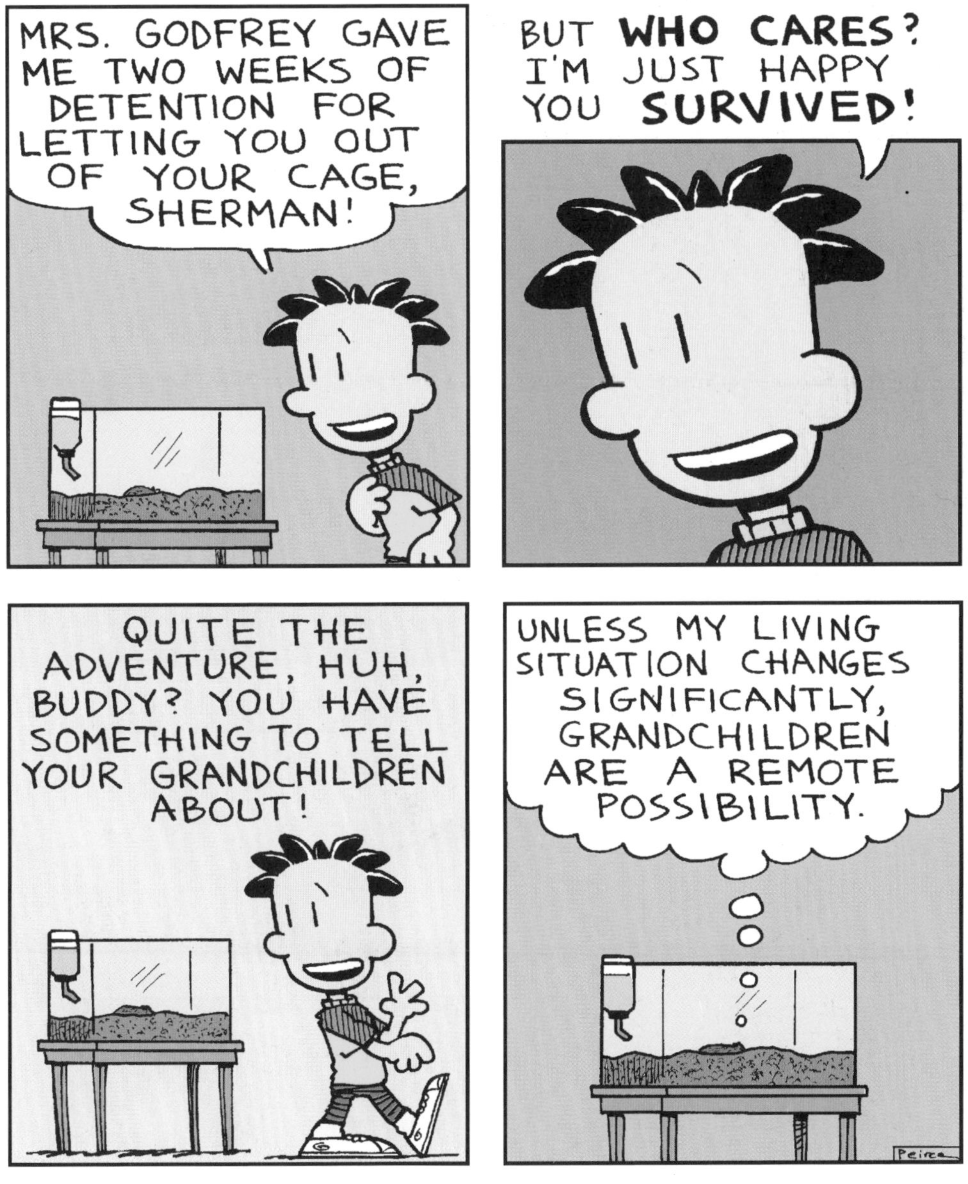
MRS. GODFREY GAVE ME TWO WEEKS OF DETENTION FOR LETTING YOU OUT OF YOUR CAGE, SHERMAN!
BUT **WHO CARES**? I'M JUST HAPPY YOU **SURVIVED**!
QUITE THE ADVENTURE, HUH, BUDDY? YOU HAVE SOMETHING TO TELL YOUR GRANDCHILDREN ABOUT!
UNLESS MY LIVING SITUATION CHANGES SIGNIFICANTLY, GRANDCHILDREN ARE A REMOTE POSSIBILITY.
Peirce

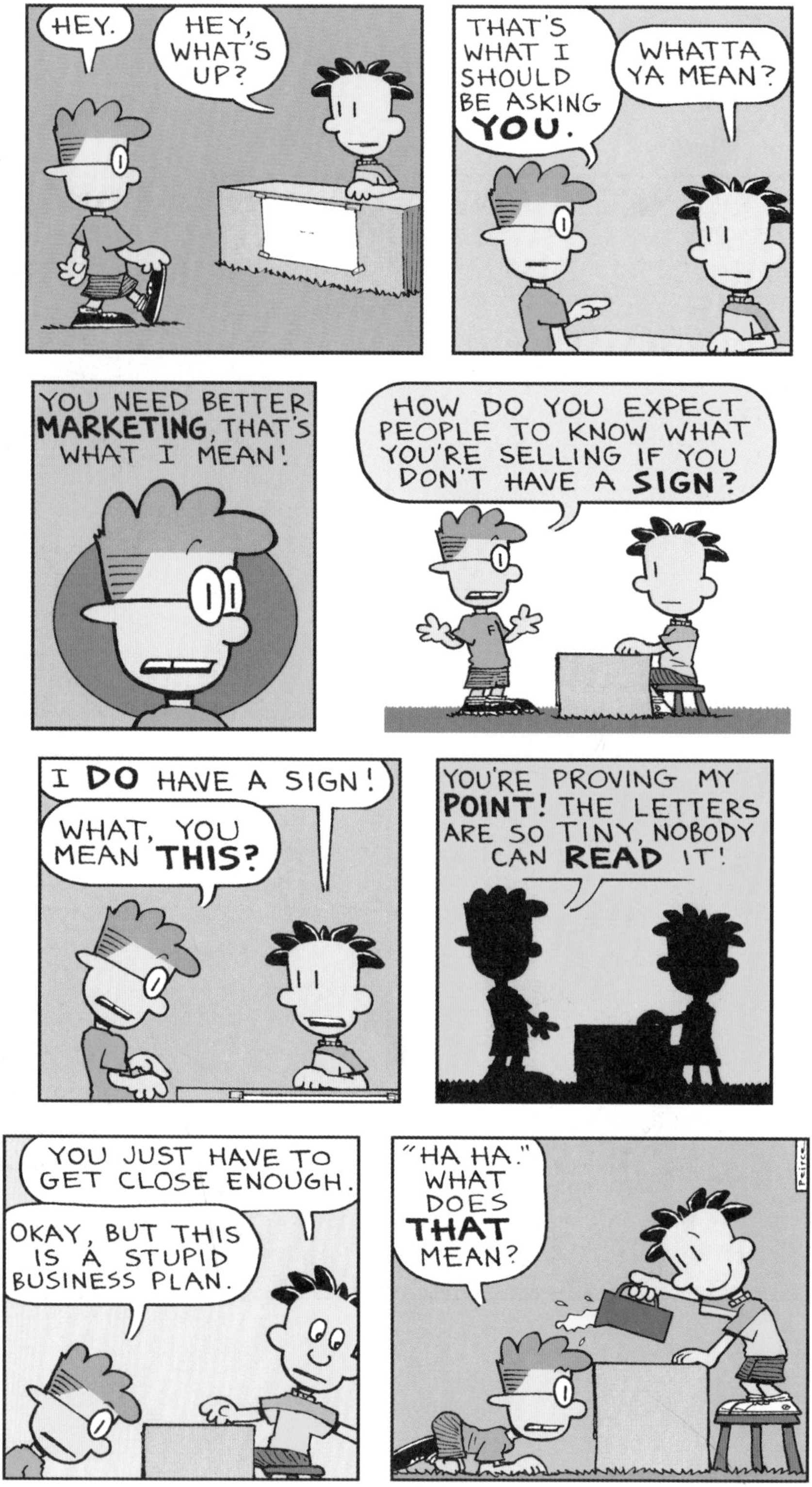
HEY.
HEY, WHAT'S UP?
THAT'S WHAT I SHOULD BE ASKING YOU.
WHATTA YA MEAN?
YOU NEED BETTER MARKETING, THAT'S WHAT I MEAN!
HOW DO YOU EXPECT PEOPLE TO KNOW WHAT YOU'RE SELLING IF YOU DON'T HAVE A SIGN?
F
I DO HAVE A SIGN!
WHAT, YOU MEAN THIS?
YOU'RE PROVING MY POINT! THE LETTERS ARE SO TINY, NOBODY CAN READ IT!
YOU JUST HAVE TO GET CLOSE ENOUGH.
OKAY, BUT THIS IS A STUPID BUSINESS PLAN.
"HA HA." WHAT DOES THAT MEAN?
Peirce

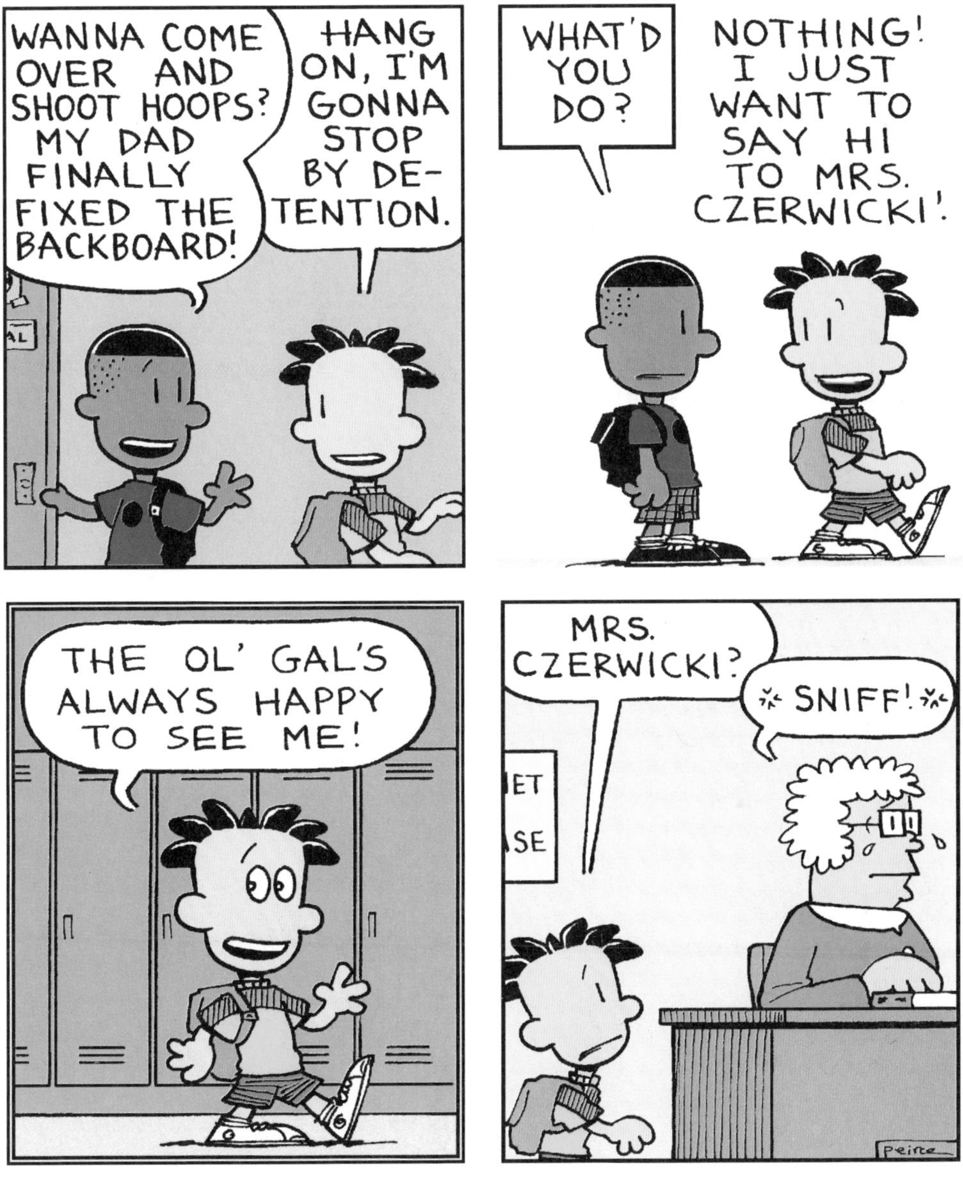
WANNA COME OVER AND SHOOT HOOPS? MY DAD FINALLY FIXED THE BACKBOARD!
HANG ON, I'M GONNA STOP BY DE-TENTION.
WHAT'D YOU DO?
NOTHING! I JUST WANT TO SAY HI TO MRS. CZERWICKI!
THE OL' GAL'S ALWAYS HAPPY TO SEE ME!
MRS. CZERWICKI?
SNIFF!
peirce

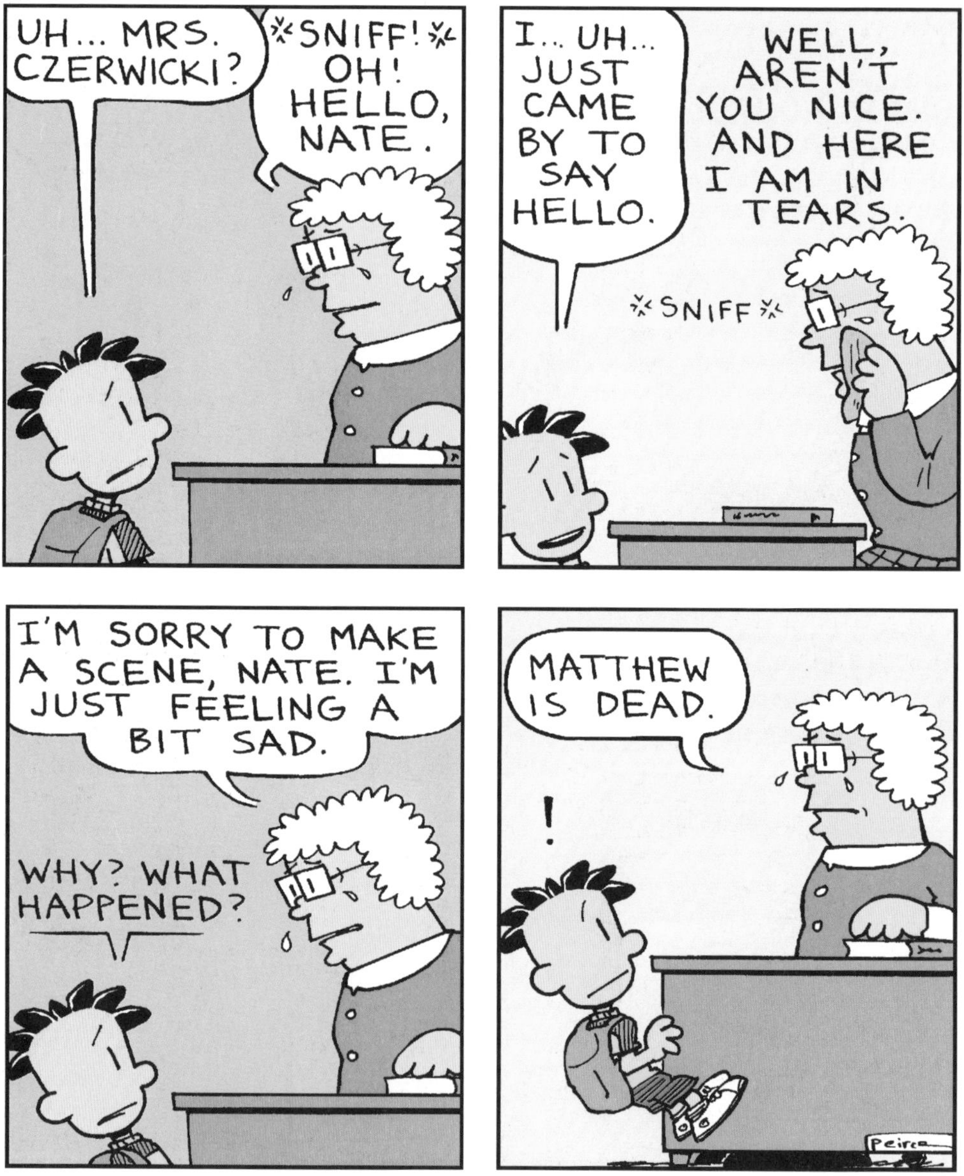
UH... MRS. CZERWICKI?
SNIFF! OH! HELLO, NATE.
I... UH... JUST CAME BY TO SAY HELLO.
WELL, AREN'T YOU NICE. AND HERE I AM IN TEARS.
SNIFF
I'M SORRY TO MAKE A SCENE, NATE. I'M JUST FEELING A BIT SAD.
WHY? WHAT HAPPENED?
MATTHEW IS DEAD.
!
Peirce

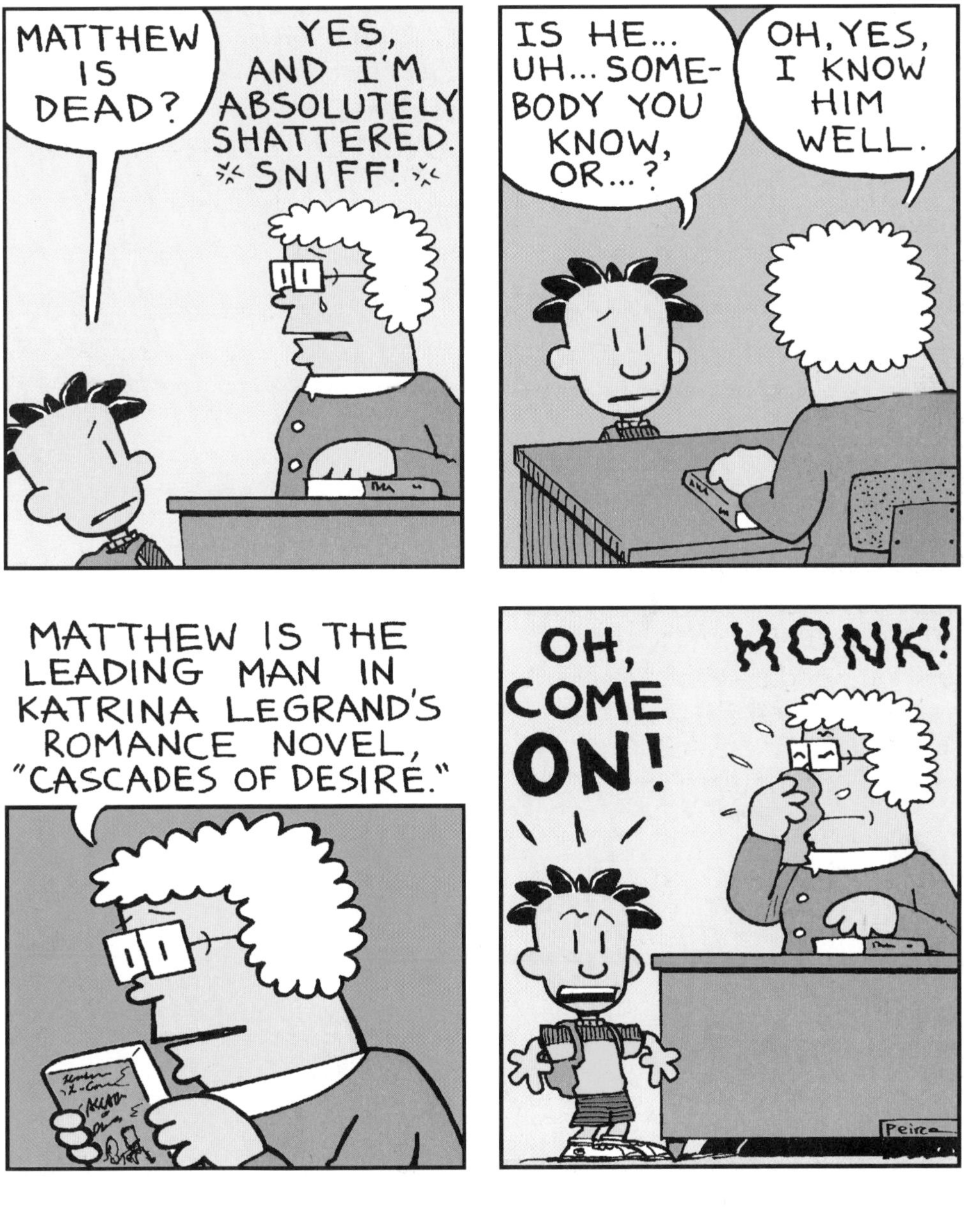
MATTHEW IS DEAD?
YES, AND I'M ABSOLUTELY SHATTERED. SNIFF!
IS HE... UH... SOMEBODY YOU KNOW, OR...?
OH, YES, I KNOW HIM WELL.
MATTHEW IS THE LEADING MAN IN KATRINA LEGRAND'S ROMANCE NOVEL, "CASCADES OF DESIRE."
OH, COME ON!
HONK!
Peirce

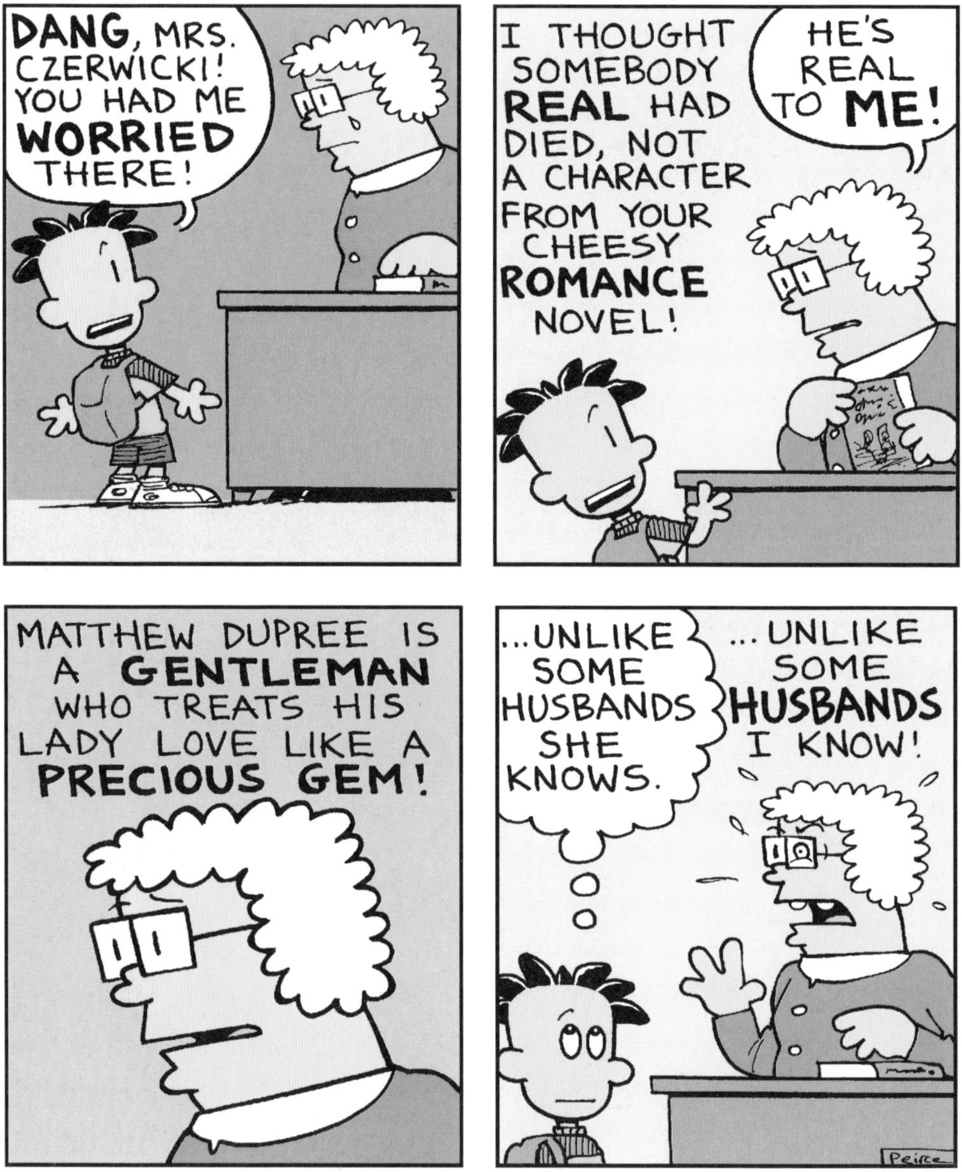
DANG, MRS. CZERWICKI! YOU HAD ME WORRIED THERE!
I THOUGHT SOMEBODY REAL HAD DIED, NOT A CHARACTER FROM YOUR CHEESY ROMANCE NOVEL!
HE'S REAL TO ME!
MATTHEW DUPREE IS A GENTLEMAN WHO TREATS HIS LADY LOVE LIKE A PRECIOUS GEM!
...UNLIKE SOME HUSBANDS SHE KNOWS.
...UNLIKE SOME HUSBANDS I KNOW!
Peirce

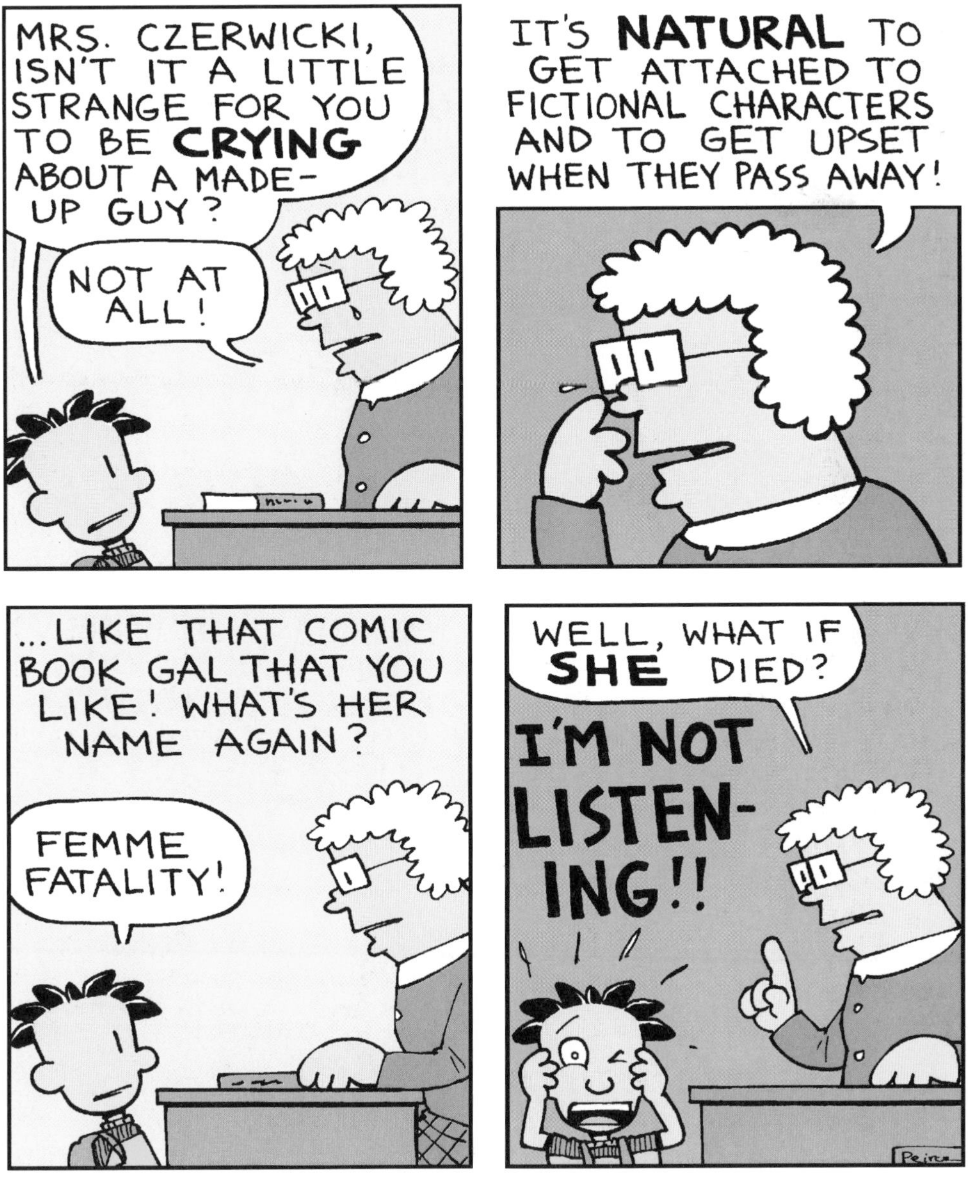
MRS. CZERWICKI, ISN'T IT A LITTLE STRANGE FOR YOU TO BE **CRYING** ABOUT A MADE-UP GUY?
NOT AT ALL!
IT'S **NATURAL** TO GET ATTACHED TO FICTIONAL CHARACTERS AND TO GET UPSET WHEN THEY PASS AWAY!
...LIKE THAT COMIC BOOK GAL THAT YOU LIKE! WHAT'S HER NAME AGAIN?
FEMME FATALITY!
WELL, WHAT IF **SHE** DIED?
I'M NOT LISTEN-ING!!

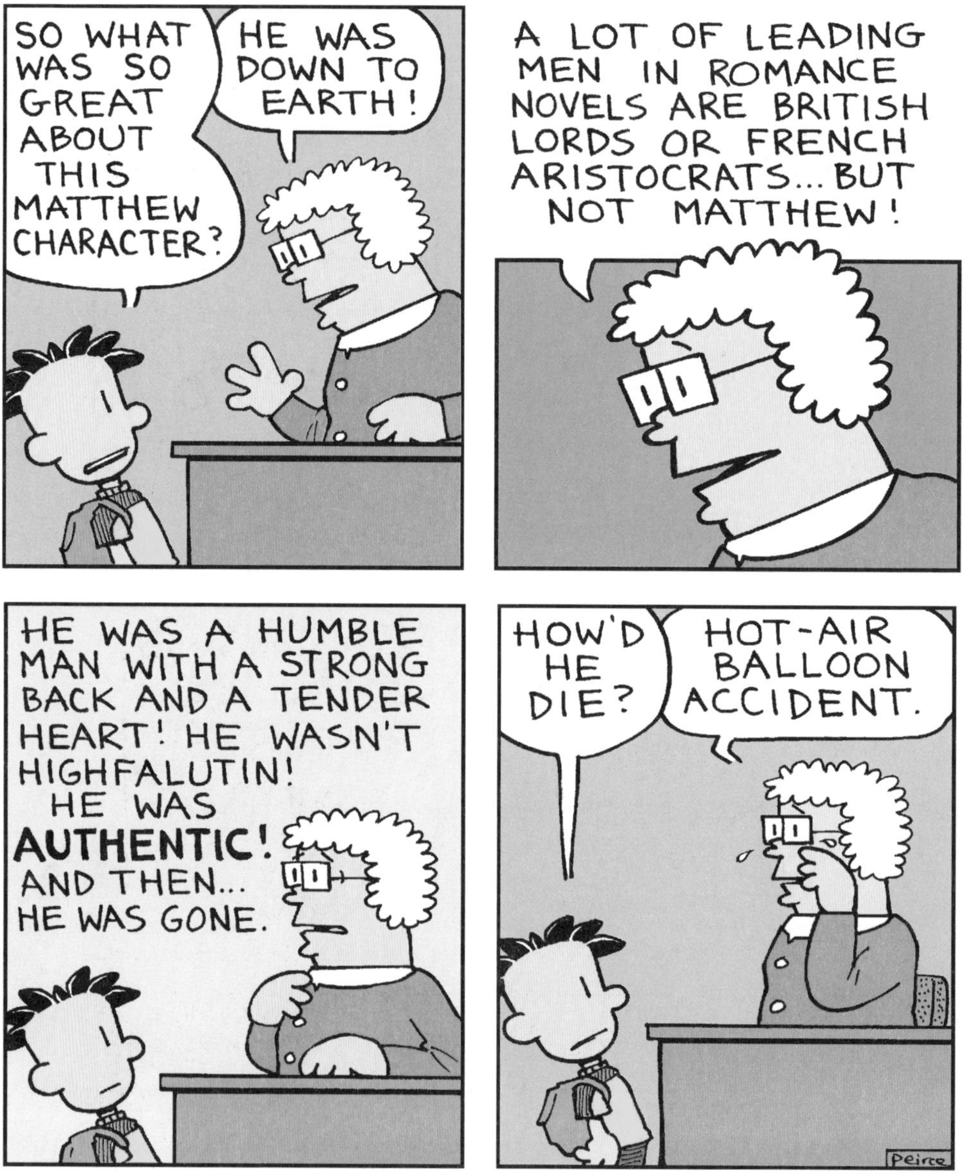
SO WHAT WAS SO GREAT ABOUT THIS MATTHEW CHARACTER?
HE WAS DOWN TO EARTH!
A LOT OF LEADING MEN IN ROMANCE NOVELS ARE BRITISH LORDS OR FRENCH ARISTOCRATS... BUT NOT MATTHEW!
HE WAS A HUMBLE MAN WITH A STRONG BACK AND A TENDER HEART! HE WASN'T HIGHFALUTIN! HE WAS **AUTHENTIC!** AND THEN... HE WAS GONE.
HOW'D HE DIE?
HOT-AIR BALLOON ACCIDENT.
Peirce

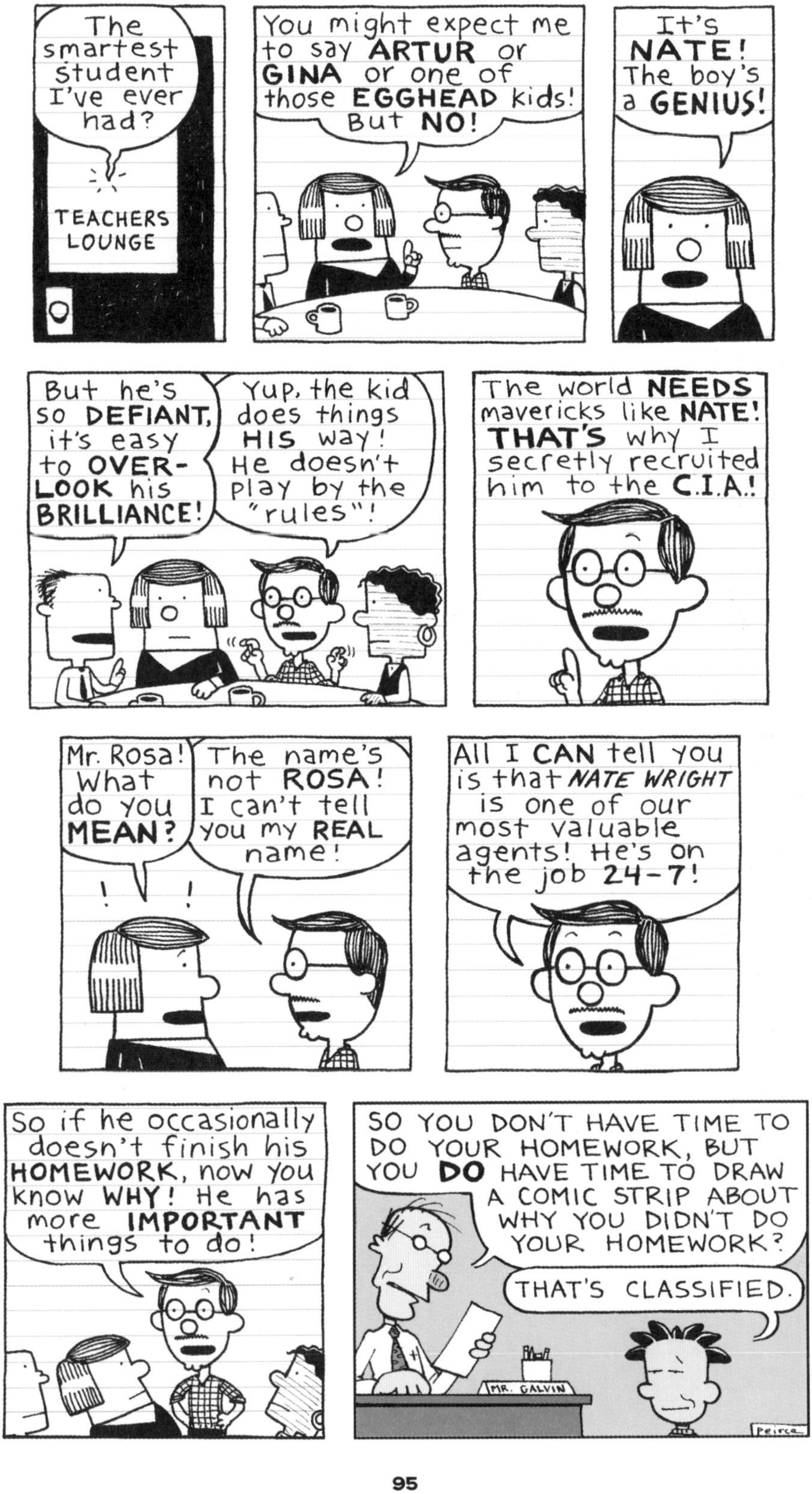
The smartest student I've ever had?
TEACHERS LOUNGE
You might expect me to say ARTUR or GINA or one of those EGGHEAD kids! But NO!
It's NATE! The boy's a GENIUS!
But he's so DEFIANT, it's easy to OVER-LOOK his BRILLIANCE!
Yup, the kid does things HIS way! He doesn't play by the "rules"!
The world NEEDS mavericks like NATE! THAT'S why I secretly recruited him to the C.I.A.!
Mr. Rosa! What do you MEAN?
The name's not ROSA! I can't tell you my REAL name!
All I CAN tell you is that NATE WRIGHT is one of our most valuable agents! He's on the job 24-7!
So if he occasionally doesn't finish his HOMEWORK, now you know WHY! He has more IMPORTANT things to do!
SO YOU DON'T HAVE TIME TO DO YOUR HOMEWORK, BUT YOU DO HAVE TIME TO DRAW A COMIC STRIP ABOUT WHY YOU DIDN'T DO YOUR HOMEWORK?
THAT'S CLASSIFIED.
MR. GALVIN
Peirce

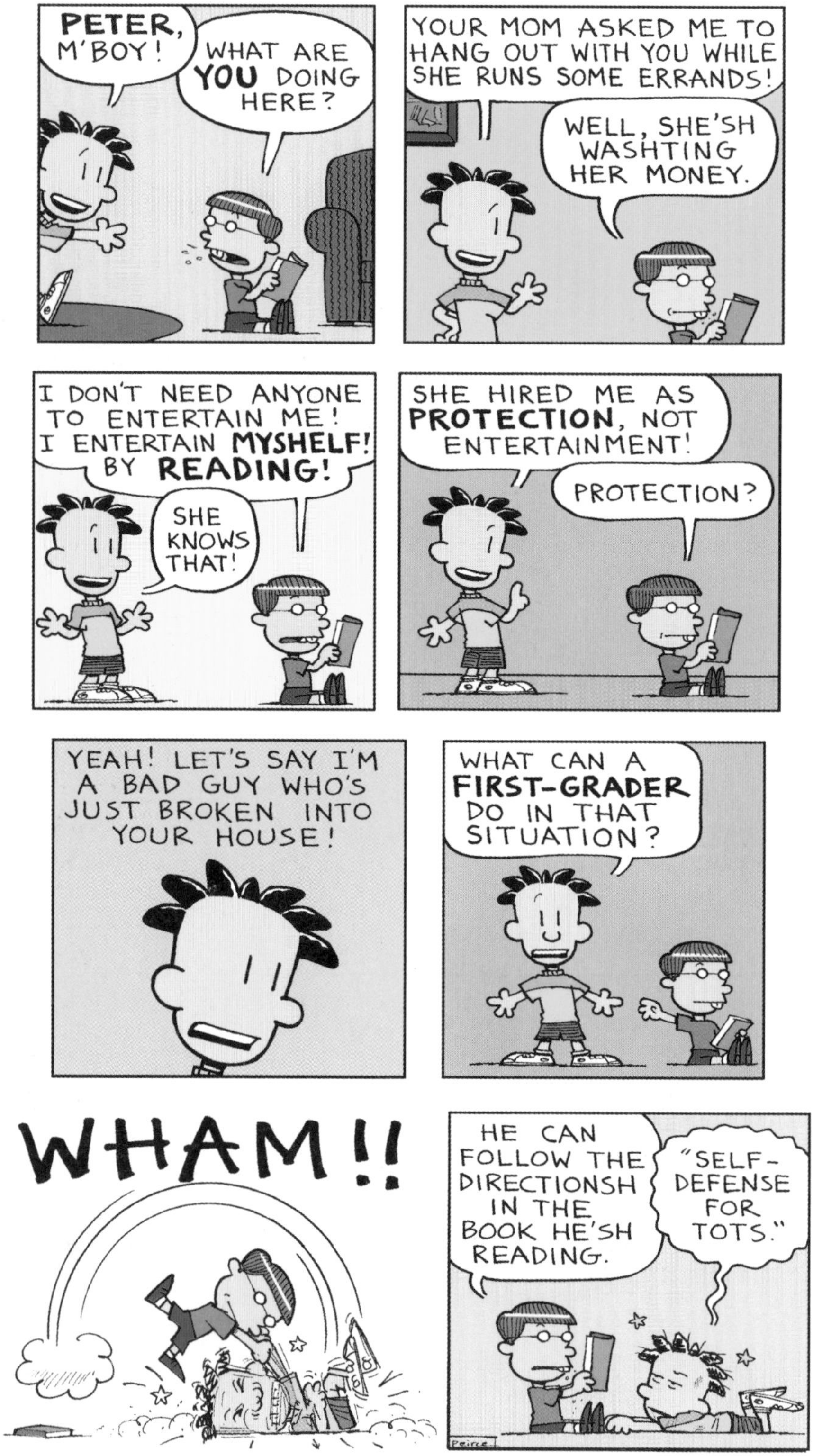
PETER, M'BOY!
WHAT ARE YOU DOING HERE?
YOUR MOM ASKED ME TO HANG OUT WITH YOU WHILE SHE RUNS SOME ERRANDS!
WELL, SHE'SH WASHTING HER MONEY.
I DON'T NEED ANYONE TO ENTERTAIN ME! I ENTERTAIN MYSHELF! BY READING!
SHE KNOWS THAT!
SHE HIRED ME AS PROTECTION, NOT ENTERTAINMENT!
PROTECTION?
YEAH! LET'S SAY I'M A BAD GUY WHO'S JUST BROKEN INTO YOUR HOUSE!
WHAT CAN A FIRST-GRADER DO IN THAT SITUATION?
WHAM!!
HE CAN FOLLOW THE DIRECTIONSH IN THE BOOK HE'SH READING.
"SELF-DEFENSE FOR TOTS."
Peirce

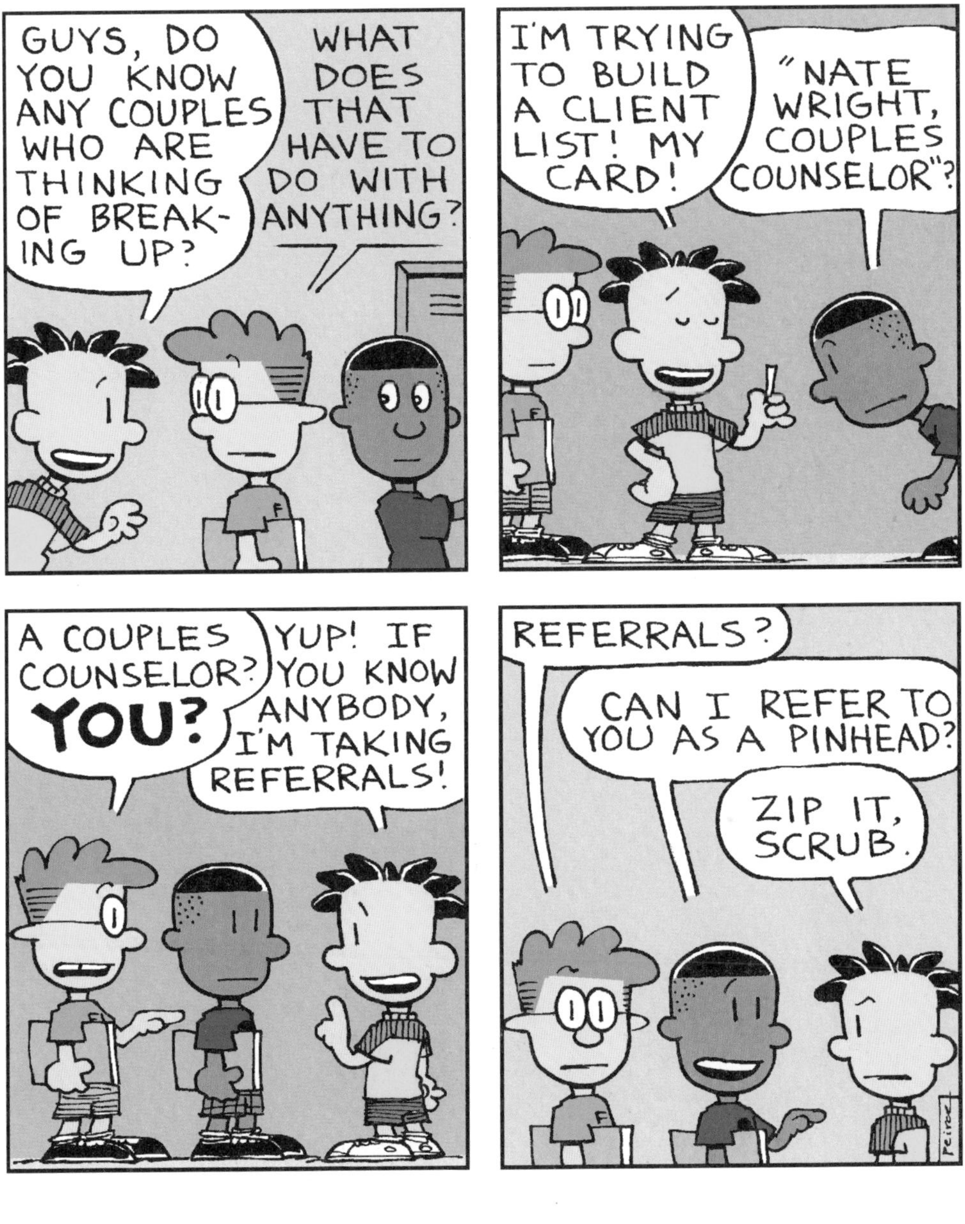
GUYS, DO YOU KNOW ANY COUPLES WHO ARE THINKING OF BREAK-ING UP?
WHAT DOES THAT HAVE TO DO WITH ANYTHING?
I'M TRYING TO BUILD A CLIENT LIST! MY CARD!
"NATE WRIGHT, COUPLES COUNSELOR"?
A COUPLES COUNSELOR? YOU?
YUP! IF YOU KNOW ANYBODY, I'M TAKING REFERRALS!
REFERRALS?
CAN I REFER TO YOU AS A PINHEAD?
ZIP IT, SCRUB.
Peirce

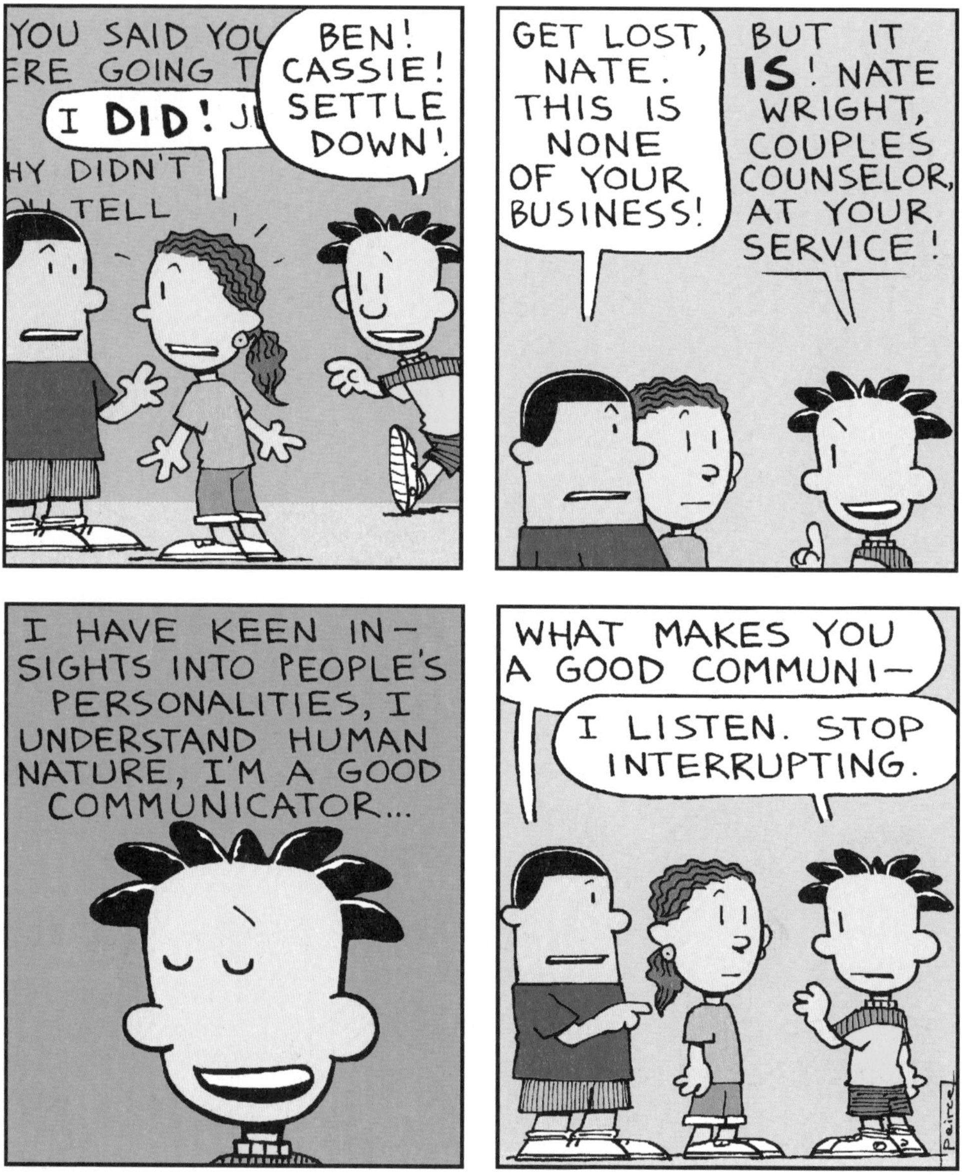
YOU SAID YOU
GOING
I DID!
DIDN'T
TELL
BEN! CASSIE! SETTLE DOWN!
GET LOST, NATE. THIS IS NONE OF YOUR BUSINESS!
BUT IT IS! NATE WRIGHT, COUPLES COUNSELOR, AT YOUR SERVICE!
I HAVE KEEN IN-SIGHTS INTO PEOPLE'S PERSONALITIES, I UNDERSTAND HUMAN NATURE, I'M A GOOD COMMUNICATOR...
WHAT MAKES YOU A GOOD COMMUNI–
I LISTEN. STOP INTERRUPTING.
Peirce

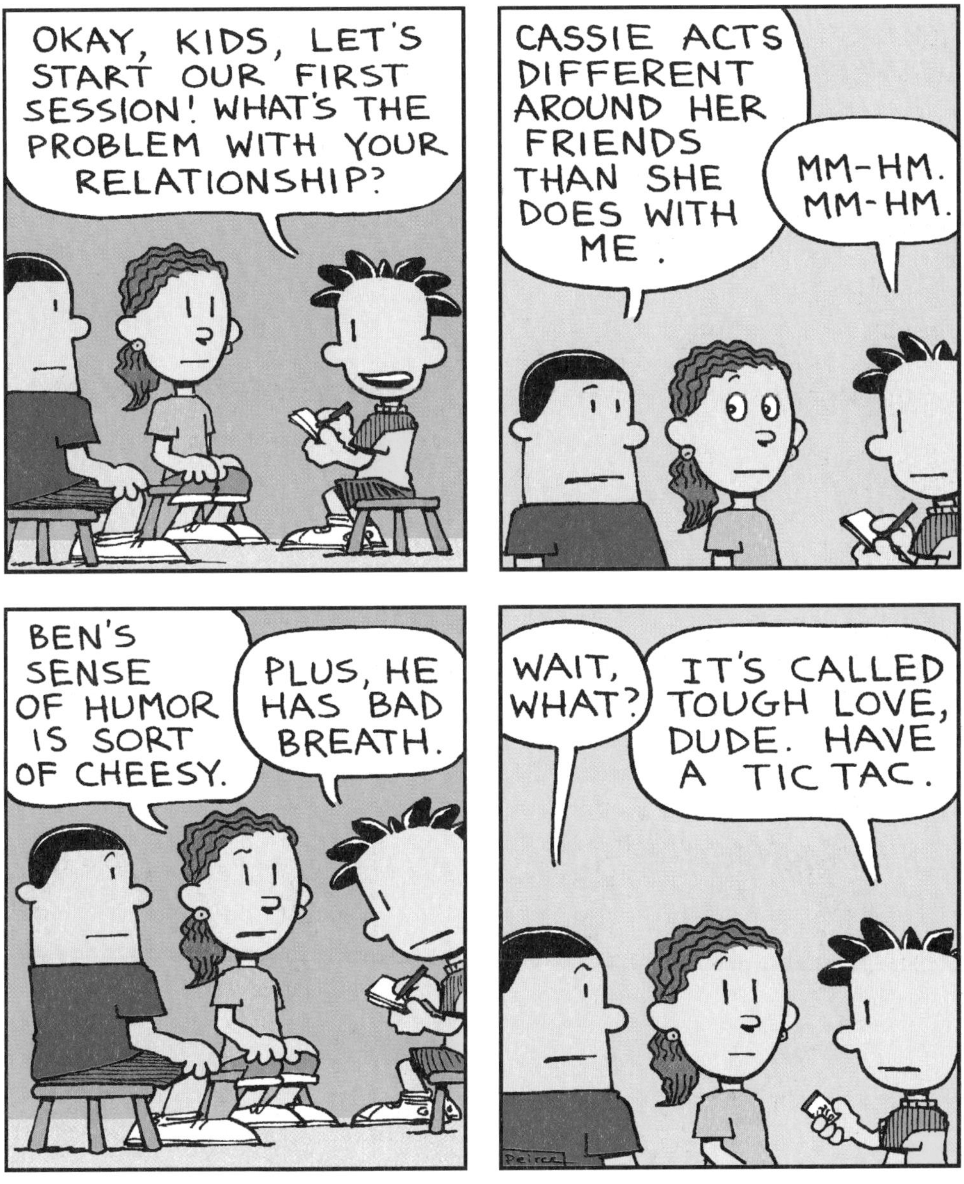
OKAY, KIDS, LET'S START OUR FIRST SESSION! WHAT'S THE PROBLEM WITH YOUR RELATIONSHIP?
CASSIE ACTS DIFFERENT AROUND HER FRIENDS THAN SHE DOES WITH ME.
MM-HM. MM-HM.
BEN'S SENSE OF HUMOR IS SORT OF CHEESY.
PLUS, HE HAS BAD BREATH.
WAIT, WHAT?
IT'S CALLED TOUGH LOVE, DUDE. HAVE A TIC TAC.
Peirce

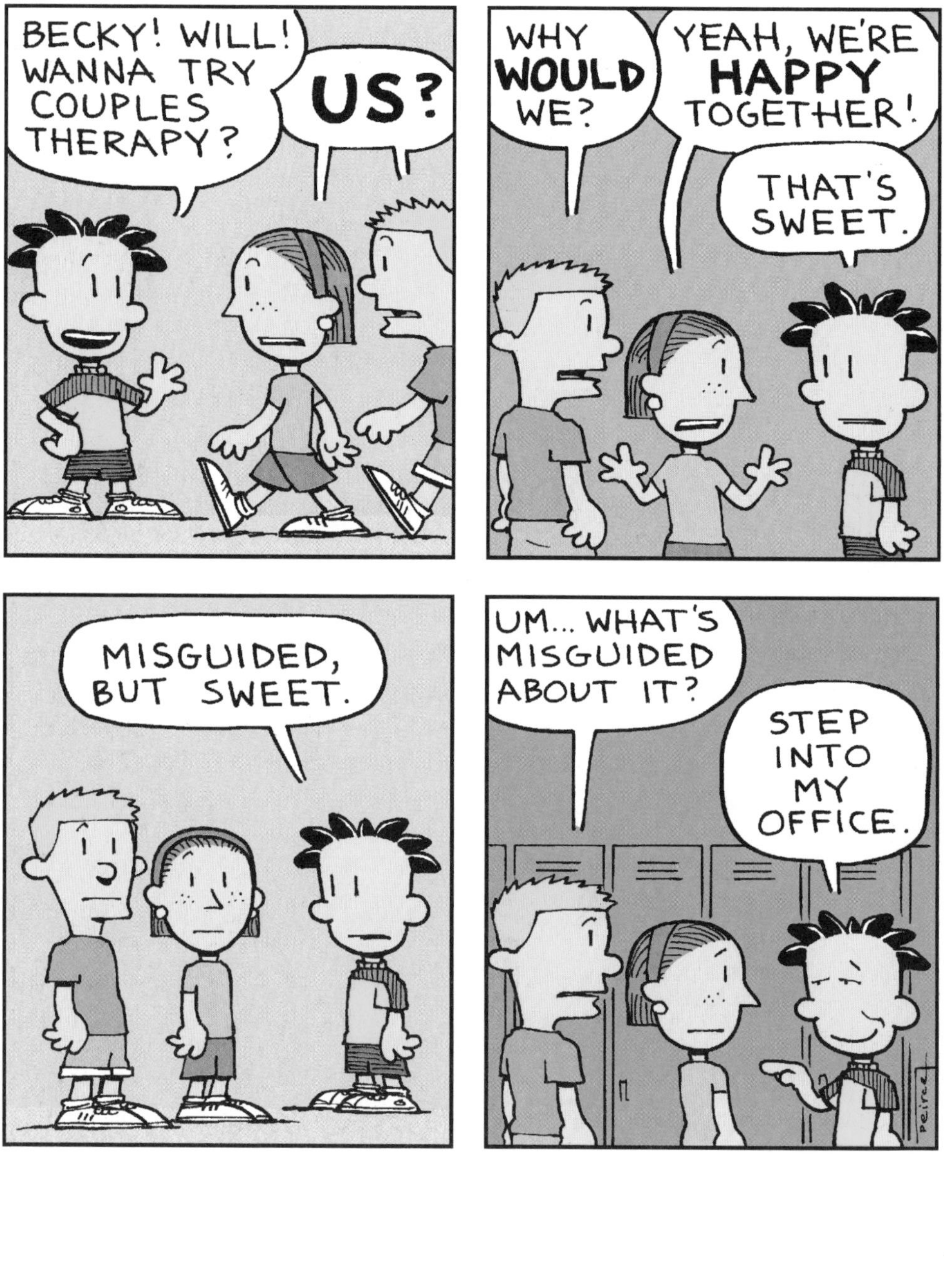
BECKY! WILL! WANNA TRY COUPLES THERAPY?
US?
WHY WOULD WE?
YEAH, WE'RE HAPPY TOGETHER!
THAT'S SWEET.
MISGUIDED, BUT SWEET.
UM... WHAT'S MISGUIDED ABOUT IT?
STEP INTO MY OFFICE.
peirce

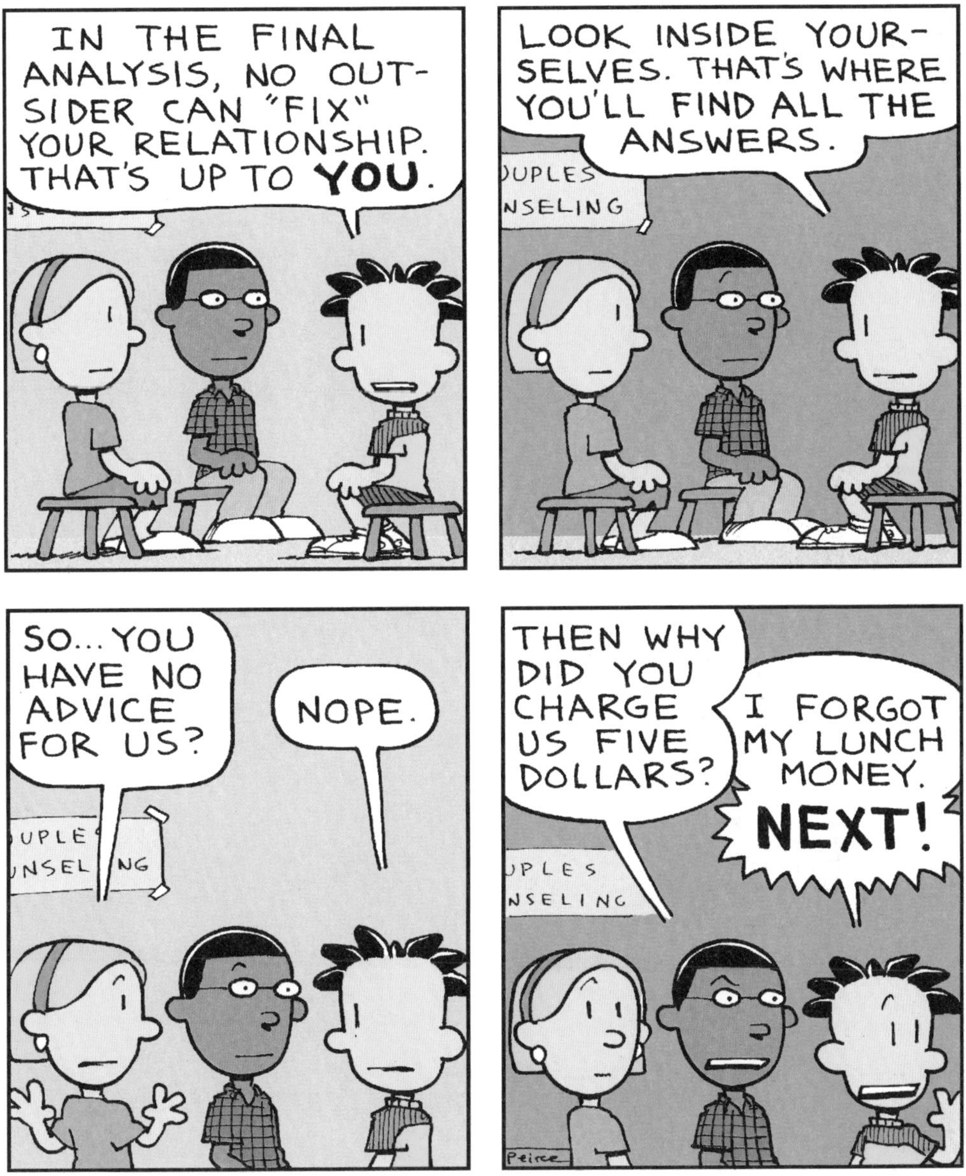
IN THE FINAL ANALYSIS, NO OUT-SIDER CAN "FIX" YOUR RELATIONSHIP. THAT'S UP TO **YOU**.
LOOK INSIDE YOUR-SELVES. THAT'S WHERE YOU'LL FIND ALL THE ANSWERS.
SO... YOU HAVE NO ADVICE FOR US?
NOPE.
THEN WHY DID YOU CHARGE US FIVE DOLLARS?
I FORGOT MY LUNCH MONEY.
NEXT!
Peirce

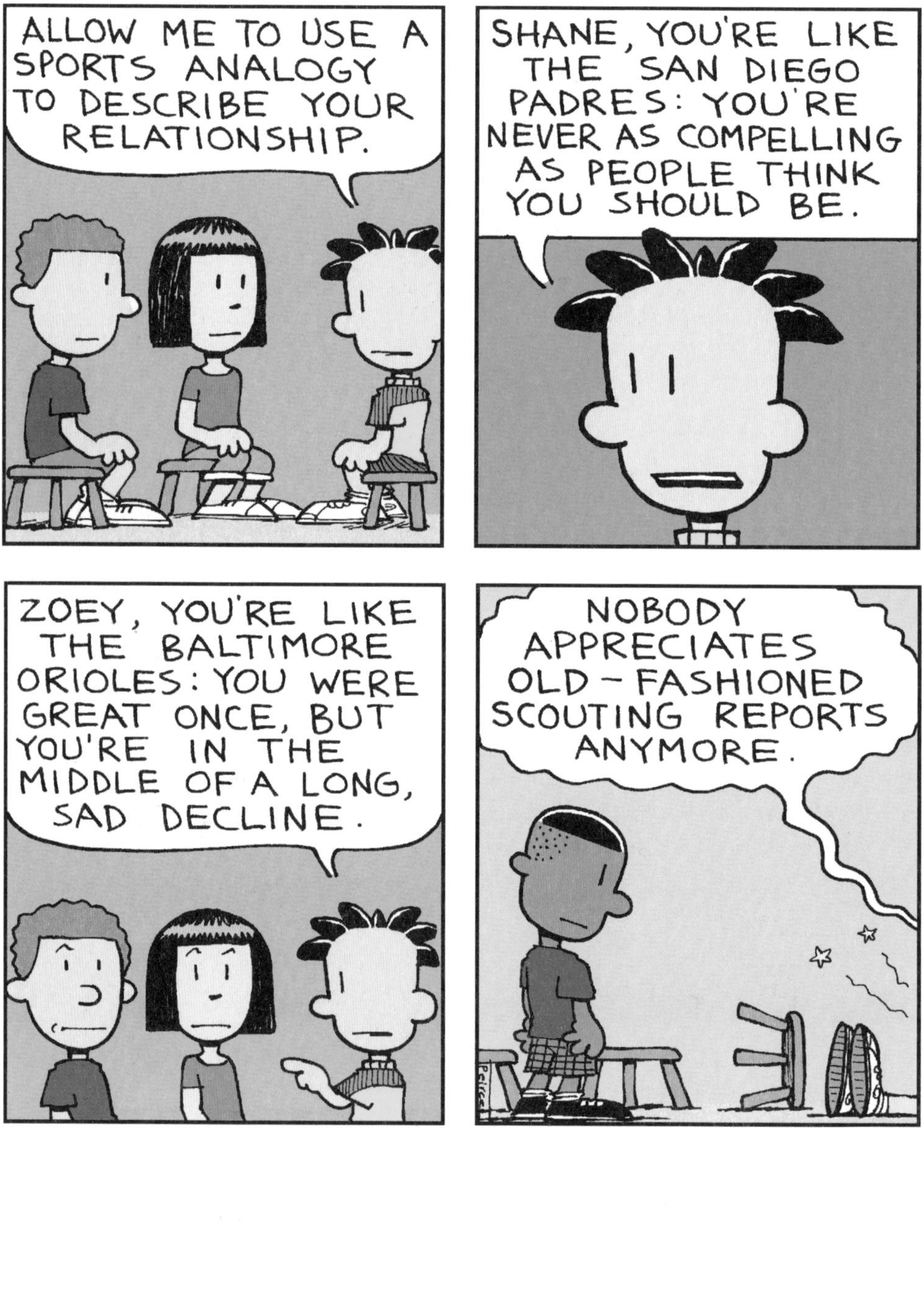
ALLOW ME TO USE A SPORTS ANALOGY TO DESCRIBE YOUR RELATIONSHIP.
SHANE, YOU'RE LIKE THE SAN DIEGO PADRES: YOU'RE NEVER AS COMPELLING AS PEOPLE THINK YOU SHOULD BE.
ZOEY, YOU'RE LIKE THE BALTIMORE ORIOLES: YOU WERE GREAT ONCE, BUT YOU'RE IN THE MIDDLE OF A LONG, SAD DECLINE.
NOBODY APPRECIATES OLD-FASHIONED SCOUTING REPORTS ANYMORE.

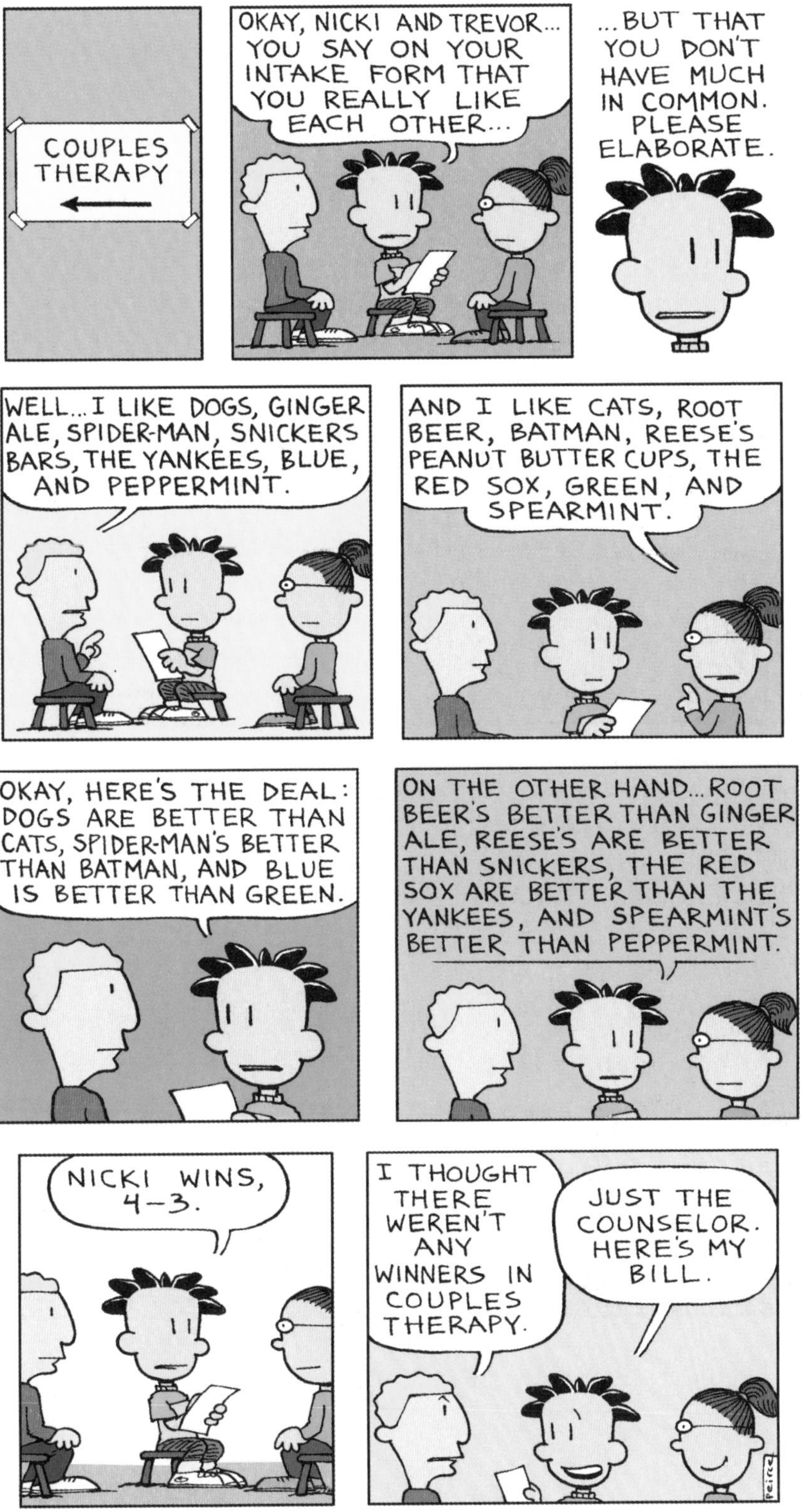
COUPLES THERAPY
OKAY, NICKI AND TREVOR... YOU SAY ON YOUR INTAKE FORM THAT YOU REALLY LIKE EACH OTHER...
...BUT THAT YOU DON'T HAVE MUCH IN COMMON. PLEASE ELABORATE.
WELL...I LIKE DOGS, GINGER ALE, SPIDER-MAN, SNICKERS BARS, THE YANKEES, BLUE, AND PEPPERMINT.
AND I LIKE CATS, ROOT BEER, BATMAN, REESE'S PEANUT BUTTER CUPS, THE RED SOX, GREEN, AND SPEARMINT.
OKAY, HERE'S THE DEAL: DOGS ARE BETTER THAN CATS, SPIDER-MAN'S BETTER THAN BATMAN, AND BLUE IS BETTER THAN GREEN.
ON THE OTHER HAND...ROOT BEER'S BETTER THAN GINGER ALE, REESE'S ARE BETTER THAN SNICKERS, THE RED SOX ARE BETTER THAN THE YANKEES, AND SPEARMINT'S BETTER THAN PEPPERMINT.
NICKI WINS, 4-3.
I THOUGHT THERE WEREN'T ANY WINNERS IN COUPLES THERAPY.
JUST THE COUNSELOR. HERE'S MY BILL.
Peirce

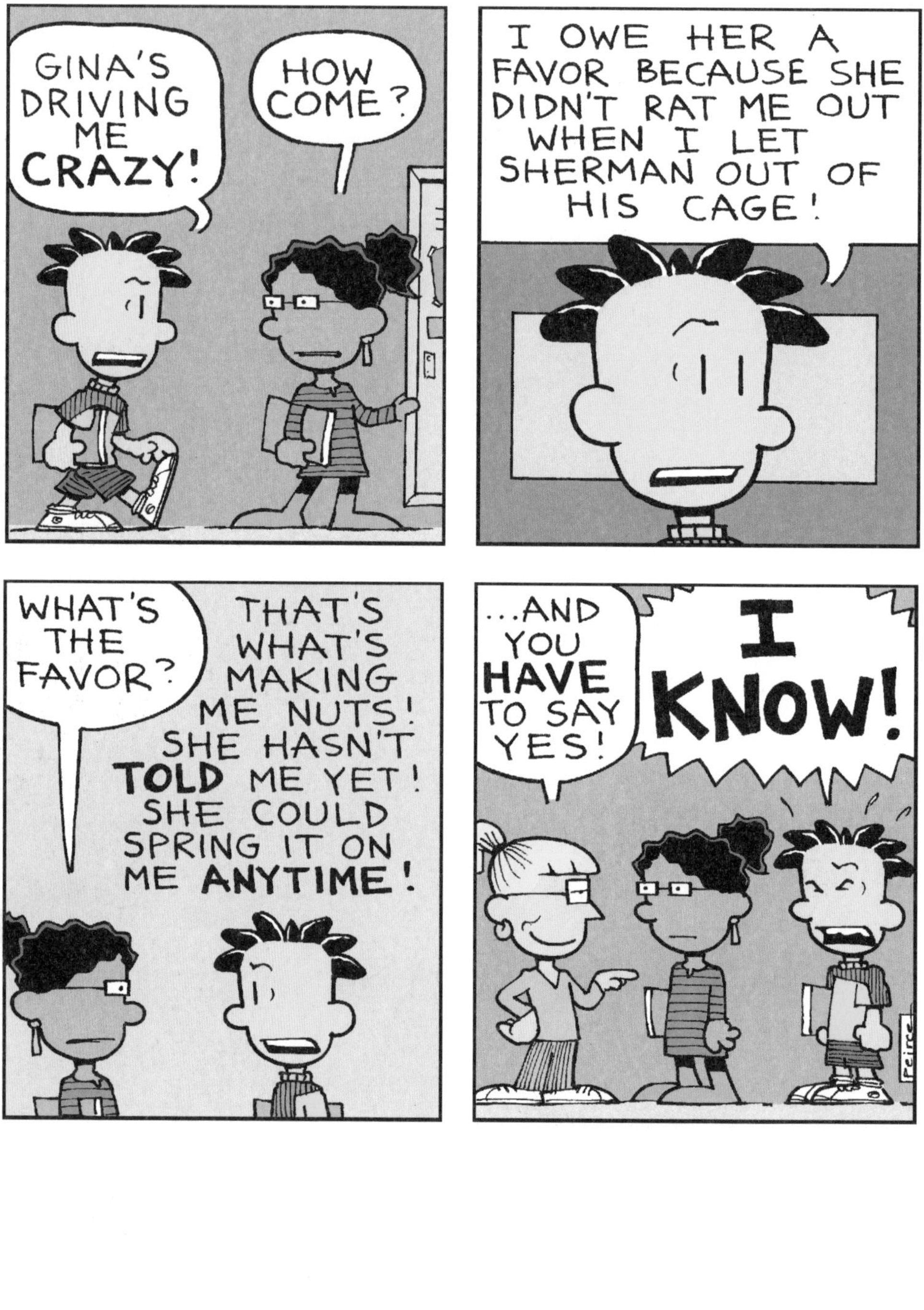
GINA'S DRIVING ME CRAZY!
HOW COME?
I OWE HER A FAVOR BECAUSE SHE DIDN'T RAT ME OUT WHEN I LET SHERMAN OUT OF HIS CAGE!
WHAT'S THE FAVOR?
THAT'S WHAT'S MAKING ME NUTS! SHE HASN'T TOLD ME YET! SHE COULD SPRING IT ON ME ANYTIME!
...AND YOU HAVE TO SAY YES!
I KNOW!
Peirce

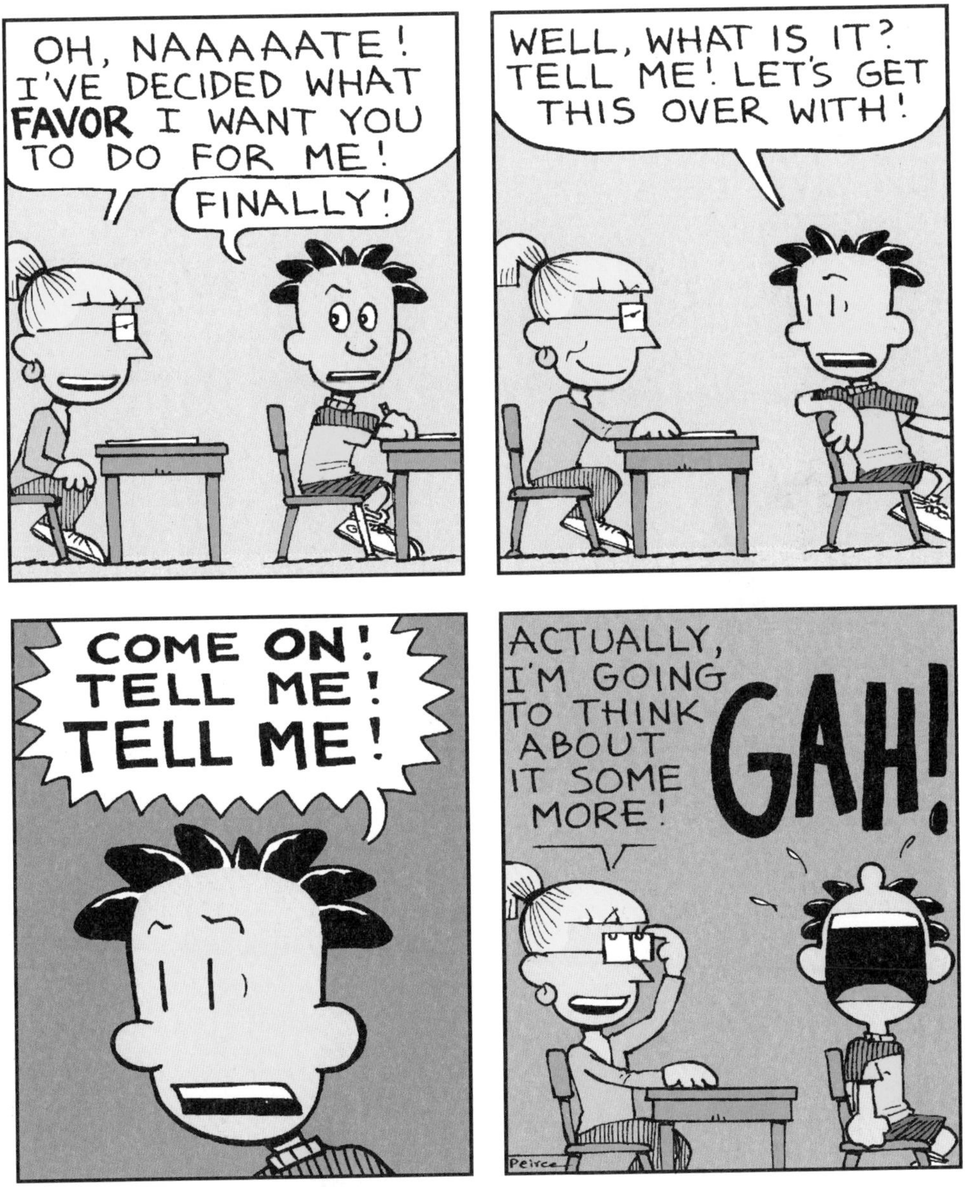
OH, NAAAAATE! I'VE DECIDED WHAT **FAVOR** I WANT YOU TO DO FOR ME!
FINALLY!
WELL, WHAT IS IT? TELL ME! LET'S GET THIS OVER WITH!
COME ON! TELL ME! TELL ME!
ACTUALLY, I'M GOING TO THINK ABOUT IT SOME MORE!
GAH!
Peirce

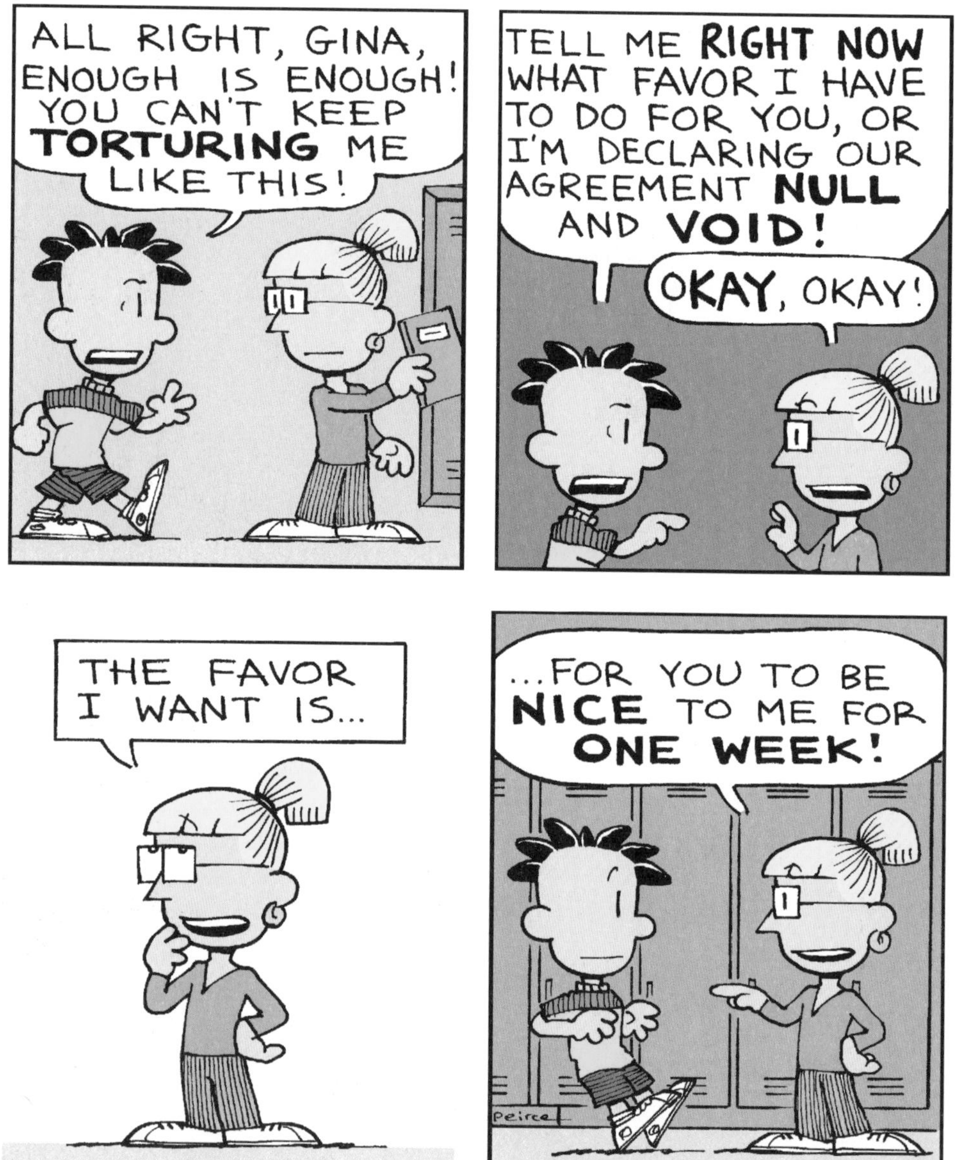
ALL RIGHT, GINA, ENOUGH IS ENOUGH! YOU CAN'T KEEP TORTURING ME LIKE THIS!
TELL ME RIGHT NOW WHAT FAVOR I HAVE TO DO FOR YOU, OR I'M DECLARING OUR AGREEMENT NULL AND VOID!
OKAY, OKAY!
THE FAVOR I WANT IS...
...FOR YOU TO BE NICE TO ME FOR ONE WEEK!
peirce

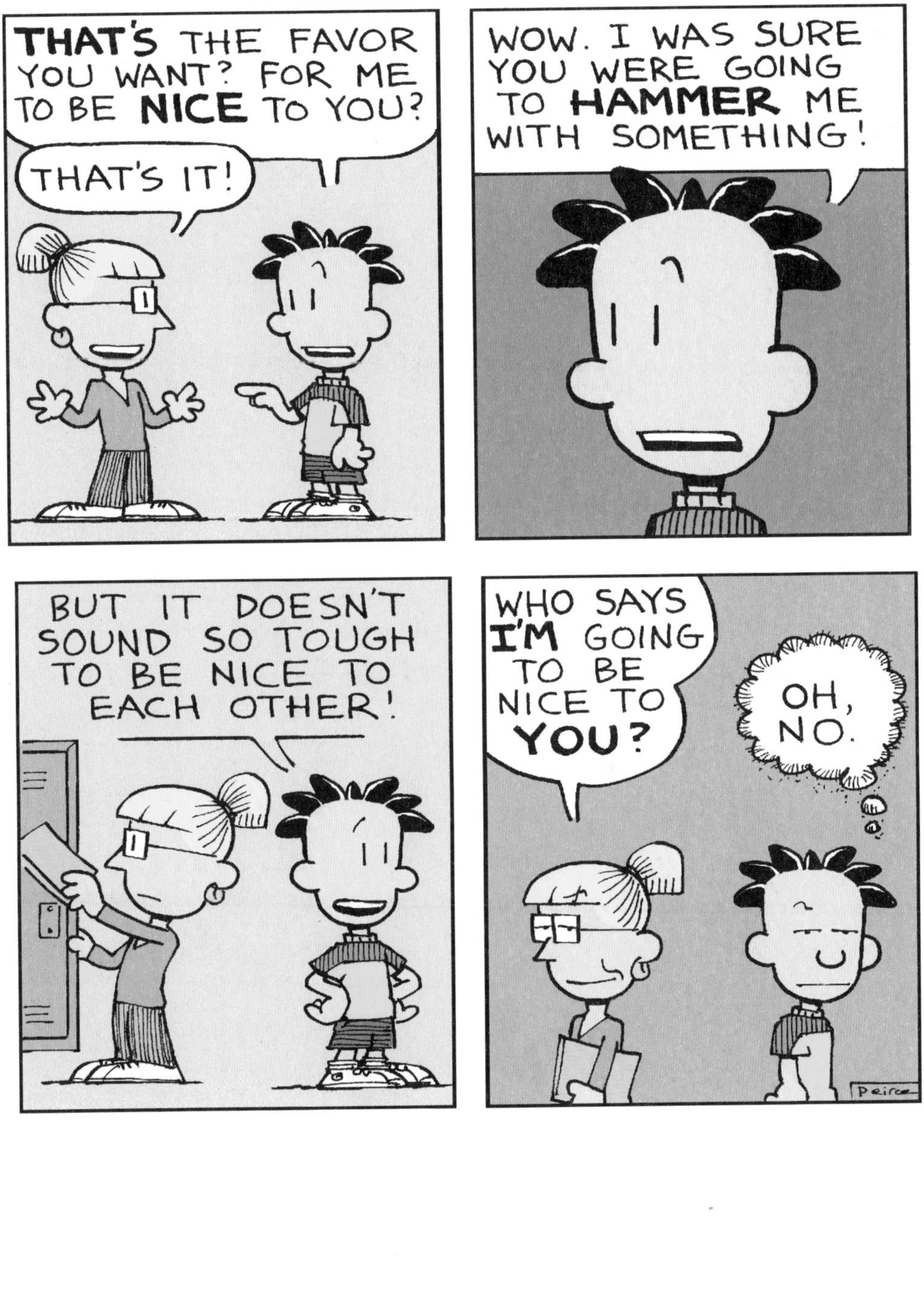
THAT'S THE FAVOR YOU WANT? FOR ME TO BE NICE TO YOU?
THAT'S IT!
WOW. I WAS SURE YOU WERE GOING TO HAMMER ME WITH SOMETHING!
BUT IT DOESN'T SOUND SO TOUGH TO BE NICE TO EACH OTHER!
WHO SAYS I'M GOING TO BE NICE TO YOU?
OH, NO.
Peirce

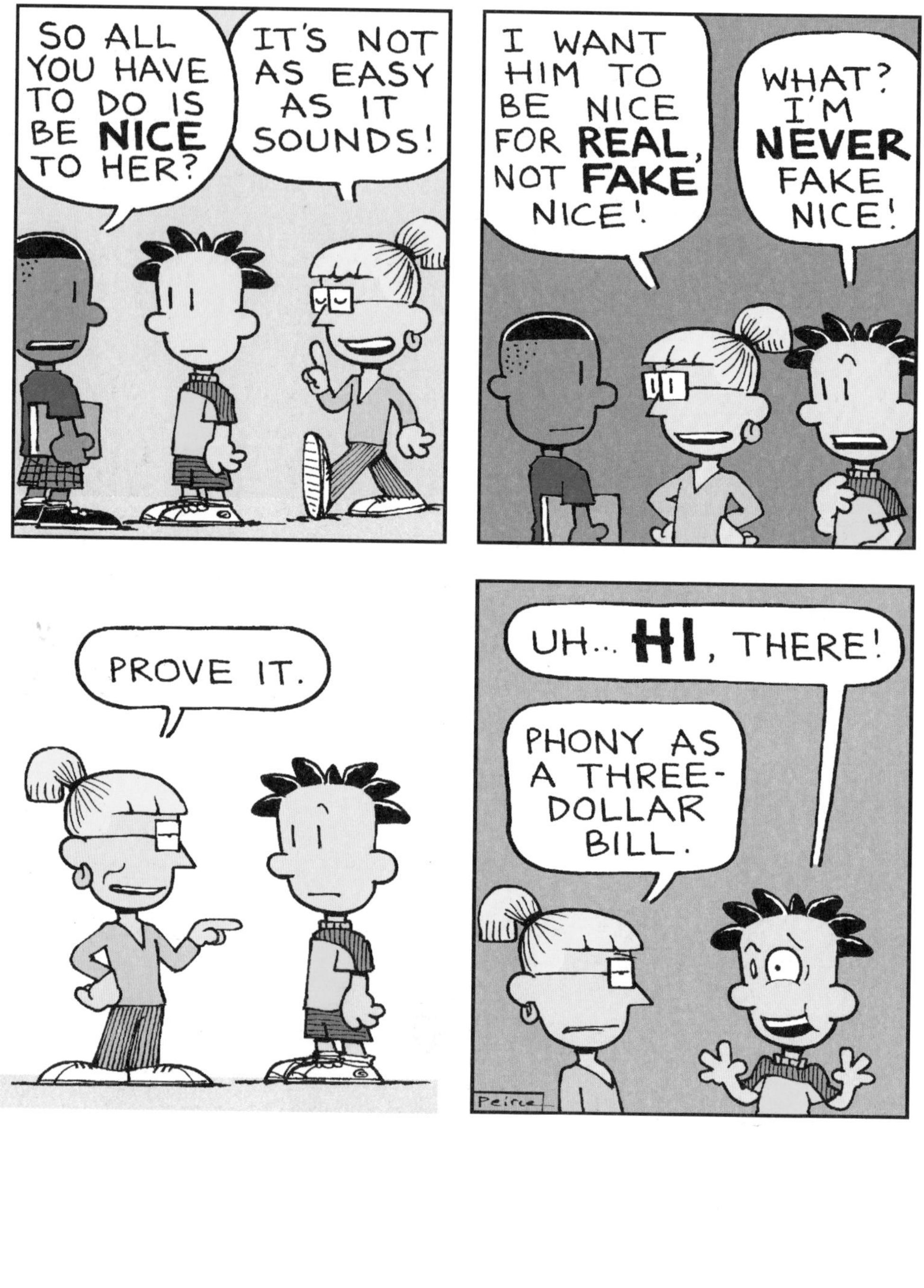
SO ALL YOU HAVE TO DO IS BE **NICE** TO HER?
IT'S NOT AS EASY AS IT SOUNDS!
I WANT HIM TO BE NICE FOR **REAL**, NOT **FAKE** NICE!
WHAT? I'M **NEVER** FAKE NICE!
PROVE IT.
UH... **HI**, THERE!
PHONY AS A THREE-DOLLAR BILL.
Peirce

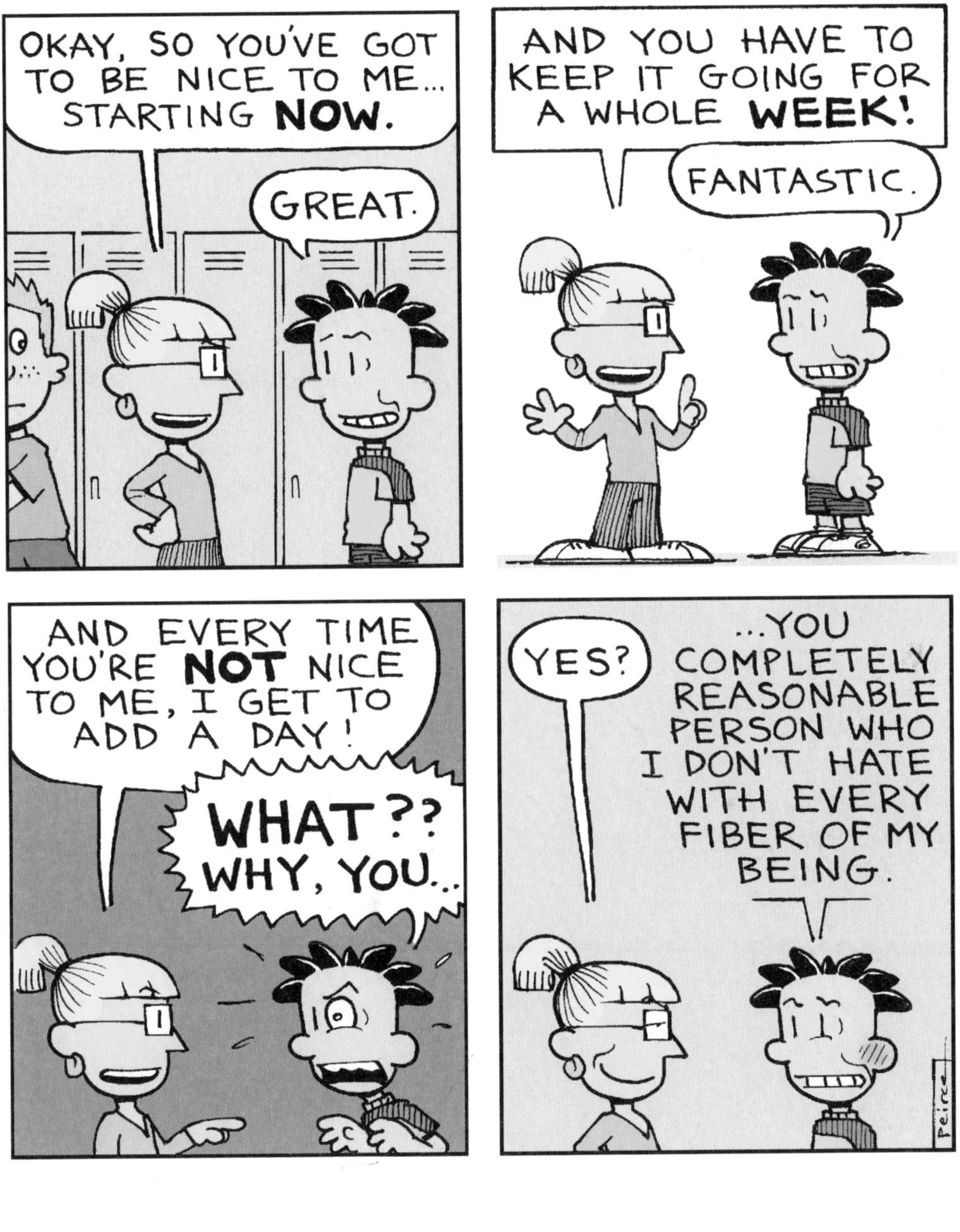
OKAY, SO YOU'VE GOT TO BE NICE TO ME... STARTING NOW.
GREAT.
AND YOU HAVE TO KEEP IT GOING FOR A WHOLE WEEK!
FANTASTIC.
AND EVERY TIME YOU'RE NOT NICE TO ME, I GET TO ADD A DAY!
WHAT?? WHY, YOU...
YES?
...YOU COMPLETELY REASONABLE PERSON WHO I DON'T HATE WITH EVERY FIBER OF MY BEING.
Peirce

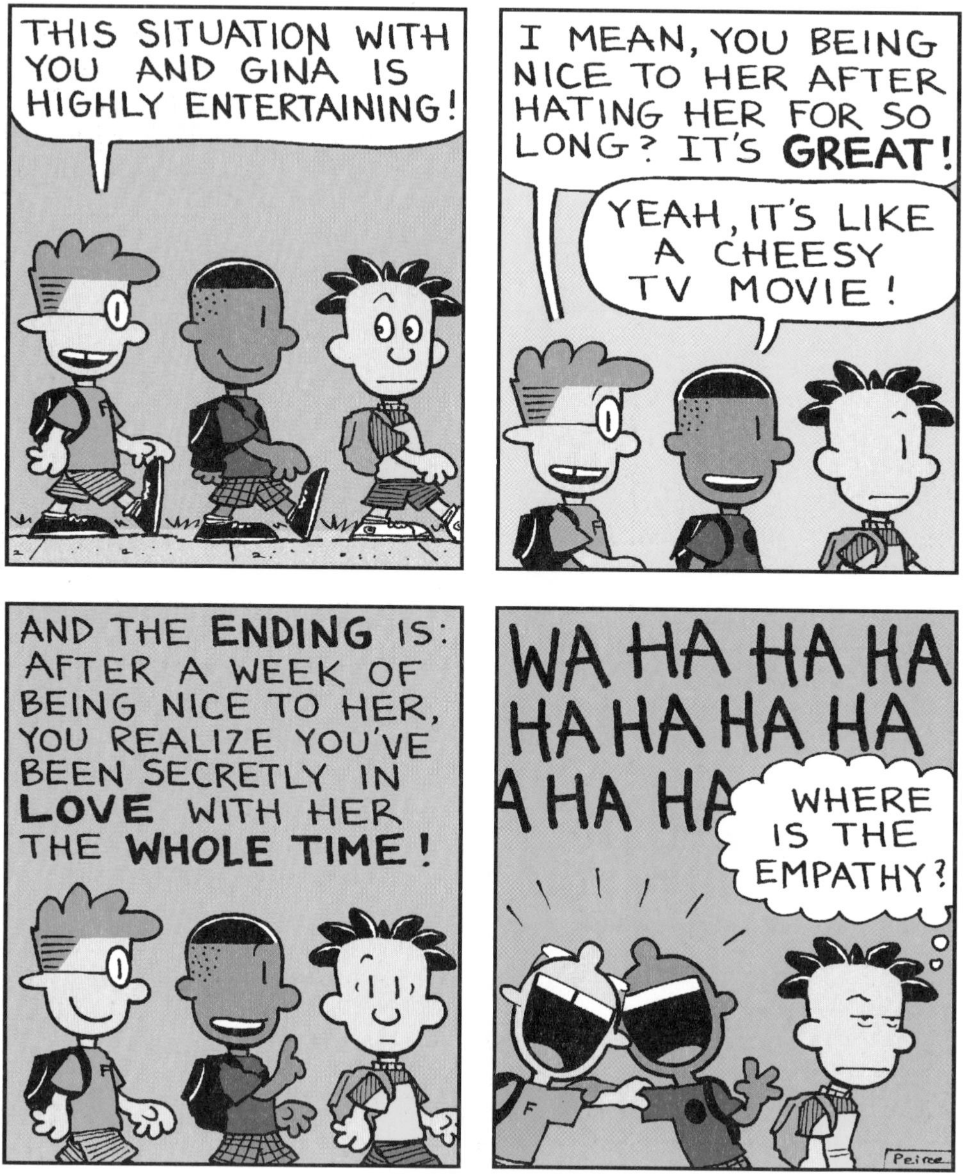
THIS SITUATION WITH YOU AND GINA IS HIGHLY ENTERTAINING!
I MEAN, YOU BEING NICE TO HER AFTER HATING HER FOR SO LONG? IT'S **GREAT**!
YEAH, IT'S LIKE A CHEESY TV MOVIE!
AND THE **ENDING** IS: AFTER A WEEK OF BEING NICE TO HER, YOU REALIZE YOU'VE BEEN SECRETLY IN **LOVE** WITH HER THE **WHOLE TIME**!
WA HA HA HA
HA HA HA HA
A HA HA
WHERE IS THE EMPATHY?
Peirce

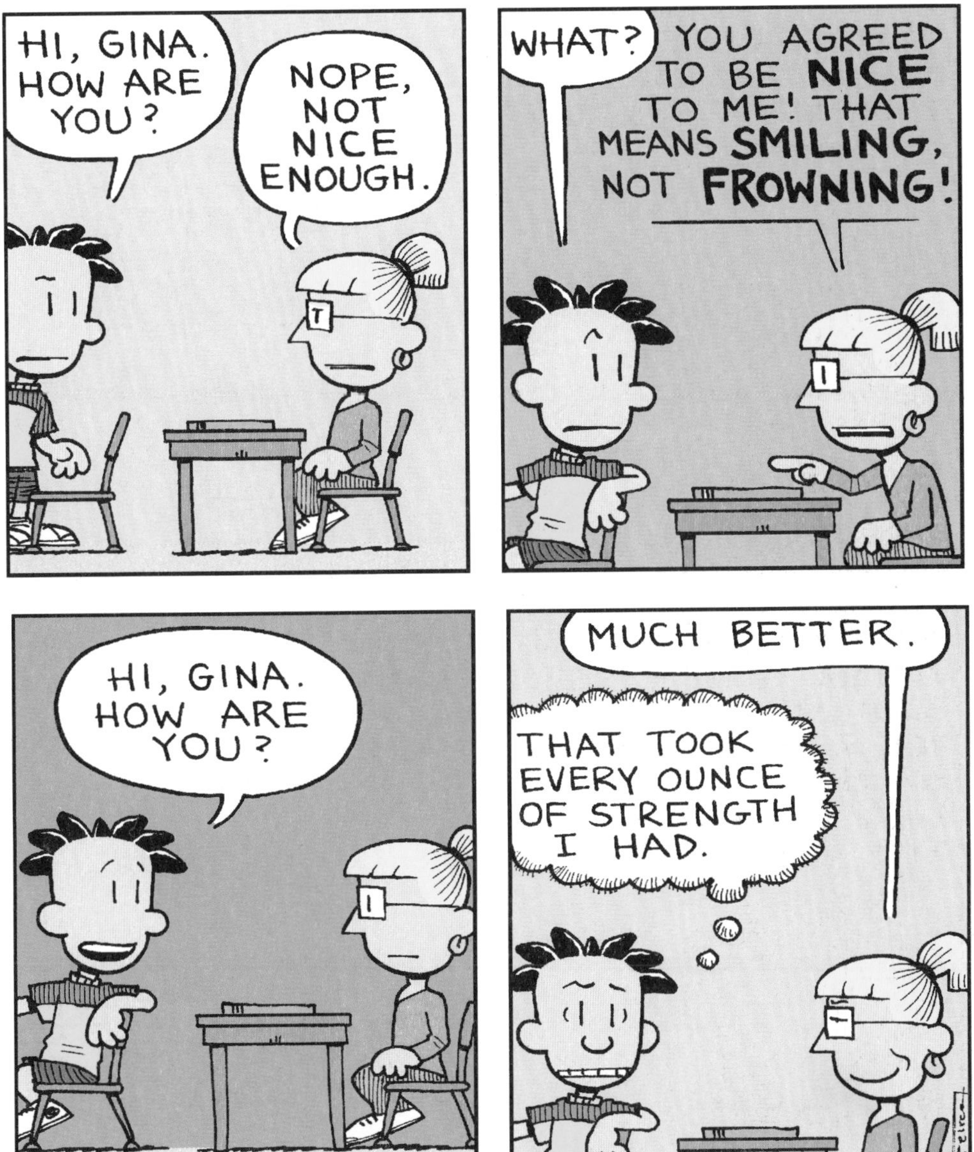
HI, GINA. HOW ARE YOU?
NOPE, NOT NICE ENOUGH.
WHAT?
YOU AGREED TO BE **NICE** TO ME! THAT MEANS **SMILING**, NOT **FROWNING**!
HI, GINA. HOW ARE YOU?
MUCH BETTER.
THAT TOOK EVERY OUNCE OF STRENGTH I HAD.

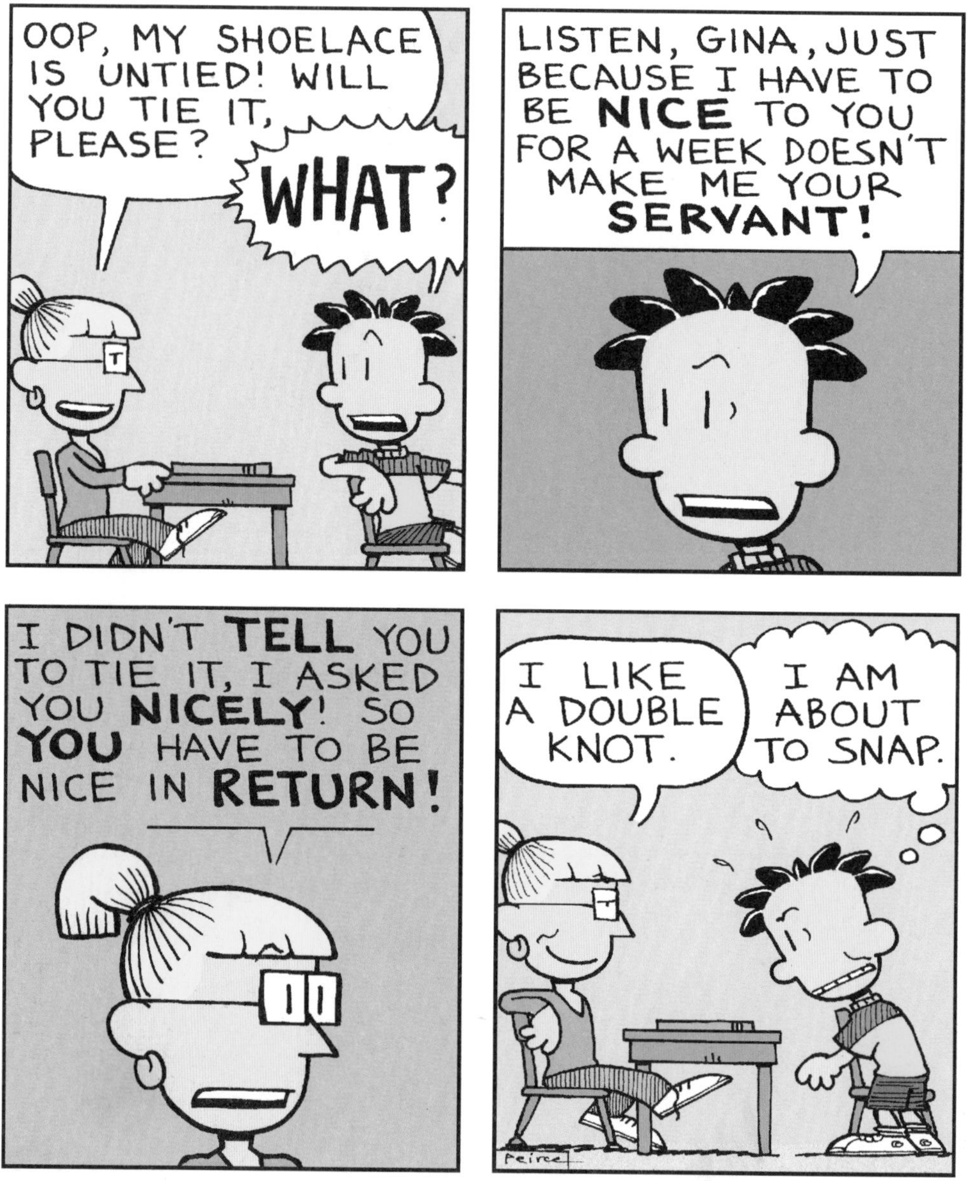
OOP, MY SHOELACE IS UNTIED! WILL YOU TIE IT, PLEASE?
WHAT?
LISTEN, GINA, JUST BECAUSE I HAVE TO BE NICE TO YOU FOR A WEEK DOESN'T MAKE ME YOUR SERVANT!
I DIDN'T TELL YOU TO TIE IT, I ASKED YOU NICELY! SO YOU HAVE TO BE NICE IN RETURN!
I LIKE A DOUBLE KNOT.
I AM ABOUT TO SNAP.
Peirce

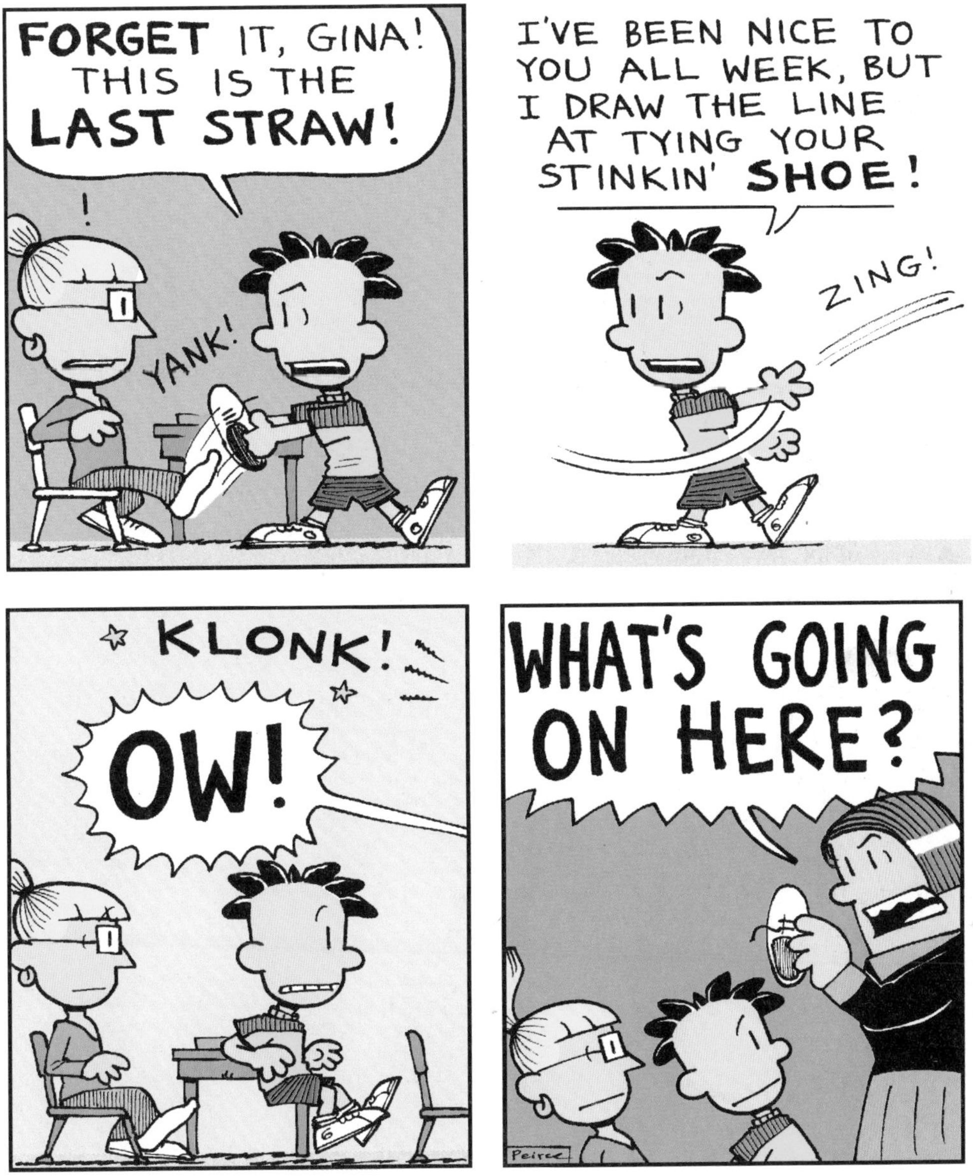
FORGET IT, GINA! THIS IS THE LAST STRAW!
!
YANK!
I'VE BEEN NICE TO YOU ALL WEEK, BUT I DRAW THE LINE AT TYING YOUR STINKIN' SHOE!
ZING!
KLONK!
OW!
WHAT'S GOING ON HERE?
Peirce

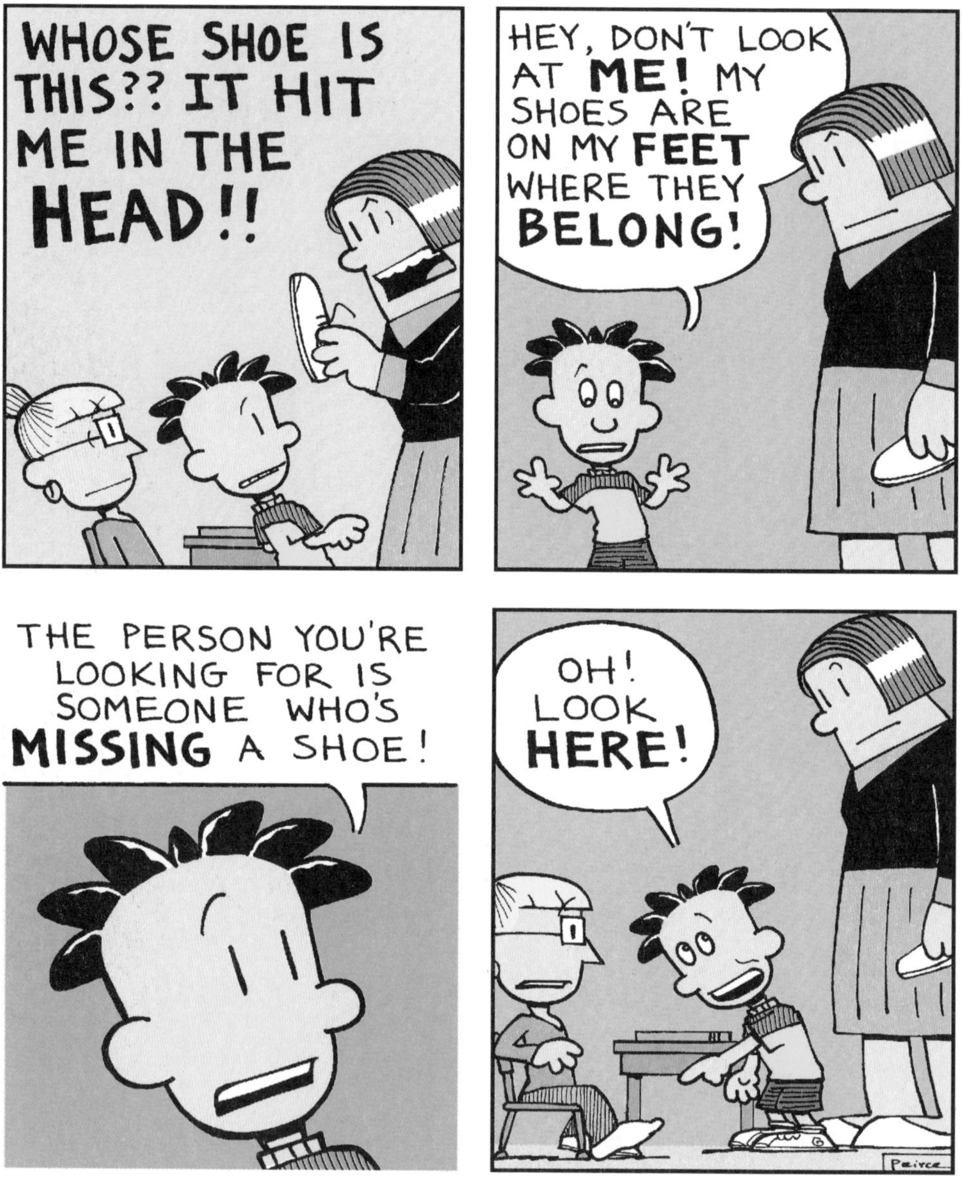
WHOSE SHOE IS THIS?? IT HIT ME IN THE HEAD!!
HEY, DON'T LOOK AT ME! MY SHOES ARE ON MY FEET WHERE THEY BELONG!
THE PERSON YOU'RE LOOKING FOR IS SOMEONE WHO'S MISSING A SHOE!
OH! LOOK HERE!
Peirce

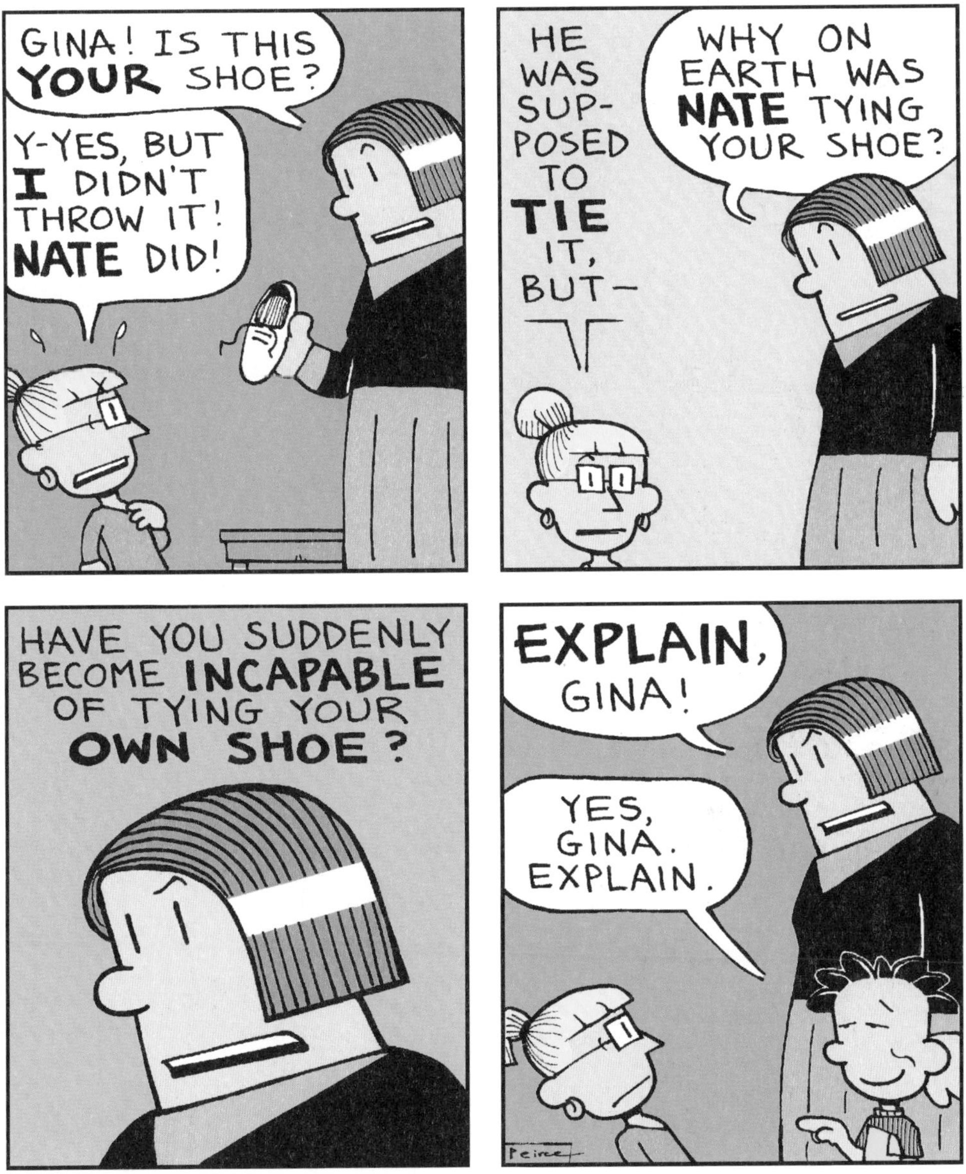
GINA! IS THIS YOUR SHOE?
Y-YES, BUT I DIDN'T THROW IT! NATE DID!
HE WAS SUP-POSED TO TIE IT, BUT—
WHY ON EARTH WAS NATE TYING YOUR SHOE?
HAVE YOU SUDDENLY BECOME INCAPABLE OF TYING YOUR OWN SHOE?
EXPLAIN, GINA!
YES, GINA. EXPLAIN.
Peirce

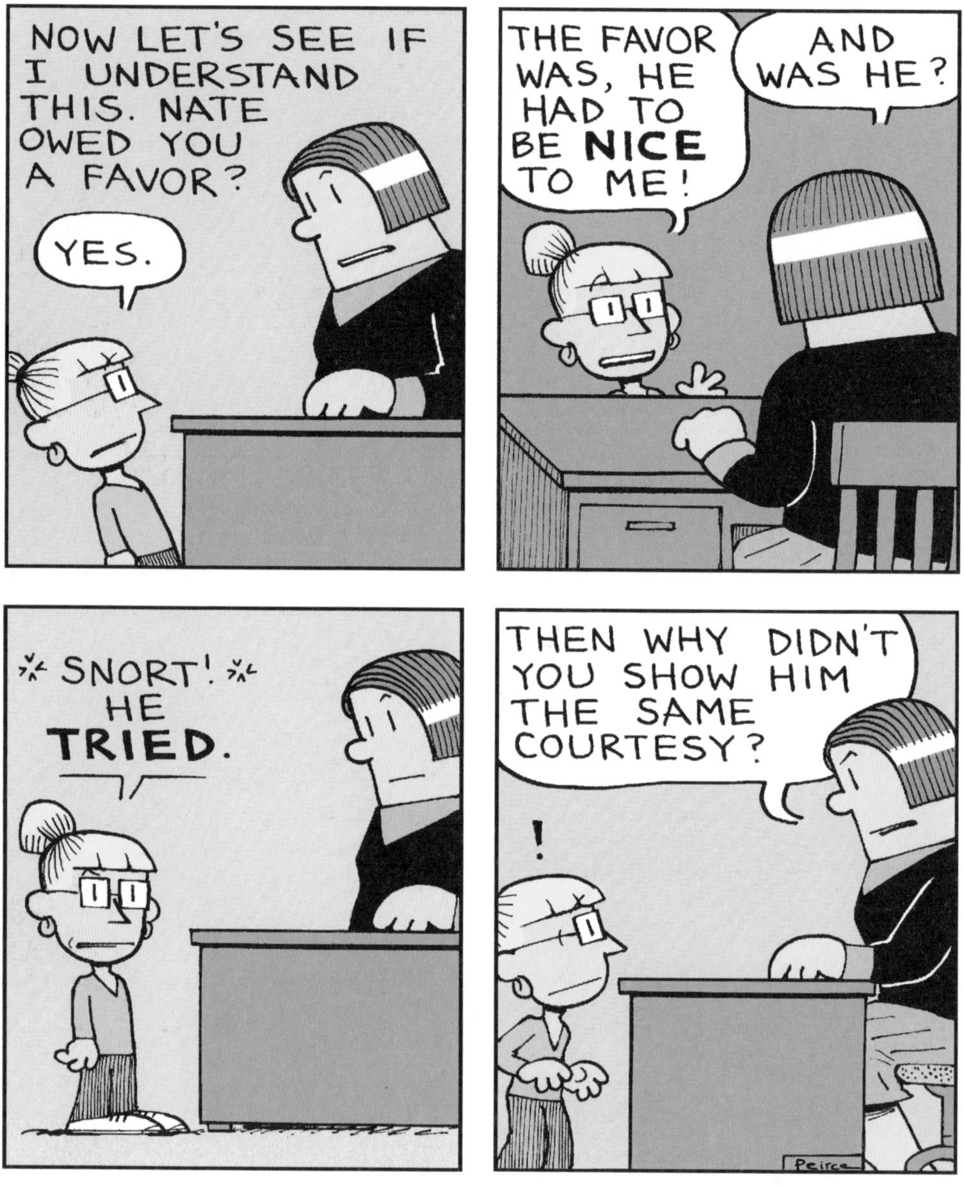
NOW LET'S SEE IF I UNDERSTAND THIS. NATE OWED YOU A FAVOR?
YES.
THE FAVOR WAS, HE HAD TO BE **NICE** TO ME!
AND WAS HE?
SNORT! HE **TRIED**.
THEN WHY DIDN'T YOU SHOW HIM THE SAME COURTESY?
!
Peirce

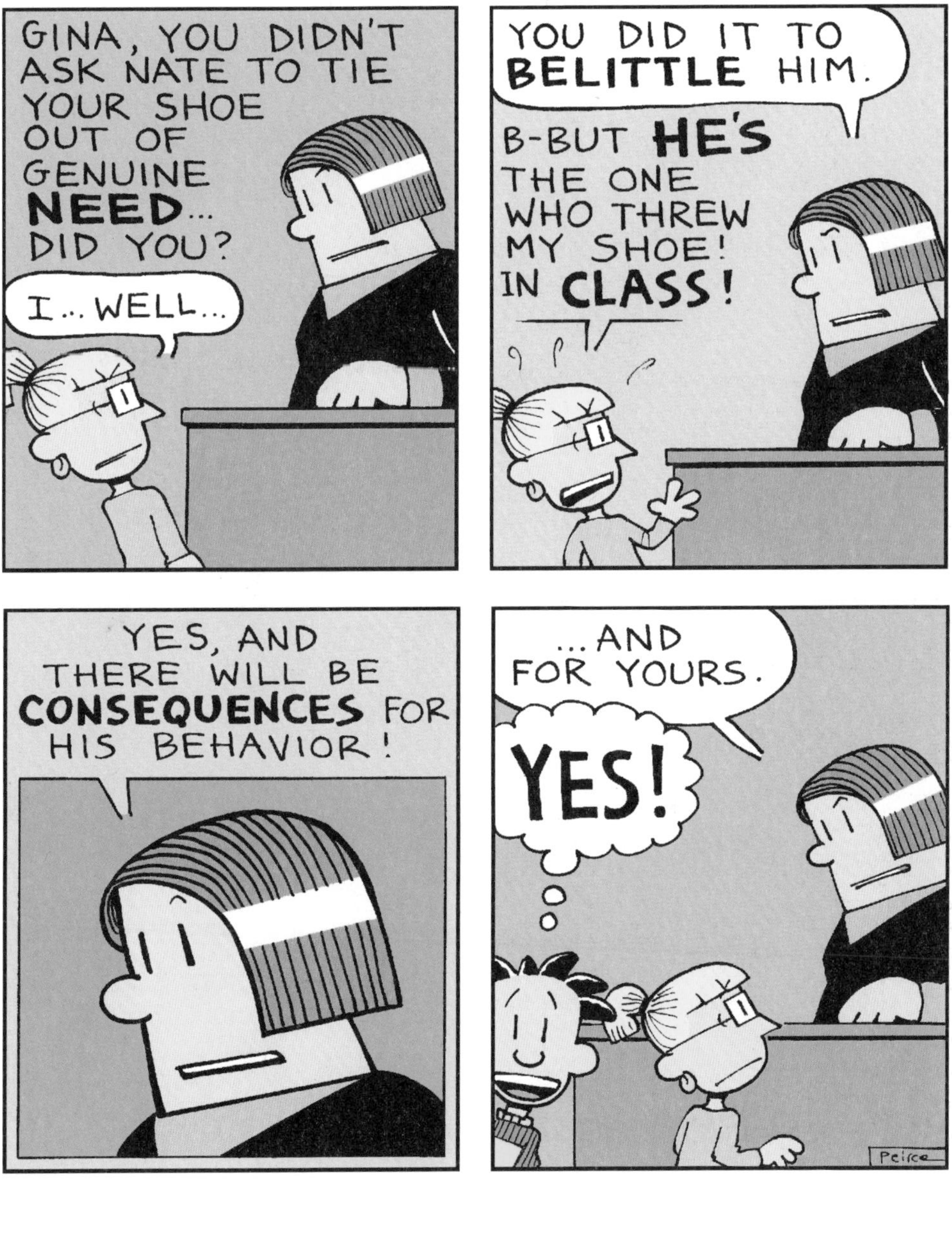
GINA, YOU DIDN'T ASK NATE TO TIE YOUR SHOE OUT OF GENUINE **NEED**... DID YOU?
I... WELL...
YOU DID IT TO **BELITTLE** HIM.
B-BUT **HE'S** THE ONE WHO THREW MY SHOE! IN **CLASS**!
YES, AND THERE WILL BE **CONSEQUENCES** FOR HIS BEHAVIOR!
...AND FOR YOURS.
YES!
Peirce

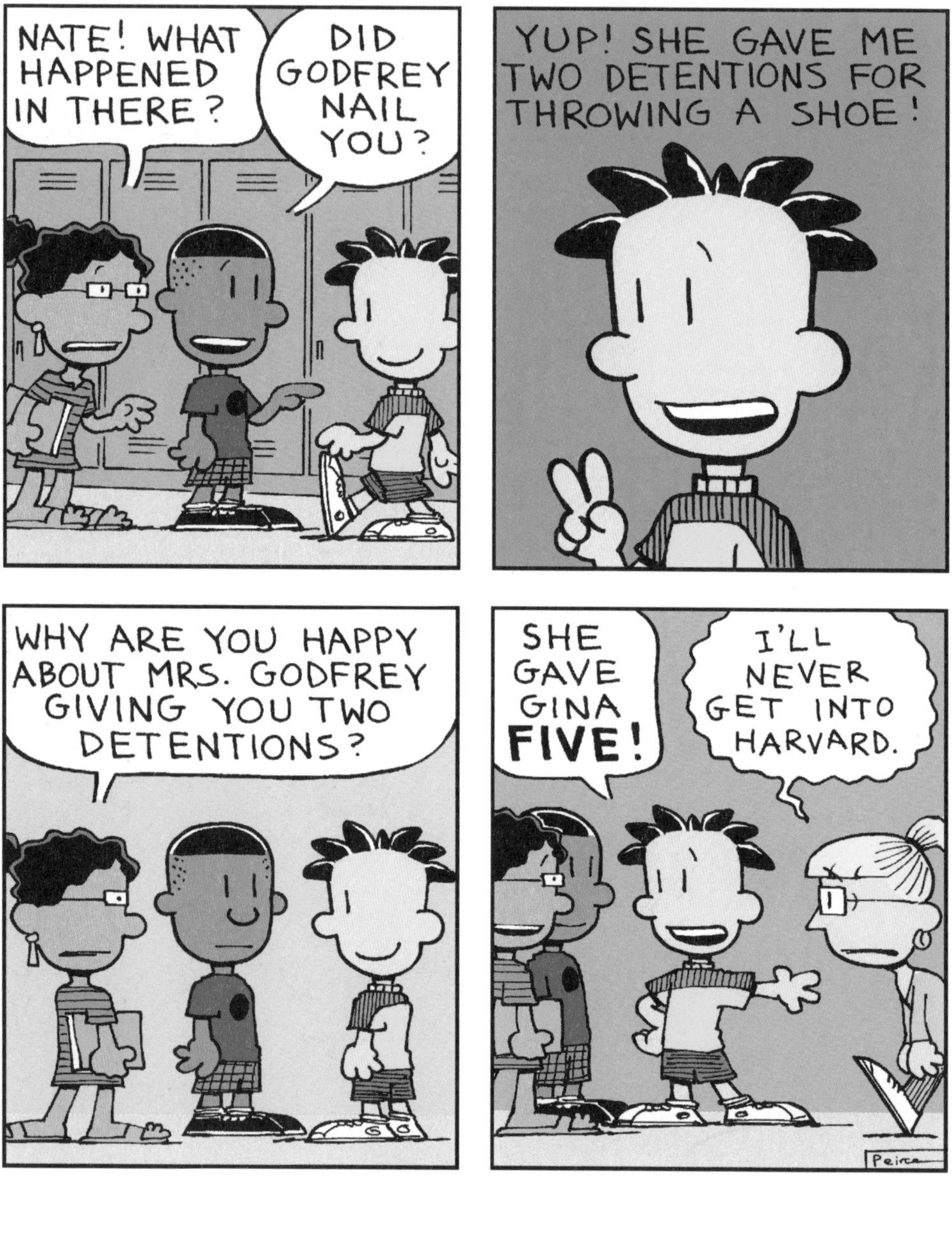
NATE! WHAT HAPPENED IN THERE?
DID GODFREY NAIL YOU?
YUP! SHE GAVE ME TWO DETENTIONS FOR THROWING A SHOE!
WHY ARE YOU HAPPY ABOUT MRS. GODFREY GIVING YOU TWO DETENTIONS?
SHE GAVE GINA **FIVE!**
I'LL NEVER GET INTO HARVARD.
Peirce

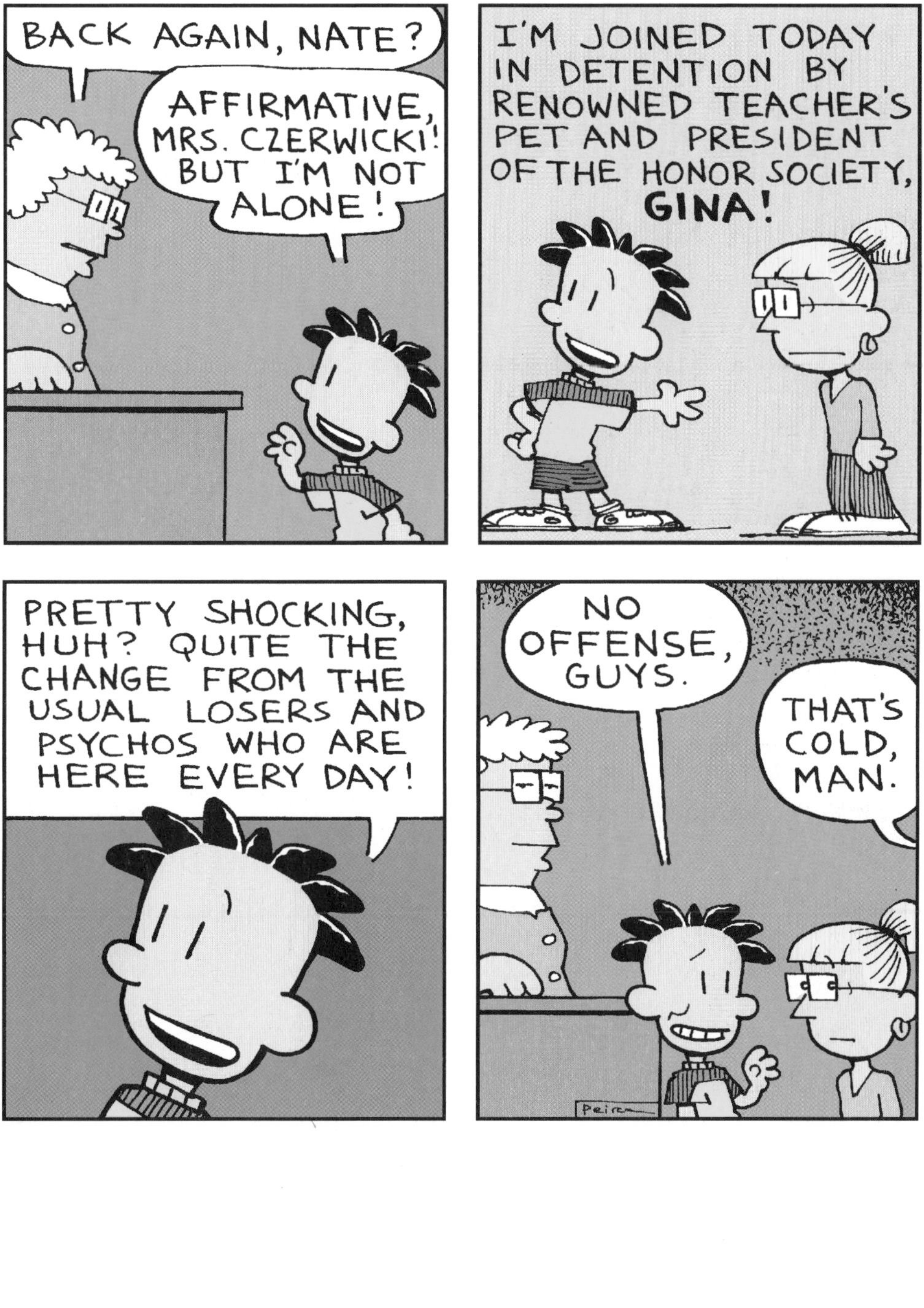
BACK AGAIN, NATE?
AFFIRMATIVE, MRS. CZERWICKI! BUT I'M NOT ALONE!
I'M JOINED TODAY IN DETENTION BY RENOWNED TEACHER'S PET AND PRESIDENT OF THE HONOR SOCIETY, **GINA**!
PRETTY SHOCKING, HUH? QUITE THE CHANGE FROM THE USUAL LOSERS AND PSYCHOS WHO ARE HERE EVERY DAY!
NO OFFENSE, GUYS.
THAT'S COLD, MAN.
Peirce

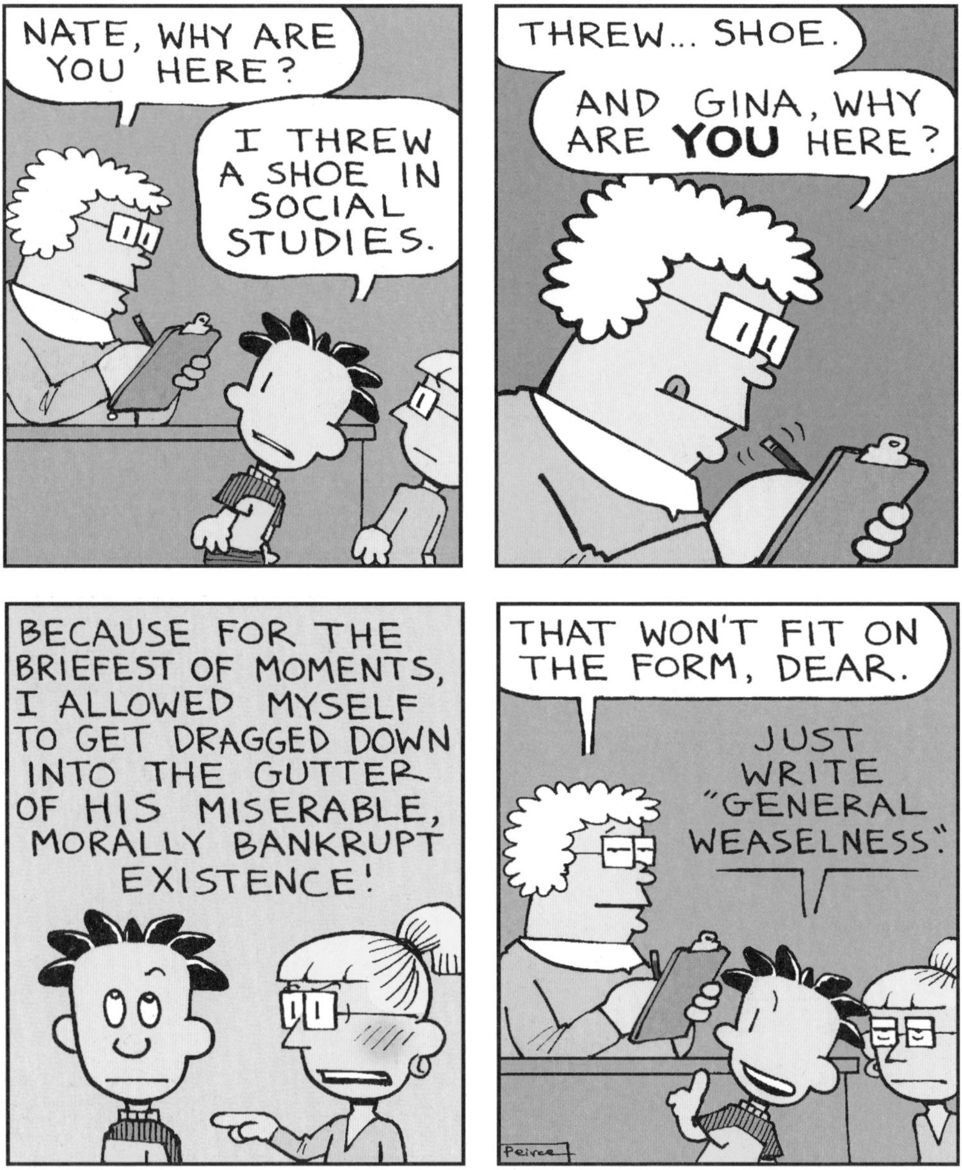
NATE, WHY ARE YOU HERE?
I THREW A SHOE IN SOCIAL STUDIES.
THREW... SHOE.
AND GINA, WHY ARE **YOU** HERE?
BECAUSE FOR THE BRIEFEST OF MOMENTS, I ALLOWED MYSELF TO GET DRAGGED DOWN INTO THE GUTTER OF HIS MISERABLE, MORALLY BANKRUPT EXISTENCE!
THAT WON'T FIT ON THE FORM, DEAR.
JUST WRITE "GENERAL WEASELNESS."
Peirce

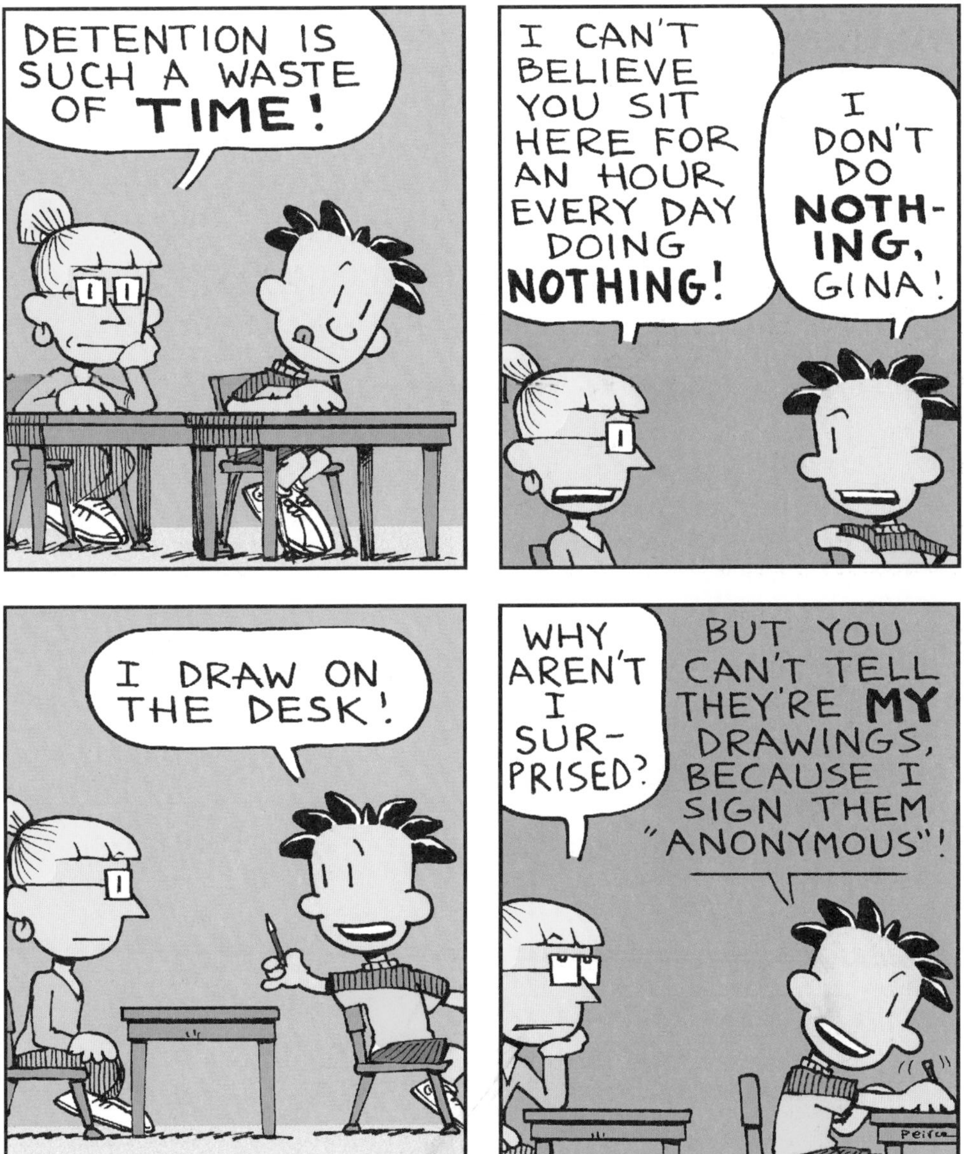
DETENTION IS SUCH A WASTE OF **TIME**!
I CAN'T BELIEVE YOU SIT HERE FOR AN HOUR EVERY DAY DOING **NOTHING**!
I DON'T DO **NOTHING**, GINA!
I DRAW ON THE DESK!
WHY AREN'T I SURPRISED?
BUT YOU CAN'T TELL THEY'RE **MY** DRAWINGS, BECAUSE I SIGN THEM "ANONYMOUS"!

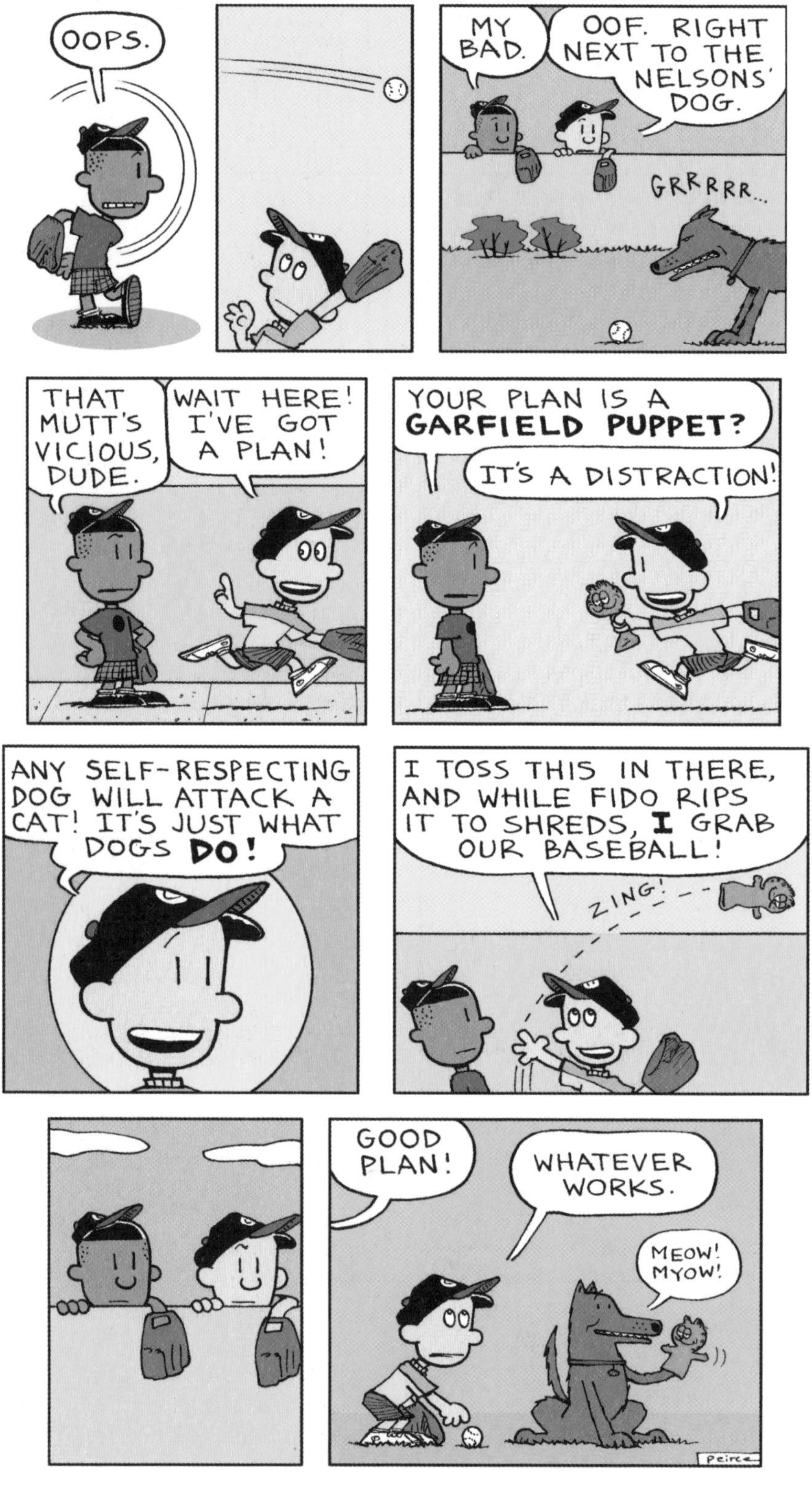
OOPS.
MY BAD.
OOF. RIGHT NEXT TO THE NELSONS' DOG.
GRRRRR...
THAT MUTT'S VICIOUS, DUDE.
WAIT HERE! I'VE GOT A PLAN!
YOUR PLAN IS A **GARFIELD PUPPET?**
IT'S A DISTRACTION!
ANY SELF-RESPECTING DOG WILL ATTACK A CAT! IT'S JUST WHAT DOGS **DO!**
I TOSS THIS IN THERE, AND WHILE FIDO RIPS IT TO SHREDS, **I** GRAB OUR BASEBALL!
ZING!
GOOD PLAN!
WHATEVER WORKS.
MEOW! MYOW!
Peirce

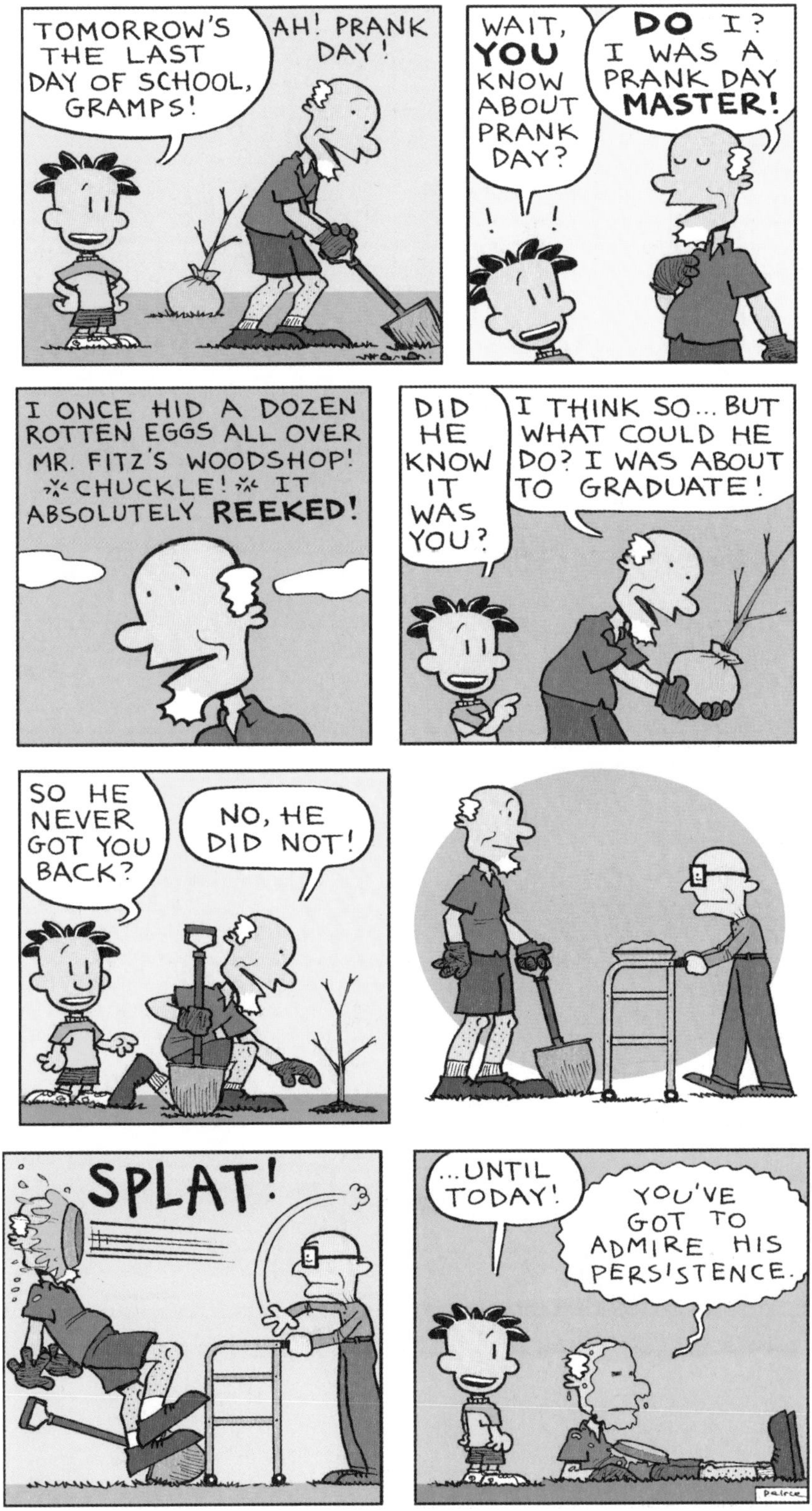
TOMORROW'S THE LAST DAY OF SCHOOL, GRAMPS!
AH! PRANK DAY!
WAIT, YOU KNOW ABOUT PRANK DAY?
DO I? I WAS A PRANK DAY MASTER!
I ONCE HID A DOZEN ROTTEN EGGS ALL OVER MR. FITZ'S WOODSHOP! *CHUCKLE!* IT ABSOLUTELY REEKED!
DID HE KNOW IT WAS YOU?
I THINK SO... BUT WHAT COULD HE DO? I WAS ABOUT TO GRADUATE!
SO HE NEVER GOT YOU BACK?
NO, HE DID NOT!
SPLAT!
...UNTIL TODAY!
YOU'VE GOT TO ADMIRE HIS PERSISTENCE.

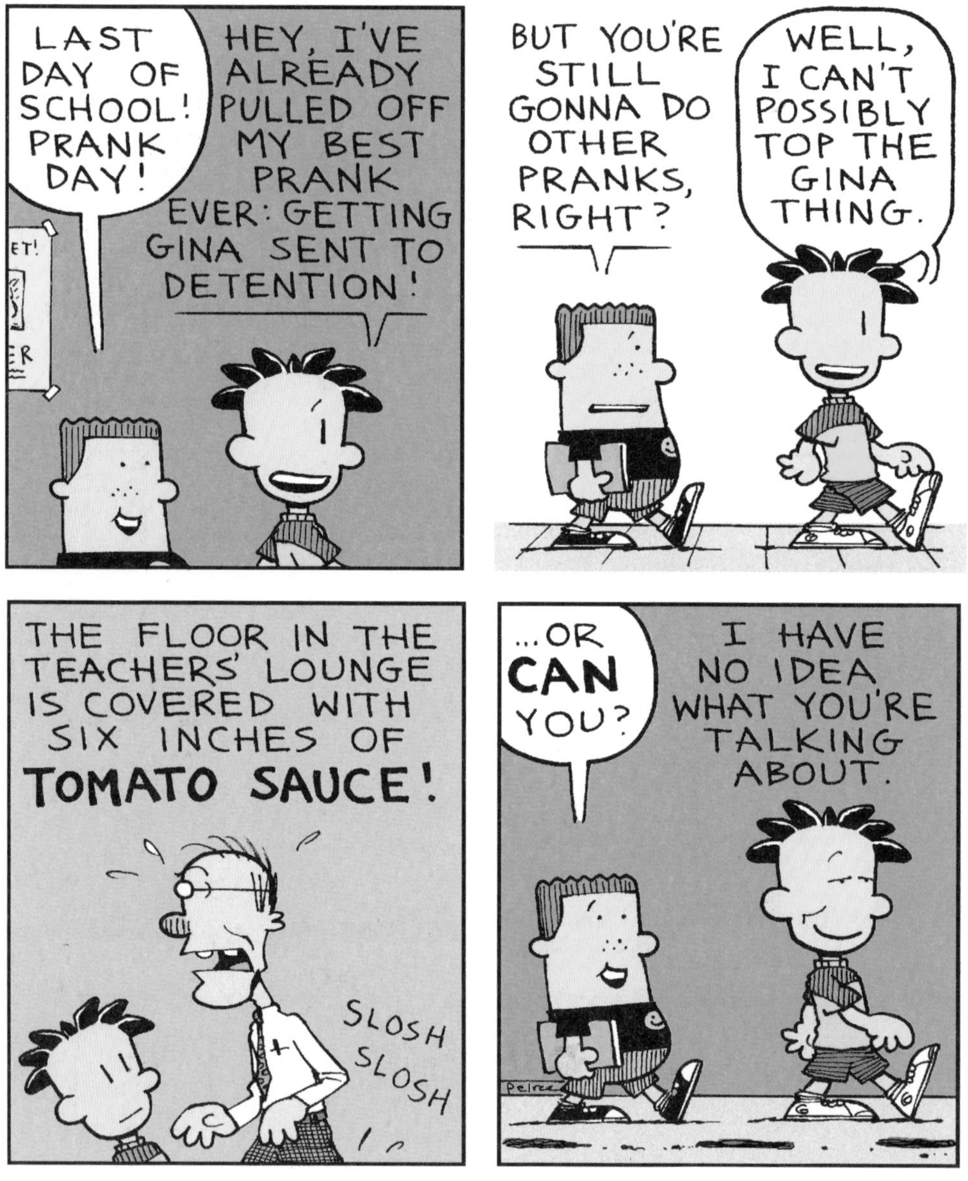
LAST DAY OF SCHOOL! PRANK DAY!
HEY, I'VE ALREADY PULLED OFF MY BEST PRANK EVER: GETTING GINA SENT TO DETENTION!
BUT YOU'RE STILL GONNA DO OTHER PRANKS, RIGHT?
WELL, I CAN'T POSSIBLY TOP THE GINA THING.
THE FLOOR IN THE TEACHERS' LOUNGE IS COVERED WITH SIX INCHES OF TOMATO SAUCE!
SLOSH
SLOSH
...OR CAN YOU?
I HAVE NO IDEA WHAT YOU'RE TALKING ABOUT.
Peirce

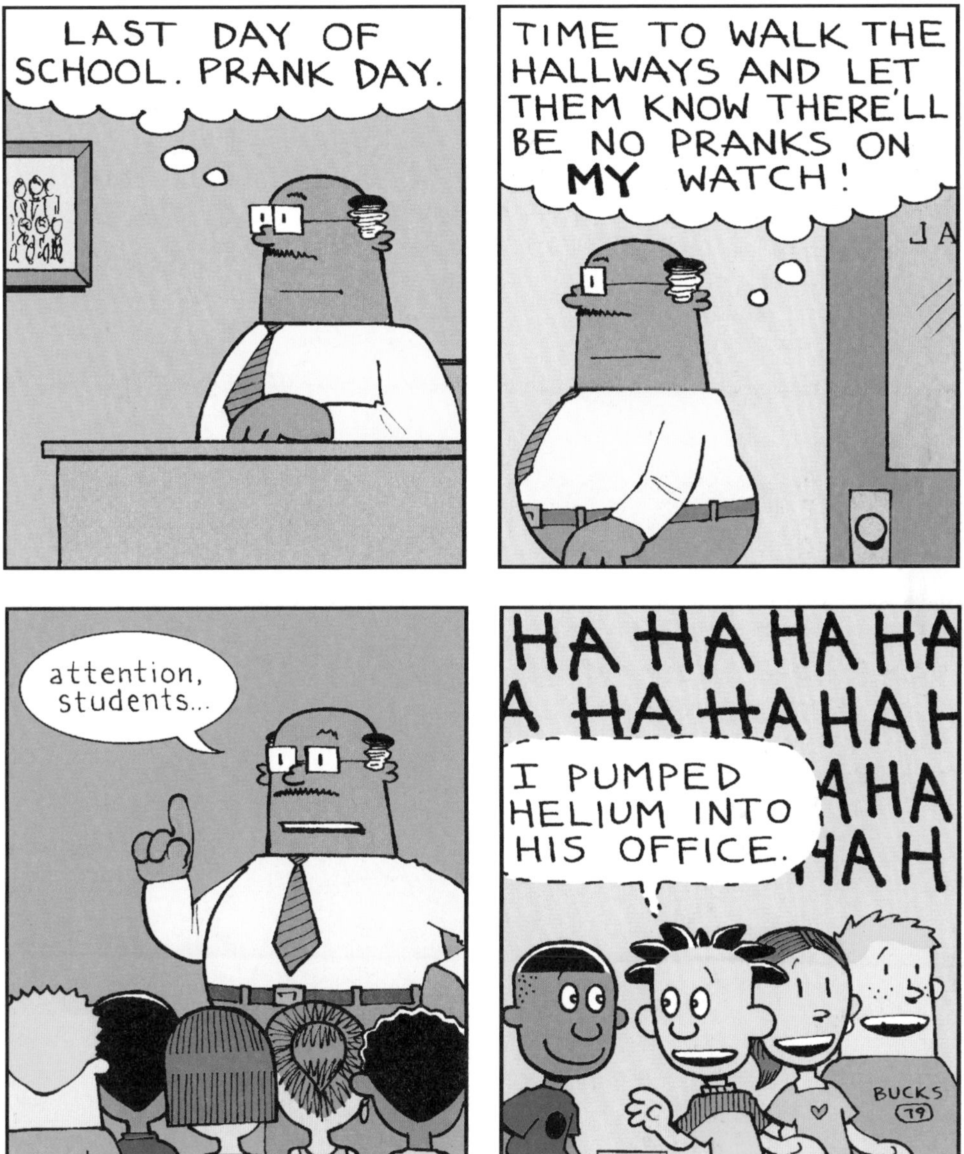
LAST DAY OF SCHOOL. PRANK DAY.
TIME TO WALK THE HALLWAYS AND LET THEM KNOW THERE'LL BE NO PRANKS ON **MY** WATCH!
attention, students...
HA HA HA HA HA
A HA HA HA HAH
AHA HA
HAH
I PUMPED HELIUM INTO HIS OFFICE.
BUCKS 79
Peirce

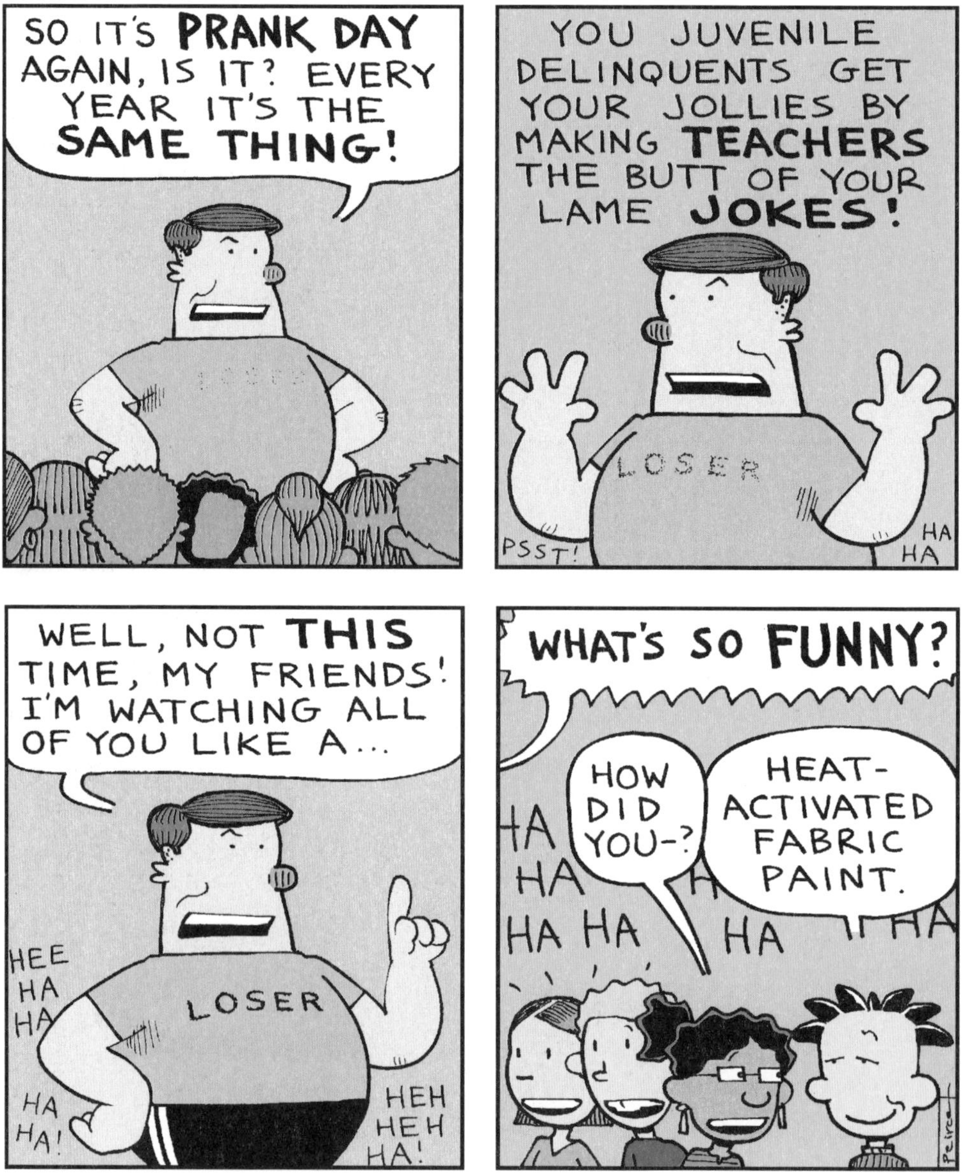
SO IT'S PRANK DAY AGAIN, IS IT? EVERY YEAR IT'S THE SAME THING!
YOU JUVENILE DELINQUENTS GET YOUR JOLLIES BY MAKING TEACHERS THE BUTT OF YOUR LAME JOKES!
LOSER
PSST!
HA HA
WELL, NOT THIS TIME, MY FRIENDS! I'M WATCHING ALL OF YOU LIKE A...
HEE HA HA
LOSER
HA HA!
HEH HEH HA!
WHAT'S SO FUNNY?
HA HA HA HA HA HA
HOW DID YOU-?
HEAT-ACTIVATED FABRIC PAINT.

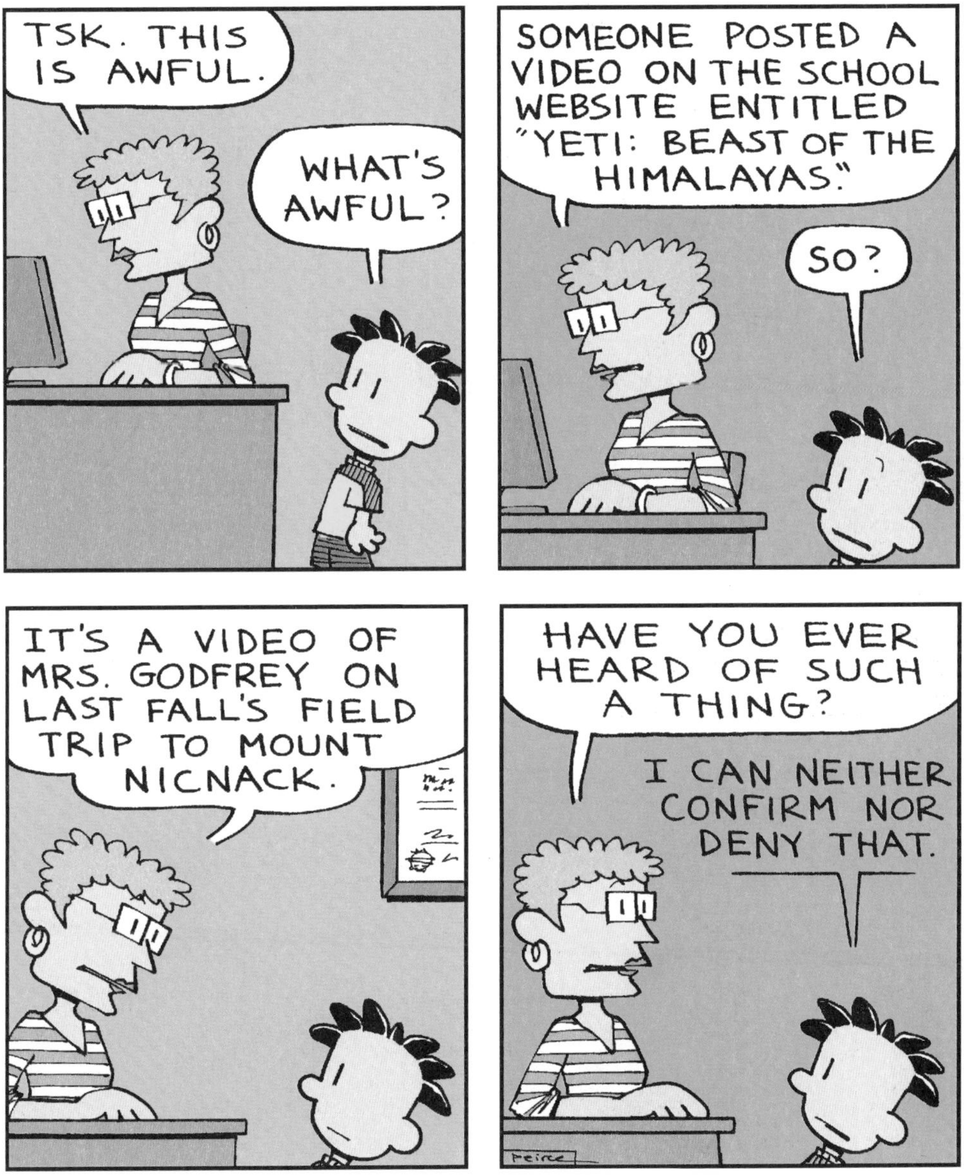
TSK. THIS IS AWFUL.
WHAT'S AWFUL?
SOMEONE POSTED A VIDEO ON THE SCHOOL WEBSITE ENTITLED "YETI: BEAST OF THE HIMALAYAS."
SO?
IT'S A VIDEO OF MRS. GODFREY ON LAST FALL'S FIELD TRIP TO MOUNT NICNACK.
HAVE YOU EVER HEARD OF SUCH A THING?
I CAN NEITHER CONFIRM NOR DENY THAT.
Peirce

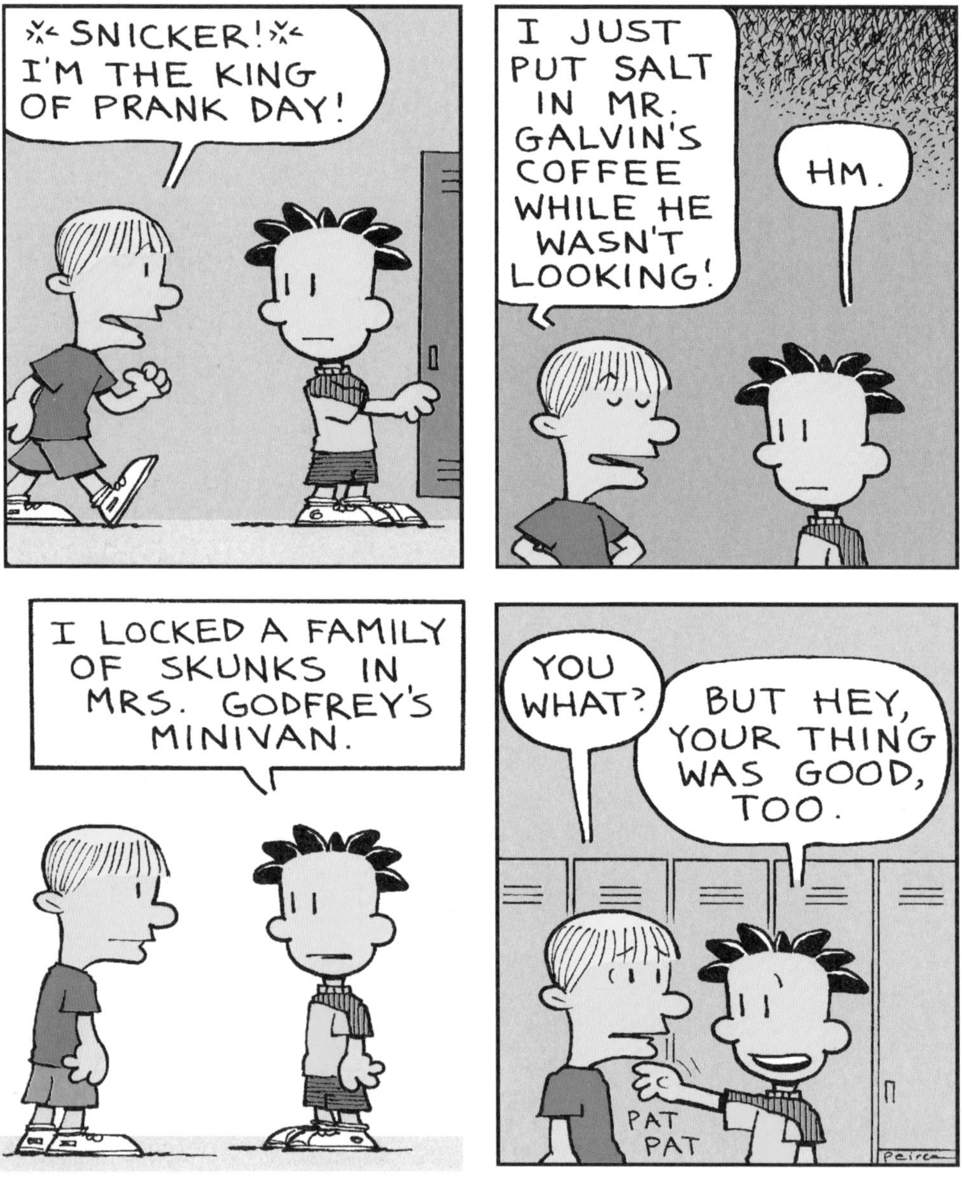
SNICKER! I'M THE KING OF PRANK DAY!
I JUST PUT SALT IN MR. GALVIN'S COFFEE WHILE HE WASN'T LOOKING!
HM.
I LOCKED A FAMILY OF SKUNKS IN MRS. GODFREY'S MINIVAN.
YOU WHAT?
BUT HEY, YOUR THING WAS GOOD, TOO.
PAT PAT
Peirce

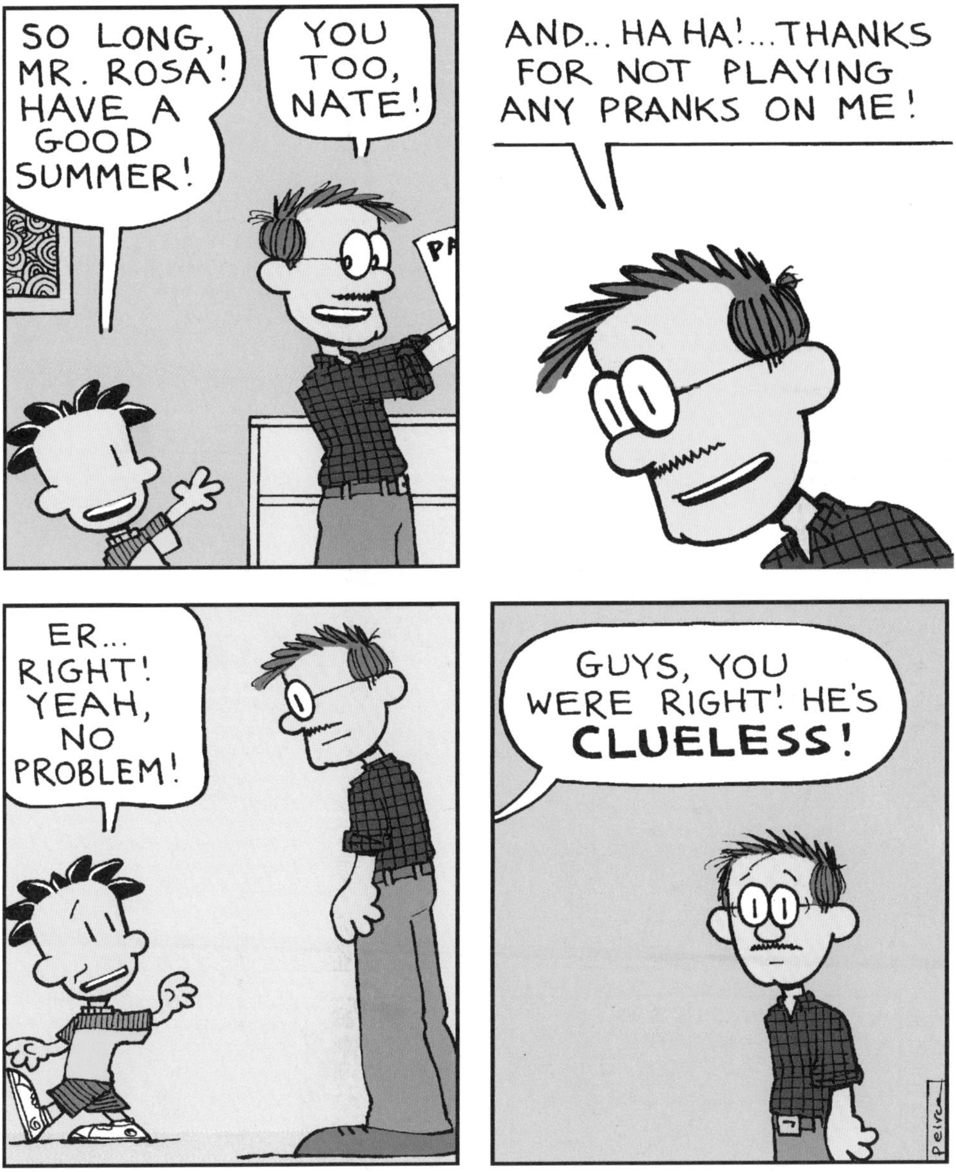
SO LONG, MR. ROSA! HAVE A GOOD SUMMER!
YOU TOO, NATE!
AND... HA HA!... THANKS FOR NOT PLAYING ANY PRANKS ON ME!
ER... RIGHT! YEAH, NO PROBLEM!
GUYS, YOU WERE RIGHT! HE'S **CLUELESS!**
peirce

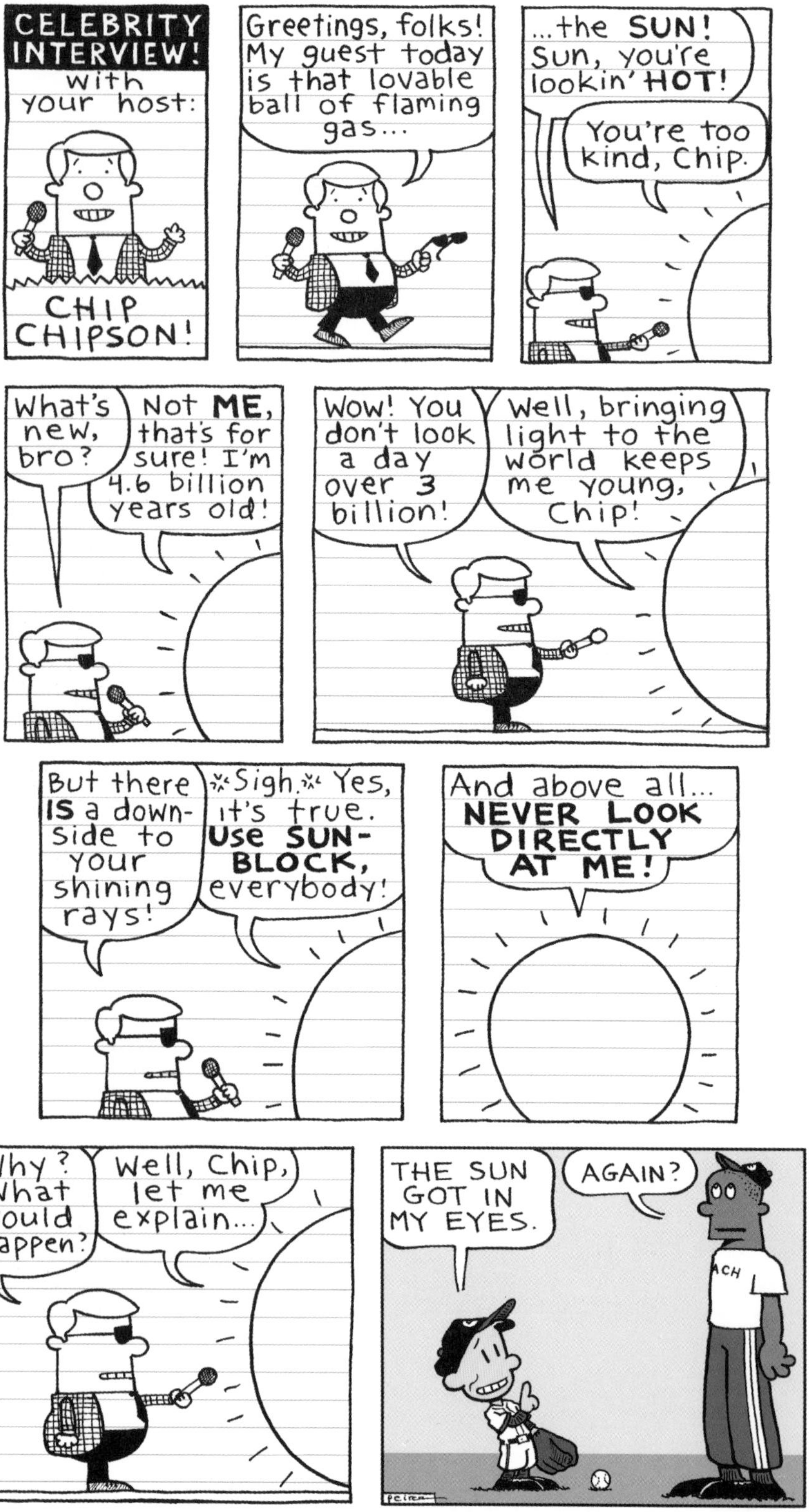
CELEBRITY INTERVIEW!
with your host:
CHIP CHIPSON!
Greetings, folks! My guest today is that lovable ball of flaming gas...
...the SUN! Sun, you're lookin' HOT!
You're too kind, Chip.
What's new, bro?
Not ME, that's for sure! I'm 4.6 billion years old!
Wow! You don't look a day over 3 billion!
Well, bringing light to the world keeps me young, Chip!
But there IS a down-side to your shining rays!
Sigh. Yes, it's true. Use SUN-BLOCK, everybody!
And above all... NEVER LOOK DIRECTLY AT ME!
Why? What would happen?
Well, Chip, let me explain...
THE SUN GOT IN MY EYES.
AGAIN?

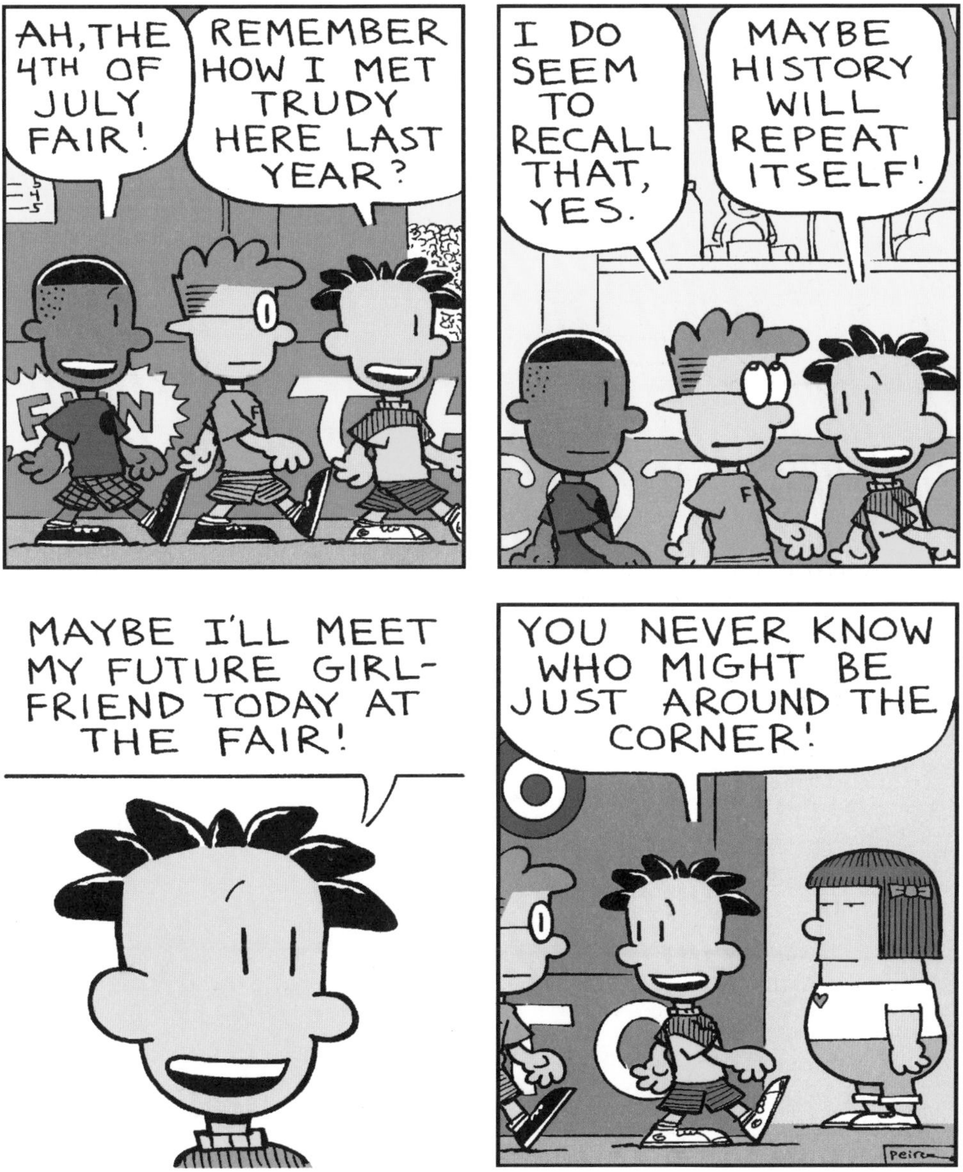
AH, THE 4TH OF JULY FAIR!
REMEMBER HOW I MET TRUDY HERE LAST YEAR?
FUN
I DO SEEM TO RECALL THAT, YES.
MAYBE HISTORY WILL REPEAT ITSELF!
MAYBE I'LL MEET MY FUTURE GIRLFRIEND TODAY AT THE FAIR!
YOU NEVER KNOW WHO MIGHT BE JUST AROUND THE CORNER!
peirce

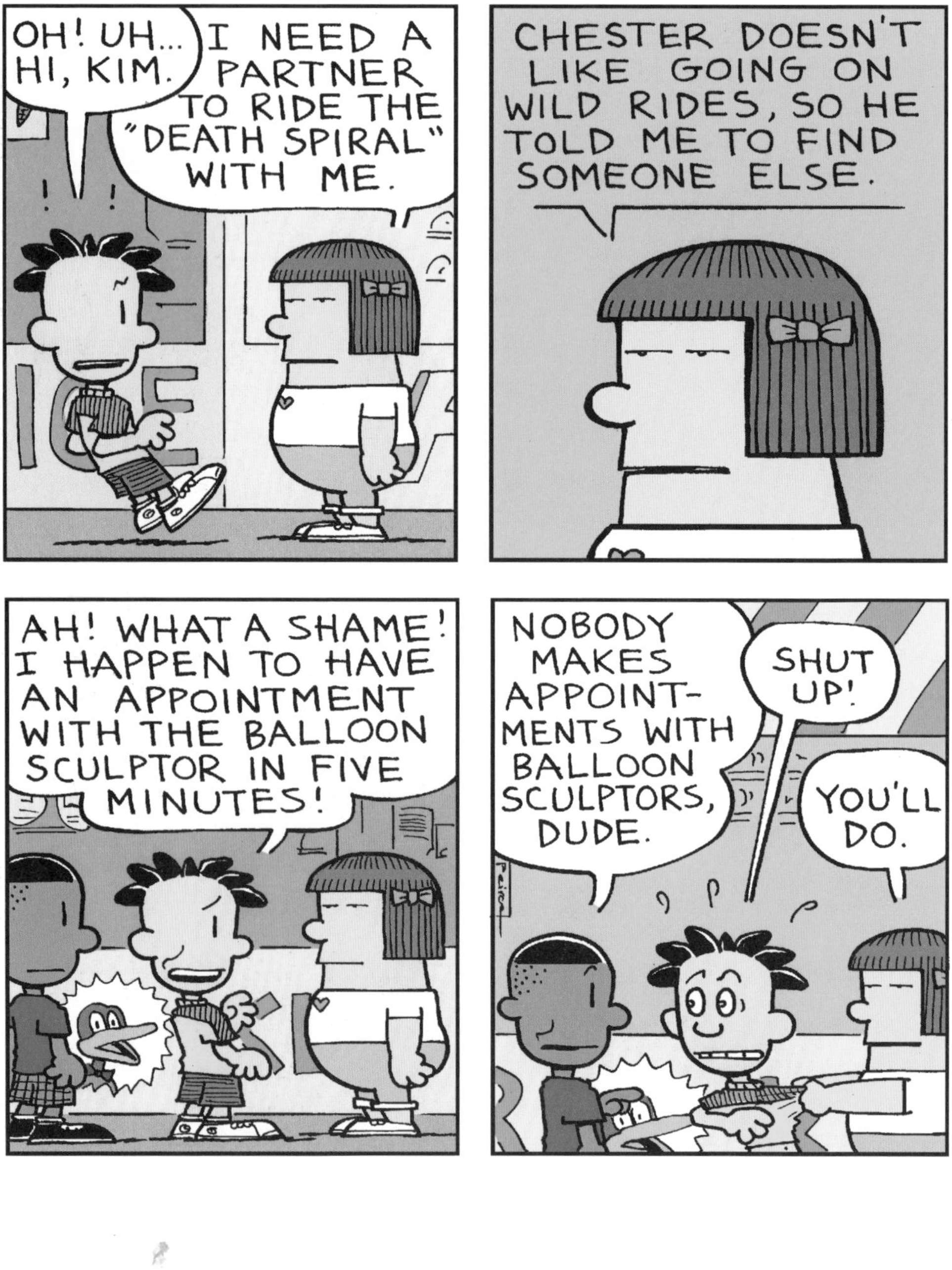
OH! UH... HI, KIM.
I NEED A PARTNER TO RIDE THE "DEATH SPIRAL" WITH ME.
CHESTER DOESN'T LIKE GOING ON WILD RIDES, SO HE TOLD ME TO FIND SOMEONE ELSE.
AH! WHAT A SHAME! I HAPPEN TO HAVE AN APPOINTMENT WITH THE BALLOON SCULPTOR IN FIVE MINUTES!
NOBODY MAKES APPOINTMENTS WITH BALLOON SCULPTORS, DUDE.
SHUT UP!
YOU'LL DO.

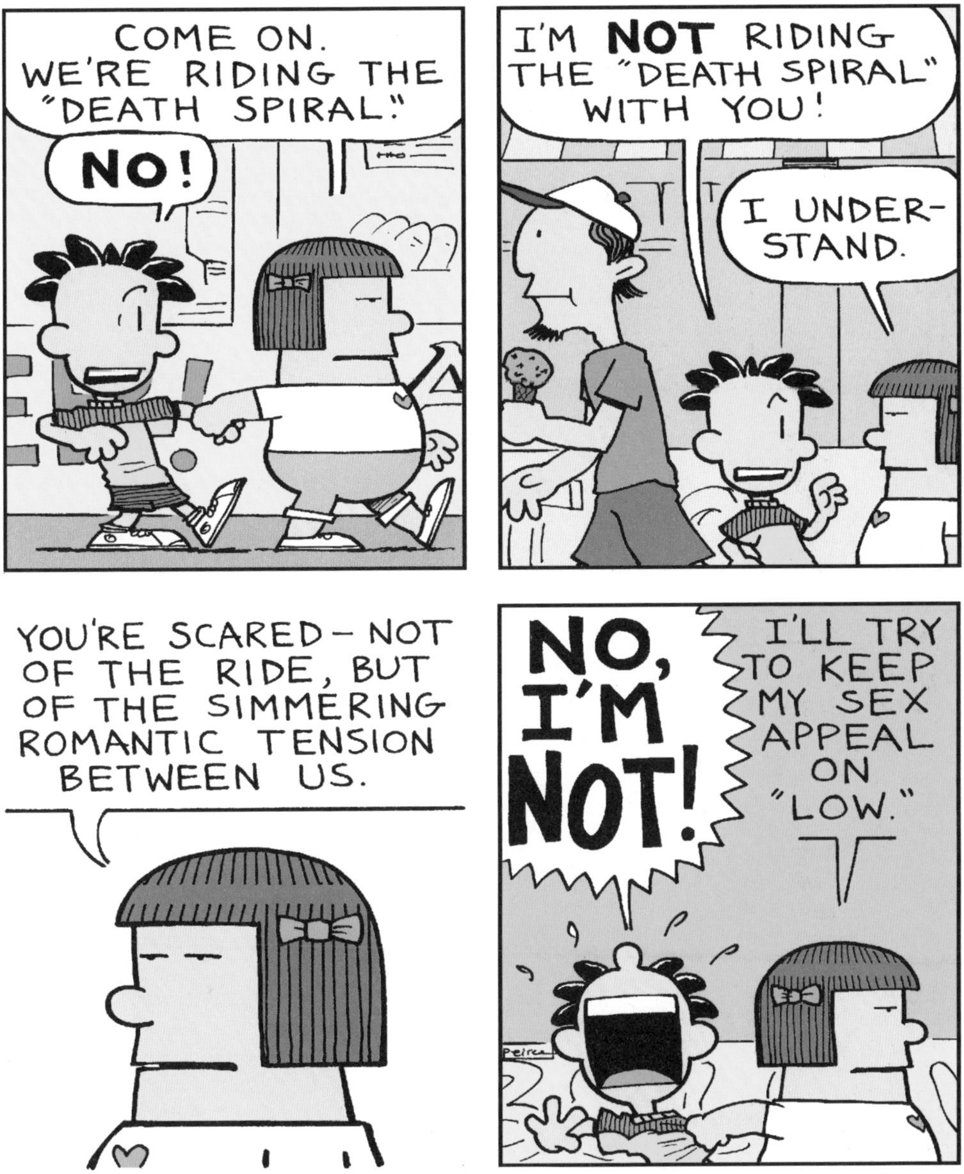

COME ON. WE'RE RIDING THE "DEATH SPIRAL."
NO!
I'M **NOT** RIDING THE "DEATH SPIRAL" WITH YOU!
I UNDER-STAND.
YOU'RE SCARED - NOT OF THE RIDE, BUT OF THE SIMMERING ROMANTIC TENSION BETWEEN US.
NO, I'M NOT!
I'LL TRY TO KEEP MY SEX APPEAL ON "LOW."

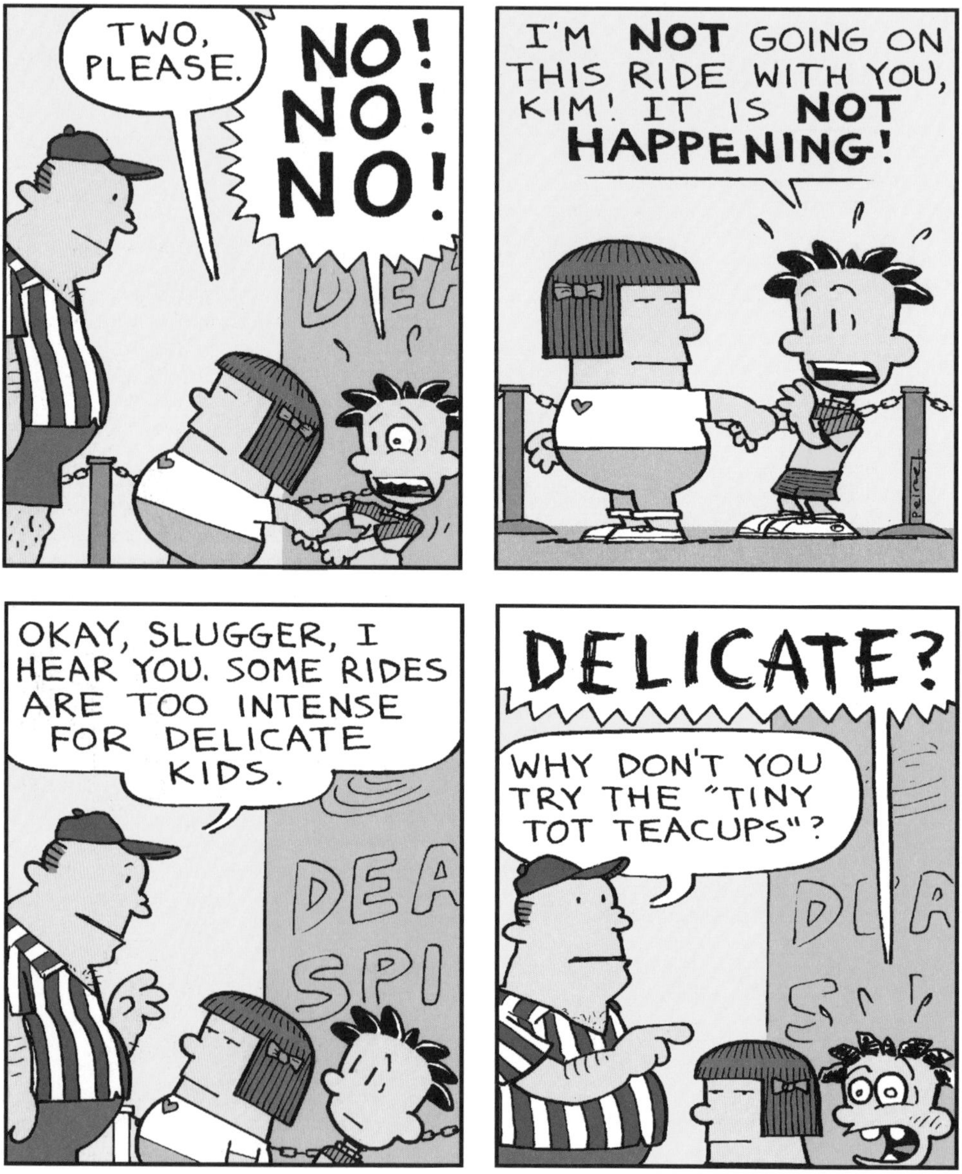
TWO, PLEASE.
NO! NO! NO!
I'M **NOT** GOING ON THIS RIDE WITH YOU, KIM! IT IS **NOT HAPPENING**!
Peirce
OKAY, SLUGGER, I HEAR YOU. SOME RIDES ARE TOO INTENSE FOR DELICATE KIDS.
DEA
SPI
DELICATE?
WHY DON'T YOU TRY THE "TINY TOT TEACUPS"?

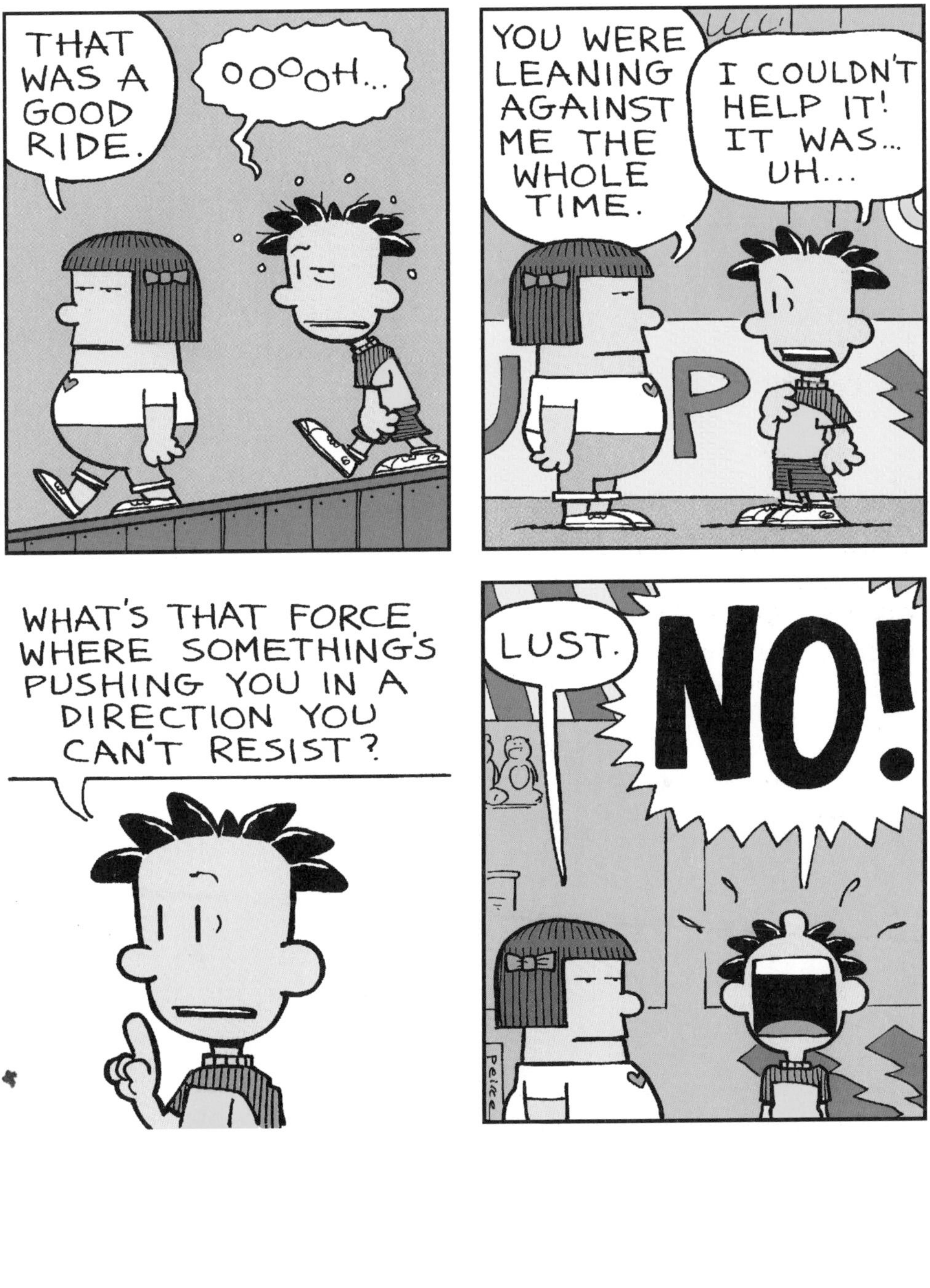
THAT WAS A GOOD RIDE.
OOOOH...
YOU WERE LEANING AGAINST ME THE WHOLE TIME.
I COULDN'T HELP IT! IT WAS... UH...
WHAT'S THAT FORCE WHERE SOMETHING'S PUSHING YOU IN A DIRECTION YOU CAN'T RESIST?
LUST.
NO!

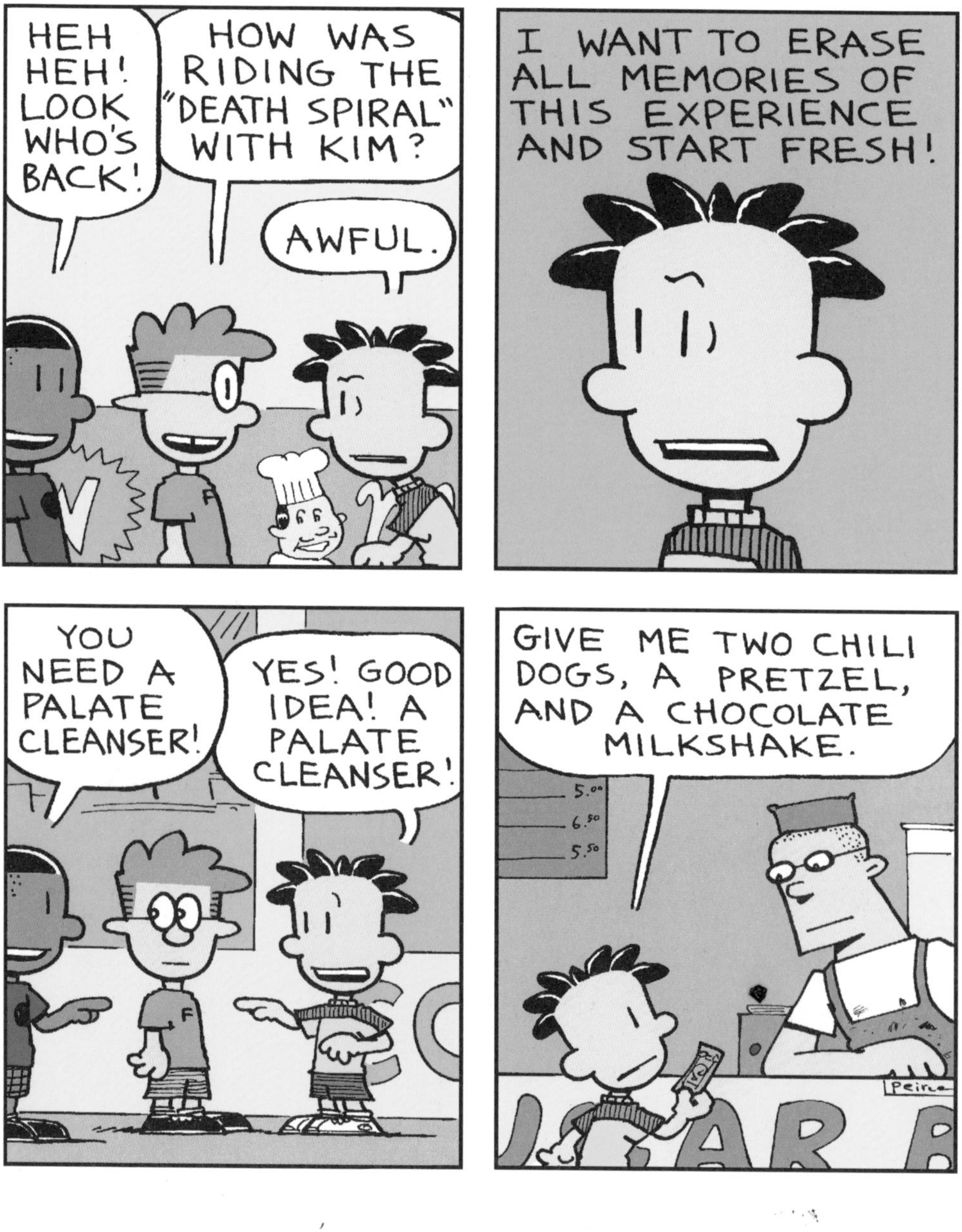
HEH HEH! LOOK WHO'S BACK!
HOW WAS RIDING THE "DEATH SPIRAL" WITH KIM?
AWFUL.
I WANT TO ERASE ALL MEMORIES OF THIS EXPERIENCE AND START FRESH!
YOU NEED A PALATE CLEANSER!
YES! GOOD IDEA! A PALATE CLEANSER!
GIVE ME TWO CHILI DOGS, A PRETZEL, AND A CHOCOLATE MILKSHAKE.
Peirce

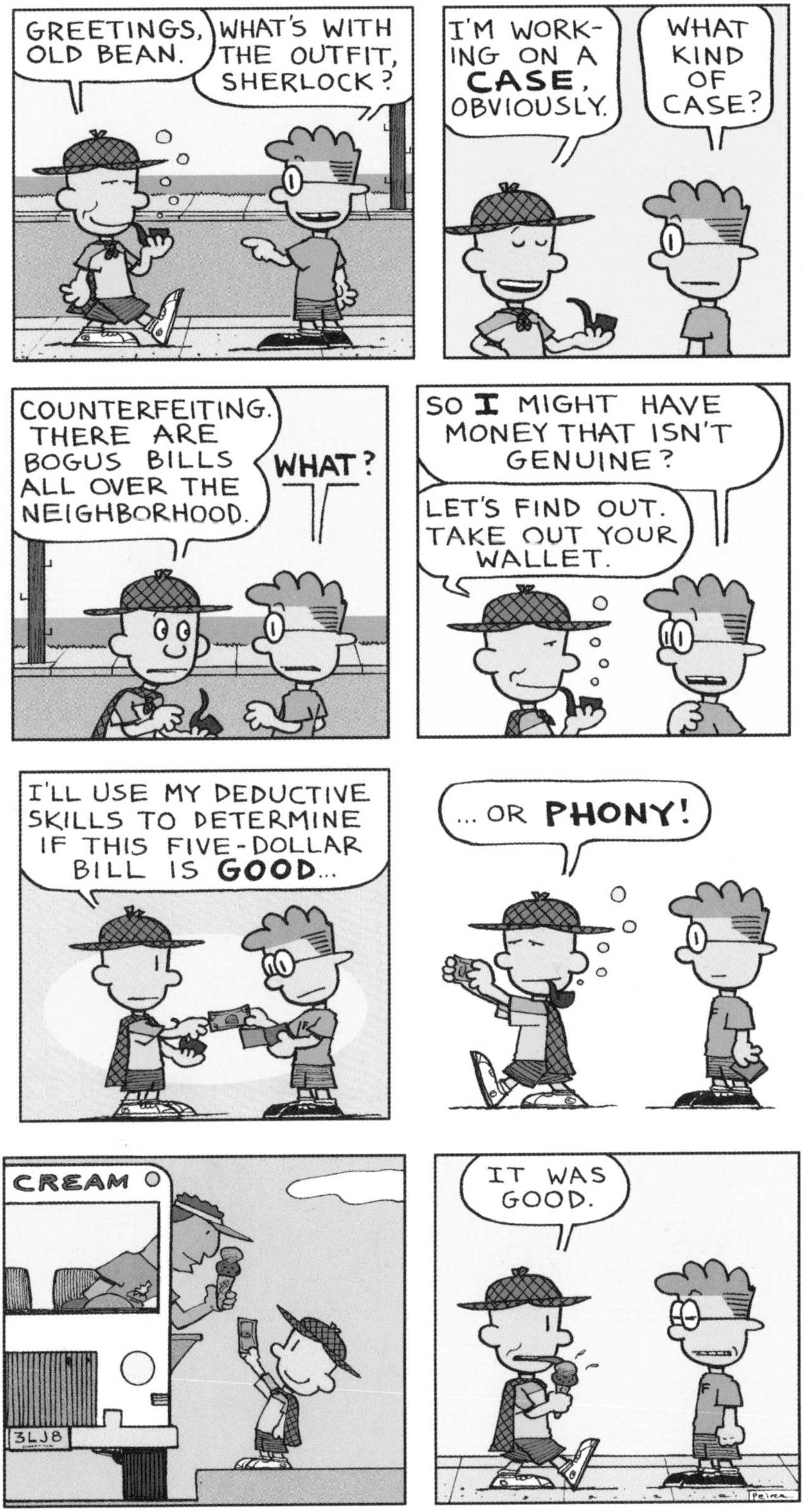
GREETINGS, OLD BEAN.
WHAT'S WITH THE OUTFIT, SHERLOCK?
I'M WORKING ON A CASE, OBVIOUSLY.
WHAT KIND OF CASE?
COUNTERFEITING. THERE ARE BOGUS BILLS ALL OVER THE NEIGHBORHOOD.
WHAT?
SO I MIGHT HAVE MONEY THAT ISN'T GENUINE?
LET'S FIND OUT. TAKE OUT YOUR WALLET.
I'LL USE MY DEDUCTIVE SKILLS TO DETERMINE IF THIS FIVE-DOLLAR BILL IS GOOD...
... OR PHONY!
CREAM
3LJ8
IT WAS GOOD.
Peirce

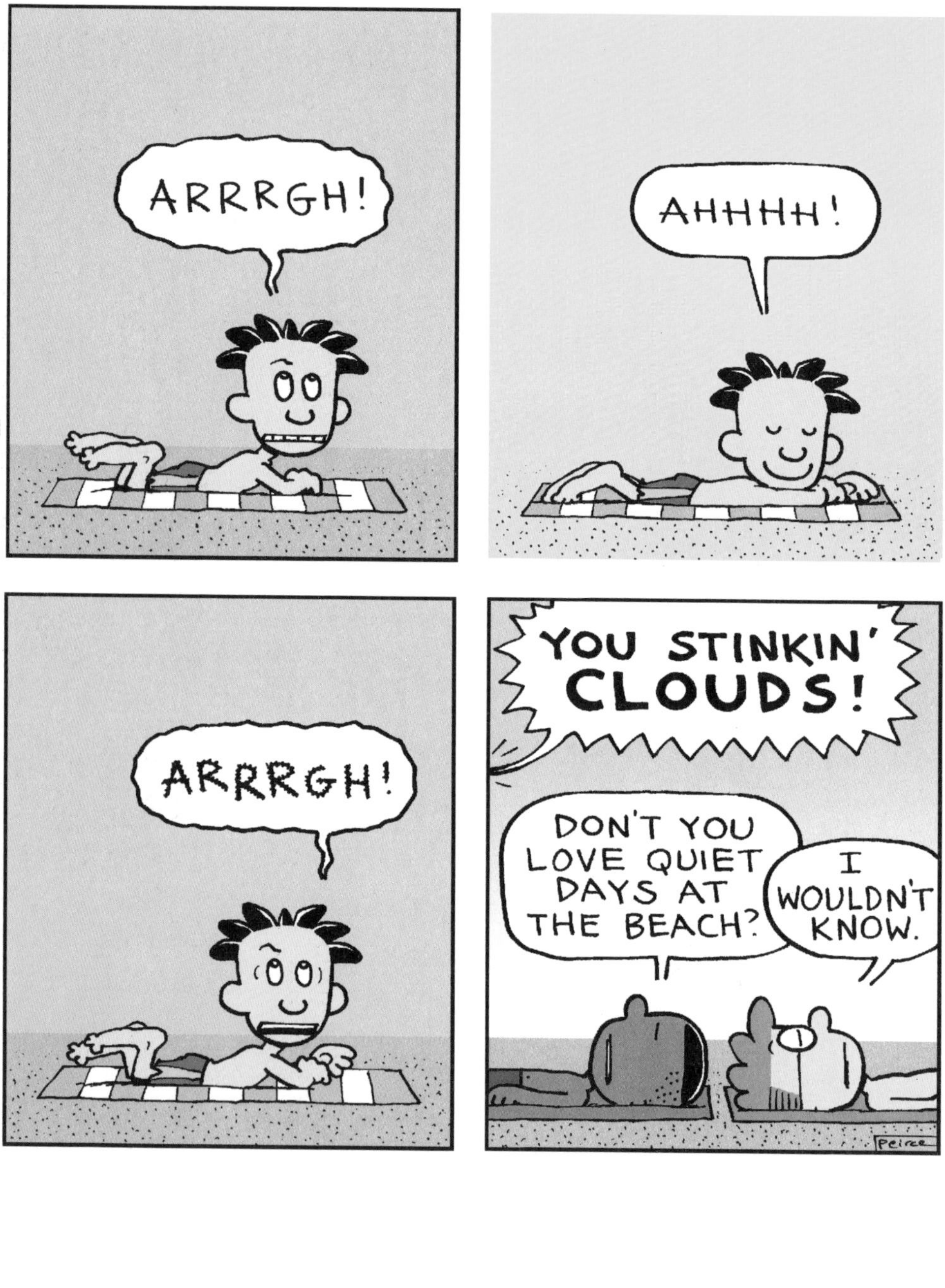
ARRRGH!
AHHHH!
ARRRGH!
YOU STINKIN' CLOUDS!
DON'T YOU LOVE QUIET DAYS AT THE BEACH?
I WOULDN'T KNOW.
Peirce

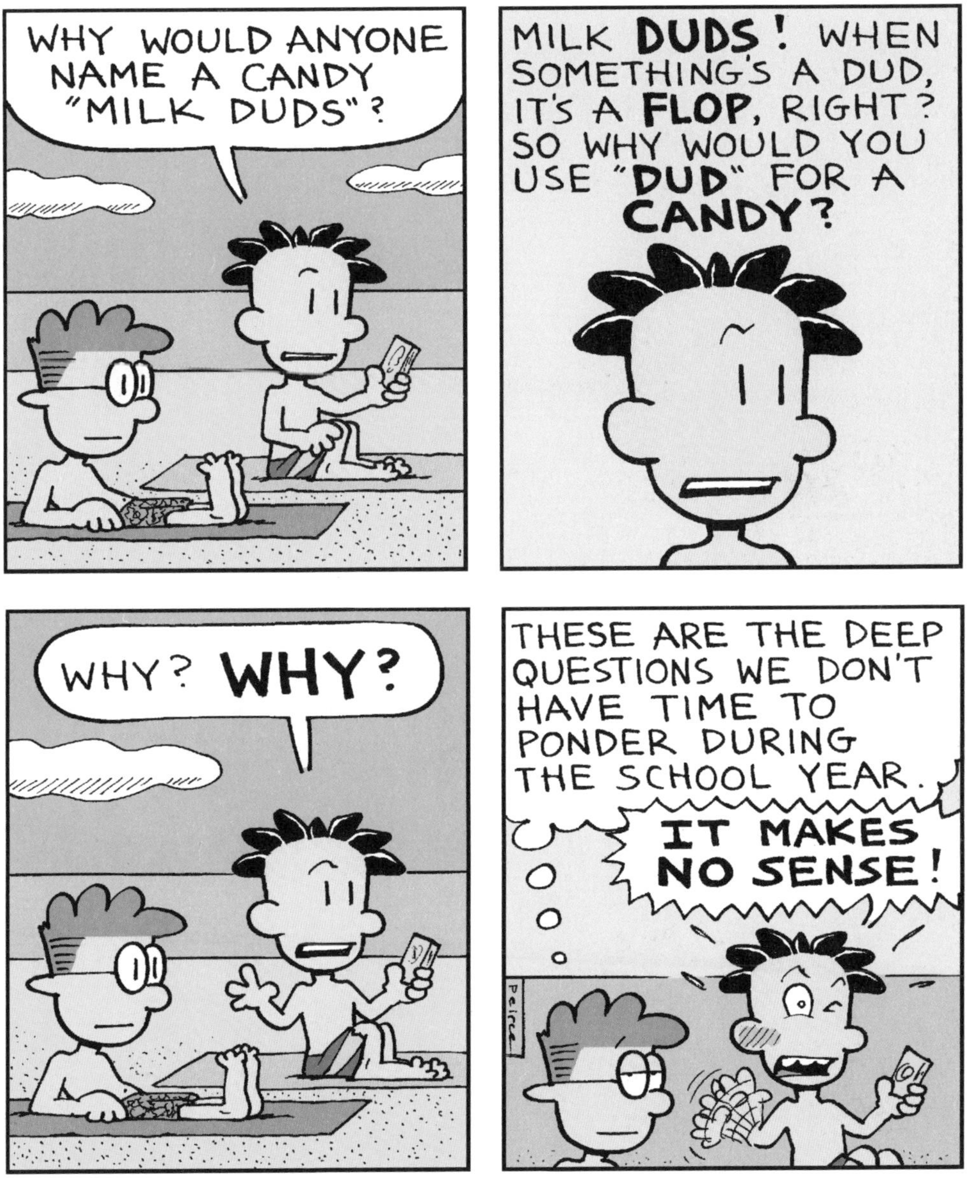
WHY WOULD ANYONE NAME A CANDY "MILK DUDS"?
MILK DUDS! WHEN SOMETHING'S A DUD, IT'S A FLOP, RIGHT? SO WHY WOULD YOU USE "DUD" FOR A CANDY?
WHY? WHY?
THESE ARE THE DEEP QUESTIONS WE DON'T HAVE TIME TO PONDER DURING THE SCHOOL YEAR.
IT MAKES NO SENSE!
Peirce

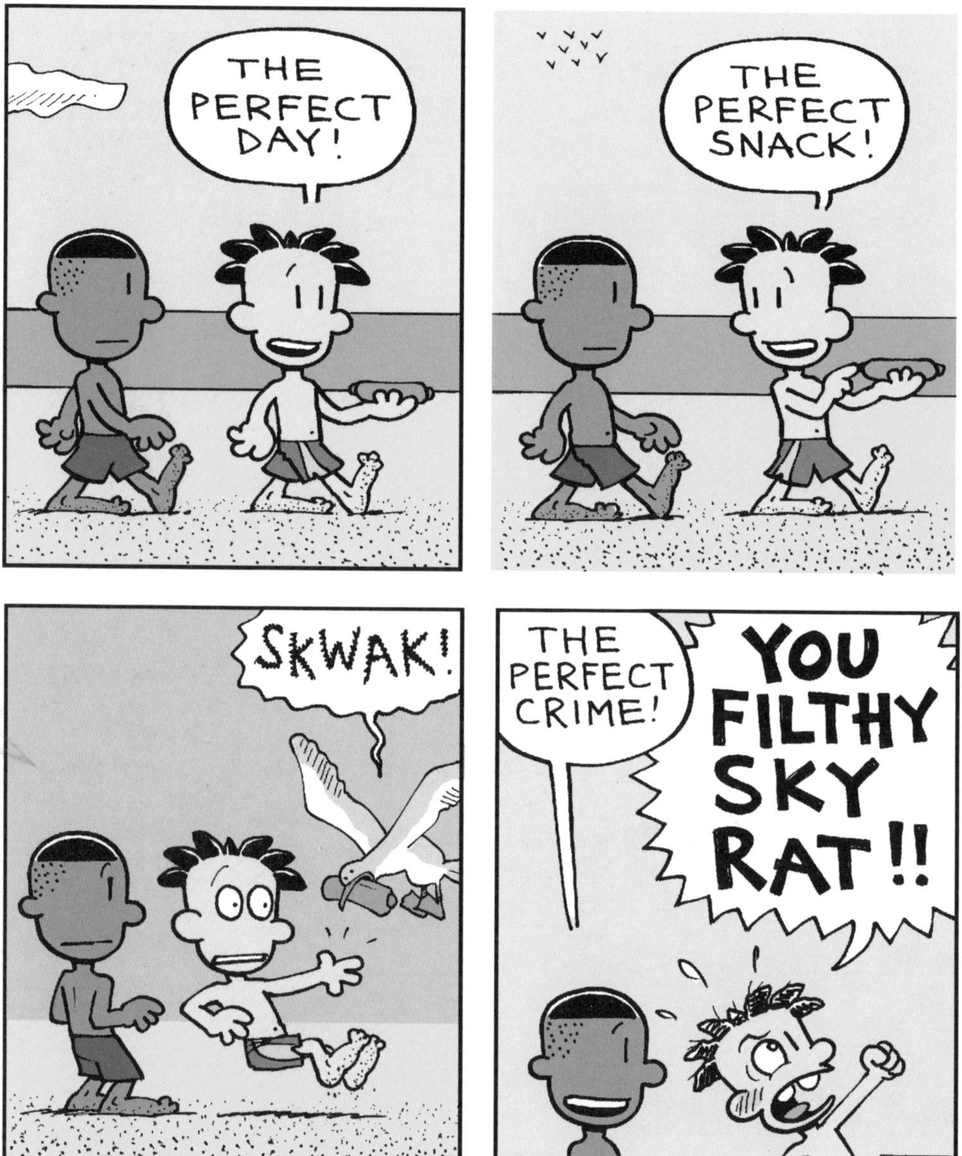
THE PERFECT DAY!
THE PERFECT SNACK!
SKWAK!
THE PERFECT CRIME!
YOU FILTHY SKY RAT!!
Peirce

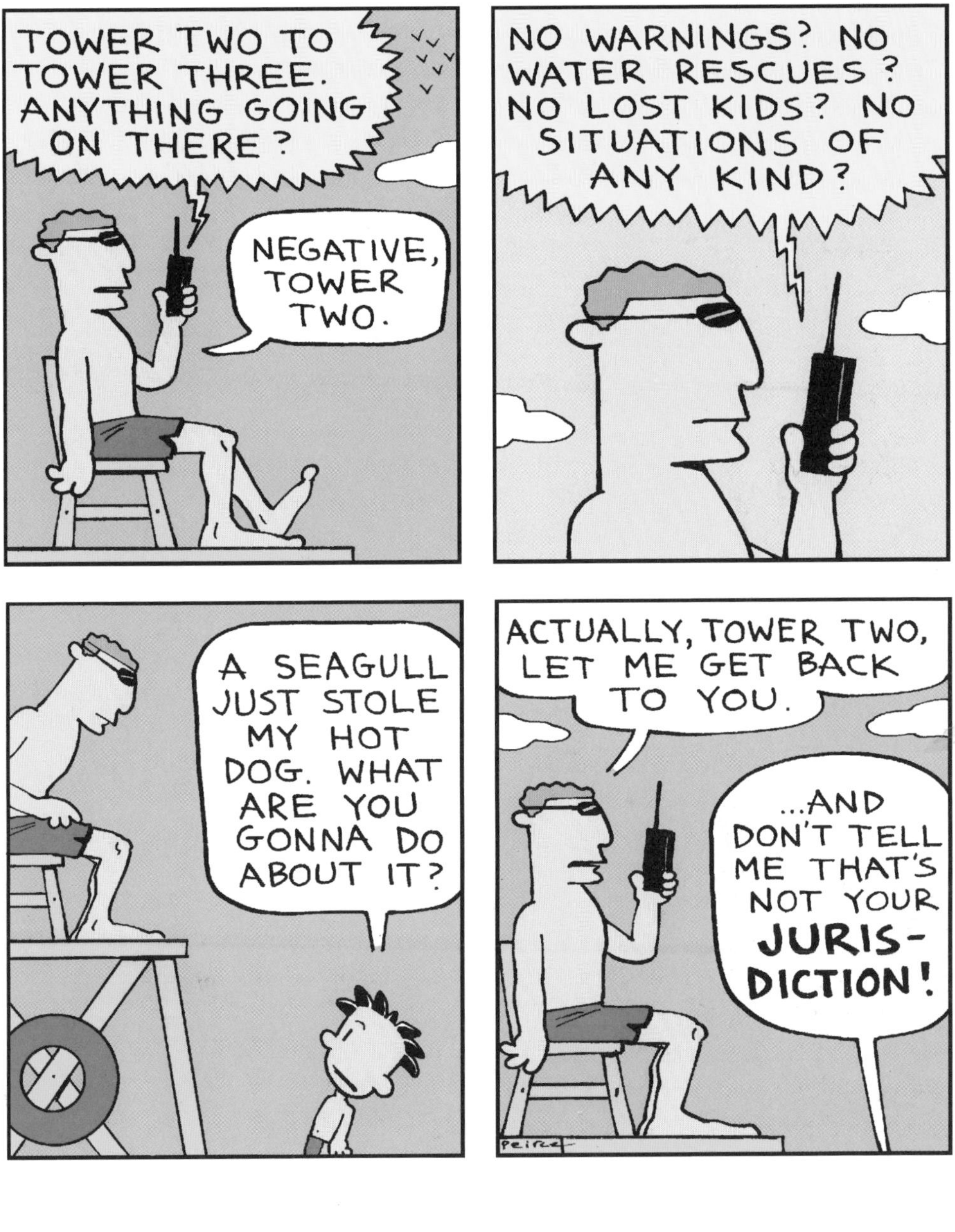
TOWER TWO TO TOWER THREE. ANYTHING GOING ON THERE?
NEGATIVE, TOWER TWO.
NO WARNINGS? NO WATER RESCUES? NO LOST KIDS? NO SITUATIONS OF ANY KIND?
A SEAGULL JUST STOLE MY HOT DOG. WHAT ARE YOU GONNA DO ABOUT IT?
ACTUALLY, TOWER TWO, LET ME GET BACK TO YOU.
...AND DON'T TELL ME THAT'S NOT YOUR **JURIS-DICTION!**
PEIRCE

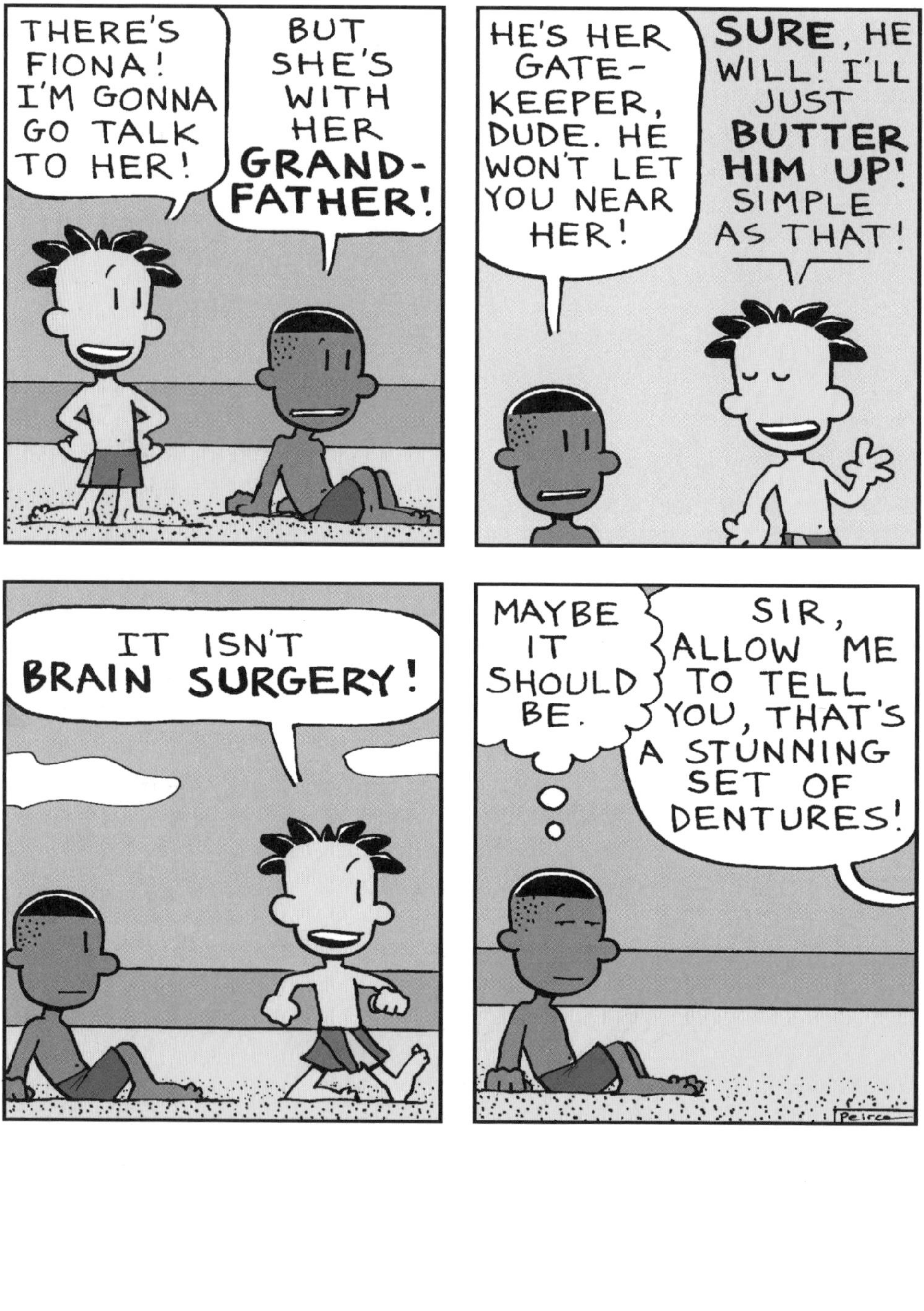
THERE'S FIONA! I'M GONNA GO TALK TO HER!
BUT SHE'S WITH HER **GRAND-FATHER!**
HE'S HER GATE-KEEPER, DUDE. HE WON'T LET YOU NEAR HER!
SURE, HE WILL! I'LL JUST **BUTTER HIM UP!** SIMPLE AS THAT!
IT ISN'T **BRAIN SURGERY!**
MAYBE IT SHOULD BE.
SIR, ALLOW ME TO TELL YOU, THAT'S A STUNNING SET OF DENTURES!
Peirce

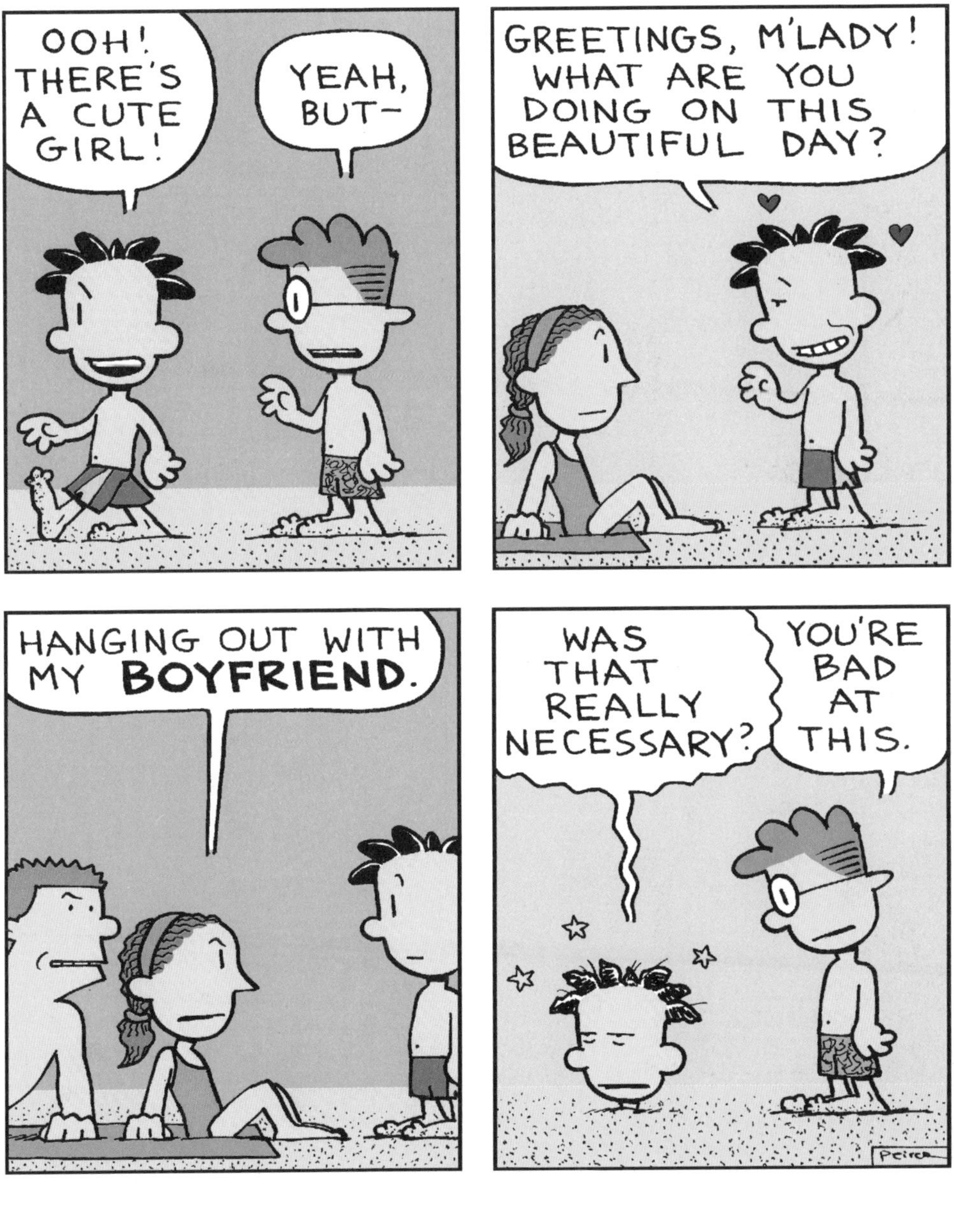
OOH! THERE'S A CUTE GIRL!
YEAH, BUT–
GREETINGS, M'LADY! WHAT ARE YOU DOING ON THIS BEAUTIFUL DAY?
HANGING OUT WITH MY **BOYFRIEND**.
WAS THAT REALLY NECESSARY?
YOU'RE BAD AT THIS.

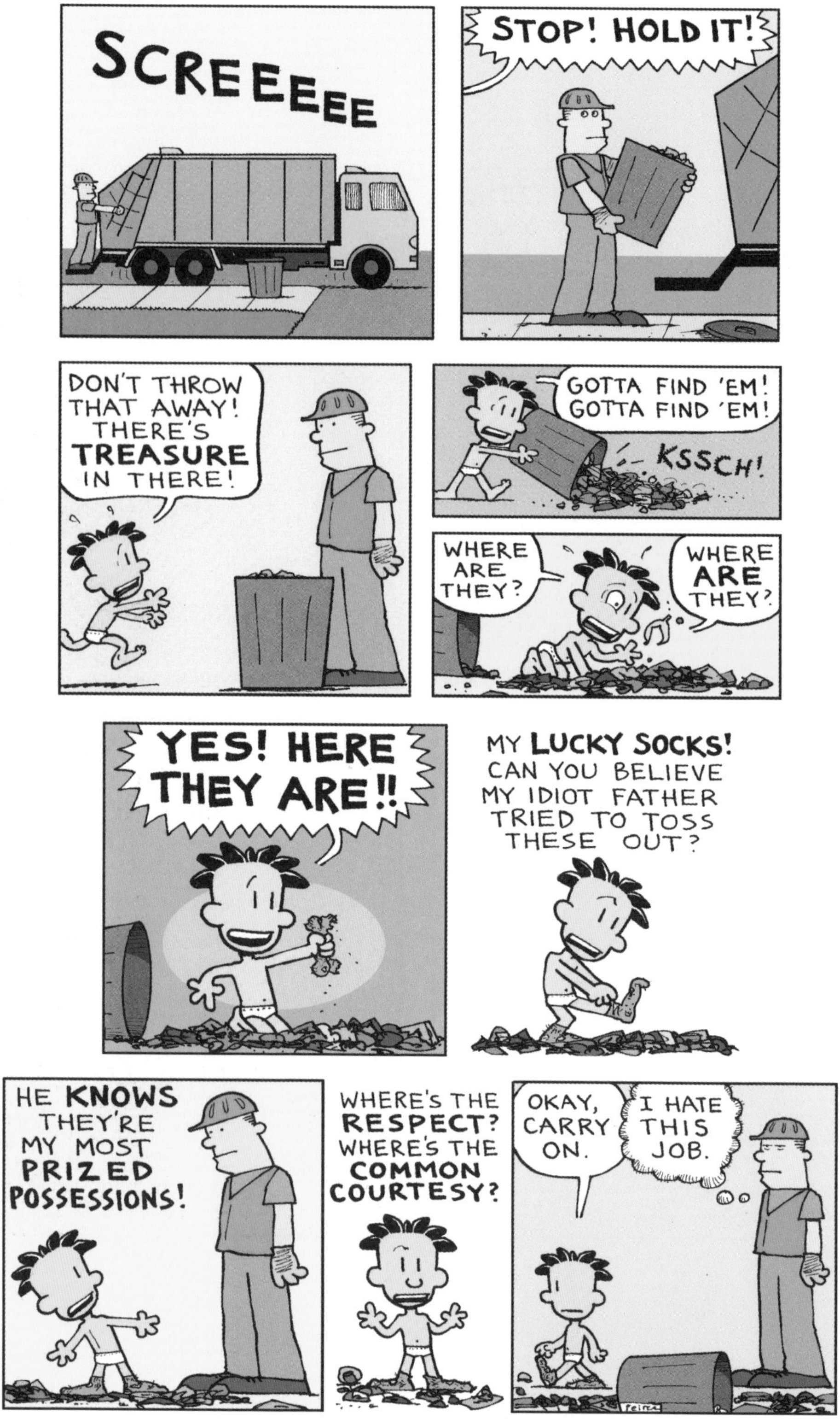
SCREEEEEE
STOP! HOLD IT!
DON'T THROW THAT AWAY! THERE'S TREASURE IN THERE!
GOTTA FIND 'EM! GOTTA FIND 'EM!
KSSCH!
WHERE ARE THEY?
WHERE ARE THEY?
YES! HERE THEY ARE!!
MY LUCKY SOCKS! CAN YOU BELIEVE MY IDIOT FATHER TRIED TO TOSS THESE OUT?
HE KNOWS THEY'RE MY MOST PRIZED POSSESSIONS!
WHERE'S THE RESPECT? WHERE'S THE COMMON COURTESY?
OKAY, CARRY ON.
I HATE THIS JOB.

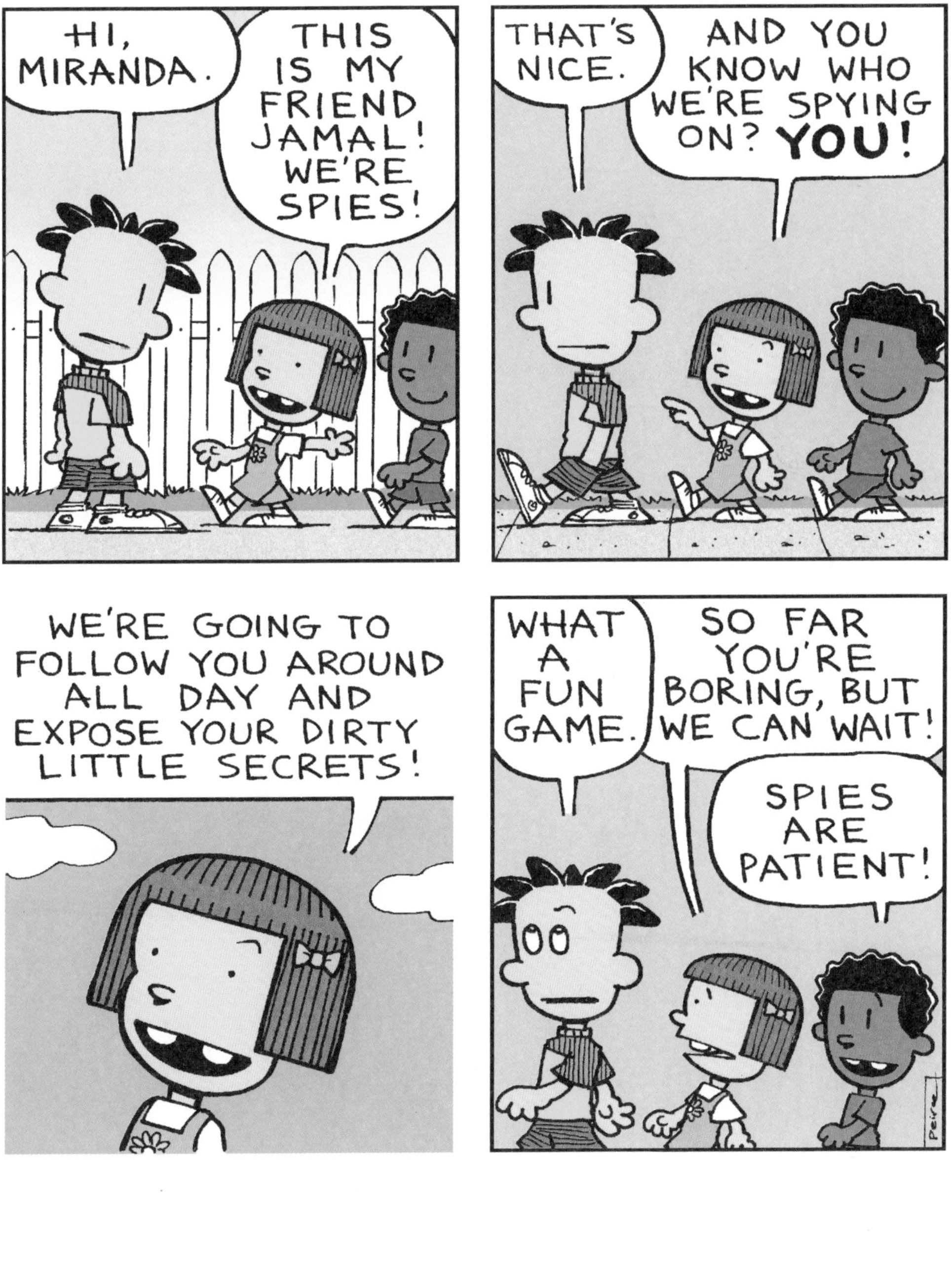

HI, MIRANDA.
THIS IS MY FRIEND JAMAL! WE'RE SPIES!
THAT'S NICE.
AND YOU KNOW WHO WE'RE SPYING ON? **YOU!**
WE'RE GOING TO FOLLOW YOU AROUND ALL DAY AND EXPOSE YOUR DIRTY LITTLE SECRETS!
WHAT A FUN GAME.
SO FAR YOU'RE BORING, BUT WE CAN WAIT!
SPIES ARE PATIENT!

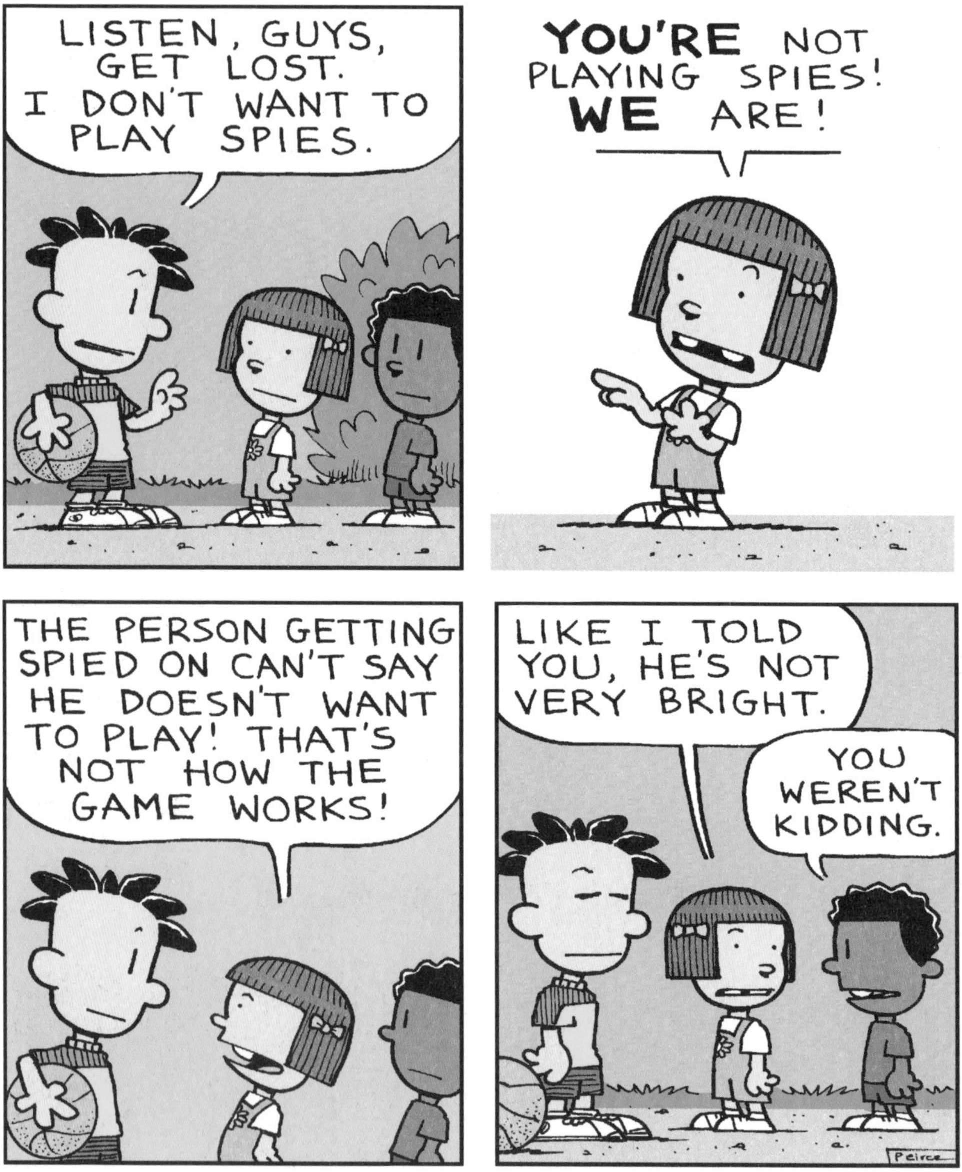
LISTEN, GUYS, GET LOST. I DON'T WANT TO PLAY SPIES.
YOU'RE NOT PLAYING SPIES! WE ARE!
THE PERSON GETTING SPIED ON CAN'T SAY HE DOESN'T WANT TO PLAY! THAT'S NOT HOW THE GAME WORKS!
LIKE I TOLD YOU, HE'S NOT VERY BRIGHT.
YOU WEREN'T KIDDING.
Peirce

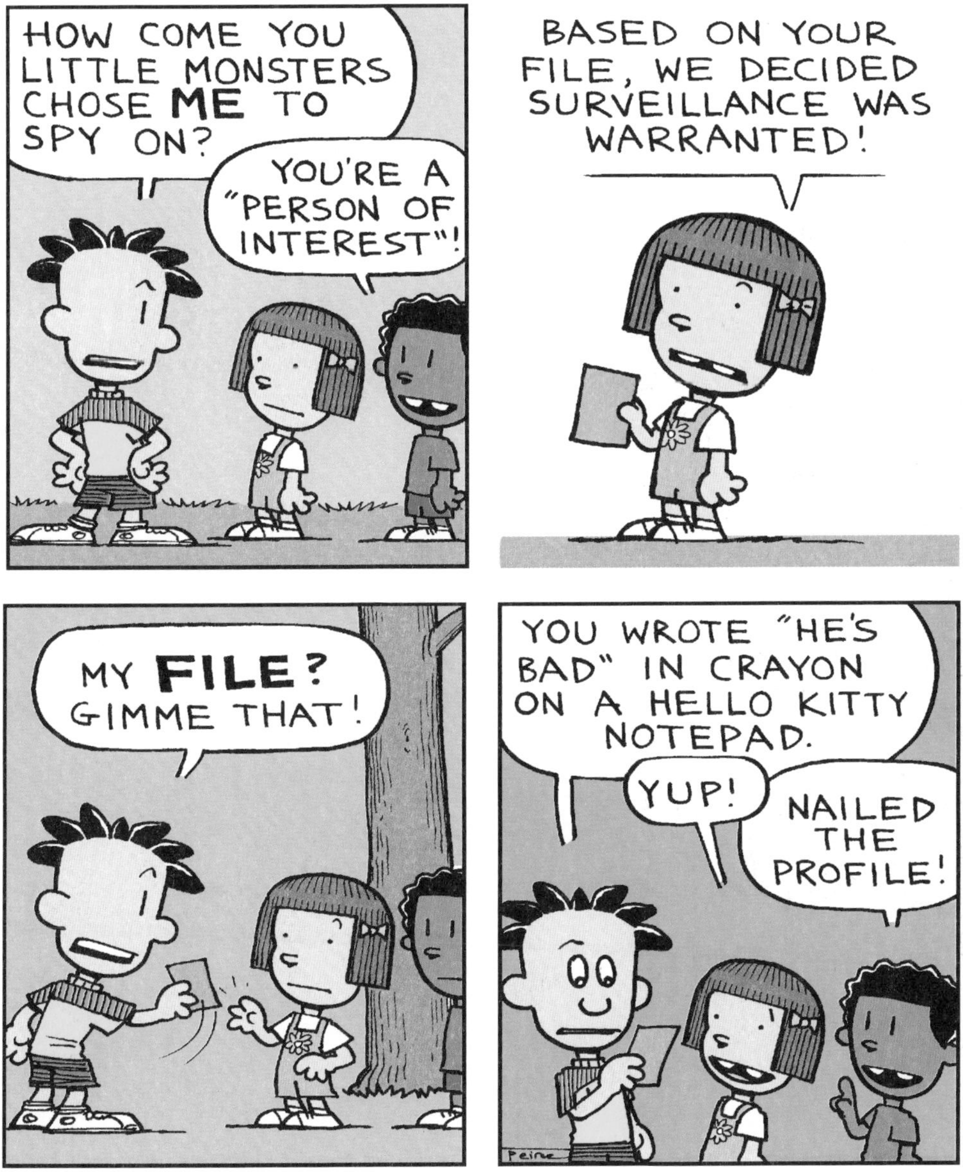
HOW COME YOU LITTLE MONSTERS CHOSE **ME** TO SPY ON?
YOU'RE A "PERSON OF INTEREST"!
BASED ON YOUR FILE, WE DECIDED SURVEILLANCE WAS WARRANTED!
MY **FILE**? GIMME THAT!
YOU WROTE "HE'S BAD" IN CRAYON ON A HELLO KITTY NOTEPAD.
YUP!
NAILED THE PROFILE!
Peirce

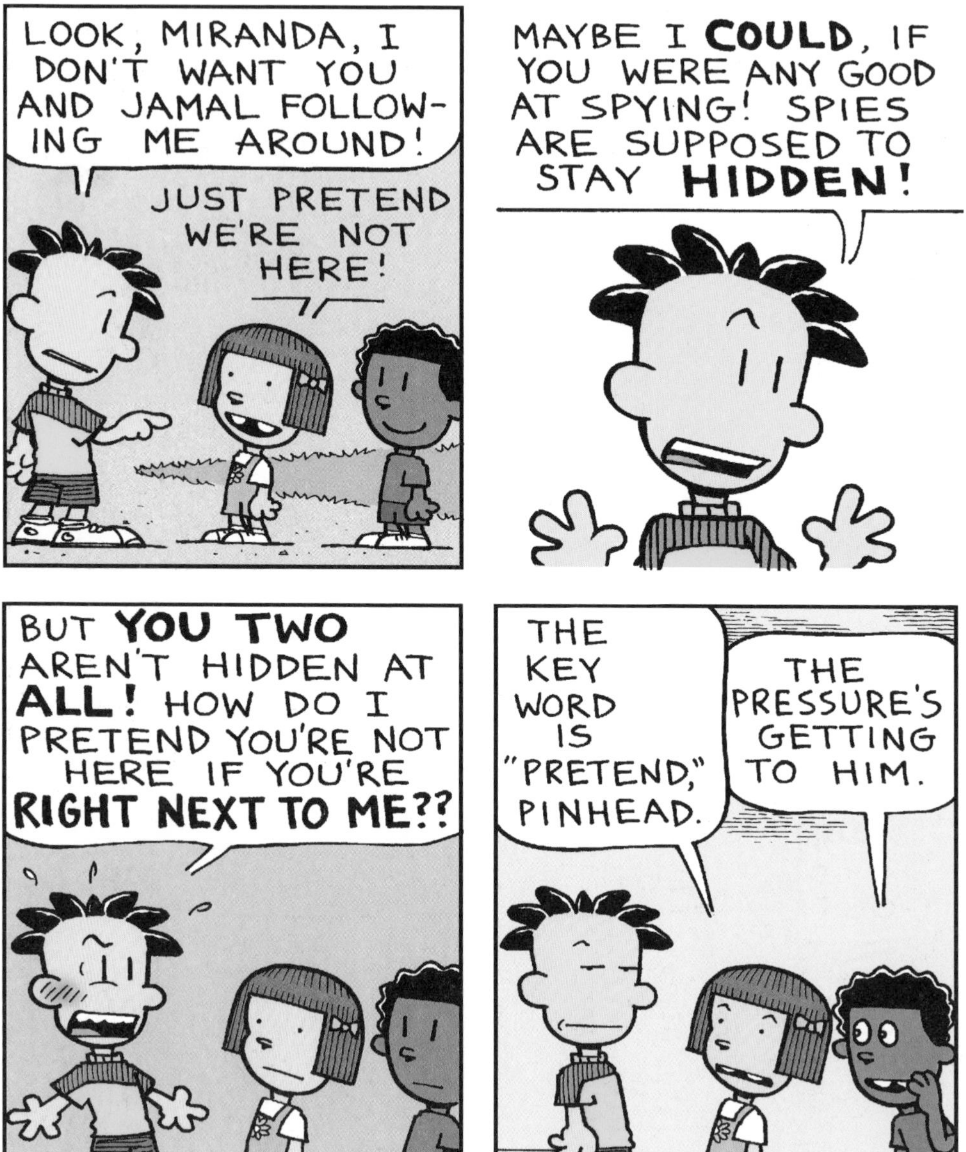
LOOK, MIRANDA, I DON'T WANT YOU AND JAMAL FOLLOW-ING ME AROUND!
JUST PRETEND WE'RE NOT HERE!
MAYBE I **COULD**, IF YOU WERE ANY GOOD AT SPYING! SPIES ARE SUPPOSED TO STAY **HIDDEN**!
BUT **YOU TWO** AREN'T HIDDEN AT **ALL**! HOW DO I PRETEND YOU'RE NOT HERE IF YOU'RE **RIGHT NEXT TO ME??**
THE KEY WORD IS "PRETEND," PINHEAD.
THE PRESSURE'S GETTING TO HIM.
Peirce

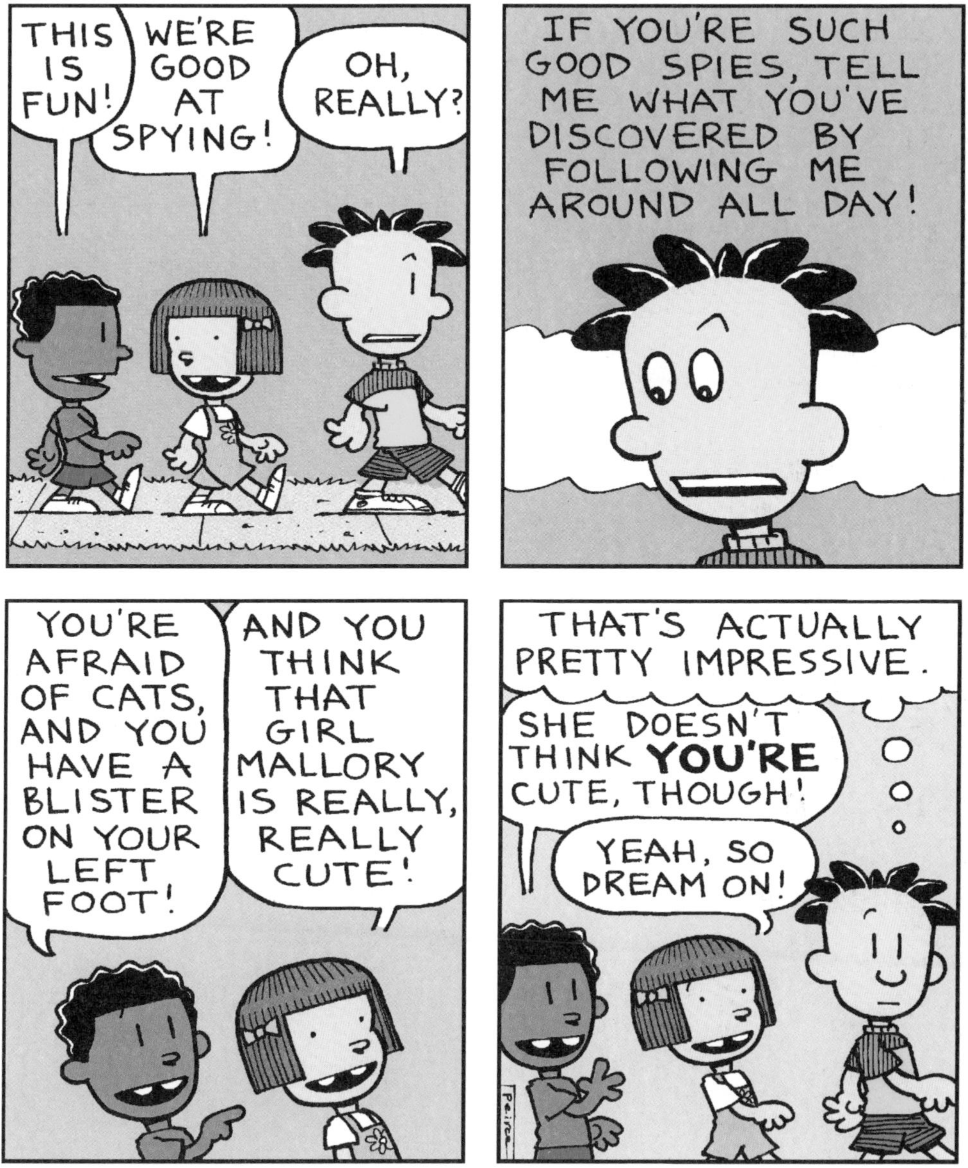
THIS IS FUN!
WE'RE GOOD AT SPYING!
OH, REALLY?
IF YOU'RE SUCH GOOD SPIES, TELL ME WHAT YOU'VE DISCOVERED BY FOLLOWING ME AROUND ALL DAY!
YOU'RE AFRAID OF CATS, AND YOU HAVE A BLISTER ON YOUR LEFT FOOT!
AND YOU THINK THAT GIRL MALLORY IS REALLY, REALLY CUTE!
THAT'S ACTUALLY PRETTY IMPRESSIVE.
SHE DOESN'T THINK **YOU'RE** CUTE, THOUGH!
YEAH, SO DREAM ON!
Peirce

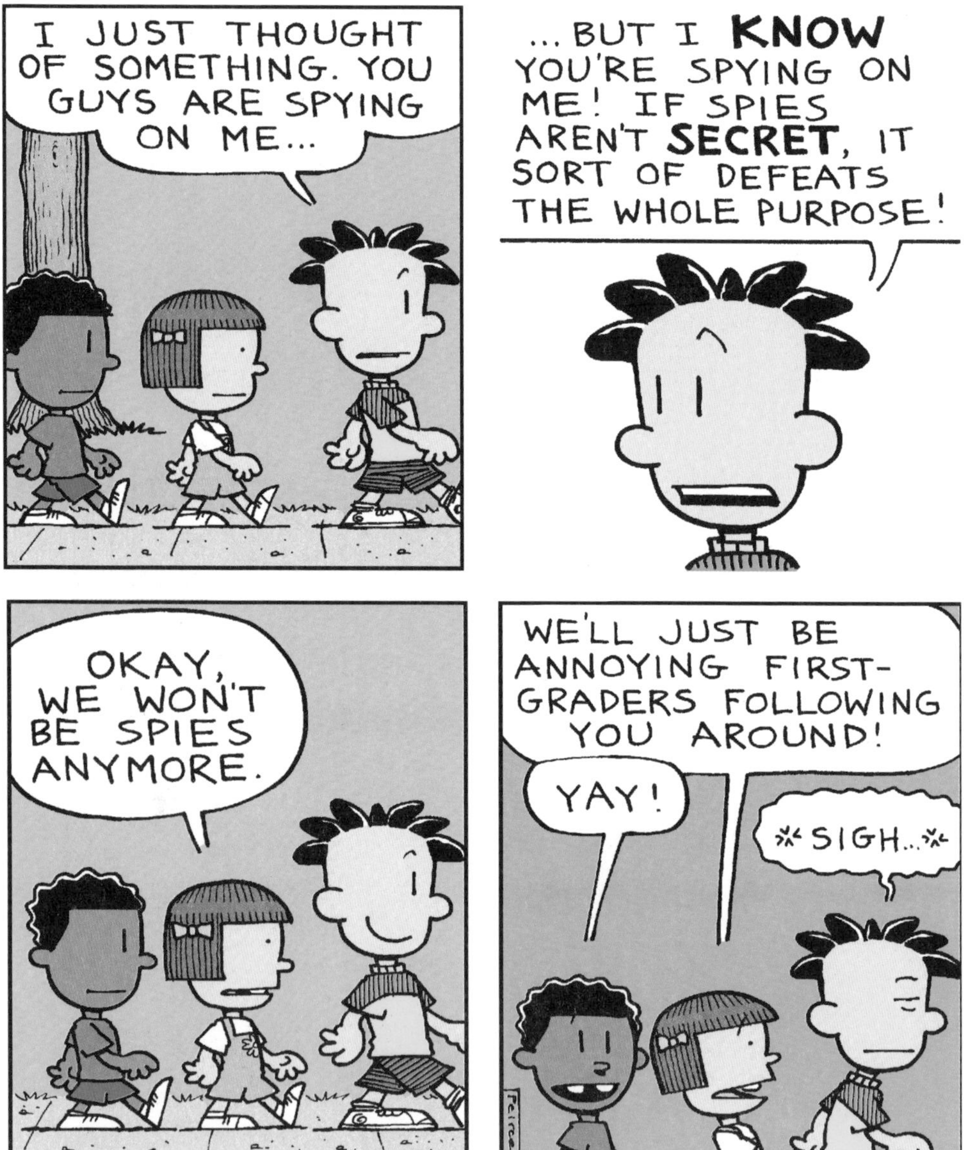
I JUST THOUGHT OF SOMETHING. YOU GUYS ARE SPYING ON ME...
...BUT I KNOW YOU'RE SPYING ON ME! IF SPIES AREN'T SECRET, IT SORT OF DEFEATS THE WHOLE PURPOSE!
OKAY, WE WON'T BE SPIES ANYMORE.
WE'LL JUST BE ANNOYING FIRST-GRADERS FOLLOWING YOU AROUND!
YAY!
SIGH...
Peirce

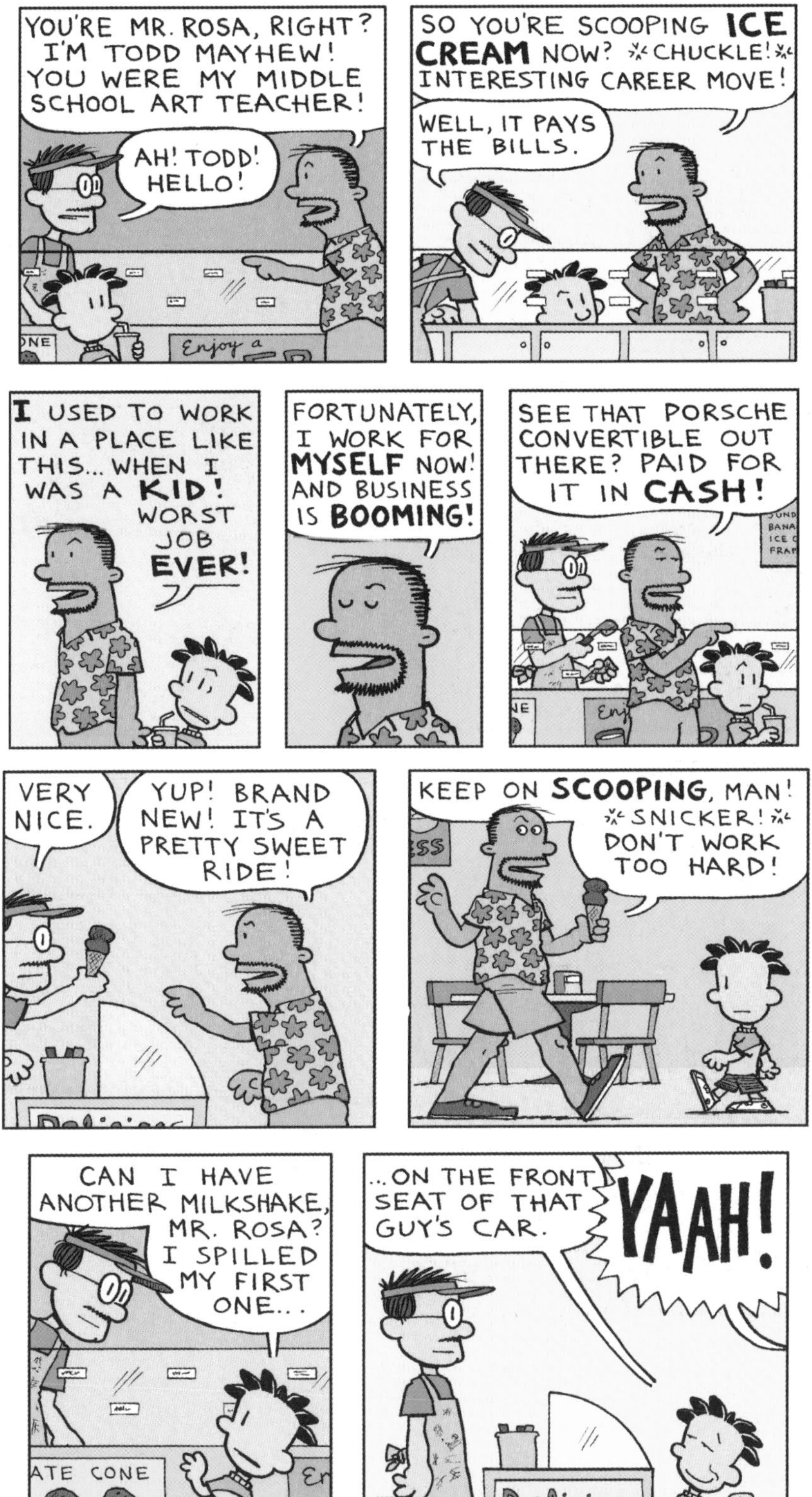
YOU'RE MR. ROSA, RIGHT? I'M TODD MAYHEW! YOU WERE MY MIDDLE SCHOOL ART TEACHER!
AH! TODD! HELLO!
SO YOU'RE SCOOPING ICE CREAM NOW? *CHUCKLE!* INTERESTING CAREER MOVE!
WELL, IT PAYS THE BILLS.
I USED TO WORK IN A PLACE LIKE THIS... WHEN I WAS A KID! WORST JOB EVER!
FORTUNATELY, I WORK FOR MYSELF NOW! AND BUSINESS IS BOOMING!
SEE THAT PORSCHE CONVERTIBLE OUT THERE? PAID FOR IT IN CASH!
VERY NICE.
YUP! BRAND NEW! IT'S A PRETTY SWEET RIDE!
KEEP ON SCOOPING, MAN! *SNICKER!* DON'T WORK TOO HARD!
CAN I HAVE ANOTHER MILKSHAKE, MR. ROSA? I SPILLED MY FIRST ONE...
...ON THE FRONT SEAT OF THAT GUY'S CAR.
YAAH!

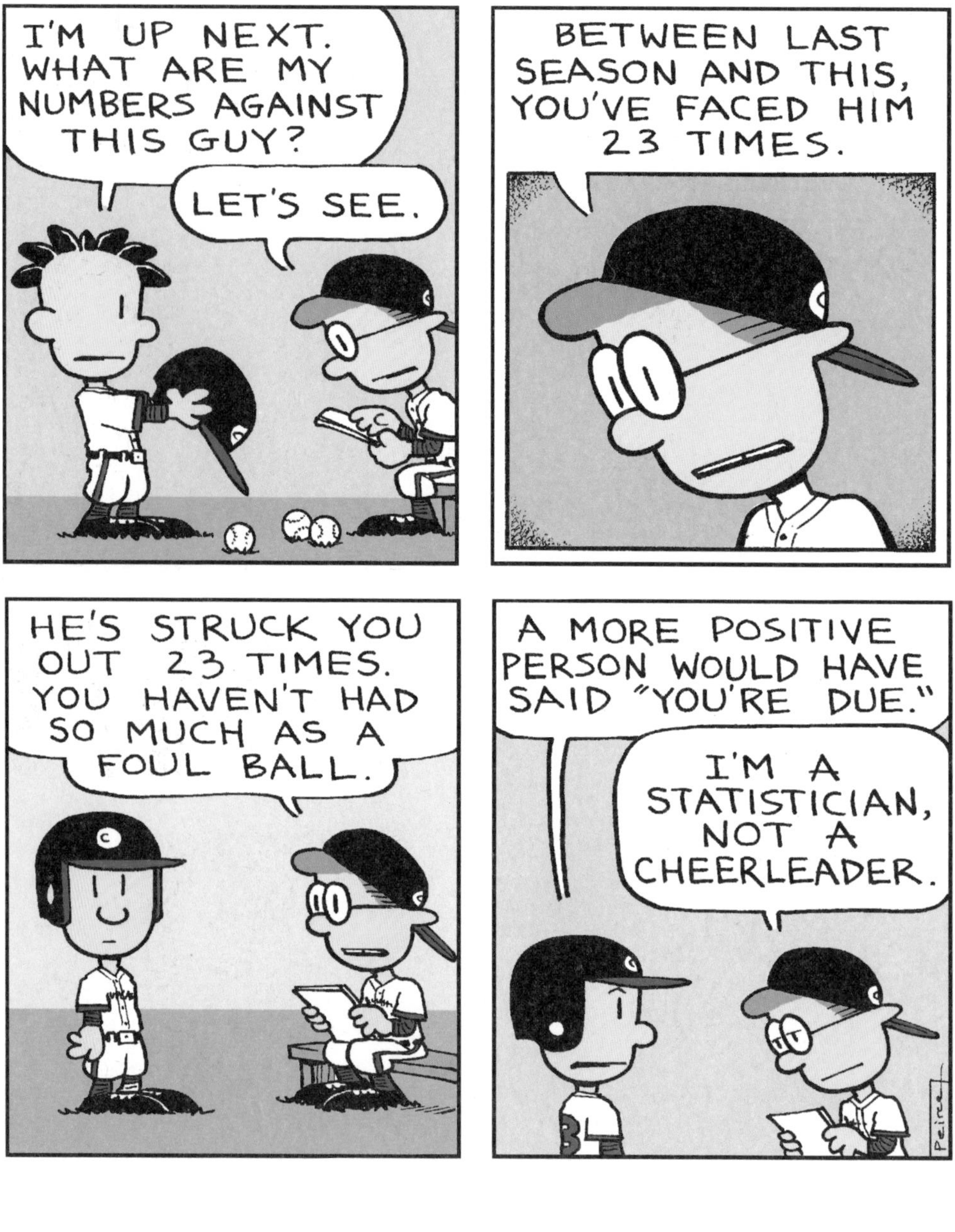
I'M UP NEXT. WHAT ARE MY NUMBERS AGAINST THIS GUY?
LET'S SEE.
BETWEEN LAST SEASON AND THIS, YOU'VE FACED HIM 23 TIMES.
HE'S STRUCK YOU OUT 23 TIMES. YOU HAVEN'T HAD SO MUCH AS A FOUL BALL.
A MORE POSITIVE PERSON WOULD HAVE SAID "YOU'RE DUE."
I'M A STATISTICIAN, NOT A CHEERLEADER.
Peirce

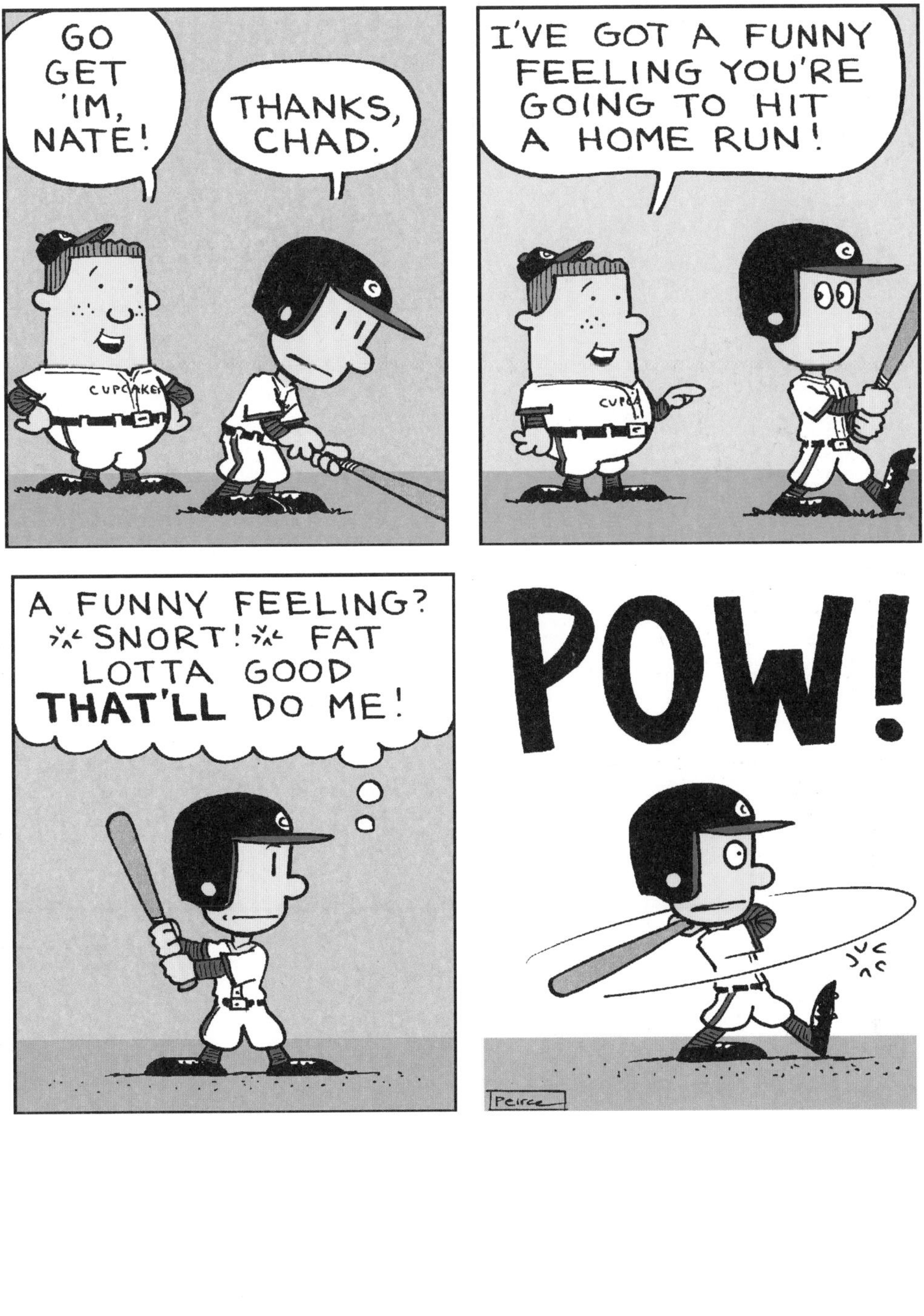
GO GET 'IM, NATE!
THANKS, CHAD.
I'VE GOT A FUNNY FEELING YOU'RE GOING TO HIT A HOME RUN!
A FUNNY FEELING? SNORT! FAT LOTTA GOOD **THAT'LL** DO ME!
POW!
Peirce

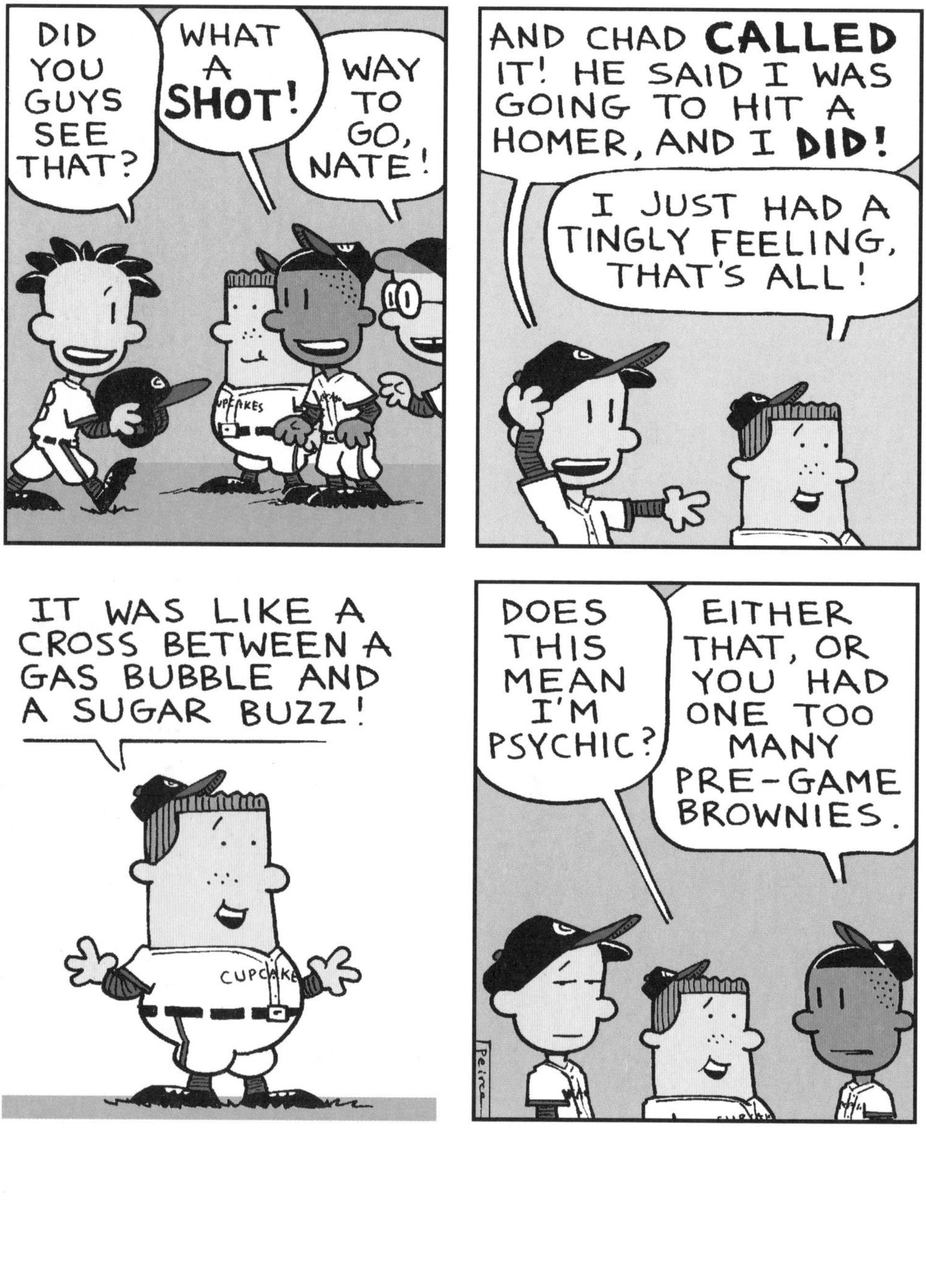
DID YOU GUYS SEE THAT?
WHAT A SHOT!
WAY TO GO, NATE!
AND CHAD CALLED IT! HE SAID I WAS GOING TO HIT A HOMER, AND I DID!
I JUST HAD A TINGLY FEELING, THAT'S ALL!
IT WAS LIKE A CROSS BETWEEN A GAS BUBBLE AND A SUGAR BUZZ!
DOES THIS MEAN I'M PSYCHIC?
EITHER THAT, OR YOU HAD ONE TOO MANY PRE-GAME BROWNIES.

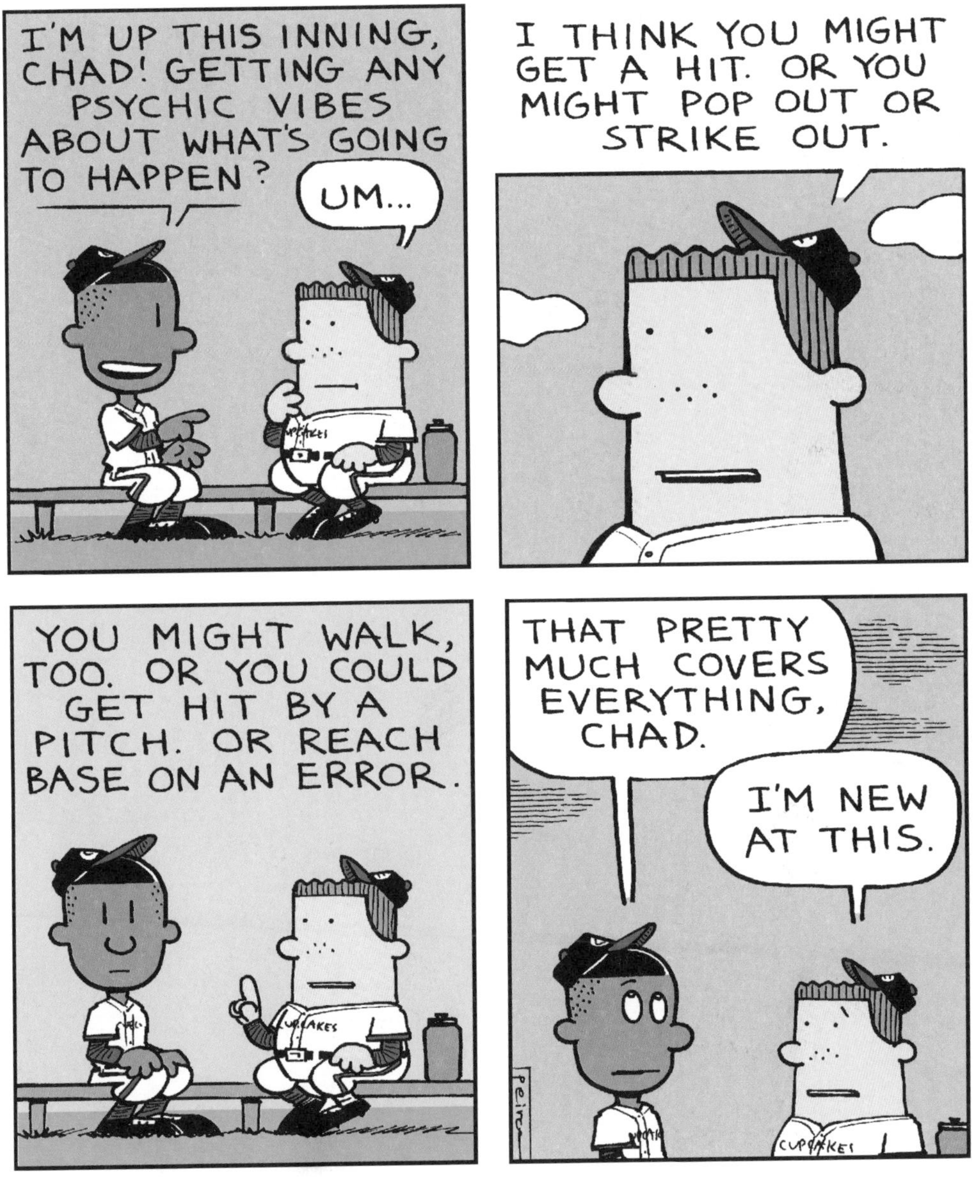
I'M UP THIS INNING, CHAD! GETTING ANY PSYCHIC VIBES ABOUT WHAT'S GOING TO HAPPEN?
UM...
I THINK YOU MIGHT GET A HIT. OR YOU MIGHT POP OUT OR STRIKE OUT.
YOU MIGHT WALK, TOO. OR YOU COULD GET HIT BY A PITCH. OR REACH BASE ON AN ERROR.
THAT PRETTY MUCH COVERS EVERYTHING, CHAD.
I'M NEW AT THIS.
peirce
CUPCAKES

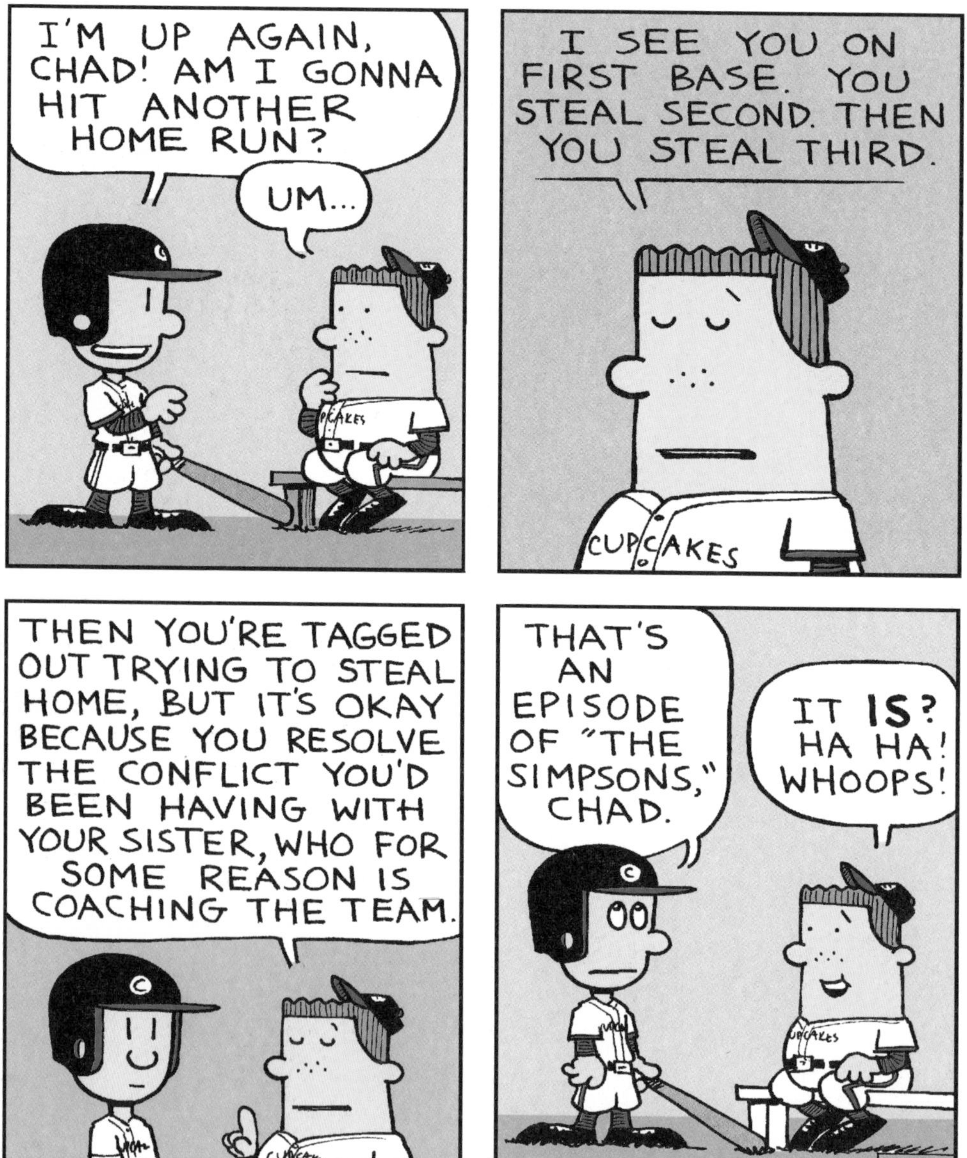
I'M UP AGAIN, CHAD! AM I GONNA HIT ANOTHER HOME RUN?
UM...
CUPCAKES
I SEE YOU ON FIRST BASE. YOU STEAL SECOND. THEN YOU STEAL THIRD.
CUPCAKES
THEN YOU'RE TAGGED OUT TRYING TO STEAL HOME, BUT IT'S OKAY BECAUSE YOU RESOLVE THE CONFLICT YOU'D BEEN HAVING WITH YOUR SISTER, WHO FOR SOME REASON IS COACHING THE TEAM.
THAT'S AN EPISODE OF "THE SIMPSONS," CHAD.
IT **IS**? HA HA! WHOOPS!
peirce

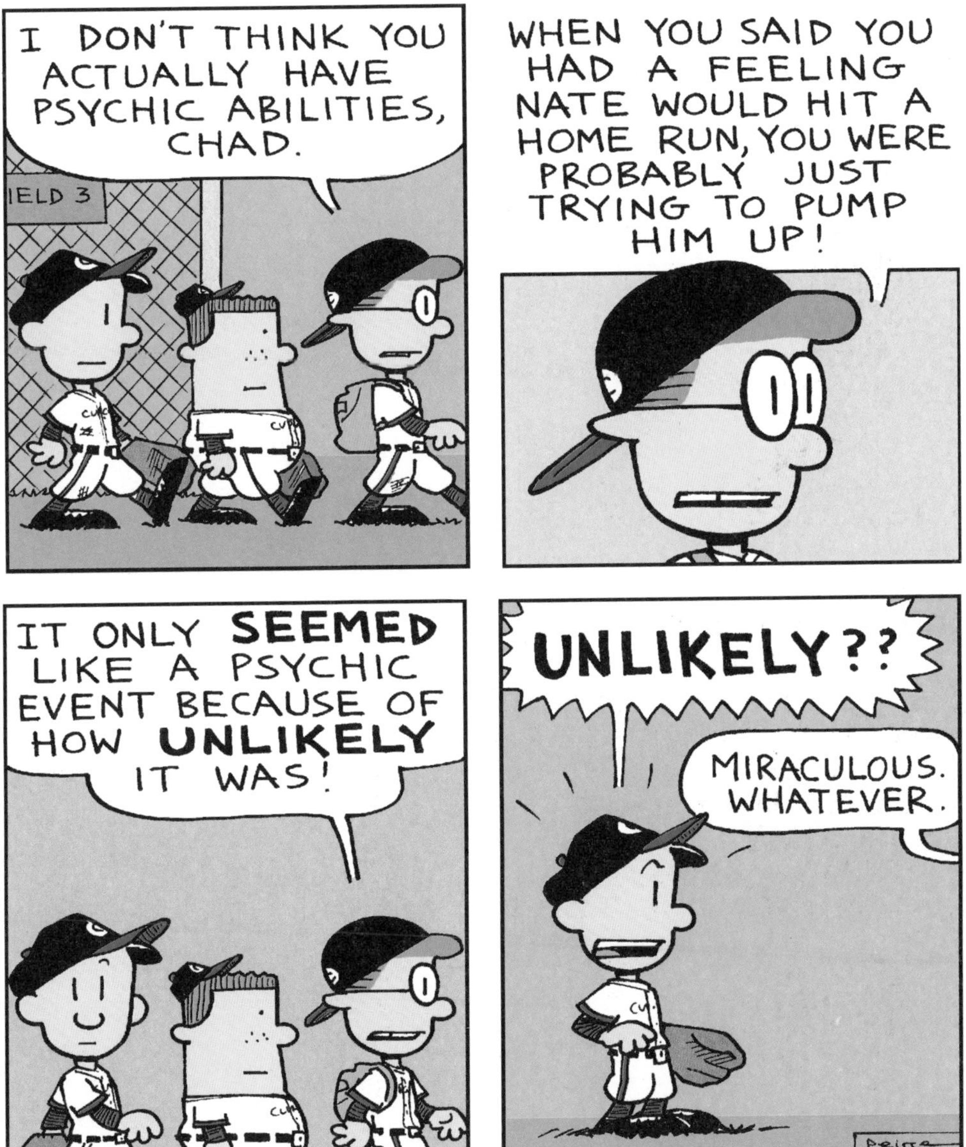
I DON'T THINK YOU ACTUALLY HAVE PSYCHIC ABILITIES, CHAD.
IELD 3
WHEN YOU SAID YOU HAD A FEELING NATE WOULD HIT A HOME RUN, YOU WERE PROBABLY JUST TRYING TO PUMP HIM UP!
IT ONLY **SEEMED** LIKE A PSYCHIC EVENT BECAUSE OF HOW **UNLIKELY** IT WAS!
UNLIKELY??
MIRACULOUS. WHATEVER.
Peirce

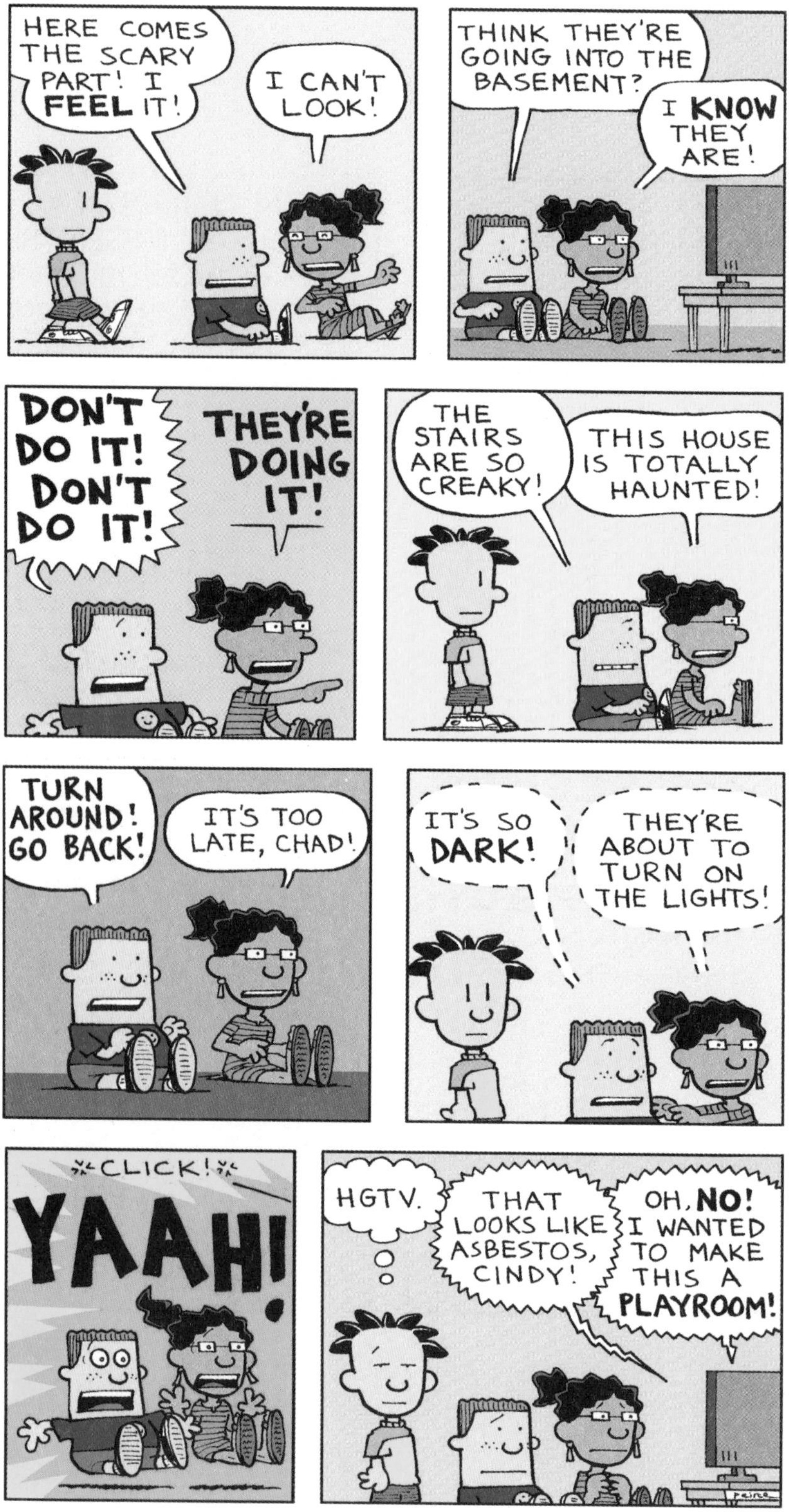
HERE COMES THE SCARY PART! I FEEL IT!
I CAN'T LOOK!
THINK THEY'RE GOING INTO THE BASEMENT?
I KNOW THEY ARE!
DON'T DO IT! DON'T DO IT!
THEY'RE DOING IT!
THE STAIRS ARE SO CREAKY!
THIS HOUSE IS TOTALLY HAUNTED!
TURN AROUND! GO BACK!
IT'S TOO LATE, CHAD!
IT'S SO DARK!
THEY'RE ABOUT TO TURN ON THE LIGHTS!
CLICK!
YAAH!
HGTV.
THAT LOOKS LIKE ASBESTOS, CINDY!
OH, NO! I WANTED TO MAKE THIS A PLAYROOM!

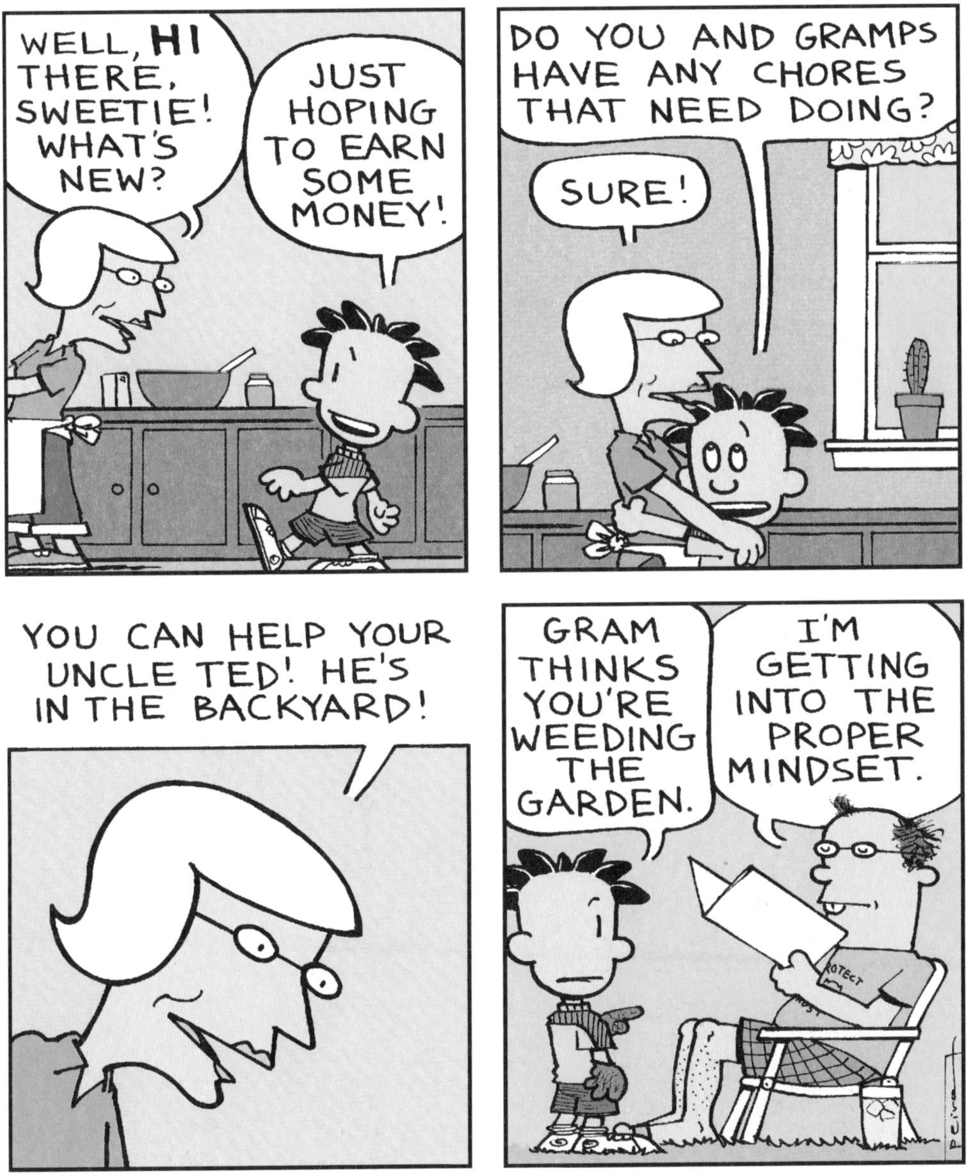
WELL, **HI** THERE, SWEETIE! WHAT'S NEW?
JUST HOPING TO EARN SOME MONEY!
DO YOU AND GRAMPS HAVE ANY CHORES THAT NEED DOING?
SURE!
YOU CAN HELP YOUR UNCLE TED! HE'S IN THE BACKYARD!
GRAM THINKS YOU'RE WEEDING THE GARDEN.
I'M GETTING INTO THE PROPER MINDSET.

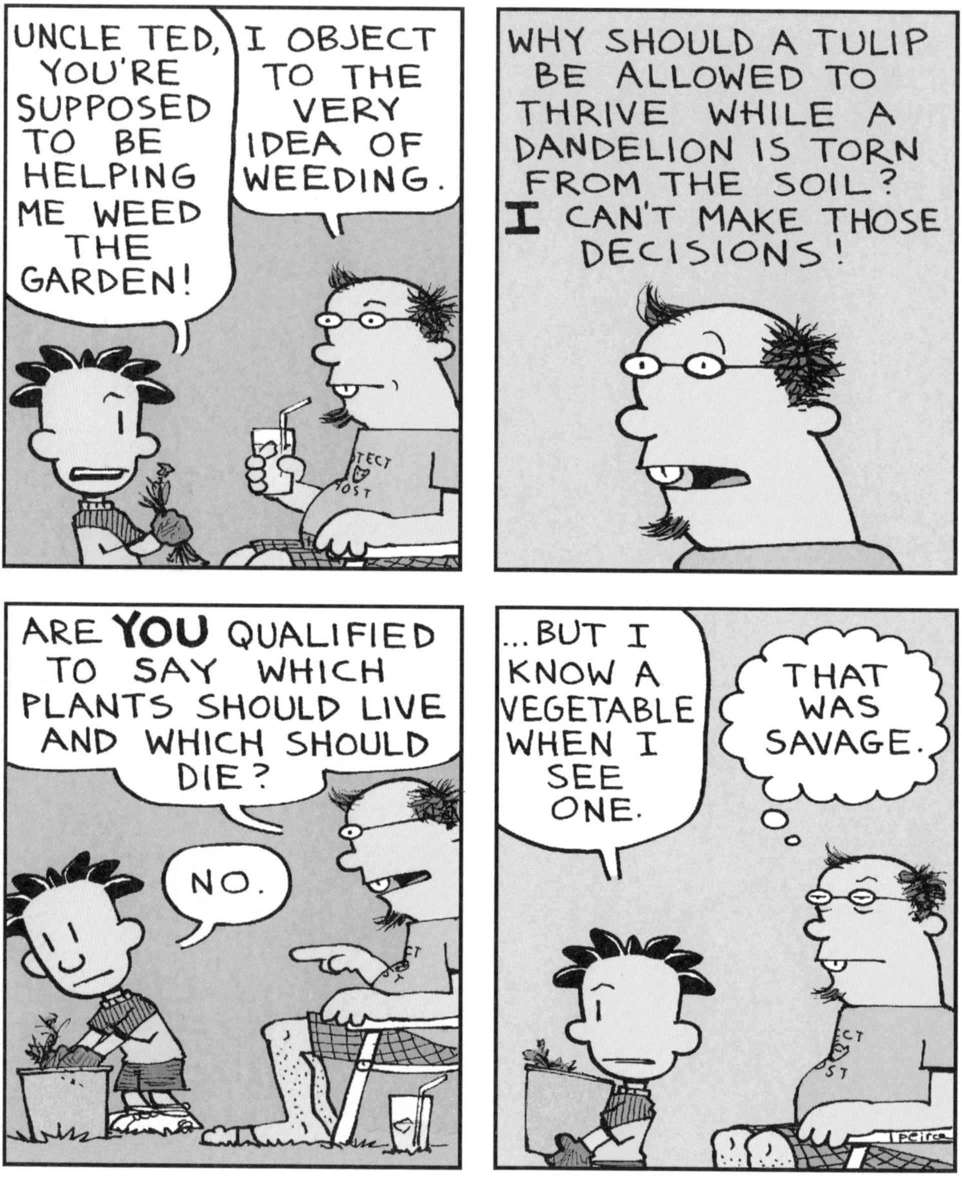
UNCLE TED, YOU'RE SUPPOSED TO BE HELPING ME WEED THE GARDEN!
I OBJECT TO THE VERY IDEA OF WEEDING.
WHY SHOULD A TULIP BE ALLOWED TO THRIVE WHILE A DANDELION IS TORN FROM THE SOIL? I CAN'T MAKE THOSE DECISIONS!
ARE YOU QUALIFIED TO SAY WHICH PLANTS SHOULD LIVE AND WHICH SHOULD DIE?
NO.
...BUT I KNOW A VEGETABLE WHEN I SEE ONE.
THAT WAS SAVAGE.

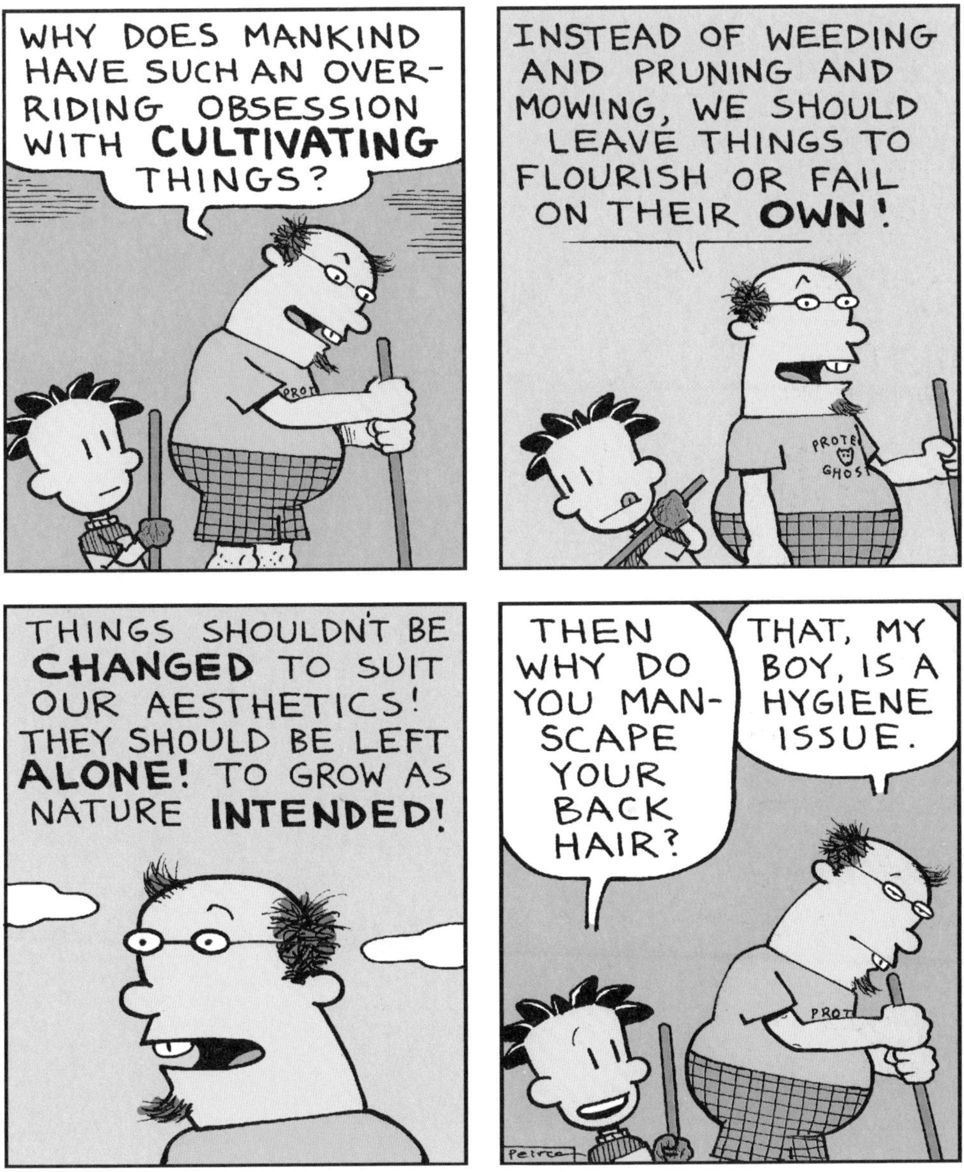
WHY DOES MANKIND HAVE SUCH AN OVER-RIDING OBSESSION WITH **CULTIVATING** THINGS?
INSTEAD OF WEEDING AND PRUNING AND MOWING, WE SHOULD LEAVE THINGS TO FLOURISH OR FAIL ON THEIR **OWN**!
THINGS SHOULDN'T BE **CHANGED** TO SUIT OUR AESTHETICS! THEY SHOULD BE LEFT **ALONE!** TO GROW AS NATURE **INTENDED!**
THEN WHY DO YOU MAN-SCAPE YOUR BACK HAIR?
THAT, MY BOY, IS A HYGIENE ISSUE.

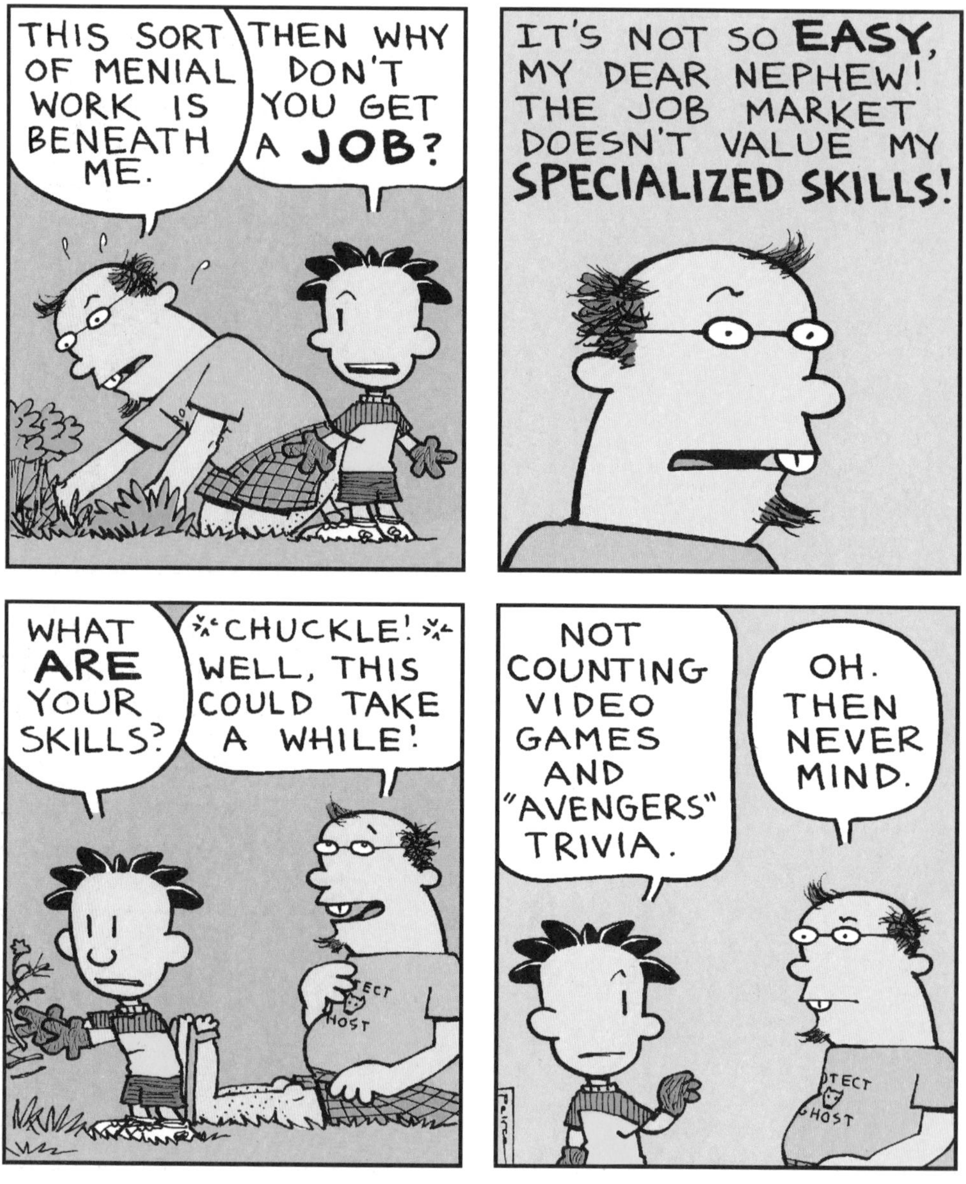
THIS SORT OF MENIAL WORK IS BENEATH ME.
THEN WHY DON'T YOU GET A JOB?
IT'S NOT SO EASY, MY DEAR NEPHEW! THE JOB MARKET DOESN'T VALUE MY SPECIALIZED SKILLS!
WHAT ARE YOUR SKILLS?
CHUCKLE! WELL, THIS COULD TAKE A WHILE!
NOT COUNTING VIDEO GAMES AND "AVENGERS" TRIVIA.
OH. THEN NEVER MIND.

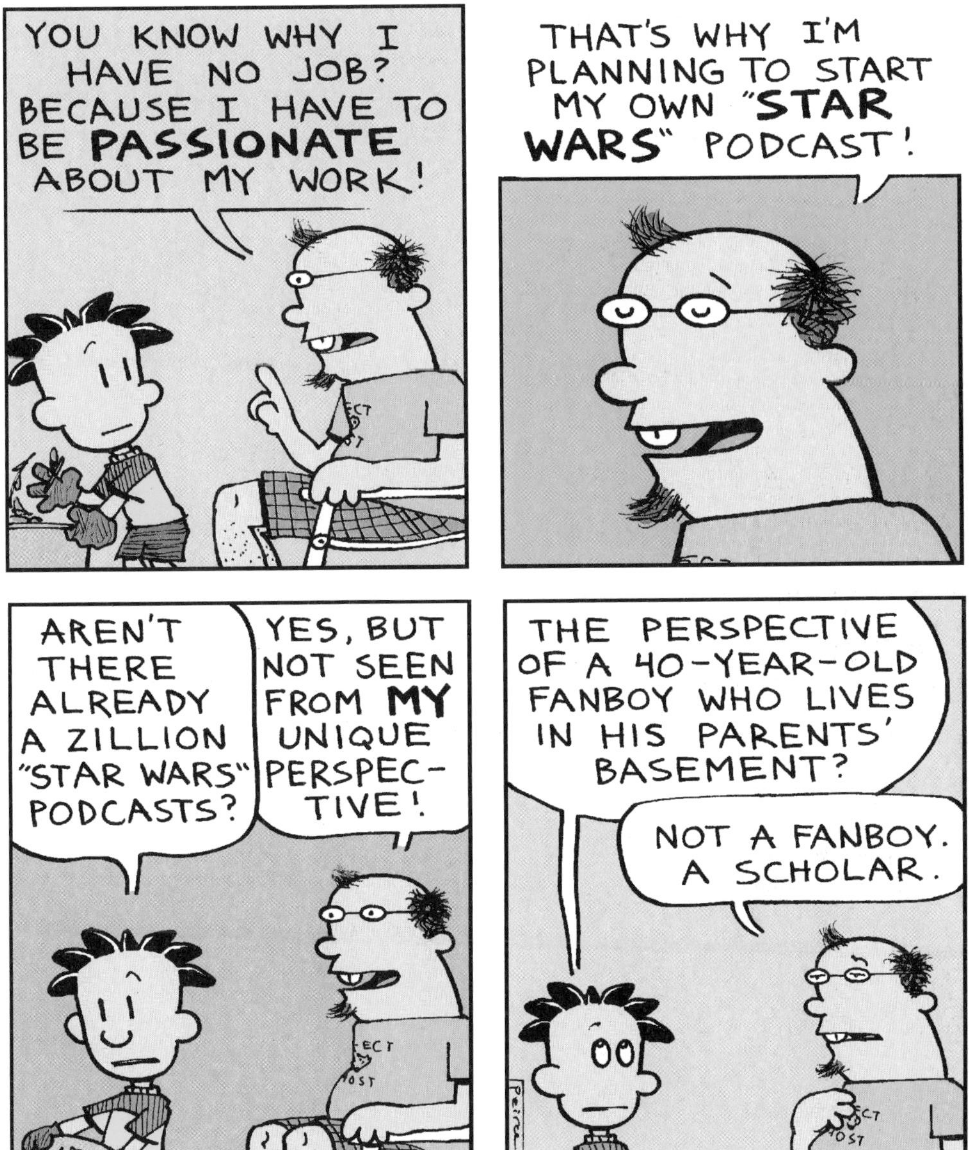
YOU KNOW WHY I HAVE NO JOB? BECAUSE I HAVE TO BE **PASSIONATE** ABOUT MY WORK!
THAT'S WHY I'M PLANNING TO START MY OWN "**STAR WARS**" PODCAST!
AREN'T THERE ALREADY A ZILLION "STAR WARS" PODCASTS?
YES, BUT NOT SEEN FROM **MY** UNIQUE PERSPECTIVE!
THE PERSPECTIVE OF A 40-YEAR-OLD FANBOY WHO LIVES IN HIS PARENTS' BASEMENT?
NOT A FANBOY. A SCHOLAR.

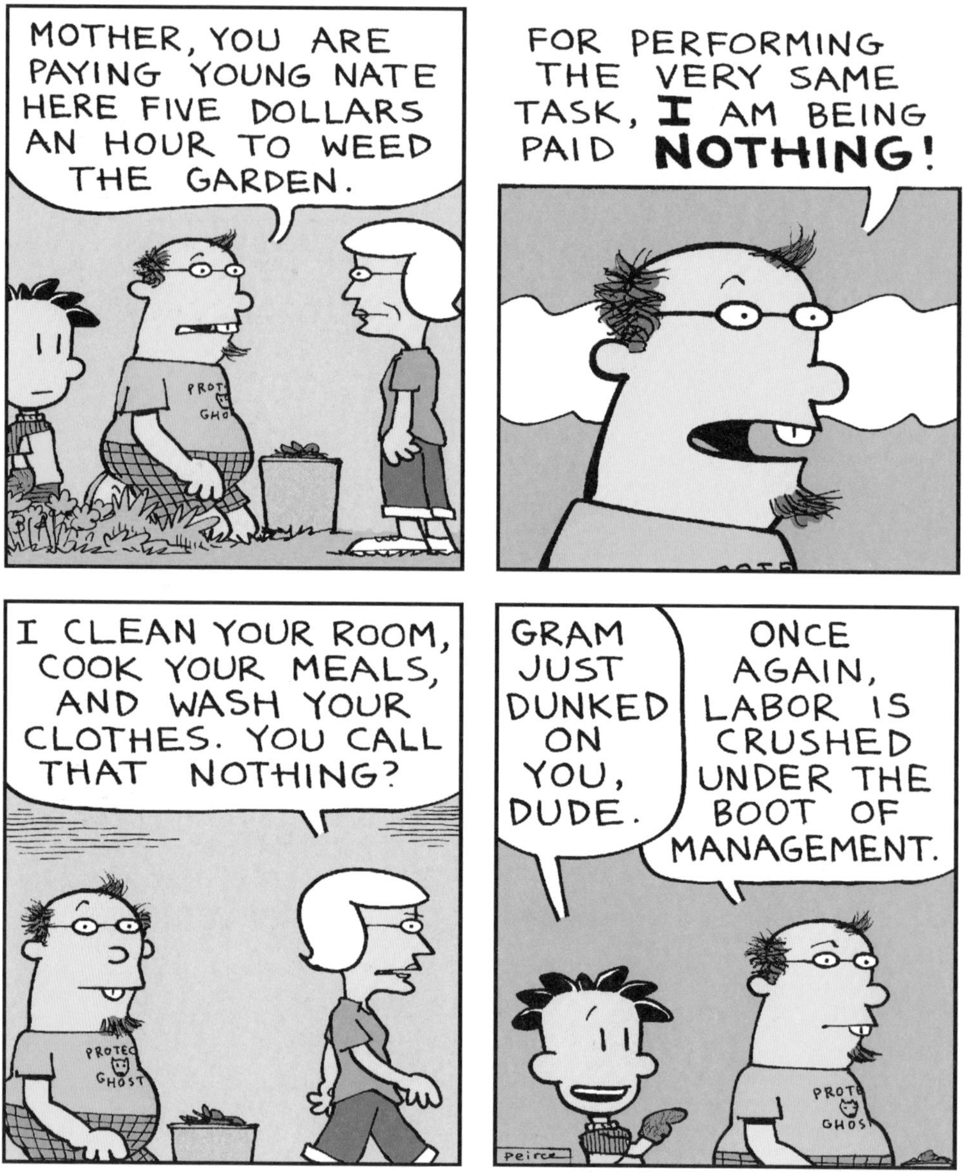
MOTHER, YOU ARE PAYING YOUNG NATE HERE FIVE DOLLARS AN HOUR TO WEED THE GARDEN.
FOR PERFORMING THE VERY SAME TASK, I AM BEING PAID NOTHING!
I CLEAN YOUR ROOM, COOK YOUR MEALS, AND WASH YOUR CLOTHES. YOU CALL THAT NOTHING?
GRAM JUST DUNKED ON YOU, DUDE.
ONCE AGAIN, LABOR IS CRUSHED UNDER THE BOOT OF MANAGEMENT.
peirce

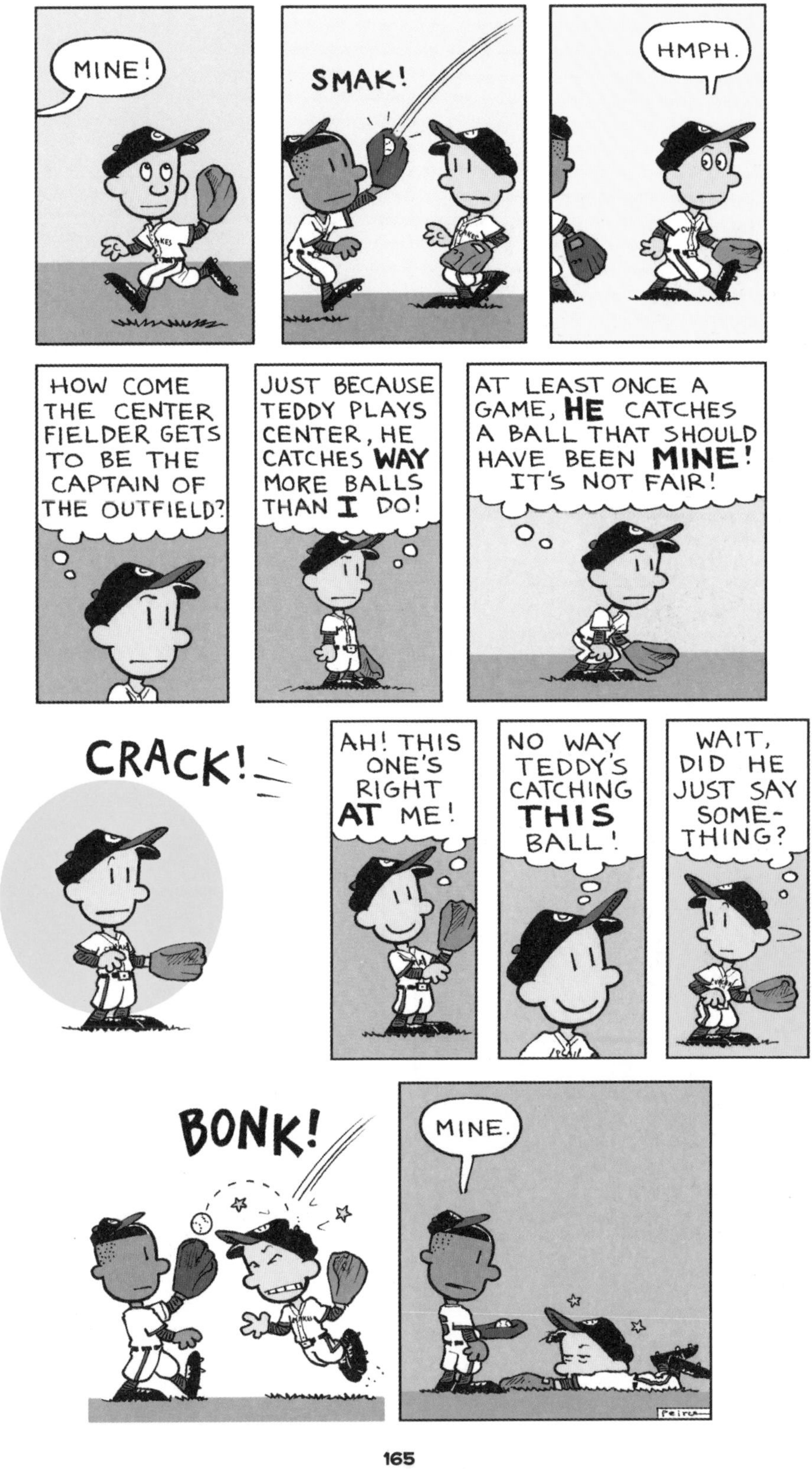
MINE!
SMAK!
HMPH.
HOW COME THE CENTER FIELDER GETS TO BE THE CAPTAIN OF THE OUTFIELD?
JUST BECAUSE TEDDY PLAYS CENTER, HE CATCHES WAY MORE BALLS THAN I DO!
AT LEAST ONCE A GAME, HE CATCHES A BALL THAT SHOULD HAVE BEEN MINE! IT'S NOT FAIR!
CRACK!
AH! THIS ONE'S RIGHT AT ME!
NO WAY TEDDY'S CATCHING THIS BALL!
WAIT, DID HE JUST SAY SOME-THING?
BONK!
MINE.
PEIRCE

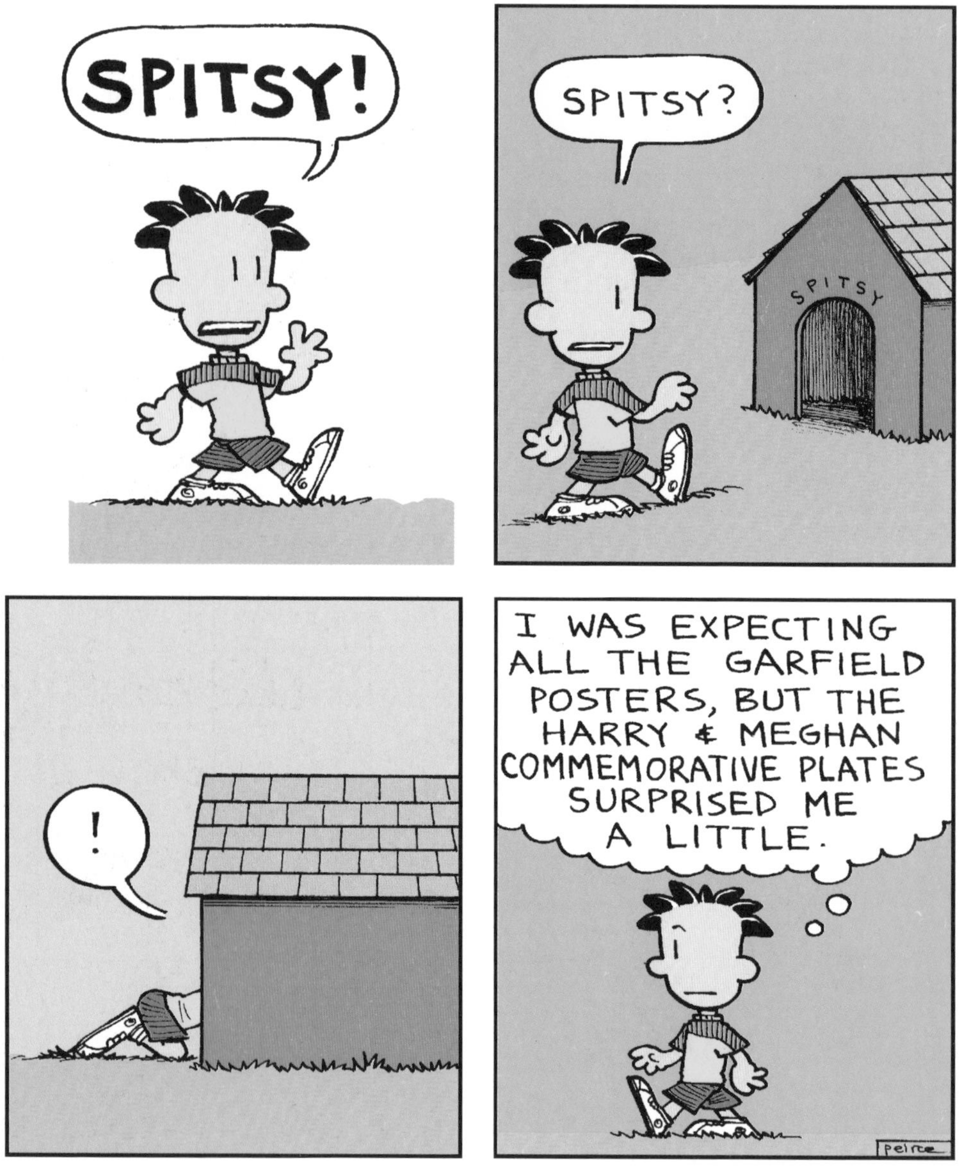
SPITSY!
SPITSY?
SPITSY
!
I WAS EXPECTING ALL THE GARFIELD POSTERS, BUT THE HARRY & MEGHAN COMMEMORATIVE PLATES SURPRISED ME A LITTLE.
peirce

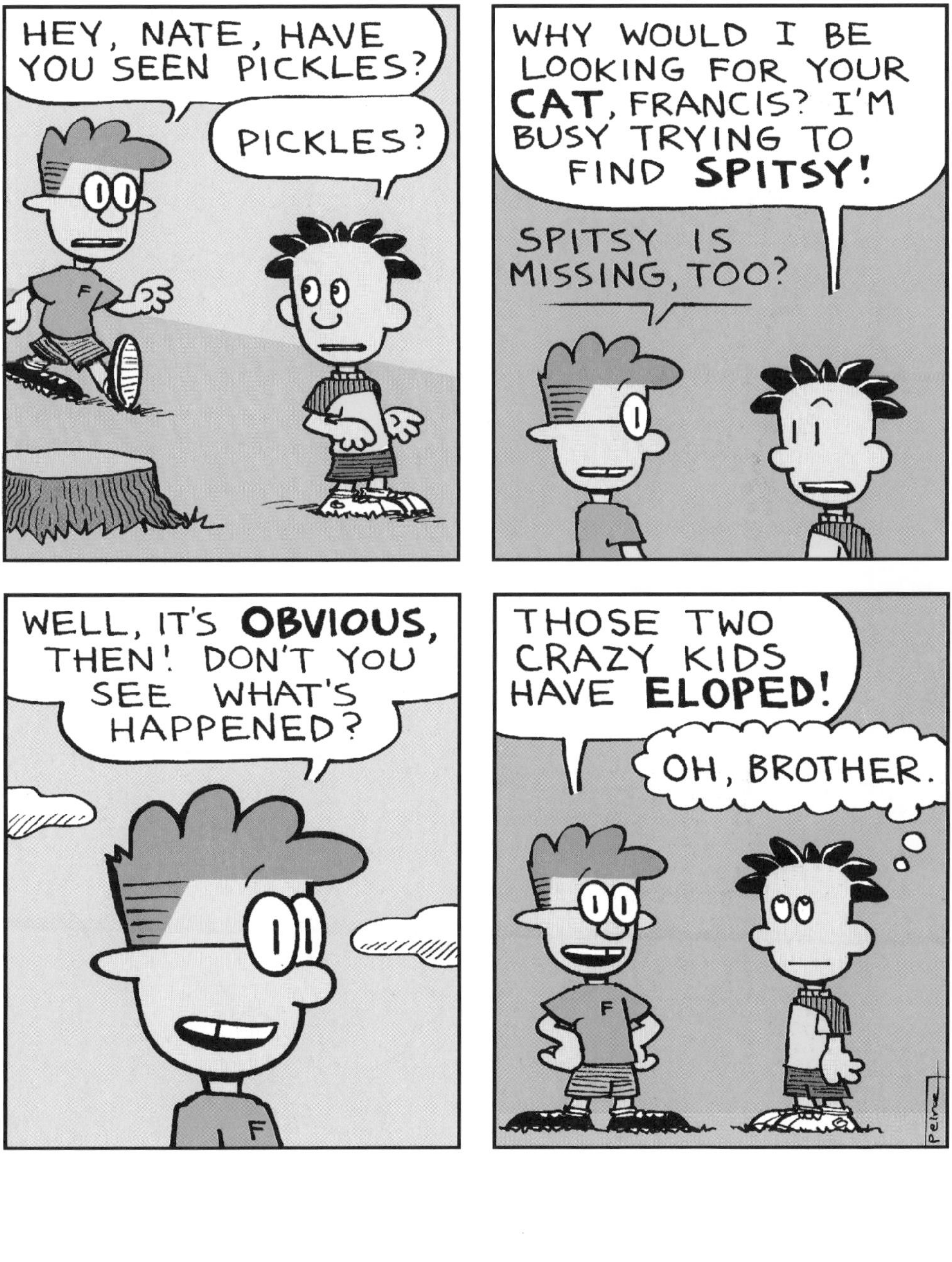

HEY, NATE, HAVE YOU SEEN PICKLES?
PICKLES?
WHY WOULD I BE LOOKING FOR YOUR **CAT**, FRANCIS? I'M BUSY TRYING TO FIND **SPITSY**!
SPITSY IS MISSING, TOO?
WELL, IT'S **OBVIOUS**, THEN! DON'T YOU SEE WHAT'S HAPPENED?
THOSE TWO CRAZY KIDS HAVE **ELOPED**!
OH, BROTHER.
Peirce

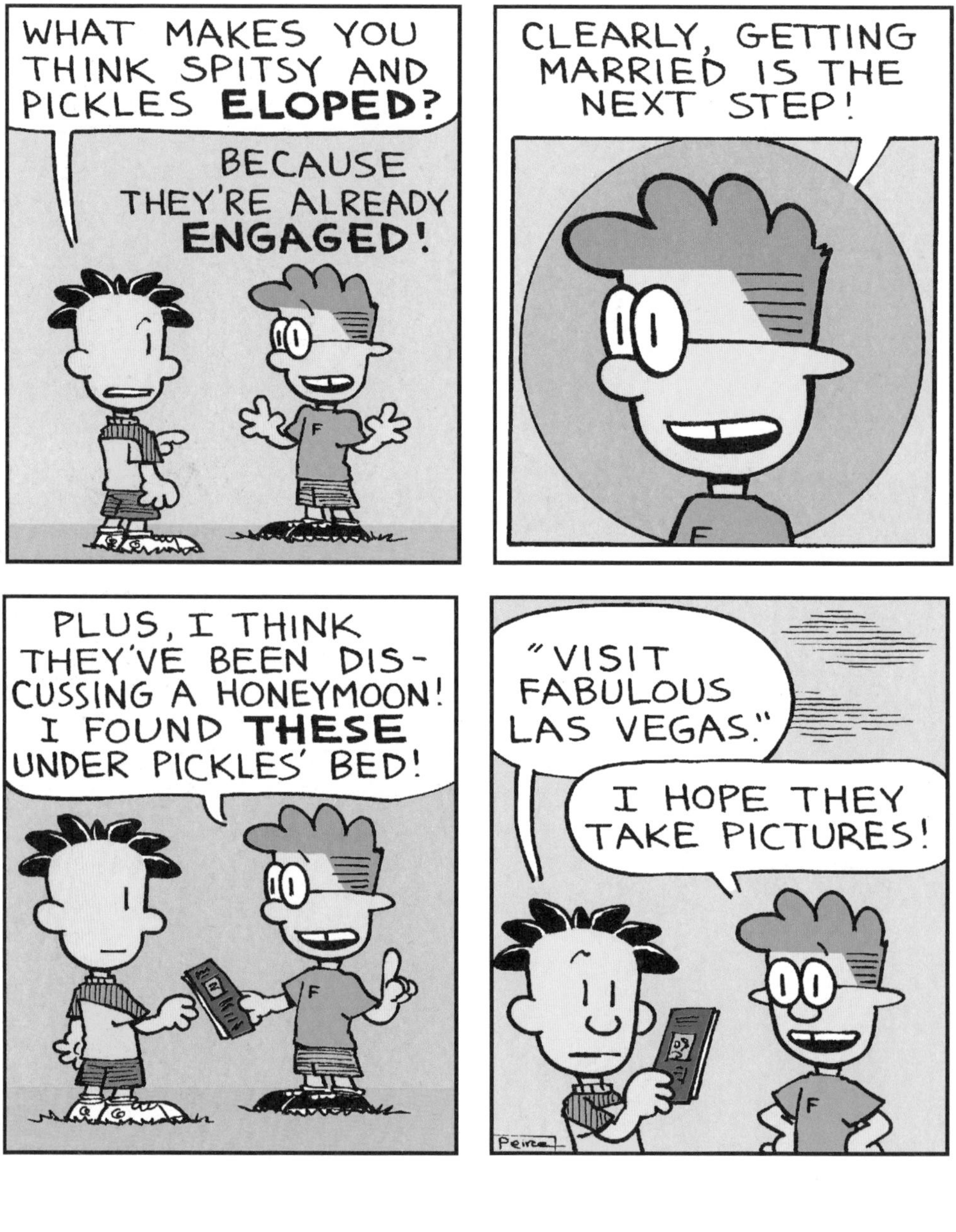
WHAT MAKES YOU THINK SPITSY AND PICKLES **ELOPED?**
BECAUSE THEY'RE ALREADY **ENGAGED!**
CLEARLY, GETTING MARRIED IS THE NEXT STEP!
PLUS, I THINK THEY'VE BEEN DIS-CUSSING A HONEYMOON! I FOUND **THESE** UNDER PICKLES' BED!
"VISIT FABULOUS LAS VEGAS."
I HOPE THEY TAKE PICTURES!
Peirce

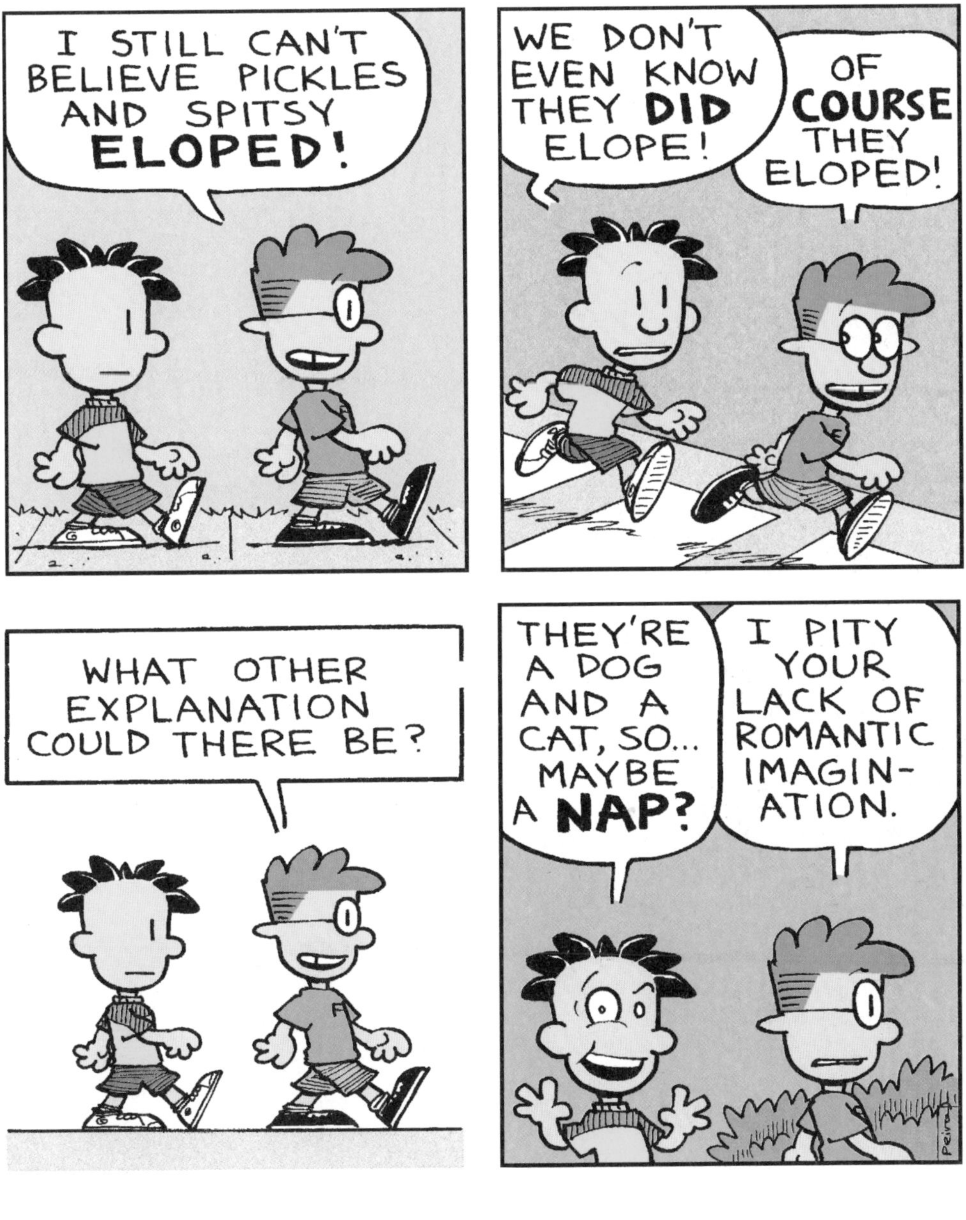
I STILL CAN'T BELIEVE PICKLES AND SPITSY **ELOPED!**
WE DON'T EVEN KNOW THEY **DID** ELOPE!
OF **COURSE** THEY ELOPED!
WHAT OTHER EXPLANATION COULD THERE BE?
THEY'RE A DOG AND A CAT, SO... MAYBE A **NAP?**
I PITY YOUR LACK OF ROMANTIC IMAGINATION.
Peirce

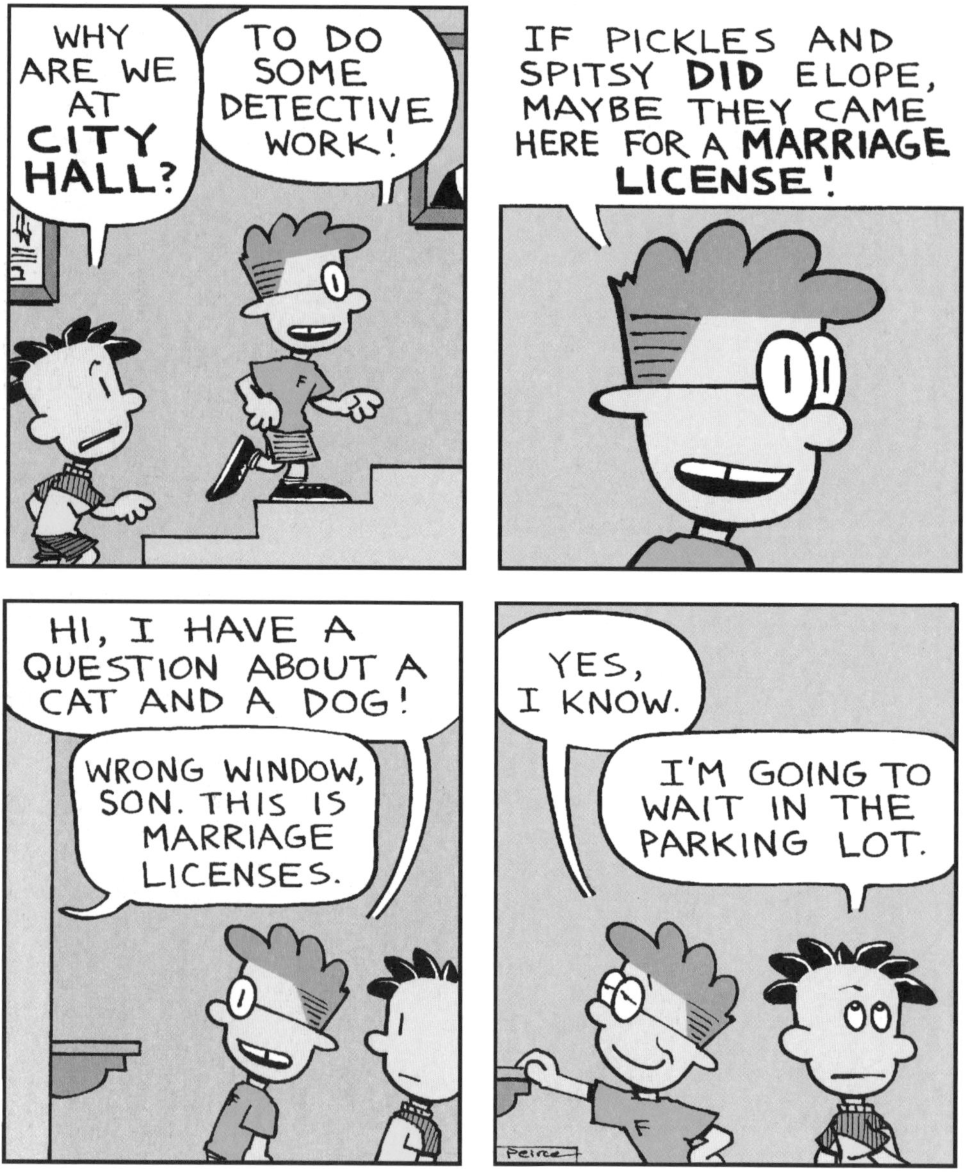
WHY ARE WE AT CITY HALL?
TO DO SOME DETECTIVE WORK!
IF PICKLES AND SPITSY DID ELOPE, MAYBE THEY CAME HERE FOR A MARRIAGE LICENSE!
HI, I HAVE A QUESTION ABOUT A CAT AND A DOG!
WRONG WINDOW, SON. THIS IS MARRIAGE LICENSES.
YES, I KNOW.
I'M GOING TO WAIT IN THE PARKING LOT.
Peirce

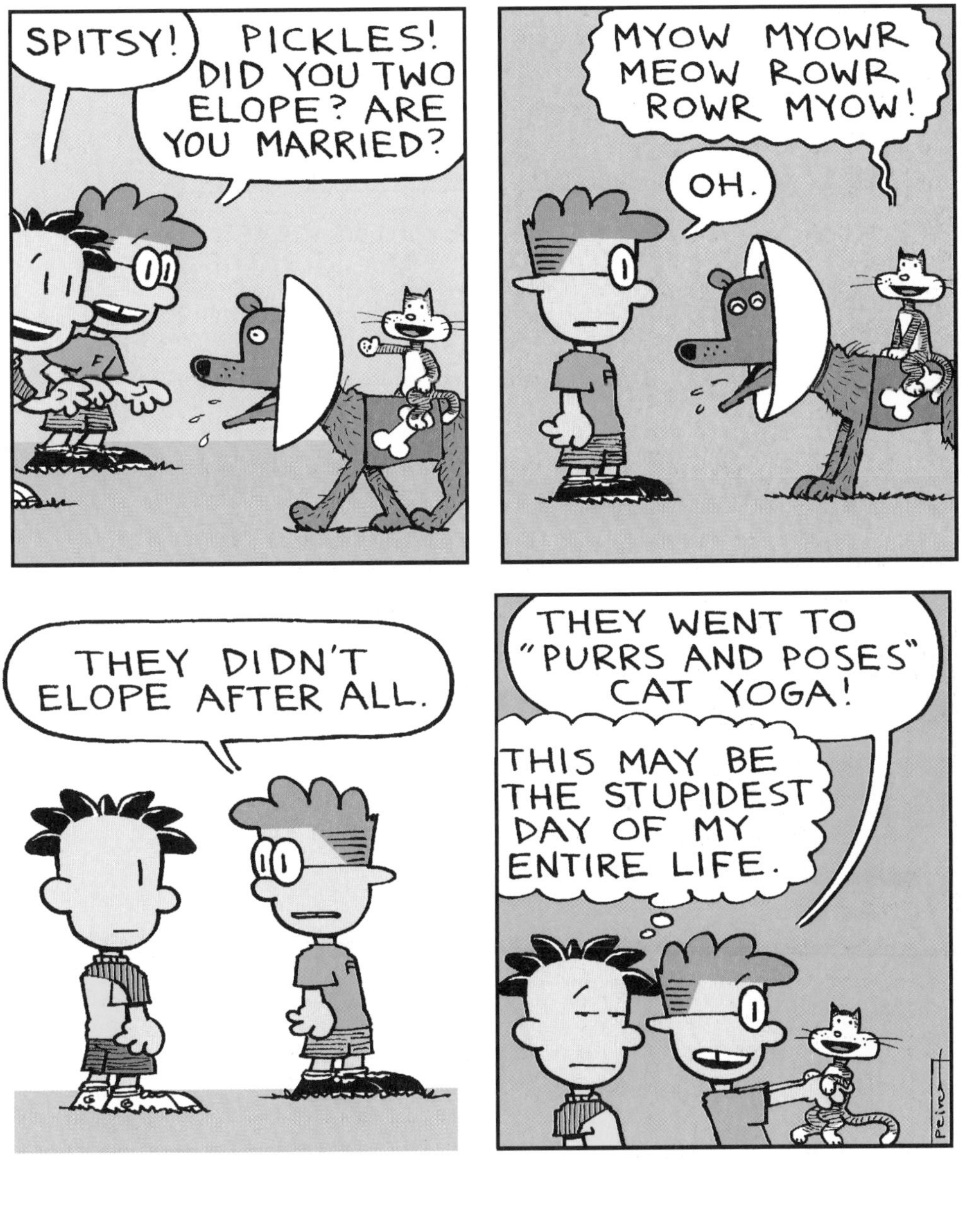
SPITSY!
PICKLES! DID YOU TWO ELOPE? ARE YOU MARRIED?
MYOW MYOWR MEOW ROWR ROWR MYOW!
OH.
THEY DIDN'T ELOPE AFTER ALL.
THEY WENT TO "PURRS AND POSES" CAT YOGA!
THIS MAY BE THE STUPIDEST DAY OF MY ENTIRE LIFE.
Peirce

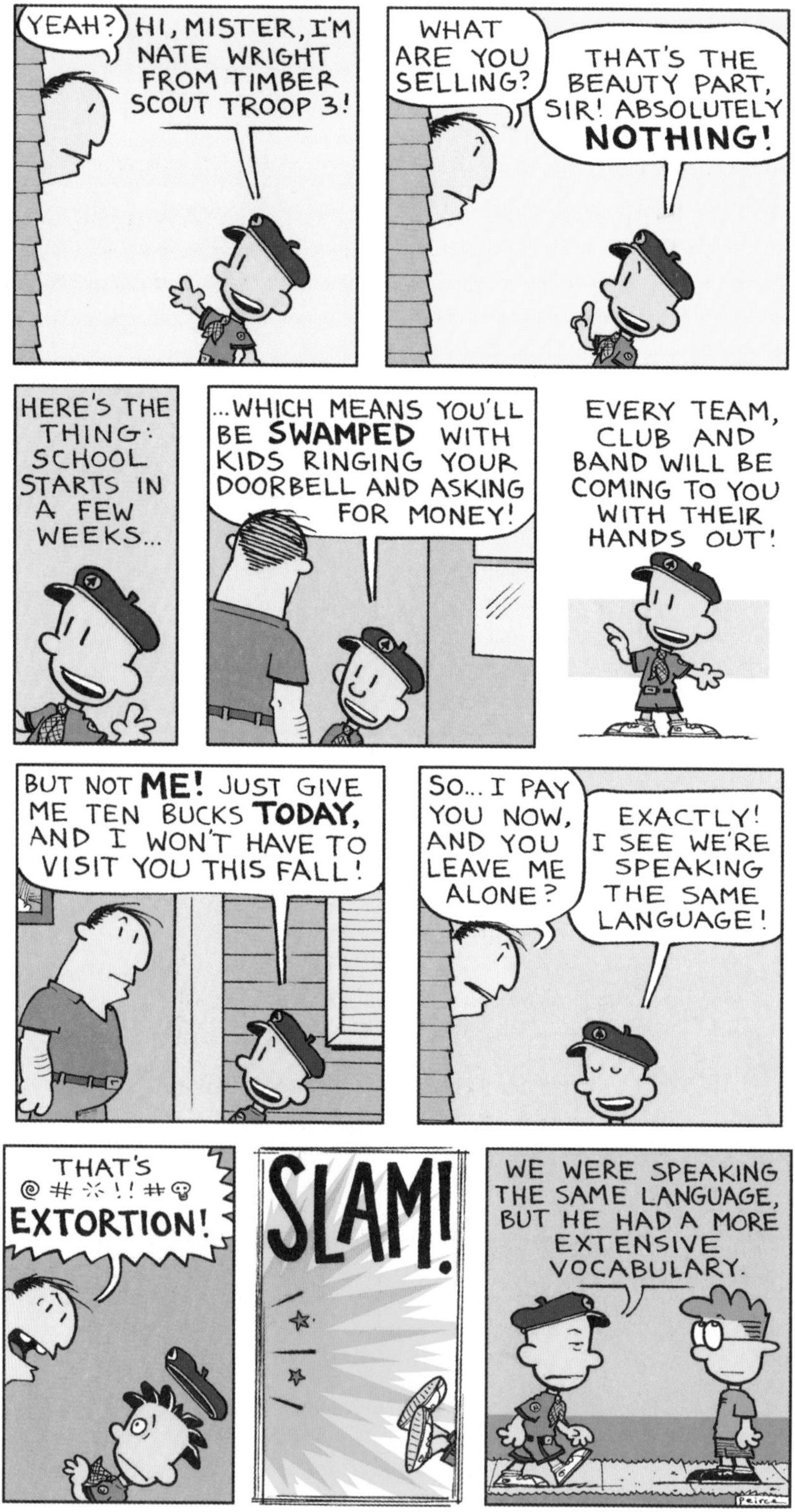
YEAH?
HI, MISTER, I'M NATE WRIGHT FROM TIMBER SCOUT TROOP 3!
WHAT ARE YOU SELLING?
THAT'S THE BEAUTY PART, SIR! ABSOLUTELY NOTHING!
HERE'S THE THING: SCHOOL STARTS IN A FEW WEEKS...
...WHICH MEANS YOU'LL BE SWAMPED WITH KIDS RINGING YOUR DOORBELL AND ASKING FOR MONEY!
EVERY TEAM, CLUB AND BAND WILL BE COMING TO YOU WITH THEIR HANDS OUT!
BUT NOT ME! JUST GIVE ME TEN BUCKS TODAY, AND I WON'T HAVE TO VISIT YOU THIS FALL!
SO... I PAY YOU NOW, AND YOU LEAVE ME ALONE?
EXACTLY! I SEE WE'RE SPEAKING THE SAME LANGUAGE!
THAT'S
EXTORTION!
SLAM!
WE WERE SPEAKING THE SAME LANGUAGE, BUT HE HAD A MORE EXTENSIVE VOCABULARY.
Peirce

Big Nate is distributed internationally by Andrews McMeel Syndication.

Andrews McMeel Publishing
a division of Andrews McMeel Universal
1130 Walnut Street, Kansas City, Missouri 64106

www.andrewsmcmeel.com

23 24 25 26 27 SDB 10 9 8 7 6 5 4 3 2 1

ISBN: 978-1-5248-7923-5

Library of Congress Control Number: 2022940887

Made by:
RR Donnelley (Guangdong) Printing Solutions Company Ltd
Address and location of manufacturer:
No. 2, Minzhu Road, Daning, Humen Town,
Dongguan City, Guangdong Province, China 523930
1st Printing—11/21/22

These strips appeared in newspapers from
February 24, 2019, through August 11, 2019.

Big Nate can be viewed on the Internet at
www.gocomics.com/big_nate.

Look for these books!

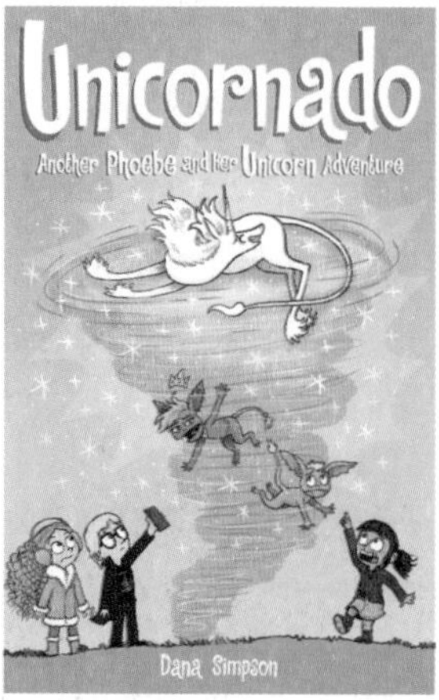
Unicornado
Another Phoebe and Her Unicorn Adventure
Dana Simpson

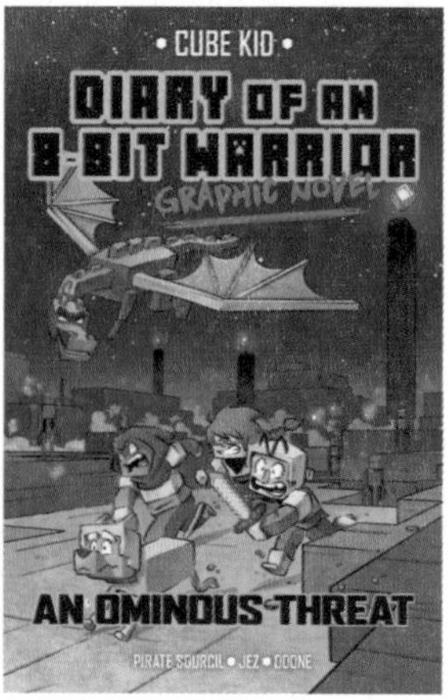
• CUBE KID •
DIARY OF AN 8-BIT WARRIOR
GRAPHIC NOVEL
AN OMINOUS THREAT
PIRATE SOURCIL • JEZ • ODONE

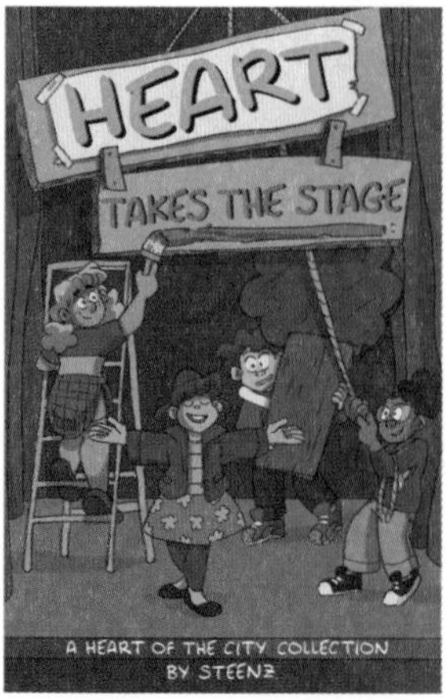
HEART
TAKES THE STAGE
A HEART OF THE CITY COLLECTION
BY STEENZ

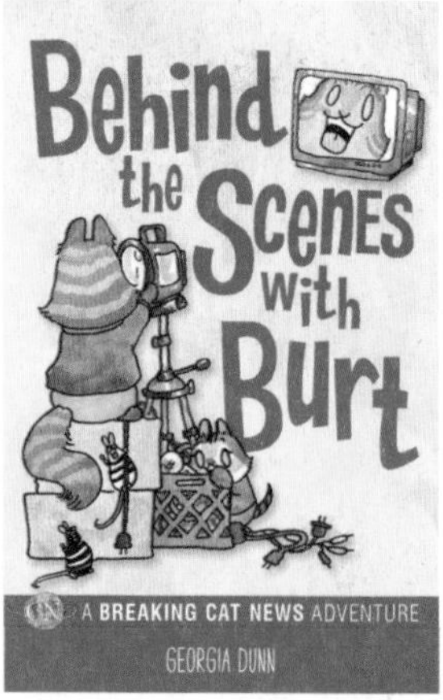
Behind the Scenes with Burt
A BREAKING CAT NEWS ADVENTURE
GEORGIA DUNN

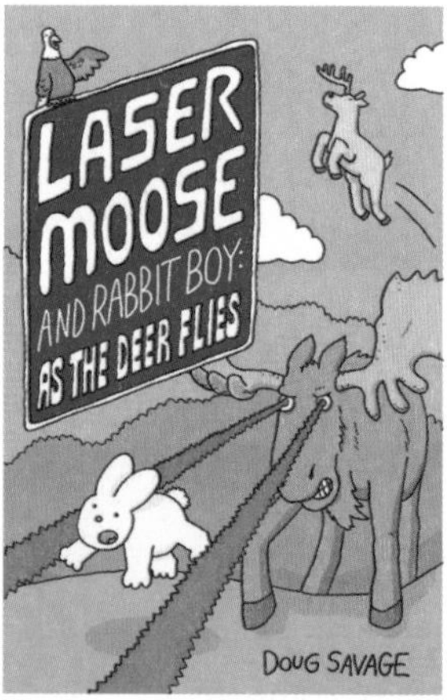
LASER MOOSE
AND RABBIT BOY:
AS THE DEER FLIES
DOUG SAVAGE

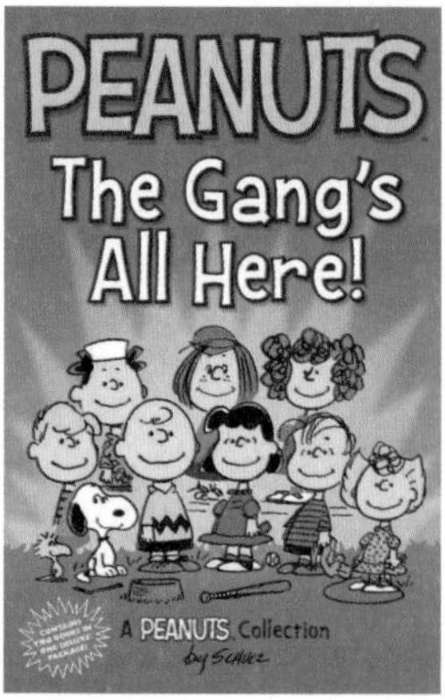
PEANUTS
The Gang's All Here!
A PEANUTS Collection

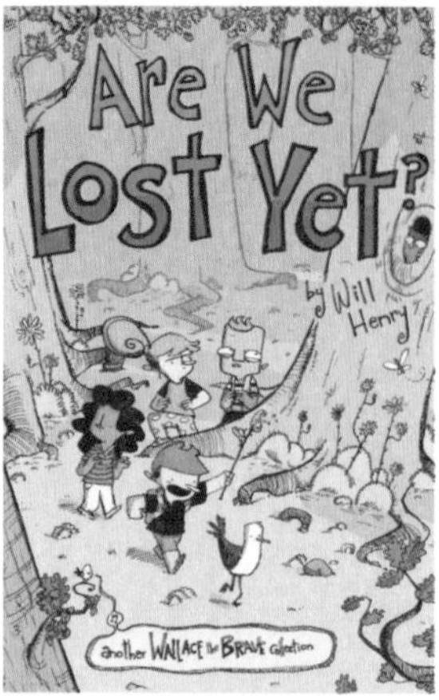
Are We Lost Yet?
by Will Henry
another WALLACE the BRAVE collection

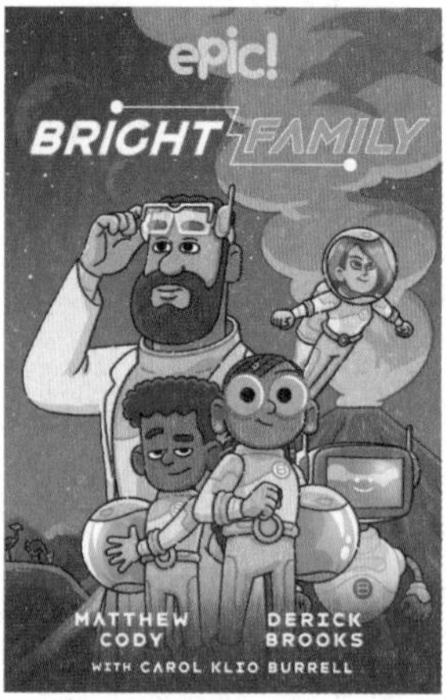
epic!
BRIGHT FAMILY
MATTHEW CODY
DERICK BROOKS
WITH CAROL KLIO BURRELL

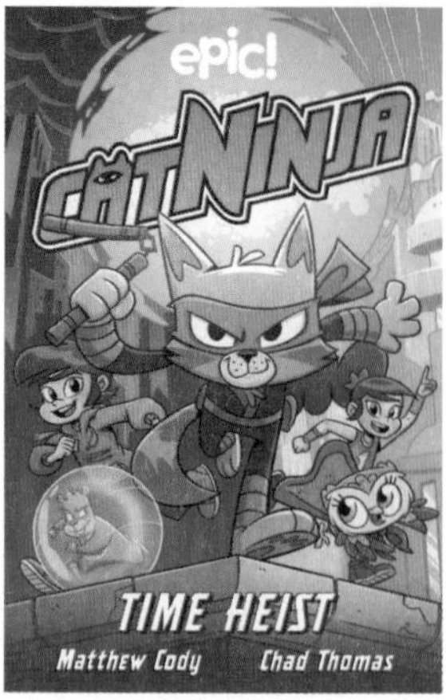
epic!
CAT NINJA
TIME HEIST
Matthew Cody
Chad Thomas

NEW GRAPHIC NOVELS
BASED ON THE HIT TV SERIES ON
Paramount+ AND nickelodeon™

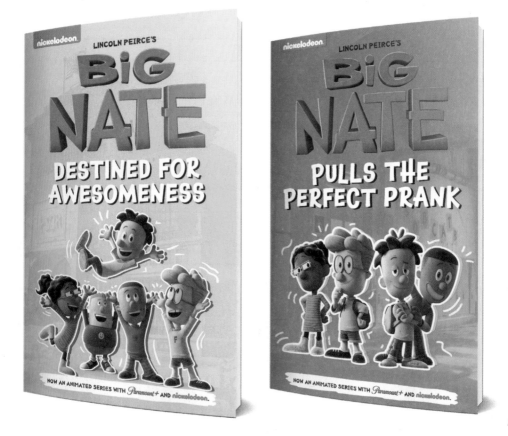

AVAILABLE WHEREVER
BOOKS ARE SOLD